SOME MUST DIE

Angie D. Comer

Some Must Die

www.angiedcomer.com

www.facebook.com/angiedcomer

Instagram: angiedcomer

In this fictional story, the geography of the United States of America is like, half-real. You can visit some of the landmarks, but don't be surprised if the path suddenly takes a detour. Names, characters, places, and incidents are either the product of the author's imagination or used fictitiously. Any resemblance to actual persons, living or dead, events or locales is entirely coincidental.

Dear Stephanie, I wrote this book for you.

Acknowledgments

I would like to express my gratitude to my extraordinary life partner, who inspires me daily, as well as her two amazing daughters, for their unwavering support.

A special thank you goes to my mom, who not only served as my first reader but also motivated me to persevere. She consistently checked in on my progress, keeping me on my toes. My dad, who has always been there for me when I needed him. My sister, who provided both laughter and tears during the difficult times, as well as invaluable editing assistance for my final version.

A special thank you to my editor, Maryann Anderson and my squad of literary warriors, Pat, Phyllis, Mary, Jill, Jan, Lori, Venita, Cam and Benae', who fearlessly jumped into the depths of my chaotic scribbles. Your commitment to surviving my initial and revised drafts is nothing short of amazing. Cheers to you, my friends!

Above all, I am thankful for God's presence in my life. Through Him, all things are possible.

Table of Contents

Part One: Leslie Jenkins and Mom, 1978

"Hope and fear are inseparable,"

Francois De La Rochefoucau.

Chapter 1: Knock, Knock, Knock

Leslie Jenkins, August 26, 1978

Summer is coming to an end and fall is beginning. The world around me feels different. I'm outside, in the backyard, lying on the ground, looking for four-leaf clovers. The skies above me are blue and the air carries a breeze of fresh new smells. I'm twelve years old and will be in seventh grade this year.

We live in a red brick two-story house with a fenced-in backyard on the corner of Locust Lane and Main Street in Tupelo, Mississippi.

"Leslie! Come in for dinner," Mom yells out the back door.

My mom's name is Vanessa Jenkins. She met my dad, Ted Jenkins, fourteen years ago. He was charming, and she was beautiful, and within six months, they were planning a wedding.

I walk inside and sit at the dinner table set for two.

My dad left with a suitcase a few weeks ago, and I haven't seen him since. I'm still trying to get used to him not coming home.

"What's for dinner, Mom?"

"How do liver and onions sound?"

"Ewww, gross!"

"Why's your face scrunching up like you ate lemons?" She laughs. "Liver and onions are so good for you!"

"Really mom?" I roll my eyes, sit down at the table, grumpy and annoyed that I have to eat something so disgusting.

"Put a smile on that face, my sweet Shirley Temple!" she says as she sets a plate of fried bologna, mashed potatoes, and Kraft macaroni & cheese. "I didn't say we're eating liver and onions; I just asked how it sounds," she winks.

"Mom!" I say and give her another eye roll. I stick my tongue out and dig into the mac and cheese.

After dinner, I ask, "Mom, can I go watch Happy Days?"

"Skedaddle, kiddo, I got the dishes."

My dad is mean to us when he drinks. He hits walls, pushes my mom around, and sometimes hurts me when he takes me to my room.

One day, after an argument with my dad, I asked, "Mom, does Dad hurt your arms too?"

She looks surprised and says, "He does sometimes when he's been drinking. Does Dad hurt you, Leslie? Let me see your arms." I show her, but he hadn't hurt me lately, so they look okay.

"Tell me if he ever hurts you Leslie. I need to know. He should never touch you in anger, do you understand?"

"Yes, Mom," I say.

The following day, Mom sat me down and said, "Leslie, sweetheart, your dad, and I have talked; honey, he's going to move into town to get help for his drinking problem."

4

"I don't understand." I say, afraid, upset, and near tears. "Does this mean your getting a divorce?"

"Honey, Dad will come visit when he's stops drinking and can be a better dad for you. His drinking causes so much hurt and pain to our family. You know that Dad loves you he's proud of you, Leslie, this has nothing to do with you!"

I begin to cry. "Then I'll never see Dad. He won't stop drinking, Mom!" I say and stomp upstairs to my room.

I lay on my bed afraid, hurt, and confused. This room is safe from Dad's terrible temper, but I'm always scared he'll hurt Mom or me. So why am I upset that he's leaving?

Mom comes upstairs, sits on the bed next to me, and says, "Trust me, kiddo, things will work out for you and me. My job is to keep you safe. I know things seem all mixed up, but they will get better." And she gave me a long hug.

"I know, Mom," I say and hug her back. I haven't seen my dad since that day. My mom seems happier, she doesn't cry anymore, but I miss my dad. I think.

The weather is on every channel as the remnants of Hurricane Anita are beginning to cross over the Mississippi. It's been downgraded to a tropical storm, but the forecast is severe thunderstorms coming throughout the night and into tomorrow.

Mom comes to the living room and says, "Bedtime, young lady."

"Mom, can I sleep with you tonight?" I ask.

"You haven't done that since you were a little kid," Mom says, then smiles, "Don't worry, I'm a little scared, too."

I snuggle up to her back and feel safe, warm, and happy.

My mom turns and hugs me; she says, "Don't forget, my boss told me I can make extra money Saturday mornings cleaning our offices. I'll leave after breakfast, but I should be home by lunch."

"Do you have to go? I don't want to be here by myself."

"Yes, I have to go sweetie; we need the money. You're twelve years old now and a big kid. I don't think you need a babysitter anymore. You're a responsible girl and can do most things on your own, and I'll only be gone a few hours." she says.

"What do I do while you're gone?" I ask.

"What you always do on Saturday mornings: watch cartoons and curl up on the couch with your blanket," she says.

The local news comes on. All the talk is about Elvis Presley. It's been one year since he died, and it's the top story, other than the weather.

Reports are coming in that people all over the United States are still mourning him. My mom loves his music; I think everyone does in Tupelo; he was born here.

"What is your favorite Elvis song, Leslie?"

"*Too much Monkey Business!*" I say.

"My favorite is *Jailhouse Rock*," she says.

Mom plays music when she cooks; it makes her happy, and sometimes she feels like dancing. We both try to shake our hips like Elvis, which is funny, especially Mom.

I start getting heavy-eyed and ask my mom if she will sing a bedtime song to me. She has the most beautiful voice. She turns off the TV and sings her favorite song, *Always* by Irvin Berlin, and as she softly sings and rubs my back, I fall asleep.

I wake up eager and proud that my mom feels like I'm a big girl and that I don't need a babysitter.

We sit at the breakfast table, drinking orange juice and eating bowls of Lucky Charms. My mom says, "Today is the first day you'll be alone at home. Are you nervous or excited?"

"Both," I say. "What if a tornado comes or the electricity goes out?"

"Sweetie, if a tornado comes, you hide in a closet, and if the electricity goes out, you can read a book with a flashlight. I'll be home before you know it."

"Okay," I say.

"Hey, would you like to go to Taco Bell for lunch?"

"Taco Bell's my favorite!" I say, "Can we go get ice cream after?"

"I think you may be pushing your luck, kiddo," she says, winking at me.

My Mom leaves at 7:30 am, and I lock the door behind her. I turn on the television, and snuggle under my soft, fuzzy, rainbow-colored blanket.

The news flashes weather warnings across the screen, saying it will be terrible weather all day. I get up and glance outside the living room window. The skies are ugly, dark gray, with steady thunder, lightning, and rain. Yuck.

I keep myself distracted by watching cartoons, Scooby-Doo is my favorite.

Around 10:00 am, I hear a knock on our front door.

Rain is pouring outside like cats and dogs, and I'm wondering who would be out in weather like this.

Mom wouldn't knock, and we never have guests drop by and I think, maybe it's Dad.

I approach the door and whisper, "Dad?" But I receive no answer.

A knock again, then a girl's voice; she sounds like a teenager.

"Can I use your phone?" she asks. "My boyfriend's car has a flat tire and doesn't have a spare."

I stand quietly by the door; I'm afraid to speak.

Knock, knock, knock.

"Please, I've knocked on all the other houses, no one is answering."

I'm worried. Mom always tells me never to open the door to a stranger and I always roll my eyes and say, "I know, Mom!"

Knock, knock, knock.

"Can you please help us? I need to use your phone. My name is Bonnie; I go to Tupelo High School."

I look out the peephole and see a girl, not much older than myself. She is soaking wet and looks worried.

Ignoring the nagging feeling, I reason this is just a teenage girl who needs help. It's just a phone call, she even told me her name, Bonnie.

As I open the door for her, a sense of unease washes over me. Suddenly, my attention is captured by a handkerchief swiftly approaching my face. The world turns from color to

8

shades of gray, and eventually fades to black as I lose consciousness.

Chapter 2: Taco Bell and Ice Cream

Vanessa Jenkins (Leslie's mom), August 26, 1978

After my first Saturday cleaning offices, I feel satisfied. We're going to get ahead. I pull into our driveway, ready to take Leslie to lunch, and notice our front door is ajar. I jump out and run inside.

"Leslie, did you leave the door open?"

No answer.

"Leslie, honey, answer me. Are you okay?!"

As I call out to her, I move quickly from room to room. Looking behind the couch, in the pantry, in the rooms upstairs, in closets, under the beds, and in the bathrooms. No Leslie.

I frantically search my mind. Where can she be? Is she hurt? Did someone take her?

My mind screams, my heart pounds, and tears begin to flow.

I call my husband, Ted. He's living at a place called The Turn in downtown Tupelo. It's a boarding house for men, where no alcohol or drugs are allowed inside, and they offer three AA meetings daily. I'm told he has already left, so I call his workplace.

"Hi Ted, did you come by and pick up Leslie for a visit this morning?" I ask nervously.

"No, Vanessa, I haven't seen her since I was asked to leave my home," he says bitterly. "Are you telling me you don't know where our daughter is?"

"Ted, I left her home this morning and went to work for a few hours. She's not here, and I'm scared!" I moan, wanting his support and help to find her.

Instead, he yells, "How could you lose our daughter, you stupid cow! She's not old enough to be left alone! You're worthless! You'd better find Leslie, or else!"

Shocked, I say, "Ted, I don't deserve to be talked to this way and will not put up with it." I hang up, stunned at his arrogance and name-calling.

He's such a bastard. How did I ever fall in love with him?

I call the Tupelo Police Department to report Leslie missing. They get to the heart of my call quickly.

When I answered who, what, when, where, and how, they assured me an officer would arrive shortly.

While waiting for the police, I search the house again, looking for any clues to be found.

"Her pillow's gone," I whisper out loud.

I also discover Leslie's school backpack and some clothes from her closet are missing. My heart is torn in two.

In my room, there's missing jewelry, an eight-track player, eight-tracks, and some cash I'd hidden under my mattress.

The police find no signs of forced entry into our home and only minor signs of a struggle. They do find a tiny smear of blood on the wall in the hallway, indicating someone was possibly hurt, but no other blood was found.

"Mrs. Jenkins, we're here to help you, I'm Detective Pace. I understand you have a missing daughter. How old is your daughter, ma'am?"

"She's only twelve years old," I say.

"Ma'am, can you bring me a recent photo, and do you remember what she was wearing this morning?" asks Detective Pace.

"Yes, when I left this morning, she was wearing a pair of Scooby-Doo pajamas and matching slippers. This is her school picture from last year before she cut her hair. It's short now." I tell Detective Pace as I take her photo off the fireplace mantle. As I pass him the photo, I think, she looks so young. She has a slight snow dust of freckles across her nose, her hair in pigtails, and her smile, with beautiful dimples. My stomach is in turmoil; I feel sick.

"My husband moved to The Turn a few weeks ago, which left our household money incredibly tight." I say, I can't control my babbling. "I left Leslie alone because I didn't have money for a sitter. I need to make money, not spend money. I took on an extra job of cleaning offices and left her alone. I feel like the worst mother ever. Oh no, I don't see her fluffy blanket," I say, crying again.

Detective Pace takes the photograph and says, "Mrs. Jenkins, you said your husband is staying at The Turn. Can you tell me when and why he moved?"

"He moved five weeks ago. He'd been drinking daily and was verbally and physically mean. It wasn't the first time, I told him I wanted a divorce, and if he didn't move out, I would file charges against him for domestic abuse. Ted got a room at The Turn the next day and told me he wanted to save our marriage. He said he would get sober and attend AA meetings and hoped I would take him back in time. I told him I wouldn't."

"Any chance he would be involved?" Detective Pace asks.

"No, I don't know; I don't think so, maybe? I called him when I couldn't find Leslie. I thought he might have come to see her or taken her out to eat. But, instead, he was furious with me, and blamed me."

"We'll send someone to speak to him immediately, and ma'am, we will also need a list of any missing items and a statement. I know this is hard, but the quicker we get the information from you, the better," says Detective Pace.

Then he gently puts his hand on my shoulder and says, "Ms. Jenkins, I've called the police station and asked for a female officer, Phyllis Baxter, to take your official statement. She will help you with any support you may need as we go through the investigation."

I nod my head, sit on the couch, and weep. I can hear the detective and other policeman speaking, but can only catch snippets; "...is and given the front door was unlocked and left open... yes... believe Leslie opened the door to her attacker," one says.

"She doesn't normally speak to strangers and never opens the door to them," I say, remembering how often we drill that into her.

Detective Pace looks around and says, "Then do you suppose that it's likely she knew whoever abducted her?"

"I don't know," I say. "My mind just keeps praying this is a mistake, that Leslie will come home at any moment."

Detective Pace says, "Contact dispatch and send officers to canvas the neighborhood and have them interview neighbors and friends. I'll reach out to the media and get a search party together. Let's plan to set up a home base in the parking lot of Saint Benedict's Church."

By 2:00 pm, neighbors, local friends, six patrolmen, and two bloodhounds were searching a two-mile radius around our home, including vacant lots and overgrown land. The rain did not let up.

Detective Pace pulls me aside and says, "Mrs. Jenkins, your husband Ted has a solid alibi for this today. We spoke to his landlord and employer. Ted was with someone the entire morning. Of course, that doesn't eliminate him, but it's a good start."

"I'm relieved to hear that. Ted isn't a good husband or father, but I can't imagine that he would want to hurt Leslie. The problem is I don't know what Ted will do when he's drinking. Part of me feared it might be him, but I can't imagine he would take her away or hurt her when he's sober."

"Yes, ma'am. I understand," replies Detective Pace. "It appears he left work after you called him this afternoon and went straight to Hank's bar. He was quite intoxicated when we found him, and one of our officers escorted him back to The Turn. Another officer stayed behind to interview the bartender and patrons. The bartender confirmed Ted was in the bar Friday night until closing and today since about 12:30 pm. So, unfortunately, he won't be able to help in the search."

Detective Pace says, "Ms. Jenkins, Saint Benedict's Church is two blocks from here, that's our designated search base. Let's head over there now, it's almost dark, and the search crew has specific instructions to check back in before nightfall when they complete their section of the mapped area."

"Vanessa, I'll leave an officer here in case Leslie comes home. I'd like you to accompany us and make a statement for the media."

"Okay," I say and stand beside Detective Pace as he speaks to all the volunteers who came to help find Leslie.

"Ladies and gentlemen of the news, media and volunteers. Our search has continued throughout the day and everyone has checked back in for the night. Unfortunately, the dogs have been unable to pick up Leslie's scent with the weather conditions," he reports. "Ms. Jenkins would like to say a few words."

I step forward, holding her photo against my chest so everyone can see her face, "I want to thank you all for coming out today and trying to help me find my daughter Leslie."

Tears begin to fall, and I look directly at the camera. "Please, if you have my Leslie bring her back to me. If you have any information, contact the police so that my Leslie can come home safe." After that, I can no longer maintain my dignity and step away from the podium.

Detective Pace says, "Folks, we will resume our search tomorrow at 8:00 am. So come early and sign in. Thank you all for coming out today."

Detective Pace brought coffee, biscuits, and gravy from The Biscuit Barn the following morning. As we drink coffee, I say, "Last night, I don't believe I slept at all. When I drifted off, I had random nightmares flashing through my brain. I keep wondering what is happening to Leslie. Where is she? Is she hurt? Has someone has hurt her, or worse?"

"Do you believe in God, Mrs. Jenkins?" Detective Pace asks.

"Yes, I do."

"Then the best thing you can do is pray. Your neighbors, friends, and people you've never met will be helping us search today."

At Saint Benedict's this morning, there is double the amount of volunteers, and the weather is better; still a light rain but not pouring.

Detective Pace steps forward to speak into the microphone, "Our focus is on areas where Leslie could have hidden if lost or injured. Remember, we will be checking all sightings, including possible sightings. If anyone has seen something, even if they aren't sure, please contact the Tupelo Police Department.

After his speech, I ask, "Detective Pace, please tell me, what can I do?"

"Ms. Jenkins, the first thing you can do is help us rule you out as a suspect. It's a standard procedure. Can you come to the station for a polygraph test? It will help solidify your innocence."

"Yes, of course, I'll take the polygraph."

"Good, I promise you, this is important."

Later that afternoon, Detective Pace calls and tells me, "Mrs. Jenkins, you passed your polygraph test. However, I want you to know your husband came in; he was subjected to three polygraph tests and failed them all. I think he has a lot to hide."

I was devastated as days turned into weeks. First, volunteers posted fliers in Tupelo at local businesses, truck stops, and restaurants. Then, going above and beyond, Detective Pace recruited volunteers to post flyers at rest areas, gas stations, and interstate bus stations within a 100-mile radius in hopes that someone would recognize my daughter's face.

The possibility of Ted being involved never left my mind. Maybe he was not responsible for hands-on kidnapping, but could he have hired someone?

When questioned by Detective Pace about his whereabouts on Friday night, Ted said, "I was drinking with a young man I hired for a short-term project. I needed extra help to meet a deadline; he worked with me for ten days. It was his last night here, and we just drank a few beers together."

"Can you tell me more about this worker?" replied Detective Pace.

"Sure can; his name is Carl Slater; he said he's from San Diego, California. Carl told me he and his brother had driven home for their grandma's funeral over in Nashville, Tennessee. He said he's working his way back home by doing short-term jobs for food and gas money. He seemed nice and was a hard worker; I invited him for drinks at Hank's since it was his last day on the job."

"Do you know how to get in touch with him or where he was headed next?

"No contact information other than an address in California, and I have no idea where he was headed. We had a couple of drinks, and he was gone," Ted said.

"Would Carl Slater have a reason to abduct your daughter Mr. Jenkins? Did you hire him to kidnap your daughter, sir?" Detective Pace inquired.

"No!" he replied. "I didn't hire him to kidnap my daughter or anything else! How would he even know I have a daughter? I don't talk about my private life with employees." Ted said.

"What was he driving, Mr. Jenkins?" Detective Pace asked.

"I never saw his car. I drove him to the bar Friday night, and he left before I did." Ted replied.

Detective Pace continues to reach out and update me as much as he can. After two months, he says, "We've had a couple of leads, Mrs. Jenkins, but they've only led us to dead ends."

"What does that mean?" I ask, frustrated.

"One lead was from a local flower shop owner, Ms. Keener. She saw something strange the day Leslie went missing. She was out on delivery, driving down Locust Lane, and saw a man and woman walking alongside the road in the torrential rain. She did not see a vehicle, and as she neared them, the man pulled down his trucker hat. Ms. Keener said she planned to stop and offer them a ride but decided not to after feeling something was off. She said the man was white, of medium build, with brown hair, and was wearing a trucker hat. He was wearing an army-type green jacket. The girl looked young, maybe 16 or 17 years old, with brown hair on the shorter side. Unfortunately, these two people were not seen by anyone else."

I gasp, "But we may have a description!"

"Please don't get too excited, Ms. Jenkins. There are other leads from Leslie's classmates. They say she would often come to school in a bad mood with bruises on her forearms and give made-up excuses. Hear what I'm saying, but don't read into it until I tell you it's solid. Ms. Jenkins, do you know why they would say these things?"

I was horrified, "Those bruises are one of the reasons I made Ted leave!" I begin to cry. "I told my daughter I would keep her safe. That is my job. I failed her. Her dad is drunk and abusive to both of us. He would always say he'd never hit us again or that he would change, but he never did. Instead, his abuse was always advancing."

"Advancing to what, Ms. Jenkins?"

"I'm not sure," I say, biting my lip, afraid to reveal what I believed.

Part Two: Samantha Archer and Mom, 1978

"There is some good in this world, and it's worth fighting for,"

J.R.R. Tolkien.

Chapter 1: The Missing Poster

Samantha Archer (Sam), December 24, 1978

My family travels every Christmas Eve from Jonesboro, Arkansas, to my grandparent's home in rural South Georgia. Our route runs through Tennessee, Mississippi, Alabama, and, last but not least, Georgia. We leave early in the morning so we can arrive before nightfall.

My PawPaw and Granny live in a small parsonage, which I learned was a home the church provides, while my PawPaw is their preacher. The church is next door to the parsonage, and both are surrounded by acres of woods and pure country living.

My grandparents are Pentecostal religious. They aren't the snake-holding type, nor the long hair and long dresses, although they believe in lifting their hands to heaven as a sign of reverence and awe, speaking in tongues and interpretation.

My PawPaw gets into his preachin'. He walks across the stage, back and forth, swinging his arms up and down and all around.

My mom says he's not yelling but passionately telling people about the love of God.

My Pawpaw and Granny have five children. Their children and their children's children visit yearly for Christmas and stay until New Year's Day.

Twenty-plus people cram in the parsonage for the next seven to ten days to bring in the New Year together.

All the kids sleep on pallets in the TV room. Parents in the spare bedrooms and on pull-out couches in the living room. Any overflow sleep in the church.

The drive to Georgia takes about ten hours along beautiful, scenic, two-lane southern roads. I have such satisfying memories of those trips with my family.

My sister Katrin (we call her Kat) is ten years old. She is cute as a button; her hair is dark, shiny, and brown. She wears it long with bangs. She always wants to play with dolls, but I always talk her into playing imaginary games instead.

My little brother, Mark, is five years old; he has short curly brown hair, a little lighter than my sister and I. He always follows us around, wanting to play, play, play.

Kat and I occupy ourselves during the ride by playing games such as *I Spy with My Little Eye*, reading Mad Lib magazines, Archie comic books, and singing super stupid, silly, and mostly funny songs!

Boom, boom, ain't it great to be crazy?
Boom, boom, ain't it great to be nuts like us? Silly and foolish all day
long.
Boom, boom, ain't it great to be crazy? A horse, a flea, and three
blind mice,
Sitting on a tombstone shooting the dice,
The horsey slipped and fell on the flea,
The flea said whoopsie; there's a horsey on me. Boom, boom, ain't it
great to be crazy?

I love riding in the back of our 1975 custom van. I look out the window into the woods as we whiz past. I gaze deep inside them, through the shadows and trees. Sometimes it's crowded, dense, and dark, other times, thin, sparse, and light.

I wonder if people live there and, if they do, why and how they ended up there. What would it be like to live like that? No school, just living. I had read a book that year called *My Side of the Mountain*. It was about a young boy who ran away from home and lived in a hollowed-out tree trunk on a mountainside. It spurred my curiosity and imagination to thoughts I had not previously encountered.

Driving through all the little towns fascinates me; some are so small that they only have one stoplight. Others have one little store with a gas pump out front. I wonder, where do these people shop for clothes? Where are their grocery stores and schools? What do they do for fun? They don't even have a skating rink!

Other towns we drive through are big cities with many shops and restaurants, and I always want to stop and explore.

Driving through Mississippi, I notice the woods changing. I can no longer scan the depth of trees and beyond; some plant completely covers them and blocks my view.

"Mom, what's covering all the trees?"

My mom is brilliant; she works at Arkansas State University. She received her Ph.D. as a plant pathologist and has a huge office and a desk with her name on her door, Dr. Stephanie Archer.

"It's kudzu, Sam," Mom says, "an invasive plant that smothers other plants and trees under a blanket of leaves. It hogs all the sunlight and keeps other species in its shade."

"It looks creepy; anything could hide under there."

"Sweetheart, there isn't anything different underneath the kudzu; it's the same woods and trees, just covered like a tent."

But I wonder if that is true. I don't want to doubt my mom, but Bigfoot, the Lochness Monster, and the Devil's Triangle were a viable part of my young imagination.

Maybe parents don't think about monsters, at least not like kids do. I see the pictures and bold headlines in magazines at the grocery store, which look like the real deal, but when I talk to my dad about such things, he pokes fun at me.

We've driven for three and a half hours when Mom says it's time to stop for a bathroom break and a bite to eat.

My mom packed lunch for us—wonder bread, fried chicken, and Ruffle potato chips with sour cream & onion dip and unsweetened iced tea to drink.

We sit at a concrete picnic table and eat lunch. The rest area is pretty and clean, with snack machines by the bathrooms. We aren't in a hurry, knowing we still have six or even seven hours left in our drive.

Our parents gave us our Christmas gifts last night. We pretended it was Christmas Eve because we were traveling today and couldn't bring them all to PawPaw and Granny's house.

Mom said, "Santa knows where we will be on Christmas Day, he will bring the rest of the gifts to their house"

My favorite gift was a camera and three rolls of film! I can't wait to start taking photographs and making photo albums.

I'm wearing one of my Christmas gifts; a new pair of jean shorts and a cute T-shirt with an iron-on patch of a Fox on the front. Underneath the fox, it reads, "Foxy... I love it!

It's a perfect day, with not a cloud in the sky. The sweet smell of honeysuckle is in the air, it feels good, and at that very moment, I knew that life and all that God gave us are beautiful and amazing.

A twelve-year-old doesn't think about time or realize the significance of how quickly life passes, not when 24 hours seems like forever. I could never have imagined how my view of the world would change in the next few minutes of my young life, not to mention throughout the next fifty-plus years.

After lunch, my sister and I walk to the bathrooms, leaving our mom to pack the leftover food.

Next to the restroom is an information board. I see a MISSING poster with a girl's photo. She looks about my age. I almost keep walking; I should have kept walking, but my curiosity wouldn't let me.

What I read and understood on the flyer was pivotal in my young life. It would be a massive part of making me into the person I would be as an adult, and it would stay with me for my entire life.

I hold on tight to Kat's hand as I read the typed and pinned information on the board. There was a photograph of a sweet-looking girl at the top of the flyer; below the photo, it read:

MISSING!

Leslie Elsa Jenkins

Last seen on August 27, 1978, Near Locust Lane and Main Street, Tupelo Mississippi

Full Description of Leslie:

Twelve years old

4'8" and 90 pounds

Curly blonde hair

Dimples on both cheeks

Hazel eyes

Pierced ears

Birthmark on left shoulder, looks like a strawberry

CONTACT INFORMATION:

If you have information, contact the Tupelo Police Department. Anonymous tips are also taken at 662-784-5185.

My sister starts tugging at my arm, bouncing around, about to pee herself. Finally, I pull myself away from the awful flyer and go inside to use the bathroom. When we come back out, I take a photograph of the flyer with my new camera.

My dad and brother exit the men's room.

"Look, Dad, a girl my age went missing."

He stops and reads the flyer. "You shouldn't worry, honey; you kids are safe with Mom and me."

He takes my hand, and we get back in the van. Dad puts in an eight-track tape, and we hit the road. The music is from the movie *Grease*, an American top forty hit this summer. Dad says, "Y'all lay down in the back and try to take a nap; the drive will go quicker." The last song I remember hearing before I fell asleep was *Hopelessly Devoted to You*.

I stir at some point and hear my parents whispering about the little girl; they sound worried. Then I finally fall asleep, but I have a bad dream: the girl was crying, sad and alone, and I couldn't find her. She was always just beyond my reach.

Chapter 2: Christmas Vacation

Samantha Archer (Sam), December 24, 1978

We arrive at our grandparent's house around dusk, and after sleeping the last few hours of the trip, it felt like transportation by magic.

All my dad's siblings are either preachers or married to preachers, and they're some of the sweetest and funniest people I know.

That night, as I am getting ready for bed, I ask my mom, "Why is Dad a forest ranger, and all the rest of his family are preachers?"

She says, "That wasn't what God wanted him to do. Instead, he has found comfort and satisfaction in nature and takes care of God's land. You know it's not bad to be different, right, Sam?"

I nod my head, and she gives me a big hug.

"Okay, off to bed, honey," Mom says.

On New Year's Eve, our whole family goes to the church to sing in the New Year together. The church members are invited to join us, and the New Year worship service has become a tradition and a packed house each year.

That is why we all come every year—to sing together.

I especially like the fun songs, where everyone stands, claps, and moves to the music.

One of my favorite songs is *I'll Fly Away*. It has a beautiful tune, and everyone gets excited and energetic!

I'll fly away, ole glory.

I'll fly away in the mornin'
When I die, Hallelujah, by and by,
I'll fly away

All the cousins hang out from Christmas Eve to New Year's Day. We play croquet, frisbee, or football in the huge front yard during the day. At night, we play cards and other games. Then for sleeping, we all crowd into the TV room where our parents make pallets on the floor for us. Then, when the lights turn off, we talk about anything and everything—what we've heard from friends, what we've overheard from our parents talking, and sometimes what we've seen on TV.

I tell them about the missing girl poster. We whisper about what could have happened. The poster says she has been missing for over four months, since the end of August. I'm scared that a girl like me is gone, nowhere to be found.

My cousin David says, "I think she was kidnapped, maybe tortured, and murdered." We all shiver at the thought.

We pray for her and finally sleep, but the discussion continues throughout the next seven days, sometimes with one cousin and sometimes with two or three.

My cousin David and I like to go arrowhead hunting. One morning after breakfast, my dad packed two bag lunches for us, and we left right after breakfast.

Wandering in the woods and finding random things and places is still one of my favorite things. We talk about everything and nothing as we explore.

"Do you think the kidnappers will chop her head off?" David asks.

"Ewwwww, David! Why do you say things like that?"

29

He smiles, shrugs his shoulders, and says, "I don't know; people are crazy; maybe she was stolen by devil worshippers."

He wiggles his eyebrows, and I roll my eyes.

We come to an old shack in the middle of the woods. It's deserted, broken down, and rotting. It looks spooky. We start looking for clues, wondering who lived here in the middle of nowhere. There are a few rusty beer cans, old candy wrappers, and a toilet seat on the steps. I'm startled by a muskrat running across the porch and let out a little gasp.

David laughs.

Ugggh, boys!

Inside the shack, there are bugs and spiders everywhere. The front room has old nasty carpet on the floor and a torn-up couch. The rest of the room is empty. The kitchen doesn't have a foundation, and the stove is in the backyard.

"She could be hidden in the woods, maybe locked up in a cabin like this." I say.

"If she were in a cabin like this, she'd probably die."

"Come on, David!" I hit his shoulder with my fist.

He shrugs his shoulders.

We continued our adventure and came to an abandoned railroad track with shabby old boxcars, run-down, faded, and forgotten. We sit on the edge of one and eat our lunch.

"You know, a kidnapper could've put her in a boxcar, and they could go anywhere unnoticed. She could be in Colorado, where it's snowing. Or in California, where the sun shines, and the weather's always warm. So maybe they aren't hurting her and just wanted a daughter," I reason.

30

He nods his head. "Kidnapped, torture, or murder. I've said it before."

I have no idea how to respond; I have to believe there are other possibilities.

Frustrated, I proclaim, "When I'm older, if no one has found her, I'll look in every boxcar, shack, city, and state; I will find her."

He shakes his head and says, "You probably won't even remember." I don't think he was trying to be mean, but it still hurt my feelings.

Part Three: Leslie Jenkins, 1978

"For in the day of trouble he will keep me safe in his dwelling; he will hide me in the shelter of his sacred tent and set me high upon a rock,"

Psalms Twenty-Seven: Five.

Chapter 1: Lucky Charms

Leslie Jenkins, August 26, 1978

After opening my front door to Bonnie, she rushes in and pushes me against the wall, banging my head.

She puts a cloth over my mouth and nose, and everything goes blurry, my knees buckle, then blackness.

When I wake, I am in a moving vehicle. All I can think of is "Stranger Danger" and how my parents had warned me, and I hadn't listened. My body is trembling with coldness, and my clothes are damp. I'm lying on my back on a bench seat, looking up at the ceiling. My heart and mind are pounding, I have to get away. I'm trying to remember what happened, but my brain is foggy.

My name is Leslie Jenkins, and it was Bonnie I trusted. Why had I trusted her?

I've been awake for a little while just listening. I hear rain on the roof and muffled voices, I just don't understand what they are saying. There's also loud music playing. It's one song that keeps repeating over and over, it's called *Dust in the Wind*.

I'm terrified to speak, but I have to pee so badly.

"Uhhhh, hey, um… hello? I have to go to the bathroom," I say, my voice shaking.

I hear a man's voice, "Bonnie, please help Leslie."

"Okay, Leslie, I'm going to help you sit up." She reaches over the bench seat, and helps me. "Crawl over the seat," Bonnie says.

We're in a van, and all the windows are covered with thick curtains except the front window.

Bonnie says, "This will probably be weird for you, but..." she pulls open a built-in closet door. "I'll close the door and turn up the music so you can pee in private." There's a small port-a-potty in the closet, and a tiny shower. I thought I'd never stop peeing. I sat wondering how to escape until I hear Bonnie call out, "Are you done?"

"Yes," I say and do the only thing I can think of when she opens the door, I push Bonnie forward, catching her off guard. I then reach for the side door, hoping I could open it fast enough to jump out.

But she catches my leg, and I fall against the door before I can grab the handle.

Bonnie says, "I wish you hadn't done that, you need to calm down."

The man says, "I knew we should have found another way to get her to come with us; this was too risky."

Bonnie says, "Leslie, we're almost at our hideout; I'll explain what's going on when we get there."

Hideout? My mind fills with dread.

"Leslie, do you understand?" Bonnie asks.

"Yes, but I want to go home!" I cry.

Bonnie lays a cloth over my face, and I sleep.

I'm confused when I wake up again, it's dark. Where am I? I'm still fully dressed, in my pajamas. I can't see anything but blackish-gray colors—no daylight or any light, for that matter. My brain is whirling. I touch and feel all around me.

I have a blanket and a pillow under me. I get on my hands and knees and crawl around on the floor; it's a cold, hard surface. I have enough room to lie down as long as I curl my legs. Then, when I lift my arms like a bird's wings, I can touch both walls beside me.

I jump up and try to reach for anything, but it's just air above me. I think I'm in a hole; I sit for a while and listen. There is water running somewhere, but the sound is far away. The smell is stale and damp, and I'm cold and hungry, and I want my mom. I bet she thinks I'm dead. My body begins shivering, and I cry out. "Someone, please help me!"

I haven't seen or heard from anyone in what seems like hours. I think I'm losing my mind. I've been yelling, shouting, sobbing, and now my throat is sore. I'm thirsty and have no more tears. Now I'm just mad.

I finally hear someone from above. "Hey, kid," Bonnie says, "I brought you a bucket to use the bathroom."

She lets down a bucket connected to a rope. I have to go so bad that I don't even question her.

"I'm done."

She pulls the bucket back up.

"Are you hungry?" Bonnie asks.

"What do you think? The last time I ate was lucky charms this morning, and they weren't so lucky, were they?" I say. I couldn't seem to help myself, I was terrified and angry, and my heart was pounding out of my chest.

"Whoa, kid," she says, "you damn sure got spunk."

"Please let me go!" I beg. "Why am I in this hole?" I ask, scared to death.

Bonnie says, "You're in the hole because when we took you out of the camper-van, you tried to bite me and kicked Carl in the balls, trying to get away from us! You're so feisty!"

I vaguely remember that happening. Everything is foggy, and I think I'm confused by whatever made me go to sleep. But, good for me!

"I don't remember," I say defiantly, trying to be brave.

She lets down a sack tied to the rope; I untie it and look in the bag. There is a bologna sandwich, chips, and a canteen of cold water.

"Look, we want to let you out of there, but we think you'll try to run away. Listen to me; we have taken you for a reason." Bonnie says.

"Just let me go!" I beg. "I won't tell anyone. Drop me off somewhere, and I'll call my mom, please!" I plead.

Bonnie leaves without another word.

Chapter 2: You Need to Calm Down

Leslie Jenkins, September 1, 1978

I'm still in this stupid hole.

So far, they've told me nothing, nor have they touched me in any weird way that I've heard adults talk about when they think you aren't listening.

I'm not sure how many days it has been. I'm living in the dark and beginning to feel a little crazy. I don't cry or plead anymore; it's useless. They aren't letting me go. I know that now.

When Bonnie came this morning, she said again that I hadn't been kidnapped.

"Not kidnapped?" I cried in total frustration. "I opened my door trying to help you, Bonnie! And you pushed me into the wall and hit my head! Then you covered my mouth with something that made me pass out, but I wasn't kidnapped?!?"

"Please calm down," Bonnie said.

"When I woke up, I was tied up and couldn't move my hands, but I wasn't kidnapped?!? You bring me food like I'm in jail and you're my guard. I use the bathroom in a bucket, but you didn't kidnap me?!"

"Okay, I get it, and I'm sorry! This isn't how things should have gone. I thought you would listen once you woke, but you tried to escape instead. If I'd let you, you would've jumped outta the camper-van going fifty miles an hour."

"Yeah, I would've," I snarled, remembering my failed escape attempt.

"Look, kid, we need to tell you what's happening, and you're making this hard. Take a chill pill, and listen, please." Bonnie said.

"I just want my mom!" I said. She shook her head and walked away.

The darkness is taking everything away from me. I lie on the stone floor with blankets underneath me and fall asleep crying.

The pillow I sleep on still smells like home, and so does my fuzzy blanket. I think of my mom; I try to see her face, but it isn't clear. I'm not angry anymore; I feel defeated. Sometimes I want to give up, but I'm unsure what will happen if I do.

I hear people talking in the distance, but I can't tell what they're saying. The one thing I do hear is music for hours and hours. They pick a song and play it over and over and over. The hit of the day is called *House of the Rising Sun*.

My thoughts are interrupted, "Good morning, Leslie. I'm going to take you out of the hole so you can bathe and shower today." Carl says.

This is unusual; I haven't seen or spoken to him since they took me. Why is he here?

"Where is Bonnie?" I ask.

Carl doesn't answer and throws the rope down with a foothold knotted at the bottom.

"Put your foot in the loop, reach up, and take hold of the rope," he replies.

I comply, and he begins to pull the loop ladder up. When I reach the top, Carl reaches out his hand and pulls me up the rest of the way. His flashlight is pointed at the ground, so I can't see his face. I only see his dark silhouette in a pitch-black room that feels very big.

We begin walking; he's holding my wrist, leading the way. I'm frightened, but I don't want him to know.

The sound of water flowing is getting louder, and I hear people talking.

Bonnie comes up and takes my hand. "Hi, Leslie, you're coming with me."

Carl turns onto a different path and says, "I'll see ya in a little bit."

Bonnie and I begin walking, and she shines her flashlight for me to see. We are in a cave. There are weird rocks everywhere—scary but beautiful.

Bonnie points and says, "The rocks coming down from the ceiling are called stalactites, and the ones growing from the floor are stalagmites. Have you ever seen or learned about them?"

"No."

"Have you ever been to any caves before?"

"No, aren't their bats in caves?"

"Yes, but you won't find any in this cave."

Walking further, Bonnie stops and says, "Okay, we're here."

In front of us is a massive, man-made wall with three sides abutting the cavern.

Bonnie says, "We built this wall around a hot spring; we use the area for bathing." Then, she turns towards me and says, "It may smell a little funny because of the sulfur mineral, but it's private, like a bathroom."

"Really?" I'm not sure if I should believe this.

"Yes, you'll see. The water temperature is warm naturally, but we also use heating stones. We burn rocks in the fire and throw them in to warm the water. It won't be super-hot, but it's the best I can do. Everything you need is behind the wall." Bonnie says.

I slowly step behind the wall and see lit candles and a big hole in the floor that looks like a tub. The music is much closer from here. They have changed the song to a catchier one. ...*I can't complain, but sometimes I still do. Life's been good to me so far...*"

I kneel and let my hand sink into the water, and it is warm. There's a towel, washcloth, soap, shampoo, and my clothes from home on a nearby rock. I pick them up and bury my face in them. They smell like home, and my heart fills with warmth and despair.

I enter the water, and it feels incredible. I haven't had a bath for who knows how many days. Then, after soaking for as long as possible, I dress in my fresh clothes. I feel happy, at least for the moment, just to be clean.

When I come out, Bonnie takes my dirty PJs and says, "I'll wash your Scooby-Doo pajamas so you can have them later." All I could think was they won't smell like home anymore, which made me feel a deep sadness.

As we walk back towards my hole, Bonnie says, "Leslie, others are here besides Carl and me. We're like a family. Would you give us a chance to explain why you are here?"

"I don't know." I pause. "No." Finally, I murmur, "I want to go home."

"Leslie, you have been here almost a week. Does it feel that way to you?" Bonnie asks.

"No... I mean, yes, I don't know. I can't seem to keep track of time."

"Please listen to me and understand. You won't be going home anytime soon. I'm not saying you can never go home. Just not right now."

I open my mouth but can't speak.

"Leslie, your mom is a good person, but your dad isn't. You don't know, but you and your mom were in big trouble, so we tried to help you. Do you understand?"

"How do you know my dad is bad? Do you know him?" I ask.

"No, not personally, but Carl knew him, and he is a bad man."

Silence.

"Leslie, do you understand?"

Silence.

"Answer me, Leslie."

"Yes ... I understand."

We arrive back at my hole, and Carl is there to lower me down. I put my foot in the loop of the rope and go back into the dark.

41

Chapter 3: Hear Them Out

Leslie Jenkins, September 3, 1978

Bonnie comes with my breakfast. I've decided to hear them out this morning.

I say to Bonnie, "I'm ready to talk. I promise I won't try to run away."

"Wow, I wasn't convinced this day would come. Give me a minute and let me get Carl so he can pull you out'ta there," she says.

Carl arrives ten minutes later, tosses the loop ladder down to me, then pulls me out of the hole.

As we're walking, Bonnie says, "You might want to squint your eyes a little bit as we get close to the mouth of the cave. You've been in the dark for eight days."

"Eight days?" I ask. "It feels longer."

"Yeah, I bet it did. You're a strong-minded kid," Bonnie says.

"Hard-headed is more like it," Carl interjects.

We veer off the path, and the music I've heard for days gets louder as we approach a vast room.

"Before we chat, we need to eat breakfast. Plus, you need to meet the others. They're in a chamber we call the living room." Carl says.

I don't respond. I'm still afraid and not sure I want to meet the others.

Walking into the living room, I find that the other people I've been hearing in the distance. They are kids like me, maybe a little older.

I see an enormous flat rock slab with breakfast laid out for us, and I am starving. The smell is making my mouth water. Somehow, they have cooked eggs, bacon, and pancakes. How did they do this in a cave?

There were two boys, Saul, and Matthew, and one girl, Sherry, waiting to meet me. The room is large and spacious. They are all sitting around on random rocks that look like seats.

Carl says, "I want you guys to meet Leslie."

"I'm glad you came out of that hole," Sherry said.

Saul and Matthew said hello.

I learn during breakfast that Carl is in charge of all the music. He chooses what to play, when, and how long it plays. I should have known.

Bonnie says, "Most of the time, Carl plays his guitar with the music, trying to learn how to play the song acoustically.

So that's why we hear it over and over, I think.

After breakfast, Bonnie and Carl take me to the mouth of the cave. There is a waterfall flowing in front of the opening. However, it isn't splashing into the cave, and it is mesmerizing. We sit by a fire pit not far from the entrance. Carl starts a fire and explains how he knew my dad and why they had taken me.

Carl begins, "Your dad hired me to work temporarily for B & B. The job was for ten days, and on the last day of the job, your dad asked me to go out for a few beers. I didn't want to offend him; he had been nice to me, so I met your dad at Dave's bar, nursed a beer, and hung out. Unfortunately, your dad continued to order one beer right after the other, with shots to boot. As a result, he got drunker and drunker throughout the evening."

My stomach is in knots, and I'm not sure if I want to hear this.

"At some point, your dad began to tell me dark secrets; and the secrets he shared, well, I couldn't forget. The thing is, Leslie, I'm so sorry to have to tell you all this stuff because you are so young, and I don't know even know how much you will understand."

Bonnie takes over and says, "Carl came back to the camper-van that night, and he was super upset. He told me that your dad is a bad man. He said your mom asked your dad to move out because he has a drinking problem."

"Yes, my dad told me he would get help, though," I say.

Carl says, "Leslie, what he told me was like a confession; he was drunk. I doubt he would even remember what he told me. Your dad said he planned to get that woman back, talking about your mom. Your dad was furious, and he said, 'She had the nerve to tell me that I can't drink in my own house. She accused me of physical and emotional abuse and inappropriate behavior with my daughter.'"

"Then the next thing your dad said sent a chill right through me," Carl continues. "That woman will be gone soon, and then it'll be just me and my little girl. I wasn't sure what he meant, so I asked him. Your dad looked around the bar and leaned in close as he spoke in an almost whisper. I'm not going to tell how, but I guarantee ya' this, we'll be burying her mother, and I'll be back home next week."

Bonnie says, "Carl comes home that night and tells me your mother's life and future are in danger. Leslie, that was on Friday night. We took you the next morning. I'm sorry we've held you in the hole for so long, but we knew if we let you out, you would run away without listening to us."

"It's true, Leslie," says Carl, "You're a fighter. Of course, we tried to give you time, but we never expected you to hold out so long."

"Did my dad hurt my mom? Is she dead? I love my mom so much. Could you please take me to her?"

"Leslie, because you went missing, your dad never hurt your mom. When your mom called the police, they searched your home and canvassed the neighborhood. The spotlight shined on your dad and your mom. That kept her safe, and we kept you safe. She is still alive and well." Bonnie reassures.

"When can I see her?" I ask.

"I don't know, maybe when the police stop looking for us," Carl says.

"Can I send my mom a note and tell her I'm alive?" I ask.

Carl looks at Bonnie and nods his head. Bonnie says, "Yes, you can do that. We may have to wait a while before we mail it to her, but it will be mailed. Get one ready, but it has to be ten words or less."

Bonnie and Carl walk me to the mouth of the cave, and we climb down the rough damp rocks behind the waterfall that lead down to the path below and a pool of water.

I look back up, watching the waterfall cascade over the edge of the cave entrance. It's gorgeous, and I can see the beauty but feel sad and confused.

Are they telling me the truth? Would my dad say those things? I was afraid he just might.

Bonnie and I head back into the cave. She says, "Let me take you to your room we've prepared."

I look around my surroundings as we walk. The cave has a lot of passages.

The mouth of the cave is dome-shaped, with dim natural light and a wide pathway through the center. We pass several chambers along the way, and Bonnie names the rooms as we pass. "That's the living room, kitchen, and the bathing area." We approach the end of the wide path, and it splits, leading in three directions.

Bonnie says, "The middle path continues deep into the caverns. The way on the left has battery-powered lights leading along the stone path to the girls' wing of our cave. The right path leads to the boys' side. We took the left path.

I look at the mattress that is on top of a wooden platform. They took a few outfits from my home and my pillow and blanket.

Bonnie pats the bed for me to sit down and sits beside me.

"I'm afraid I'll never see my mom again." I say.

"You will, just not now," Bonnie says.

My eyes fill with tears, and I cry.

"Would you like me to hug you? I don't know what to do to make you feel better." Bonnie says.

"No," I say and shrug away from her. "I don't want to be hugged by YOU. I just want my mom!"

At this point, my crying becomes more like a baby having a temper tantrum, and I pull the blanket over my head. I begin to hiccup. I feel so homesick, scared, and overwhelmed.

Bonnie sits beside me and doesn't move until the hiccups begin to subside. Then she slowly scoots closer and says, "I haven't seen my mother since, I was twelve."

Chapter 4: Dr. John David Scheffler

Vanessa Jenkins (Leslie's Mom), October 23, 1978

I started seeing Dr. Scheffler two weeks after Leslie's disappearance. It's been two months now.

Today, I have hope when before I felt hopeless.

"Doc, I received a large envelope in the mail two days ago. Inside was a postcard with my daughter's handwriting and her Scooby-Doo PJs!" I say. "The note read, *Mom, I love you. I'm okay. I'll find you.*"

"That's fantastic news, Vanessa," replies Dr. Scheffler.

I say, "The police seem to believe the note is real, but they think that Leslie may have been forced to write the message, or they may be trying to mislead the investigation. The postmark is from Tupelo. Detective Pace told me there were no fingerprints on the postcard or envelope except my daughter's."

"How does that make you feel, Vanessa?" asks Dr. Scheffler.

"Angry and upset that they aren't taking the lead seriously. But it was from Leslie; I know it, without a doubt, and it gives me hope. I believe she is still out there, alive, and that I'll see her again. So, the weight of not knowing if she's dead or alive is gone."

"How did you feel when you opened the package when you knew it was from her?"

"I felt dizzy, overwhelmed, and scared. Then hopeful, I sat down and cried."

"That's all a very normal and healthy reaction, Vanessa," notes Dr. Scheffler.

"I miss Leslie so much," I say. "They also told me that my husband, soon-to-be ex-husband, has finally been cleared by the police.

"That's more good news. Do you feel relieved?" Dr. Scheffler asks.

"Yes, but it won't change how people perceive me; they've already made up their minds either way. Many of my friends have been there for me. Most of them mean well, but inevitably they say the wrong thing. It's probably hard to know what to say.

"Neighbors and townsfolk all know me; even though I don't know them, I'm sure they wonder if I'm involved. They stop me on the streets, in grocery stores, and even knock on my door at home, thinking they will help me by speculating on what might have happened. Which only stresses me out. Others avoid me altogether, even some whom I thought were my friends."

"Yes, hard times bring out the best in some and the worst in others," Dr. Scheffler replies.

"You think?" I laugh bitterly. "Anyway, I'm returning to work next week. Mr. Pearson has been very kind and supportive of me for the past few months. He kept my job open and used a temp service until I could pull myself together."

"You seem to be coping well today, Vanessa. But we will still need to see each other for a long time. You've been

49

distraught since the day she went missing, and that is not something you will get over so quickly," he says. "You are headed in the right direction, though, and I'm happy to see the progress."

Chapter 5: Gypsies, Tramps, and Thieves

Leslie Jenkins, September 6th, 1978

When I first learned my kidnappers were runaways, murderers, and thieves, it was September 6th, 1978, three days after I came out of my hole.

"Bonnie? Why a cave? Why do you live here?" I ask.

Bonnie says, "Yeah, I guess it's time you know more about our little family. So here goes, I was supposedly kidnapped by Carl, so he is a person of interest in my missing person case down in Orlando, Florida. The police would love to find and charge him with kidnapping, arson, and murder. That's why we changed our names."

"Murder? Changed your names?" I ask.

"Yes," she says simply. "Then, there's Saul. He was held captive, tortured, and was a prisoner in his foster dad's basement. Carl found foster dad and did what he had to do. No other kid will be hurt by this man; Carl made sure. The police don't close cases with murder involved, and we aren't sure if Carl left fingerprints, but it's possible."

"Murder?" I ask again.

Bonnie ignores me and continues, "There's Matthew. His mom was mentally, emotionally, and physically abusive to him and his sister. We aren't entirely sure if she even went to the police to tell them he went missing. We think she pimped out her daughter, who knows what she did to Matthew. He hasn't said."

"Pimped out?"

"Then, of course, there's Sherry; I think an evil guy in Texas is still looking for her."

"I'm confused," I say.

"Sorry, I know it's a lot. We don't want Carl to end up in jail. So that's why we keep low profiles. Does that make sense? We live in the cave so we can stay in the shadows. Oh, and you'll need a new name."

"A new name?"

"Yes, we've all changed our names, and we can't call you by your real name in public. That would be a mistake." Bonnie says.

"Does everyone steal and kill?" I ask.

"No," she states.

"Bonnie, is Carl bad?"

"He's a guy who was abused and stood up for himself. Now he stands up for others. Look, Leslie, we rob homes only when needed and keep our heads down as best we can. Our future is good; we take what we need and care for each other. Do you understand?"

I nod yes, but I don't understand at all.

Part Four: Chris & Brenda, 1954-1972

"Everyone is a moon and has a dark side which he never shows to anybody,"

Mark Twain.

"You never forget a person who came to you with a torch in the dark,"

Unknown.

Chapter 1: Life of Shadows

Chris Finch, April 1954 - April 1969

My name is Chris Finch—not Christopher, just Chris. I don't have a middle name. My mother, Earlene, died during childbirth, and my father, Lee, didn't remember what my mom had chosen for my middle name. So, he decided nothing.

I was born on April 15, 1954, and grew up on a farm in Paragould, Arkansas. We lived in an old, wooden, two-bedroom shack that had rats and smelled like cigarettes. The front yard was mostly bare, with a large white oak tree and a dirt road leading to the house from the main road.

My dad was a bitter man. He was angry at my mom that she had died and mad that he had to raise his son alone.

My dad worked on his farm from sunup to sundown. So, when I was a baby, he would have our closest neighbor, Mrs. Jacobs, come over to babysit. She would bring her son, Stevie, make breakfast and lunch, and leave shortly after. I was left in my crib for the rest of the afternoon, alone, until my dad came in from the corn fields.

He had no woman to help him raise me, so he just did what he always did: he worked.

In his mind, his son had killed his wife, and he didn't know how to love me.

When I was five years old, I remember sitting on the porch steps, waiting for Daddy to come home for dinner. He was in a bad way when he walked up into the yard. He looked right through me and never said a word. Then, he walked up the porch steps and into our house.

He usually cooks eggs and bacon when he gets home after work in the evenings. I went to the kitchen, but he wasn't there. I looked around the house and found him in bed.

I hadn't eaten since lunchtime and was starving. I pushed a chair against the countertop and climbed up to get to the cabinets. We had a little bit of peanut butter left, and I liked peanut butter. I got a spoon, sat at the table, and ate.

Then I went to bed, too. We had no TV—only radio. There was nothing else to do but catch fireflies in a jar or lay in the grass and watch as the moon and the stars came to life.

I only remember this so clearly because he came to my room the following day and jerked me out of bed. First, he stood me up facing the wall, and then he whipped me with his belt over and over. I was crying hard. I didn't know what I had done.

As he swung the belt, I kept saying to him, "Daddy, no, please stop, Daddy. What did I do, Daddy? You're scaring me; please stop!"

He never answered me nor said a word. When he left the room, I lay on my bed, buried my face in my pillow, and cried. I didn't understand.

I smelled breakfast cooking but was afraid to leave my room. When I heard Mrs. Jacobs come in, I ventured out. Mrs. Jacobs continued to babysit me until I went into kindergarten.

I never learned what I did wrong, but that was the start of many years of what I now know was abuse.

I went to kindergarten at Woodrow Wilson Elementary School in East Paragould.

Mr. Jacobs would pick me up and take me to school each morning with Stevie. In exchange, my dad promised to give the Jacobs enough corn to last through the winter come harvest time in September or October.

Stevie hated me, but he pretended to like me in front of his parents. At school, he was my tormentor.

I had a tough time in school because Stevie and all the other kids made fun of my tattered clothes, and because I was so skinny, they called me a scarecrow. They would "accidentally" trip me or talk in front of me—about me. I'd get angry and defend myself, and the teacher would call me out and I would be in trouble and humiliated by the teacher.

I would get my hand paddled or put it in a corner for punishment. The teachers never noticed them picking on me, making me angrier.

One day, many years later, when I was 11 years old, my sixth-grade teacher, Mr. Boone, brought me home from school at lunchtime to speak with my father about my misbehavior.

"Mr. Finch, I'm sorry to tell you this, but your son is not suited in behavior or attitude for our particular social environment."

"You mean school? Really?" My dad looked at me.

"Yes, sir. For example, today, we were on the playground during recess. Chris walked up to one of the little girls, Jenny, who was minding her own business, brushing her doll's hair. Chris snatched the doll and ran to the edge of the playground and threw the doll as far as he could away from school property. Jenny started crying, and he walked away and never looked back."

"Dad!" I cut in. "She stole my lunch bag, then threw it in the trashcan! I was paying her back! I told Mr. Boone, but he doesn't believe me, and of course, Jenny denied it."

"Mr. Boone, did you check the trash?"

Mr. Boone's whole face blushed a deep red.

"No, Mr. Finch, I did not, but I don't believe Jenny would lie about such a thing. Sir, we cannot tolerate this conduct at school, and it is a consistent problem with your son."

"I guess not," Dad replied in his slow Southern accent and looked at me.

Silence.

Mr. Boone seemed uncomfortable, then said, "Mr. Finch, we have tried correcting him on many occasions. It doesn't seem to do any good. He says he's picked on, but he's doing the picking. Our decision is suspension from school for two weeks as punishment. Another alternative would be for you to homeschool the boy."

"I see," Dad replied. "Boone, I'd like to talk to my son alone. I'll let you know what I decide. Just give us a few minutes."

Mr. Boone rose, walked to the porch, and sat in the swing.

When he was out of earshot, he asked me, "Do you want to go back to that school boy? Or do you want to work on the farm with me? I could use the help."

Wow, I thought to myself. I assumed I would be in serious trouble, whipped for sure, and told to stay in my bedroom. I wondered, *does Dad want me to quit school?*

"I'd rather never go to school again. The kids are mean, and I hate them. I wanna work on the farm with you," I replied.

We walk outside to the porch, Dad says "Mr. Boone, I'll teach the boy some math, reading, and history. He's going to be a farmer anyways, and the school don't teach that."

"Okay then," said Mr. Boone, as he got up to leave, "I'll let the Jacobs know they no longer need to be giving the boy rides to and from school."

I began working in the cornfields every morning, and Dad started to teach me what he knew about math, reading, and history in the late afternoons. This lasted for a week.

"Chris, it's going to get hot and dirty in the summertime. You'll be outside in the cornfields all day since you aren't going to school. Do you understand me, boy? Even in the summertime, when the heat is at its worse, and most kids play."

"Yes, sir," I said.

If I thought the relationship between my father and I was difficult before, it soon became horrendous.

Working in the fields was sweaty, buggy, and sometimes itchy, but I worked hard and never complained. But no matter the task or how well I did it, my father always corrected me. Whippings were a weekly occurrence.

As my father put welts on my bottom and back, I would feel an intense desire to grab the belt and lash back out at him. But instead, I became quiet, withdrawn, and moody, wanting desperately to turn the tables and hurt him back.

Then, the worst happened. It began as a new punishment.

At the age of thirteen, my father came into my room one night. He said, "The devil has taken me over, and the devil wants his due, so stand up and face the wall. Now, pull down your shorts, boy."

I did as Dad told me; I knew I was fixing to get a whipping. I would close my eyes and not mutter a peep; I wouldn't give him the satisfaction of crying.

So, it surprised me when I felt my father grab my hips. He said, "You owe this to me, boy. Now be still." I froze, mortified, while my father committed the most sinful act a man could do to his own son.

Horrifying. The memory won't go away. Lee, whom I could no longer think of as my dad, told me it was because I killed my mother that I owed him his due.

I was angry and sick to my stomach. I loathed, hated, and wanted to kill my dad. I stayed as far away from him as possible.

One afternoon, I was at the house alone. Lee had driven the truck to town for groceries, and I found my mom's stuff in our crawl space.

He must have boxed it all up after she died and, not knowing what to do with it, put it out of sight and mind.

Before that day, I hadn't noticed the crawl space in the back of the hall closet.

I found four small cardboard boxes filled with photos, clothes, and a small cedar chest that held Mom's wedding dress. The chest smelled like mothballs.

But the best find was my mom's guitar.

I picked it up and marveled; it was a Fender Wildwood Acoustic Guitar. I knew Lee would be home soon, so I backed out of the crawlspace, took the guitar and a photo of my mom to the barn, and hid them in the loft.

I don't know why I hid them, but I guess I figured he wouldn't let me keep 'em if I told him.

After that, when Lee would go to bed in the evenings, I would head out to the barn and learn how to play the guitar with my radio. My first attempt at playing my new guitar was to a song called *White Rabbit*. I had a lot of work to do.

In the barn, I would release my anger. I threw bales of hay from one side of the barn to the other. I punched and pounded the walls, making my knuckles bloody and bruised. I was angry most of the time. I was stuck on a farm with no one around but Lee. I should have stayed in school.

As time passed, my desire to kill Lee and my hatred of him grew.

Today is my fifteenth birthday, and I'm now taller than Lee; my muscles are bigger, and I believe I'm stronger. I've decided it's time for him to die.

After more than two years of planning, I know I can take him if it becomes a fight. I have every detail thought out. Tonight, will be fitting; he will die on the same day my mother died and on the day I was born.

We never celebrate my birthday because of my mother, but we never celebrate anything. When Lee comes in from the fields, I have plates on the table and dinner on the stove.

"What's this?" the old man grumbles.

"Dinner," I reply. "I cooked us some fried chicken and cream corn."

It wasn't the first time I'd cooked chicken and corn, but the occasions were rare.

He fussed around, put his shoes up, returns to the table, and sits down. I serve him his last meal. As he eats, I can't help but think to myself, *you'll never have to see this asshole again.* And I smile.

"Whatcha smiling at, boy?" he says.

"Nothing, Dad." We eat in silence.

When he went to bed, I set my plan in motion.

I go to the kitchen, where Lee hides his cash. He has what I guess he thinks of as a secret hiding place—what a dumbass. The money is in the back of a kitchen cabinet in a coffee can. Spices, sugar, and flour sit in front of the can; I suppose Lee thought it would be a good camouflage.

I found his savings a couple of years ago. I'd never touched it, but I've watched it grow ever since.

We have a good crop season this year and the past several years. The can is almost full, I grab the can and stuff it into the bottom of my backpack. Then continue to fill my pack with clothes, a razor, shaving cream, shampoo, and a few eight-track tapes, hoping wherever I end up there will be a player. Finally, I have my backpack ready to go.

Lee smokes cigarettes and always leaves them lying around the house. I'm not one to smoke, I tried them once, and they disgusted me. They always make me think of him. But tonight, I will embrace the odor. I will light a cigarette and deeply inhale when I do so.

Lee finally goes to bed, and I wait over an hour. Then, I pick up my pillow and walk into his room to shake him awake. "Dad, there's a fire." I want him to know what is happening to him in the last moments of his life.

Lee reacts faster than I expected for an old man, but I am quicker. I jump on top of him and pin him to the bed by straddling his stomach, so I will have a more advantageous push position. Then, I slam the pillow down over his face, smothering him.

I feel him struggle against me, fighting to stay alive.

I laugh and laugh as he breathes his last breath. I light a cigarette and deeply inhale, then put it between his fingers as he lay dead in bed.

His bed is by the window curtains, which go up in flames quickly. Since our home is wooden, it was like matches once the fire started.

I return to the kitchen, grab my backpack, and go outside to put it in the barn with my guitar. I figure and hope that I can come back for it later.

The Jacobs down the road must have seen the fire and smoke coming from the house and called the fire department because I can hear the sirens in the distance.

I go back inside through the kitchen. It is getting hard to breathe; the smoke is getting thick. I have to move quickly. I take Lee's arm, pull him out of bed, and drag him out of the house.

I wait for the firefighters, kneeling beside Lee's dead body. By the time they arrive, the house has burned almost to the ground. The firefighters contained the fire, but it's hot and burned for hours after.

When the scene begins to calm down, a policeman, Sheriff Gilmore, approaches me and asks, "Can you tell me what happened here, son?"

"Yes, sir," I say, "I woke myself up coughing, then began to smell smoke. I got outta bed, went into my dad's room, and saw it was on fire. I could hardly see my way to him, so I crawled on the floor to reach his bed. I shook him, trying to wake him, but he didn't move. The smoke was so bad I just grabbed my dad's arm, pulled him out of bed, and got him on the floor. I didn't know if he was breathing or not. Everything was happening so fast. I pulled him outside and tried to wake him up, but I couldn't. He's dead, isn't he? Is my dad dead?" I ask. Then I burst into tears because I assumed most people would if they thought their dad was dead.

No one appeared to suspect foul play. Instead, they all seemed to feel sorry for me and my loss. That is, except for maybe Sheriff Gilmore. He had a funny look on his face after I gave him the details. Maybe I shouldn't have fake cried.

Chapter 2: Uncle Don

Chris Finch, April 15th, 1969

I have no relatives in town, so Sheriff Gilmore offers to take me to his house for the night. I stay in his spare bedroom and lock the bedroom door as I sleep. In the morning, I was given a towel and some clean clothes and told to bathe.

Sheriff Gilmore says, "Looks like your dad has a brother living in Orlando, Florida. I reached out to him this morning. He's driving up from Orlando and should be here tonight."

I watched TV all day at the Sheriff's house. I knew about televisions but had never seen one before now. I watched the Brady Bunch, Gunsmoke, the Beverly Hillbillies, and The Carol Burnett Show. It was eye-opening, and I was fascinated. I didn't know life could be so different.

It was early evening when my uncle got to the Sheriff's house. He looks a lot like my dad, with the same brown hair, hazel eyes, and sinewy muscular build. Only healthier.

The Sheriff speaks with my uncle for a few minutes, and we leave. My uncle's car is a light blue 1967 Ford Mustang Fastback— a super sweet ride.

"Chris, would it be okay with you if we stay at a hotel tonight? I'll get us two beds. I've driven all day and want to eat dinner and get some sleep before heading back to Orlando."

"Yeah, sure," I say.

He nods his head, and we find the Twilight Hotel in town, check-in, and walk to the Main Street Cafe. We eat country-fried steak with homemade gravy, french fries, and apple pie with ice cream for dessert. It tasted so good. I've never eaten at the Cafe, and I feel happy. No, not happy. Satisfied.

The following day, as we are getting ready to leave, I ask Uncle Don, "Can we go by Dad's house to see if anything was left? I'm sure there's not much, but my guitar is in the barn. Maybe I'll find some other stuff."

"Sure, Chris."

I walk around the home's foundation and see nothing but burnt trash. I go to the barn and grab my guitar and backpack. Then to Lee's truck and find some tools and a shotgun. My uncle doesn't question a thing.

I hop in the Mustang, never to look back. The bastard got what he deserved. I'm not sure what will happen to his land or his truck, but I don't want either.

The following morning, we arrive at Uncle Don's. He says, "Chris, my home is a split-bedroom floor plan, so you will be on the right side of the house, and we'll share the living room and kitchen area."

His home is neat and clean but smells like an older person, and I wondered why older people have different smells.

As he's giving me a tour of the home, he says, "Son, I'll take care of your financial needs and give you a place to live until you turn eighteen. My one stipulation is that you have to go back to school and graduate; this is non-negotiable." He turns and looks at me sternly. "I know you've missed a lot and will have to catch up, but I'll enroll you in summer school and give you books to read in the evenings until school begins in the fall."

65

"I don't want to go to school. I don't fit in, Uncle Don."

"What do you mean?" he asks. "People only know what you tell or show them about yourself. I'll teach you some tricks on how to deal with the other kids."

Fast forward to late July, my uncle tells me, "I finally got a letter from the school today. They're starting you in ninth grade. You did a fine job in summer school, but you're still starting way behind the curve. I'm going to enroll you in summer school each year, so you can catch up and graduate on time."

"Please no, Uncle Don!" I say miserably.

"Yes, Chris. And on the day, you turn eighteen, you can choose to do whatever you want with your life. Until then, I will take being your guardian seriously."

My uncle has never bothered me or touched me in the wrong way. After arriving at his home, he told me he was a family psychologist. He said, "Chris, your father and I were abused by our dad, your grandfather. Because of that, I left home as a young teen and broke our connection. I tried to get Lee to leave with me, but he was too scared. After leaving, my mind was constantly tortured, and I struggled to cope with the trauma that happened in my youth. I had nightmares and flashbacks of awful things."

I nodded my head, knowing exactly what he meant. "I have them all the time, too," I said.

"Chris, it's a long story, but eventually, I was able to go to college and became a family psychologist. It saved me. Unfortunately, the concept of domestic and child abuse isn't recognized by many people. Most see it as private family business or taboo to speak about. I'm hoping to change the perception. Know this Chris, I'm here to support you every step of the way. You can talk to me about anything, and I will listen without judgement."

It was tough to tell my uncle what had happened to me initially. I was embarrassed and angry and wondered if I was to blame for what happened.

With time, though, I felt safe enough with him to share my living nightmare and my current struggles to cope with the trauma and the guilt of my dad's actions and my reactions.

My uncle said, "I'm glad we're talking about this Chris. My first suggestion is compartmentalization, it will help keep your mind organized, making your emotions and feelings more manageable.

Chapter 3: School Daze

Chris Finch, 1969 - 1971

I wouldn't say I liked school and I hated my uncle for making me go, at least for a little while. I didn't want to go, and I acted like a huge brat. I was a loner throughout ninth grade, but reading, studying, and, yes, school grew on me as the year passed.

In May, when school let out, I began to look for a job that I could do on weekends.

Jake's Auto Repair hired me for my first real job. Jake started me off with grunt work but quickly taught me more valuable skills once he saw how hard I worked. I found the job to be therapeutic. I could work on a car for hours, not even realizing I had been doing so. It didn't feel like work to me; it felt like puzzles.

One late afternoon, my boss, Jake, says, "Chris, I know your uncle brings you to work, well let me tell ya', I have a fifteen-year-old beater sitting in the auto yard behind the shop. It needs more work than I'm willing to put into it. If you want it, I'll sell it to you super cheap, say $200. I can take some of your weekly paychecks until you work it off. Would you want to do that, Chris?"

"What kind of car?" I ask.

"It's a 1955 Chevrolet Bel Air. Two-door, hardtop with high mileage, faded paint, damaged front fender and bumper. Know this, Chris; this car was driven hard by a rich young kid that used it for street racing. You'll be a fine mechanic if you keep that thing running," he says.

I say yes. Eventually, I added a bumper and fender from the junkyard. The next week, brakes. You name it, and I fixed it. After that, my life was school, fixing my car, and working at Jake's on weekends throughout the tenth grade.

In eleventh grade, I was still a loner and thought maybe I always would be. That's when a girl asked me to go to the prom with her. She was in my biology class and sat next to me. I wondered why she asked me to the prom, out of all the other guys. She's one of those girls the football players want to date.

I told her yes, went home that afternoon, and talked to my uncle about her.

"I've never been on a date, held a girl's hand, much less kissed a girl. What do I do if she likes me like that?" I ask him.

"Do you like her, Chris?"

"I don't know; I think she's pretty. She has long blonde hair and brown eyes, a beautiful smile and she's nice. I've never thought of her in a girlfriend sorta way."

"What's this girl's name?" he asks.

"Her name's Sandy."

"My advice Chris? Go and have fun. Expect nothing from her or yourself. Just go to the prom and dance with your biology classmate."

"You make it sound easy," I say.

He laughs and says, "No, not easy. Over the next month, we'll have to pick out a tux, order a corsage and boutonniere, find a place to take her for dinner, and last but not least, do you know how to dance?"

"Oh no … not at all," I say, embarrassed.

"Don't worry. I have a friend at my AA meetings who teaches dance classes. I'll pay for you to take a few lessons from her."

"Okay, thank you."

When the big night finally came, I felt sick to my stomach. I thought I would vomit walking into the gym. The lights were dim, the glitter ball was spinning, and the music walking in was *"I Feel the Earth Move."*

Most students were already dancing. We grab punch. I feel awkward, and we stand around until *"Go Away Little Girl"* comes on. Sandy smiles at me and asks, "Well, are we gonna dance?"

I nod, and as we sway side to side, I begin to relax, and we dance the rest of the night. It felt like we were in our own little world.

When a jock tapped my shoulder and asked if he could cut in, I was glad my uncle had prepared me for the possibility. I nod my head at Sandy and begin to walk away, but Sandy grabs my hand and pulls me back to her, and says to the jock, "I'm with Chris."

The jock looks pissed, but he walks away. I thought, *what did I do to deserve someone like her?* I still feel the deep sad stench of unworthiness from my childhood.

The final dance of the night is *"I'll Be There"* by the Jackson 5. Driving home, I ask her if she would be my girlfriend. She says yes, and my heart skips a beat. I finally truly believed in my head that she likes me.

I spent the rest of my junior year studying with Sandy at the library after school. We became good friends and talked about anything and everything. When school let out for summer, we went on hikes, had picnics, took long car rides, and went to the movies.

In August, the week before the start of our senior year, Sandy tells me her parents and her best friend, Tina, are going to take a last-minute weekend boating trip.

She calls me Saturday morning and says, "We're having fun, but next time you're coming with us."

"I'd love to. Let me know when and I'll ask off work."

The following day, I am watching TV with my uncle when a breaking news story comes on.

"A tragic boating accident in the West Palm area left one teenager dead and three people injured last night. Officials with the U.S. Coast Guard reported the boat hit a channel marker, capsized, and all four people were tossed overboard. The crash happened around 7 PM, and all were airlifted to the Methodist Hospital. The police informed us that a 17-year-old high school senior from Orlando, Sandy Foster, was on the boat that crashed and died at the scene from a fatal injury to the head."

"I just talked to her yesterday," I say as I sit stunned in my chair, devastation. I can't believe she's gone. Over the next few months, I was inconsolable.

Sandy was pure and kind, my friend, my first kiss, and my only girlfriend. She was a presence that brightened every room she walked into. She was a beautiful soul, and I'll never forget her.

Chapter 4: Move On

Chris Finch, 1971 - 1972

My coworker, Frank, has been asking me to hang out with him on the weekend for months. Frank is nice, but he's older than me by about ten years.

"Come on, man. You have to get out and try to move on. I know you loved Sandy, but she would want you to be happy," Frank tries to talk me into it.

One day, I finally give in and met up with him, and he becomes my friend. Frank takes me to my first theme park, deep sea fishing, and exploring the Everglades National Park. He teaches me to shoot my dad's shotgun, drink beer, and smoke pot. Frank likes beer and pot a lot. I'll have one or two beers, but he'll have six or eight.

Pot reminds me of cigarettes, which makes me think of my dad, so I didn't enjoy that experience at first.

But then I did. It numbed my pain of loss, at least for a while. Then it didn't anymore, so I told Frank, "I'm done with getting high."

Frank said, "Your loss man. More for me!"

Since I took my uncle's advice to go to summer school each year, I'm now a senior and have all my credits for graduation.

One day, I say to him, "Uncle Don, I've been thinking that I want to travel when I turn eighteen."

"Son, if I could return to eighteen years old and travel, I would. Where d'ya wanna go?"

"I don't know, everywhere? I've never gotten used to the Florida swamps or year-round warm weather. I want to go and see different places. I want to find my place, my home. I've been considering buying a drivable RV if I can afford one or maybe a camper-van. What do you think? Is it a good idea?"

"For a quest such as yours, I think it would be perfect for you," he replies.

"Do you have that much money saved?" he asks. "I know you've been saving your work money from Jake's, but an RV or camper-van sounds expensive."

"Yeah, I have enough. The night the fire burned my dad's house I grabbed a coffee can from the kitchen cabinet We used for saving money. It was all we had that was worth anything. I knew he had been saving money for us, but I didn't know he had almost $4000 in the can. I haven't spent a penny of his money and saved over $2000 working at Jake's. I added it all up, and I have $5820."

"Whoa, money pockets!" my uncle says. "Okay, let's go tomorrow after school, if you aren't working."

I pull into the VW dealership the following afternoon. Eddie is the salesman on duty. He is a slight man, around thirty-five, with red hair and freckles on his face; he looks like a nice person. His face makes me think of Opie Taylor from the Andy Griffith Show.

When he first saw me, I'm sure he didn't think much would come of a sale because I'm a teenager, but he treated me like an adult anyway.

I tell Eddie, "My father passed away and left me an inheritance, and I've been trying to decide what to do with the money. I'm staying with my uncle right now. He said he

73

would meet me here; I'm considering traveling when I turn eighteen and am interested in your VW camper-van. Can we take a look inside and find out the pricing?"

"Okay, yeah, let's take a look," Eddie says.

My uncle pulls into the lot and joins us. We walk around the outside of the van first.

Eddie says, "It has the long window in the back of the van. The side panels have windows with curtains,"

As Eddie opens the passenger-side sliding door, I see the inside for the first time. He says, "This is a custom van, so notice the expandable divider between the driver area and the back of the van for privacy. Behind the passenger seat is a waist-high refrigerator with a small freezer and cubbies above that can be used for storage."

"Cool!" I exclaim.

Eddie smiles, "Now, the tall closet behind the driver's side is special. So go ahead and pull that door open."

"Okay." I say as I open the door. "Whoa!" I see a sink with shower-head above and a potty underneath. What the heck?"

"Yea, cool huh? When you enter the closet, step over that ledge at the doorway. The ledge keeps the water in the closet, and drainage access is behind the potty." He leans forward. "See?"

"Yeah," I say. "Wow, dude! I never expected there would be a toilet or shower!"

Eddie continues and show us the fold-down bed in the back and the pop-up tent on top.

"I've never seen anything like this," my uncle remarks.

"We've been selling these for a few years, but this is a limited edition," Eddie smiles. "Do you have questions?" he asks.

"Not right now; I feel overwhelmed. Can my uncle and I talk about it and come back tomorrow?"

After we get home, my uncle says, "Chris, I'm on board. If we can agree on a price with Eddie, that is. We can put it in my name if you want, and when you turn eighteen, I'll sign it over to you."

We go back the following day and get the camper-van.

Chapter 5: Brenda's Birthday

Chris Finch, April 15th, 1972

I met Frank's daughter, Brenda, on her twelfth birthday.

I finally turned eighteen, and Frank thinks it's cool that I have the same birthday as his daughter.

"Hey Chris, come over to my house tonight. I'm giving Brenda a little birthday party. Then after, we will have an adult party for you."

"Thanks, man, but I think I'll just stay home tonight," I say as I think about how awkward that would be.

"What, man? Can't you come over and have a few beers on your birthday? Come on; you can meet the family."

When I shake my head no, again he says, "Chris, I thought we were friends." He is really heaping on the guilt.

I think and shrug, "Okay, I'll drop by man. I'm not a big party guy. You know that."

Frank rolls his eyes.

I'd heard about Brenda and Jenny, of course. Frank told me his wife Jenny got pregnant at sixteen; Frank was seventeen. Frank told me her parents are very religious and saw this as rebellion and an offense to God. They felt it was their duty to separate themselves from her sin, so they kicked her out. All I can do is wonder what is wrong with people.

Jenny and Frank don't have a lot of money. Jenny works at Pizza Hut for tips, and Frank at Jake's Auto. They do their best, but they live in a cheap rundown house on Mercy Drive on the edge of town—not the best neighborhood.

Jenny waits on tables for tips at lunch, then gets home in time to meet Brenda's school bus while Frank works. When Frank comes home, he takes over the child-watching duties and begins drinking. Jenny goes back to work for the evening shift.

When Jenny comes home at night after her late shift, they drink together or fight, sometimes both. On the weekends, they have friends come over to party hard, and the cycle continues. They have no clue how to raise their child, and Frank says smoking pot gets them through each day.

When they wanted to give Brenda a birthday party, she didn't want one. Frank tells me, "She says she has no friends at school to invite. How can she be at school all day and have no friends? No one ever comes over and spends the night with her, and she is never invited to anyone's home for a sleepover. Or, if she is, she doesn't ask us if she can go."

I don't know how to respond to Frank because I think from what I know, Brenda has probably had to mature beyond her age with parents that party all the time.

I show up to the party with a present in hand. Frank answers the door.

"Chris, dude, I'm so glad you came! I had a bet with Jenny, and I just won. Oh, hey, I'd like you to meet Brenda."

"Brenda, birthday girl, get over here and meet Chris." She comes over and looks up at me.

"Nice to meet you, Brenda. Your dad tells me we have the same birthday," I say.

She nods her and quietly says, "Happy Birthday."

"Happy Birthday to you too, Brenda," I say, handing her the present.

Frank says, "Brenda, go put that with your other presents."

As she begins to walk away, Jenny says, "The cake is your favorite, Brenda; yellow Duncan Hines with chocolate frosting and sprinkles on top!"

Brenda gives no reply, just a brief smile that never touches her eyes.

Across the room, Jenny is setting the table. She says, "Hi, Chris! It's nice to meet cha."

I wave to her. "You too, Jenny."

The party begins thirty minutes later with ten adults, including myself, Frank, and Jenny.

"Everyone, listen up! Gather together around the table," Jenny says. "Brenda, come sit in front of the cake; I want to get a picture of you!"

We sing *Happy Birthday*, and Brenda blows out the twelve candles.

"Did you make a wish?" Frank asks.

She nods her head.

"What did you wish for?" Frank asks.

She looks up at him and then back down at the cake.

Jenny says, "Frank, don't tease her. You know she can't tell her to wish, or it won't come true!"

He winks, and Jenny begins cutting the cake.

We all eat cake, and then Brenda opens her few presents. She got pop rock candy, a pet rock with a cute face and a pipe cleaner for hair, coloring books and crayons, Flintstone's Weeble Wobbles, a game called Connect Four, tennis shoes, and a Barbie doll that I picked up for her this afternoon.

After cake and presents, it pretty much becomes an adult's party when *Led Zeppelin's, Whole Lot of Love,* begins to play.

Everyone is getting stoned, drinking, acting foolish, and playing Pin the Tail on the Donkey. *Ugh.*

I sit in a recliner in the living room, with a view of the hallway and living room. The kitchen is behind me.

When Frank asked me to join the fun, I gave him a thumbs up and said, "I'm good, man." He seems satisfied and goes back to partying.

Brenda sat quietly at the coffee table, watching the adults as they amused themselves. She seems to be unhappy. I wonder why, other than having reckless parents and being neglected.

Eventually, the party is in full swing—loud laughter and obnoxious conversations. Finally, Frank and Jenny tell Brenda good night and send her to her room, and the party continues.

I remain sober. I still hold my first beer in hand, watching men and women acting like they're having a good time. To me, they look out of control, messy, and stupid. I think I'll give it five more minutes and leave.

I observe a man twice my age going to the bathroom down the hall. But instead, he turns into Brenda's bedroom. I am shocked.

Is he so drunk that he made a mistake? I wait to see if he would return, but he doesn't.

What is he doing in her room? I thought I must be seeing things; this couldn't be right. I'm going to check right now.

I quickly get up and go to the room to find the man leaning over Brenda.

He was a big boy, at least 6'2, compared to my 5'10', and weighed a hundred pounds more than me.

However, I surprise him and yank him backward, away from Brenda. He stumbles, catches himself, and turns around to face me. He is very pissed off and extremely drunk. He begins to come towards me.

"You sick son of a bitch!" I say between clenched teeth.

The man must have seen something in my eyes. He starts to step back, I push him hard, and he falls backward. I watch as his head hit the corner of Brenda's dresser, and I hear a sickly cracking sound as he drops to the ground.

Oh shit!

I bend down and shake his shoulder. He isn't moving, so I check for a pulse and can tell things have gone very wrong. His eyes are wide open, and he is unmoving.

Brenda is staring at the man on the floor.

"Brenda, would you turn over and close your eyes tight," I ask.

She does as asked, and I pull the body into the girl's closet and shut the door.

Then I squat down near Brenda's bed, but not too close, and say. "Okay, you can turn around and open your eyes."

She does and asks, "Is the bad man dead?"

"Yes, he is. It was an accident. I didn't mean to kill him; I just wanted to get him off you. Please don't tell anyone I killed him, honey."

"Okay," she says.

"Brenda, I know what was happening to you; with the bad man," I say. "It happened to me too, when I was a kid."

She just stares at me.

"Has this happened before?"

She nods.

"A lot?" I ask.

She nods again.

"Brenda, does your mom or dad know what's happening to you?"

She stares at me, looks down, and then shrugs her shoulders.

"Brenda, I told you that it happened to me too, and when it happened to me, I just wanted to run away. Do you want to run away sometimes too?"

She nods slowly.

"Would you like to leave this place and go far, far away with me? I promise to protect you from the bad men and never let something like this happen to you again," I say.

She looks at me intently but doesn't respond.

"You can say no if you don't want to go," I say.

Then she nods her head slowly. *Yes.*

"You want to go? Are you sure, honey?"

81

Again, she nods her head. *Yes.*

"Okay, turn over in your bed and wrap up in your blanket. I'll make sure no one else comes in this room tonight. Do you understand me?"

She gives me another nod. *Yes.*

I return to the party and sit vigilantly in the chair with a view of the hall. Finally, people begin leaving the party. Frank tries to keep it going by starting a game of shots.

"Chris, have you seen Redbud?" Frank asks.

"I don't know, which dude is Redbud?" I ask.

Frank walks down the hall, goes directly to Brenda's room, looks in, closes the door, and then looks into the other bedroom and bathroom.

Walking back up the hall, Frank asks, "He has the long-braided hair, tall and pretty hefty dude. Did he leave?"

"Yeah, you know, I think I did see him leave a little while ago," I say and think, *Redbud's in the closet, dude.*

"That's funny 'cause he usually spends the night here when we party," he slurs.

Does Frank know about Redbud and allow it to happen, I wonder?

"Do you need another drink, Chris?" Frank asks as he stumbles towards the refrigerator.

"No, man, I don't need another drink, I'm wasted," I lie.

"You know what, Chris? Since Redbud left, you can crash in Brenda's room."

"Dude, don't you think that would be awkward, me sleeping in your daughter's room?" I point out.

"Nah, man," he replies nonchalantly.

"I might crash on this recliner chair instead. Would that be okay?" I ask.

"Well, I reckon that's okay, man." He replies as he drinks his beer.

Jenny has passed out, so I ask Frank, "Does Jenny allow men to sleep in her daughter's room too? Or is this a between guys thing?"

He looks at me hard and long. I guess he wasn't sure what to say.

"Why do you allow it, Frank?" I say with a sincere lack of understanding.

"Look, dude, don't get all high and mighty on me. And don't judge me!"

"Okay, okay, man," I say, though I hated myself for uttering those words because I wanted to kill him.

I pretend to pass out in the reclining chair, but I am figuring out an exit plan. I believe Jenny allowed this to happen by not being present, and Frank is responsible for ensuring his child's safety. Neither of them deserves to be parents.

I knew what I had to do. I wake Brenda and ask, "Are you sure you want to leave with me?

She nods. *Yes.*

I take her to my camper-van and lock her inside. "I'll be back in just a few minutes, Brenda."

I find Frank's zippo and lighter fluid; the fluid feels full in my hand, and I squeeze the bottle, soaking Brenda's closet,

Redbud's clothing, the carpet, walls, and the door. I then light the curtains on my way out.

I sneak Brenda into my uncle's house, and she sleeps on my bed as I lie in my sleeping bag on the bedroom floor. I can't sleep worrying and wondering what we were going to do.

In the morning, I wake Brenda before leaving for work. I kneel and say, "Morning, Brenda. I need to go to work for a little bit, get some supplies, and then I'll be back, okay? Please don't open the bedroom door. My uncle lives here. He's nice and won't hurt you, but I don't want him to know you're here. Okay?"

She nods.

"I set some milk and Little Debbie cakes on the dresser for your breakfast. I know it's not a great meal, but I will be back for you around lunchtime. If you need to pee, use the connecting bathroom, but don't flush, or my uncle will hear."

She nods yes and puts a finger to her lips.

That made me want to cry. How weird; I've never felt that feeling before. Although I didn't know what it was then, I loved Brenda like a little sister. I wanted to take care of her and protect her from evil.

When I arrive at work, my boss greets me, "Good morning, Chris! Hey, I haven't seen Frank yet. Did his daughter have a good birthday?"

"Well, I'm not much of a drinker, so I left the party after we finished the cake and presents. But yeah, I think the little girl had a good party," I lie.

He pats my shoulder. "He's probably hungover. He'll get here when he gets here." Then, he says, "I'm proud of you, son; alcohol is the devil's drink."

I don't know if that is true, but I do know that some people who drink it are evil.

A detective shows up at Jake's Auto around 10 a.m.

Jake calls us over, and he looks shocked. Frank's house had burned down during the early morning hours—one dead, two in critical condition.

Jake is devastated. Frank had been working for him since he was 17; he was family.

My heart is hammering. One dead, two in critical condition? I saw the smoke detectors in the house. They were in the hallway, the living room, and the kitchen. Brenda's room should have burned, but the alarms must have gone off, waking Frank and Jenny. *Shit*.

Detective Sellers approaches me. "Hi, Chris. Jake tells me Frank had a party last night for his daughter's birthday. Did you know his daughter?"

My heart is pounding like crazy. "No, sir. Frank invited me because I have the same birthday and he's, my friend. Initially, I told him no, but he made me feel guilty, so I went."

"Can you tell me when you left Frank's last night?"

"I'm not sure. I stayed until after the cake and presents. I'm not a big party person," I say.

"So, you stayed for the presents being opened?"

"Yes, sir, that was right after cake."

"Did you notice anything unusual last night?"

85

"No, sir. After the cake and presents, the adults started having their party, and Brenda was sent to her room. When the party started to get wild, I decided to leave."

"What do you mean by wild?" he asks.

"They were rolling some doobies and doing shots. As I said, I'm not much of a partier."

"I thought you said you left after cake and presents," Detective Sellers responds.

"Well, I did, but not right after," I reply.

"Chris, can you give me a more specific time?"

I think for a minute. The detective is writing all this stuff down, and I am worried. "I can guess it was a little after 9 p.m."

Detective Sellers says, "Okay, thanks, Chris. I'll be in touch if I need more information later. If you think of anything, please get in touch with me."

Jake closes the shop for the rest of the day and tells us to go home.

I leave work and stop at a gas station to fill the campervan, then go inside to get a map of the United States and a newspaper.

My mind is worried about the aftermath of Brenda's home burning down. Although I'm guessing the police believe she died in the fire, there was no mention of a child's body.

I look in the newspaper, but it only mentions the burned house and one body, with no details.

I pull up to my uncle's house and go inside. He was at his daily AA meeting down at the Starlight Diner for lunch. Thank God for the small things.

I know we have about 45 minutes before he returns home, so I open the closet door and tell Brenda to come out.

I grab the new duffel bag my uncle gave me for my birthday and shove my eight-track collection, a pack of soap, shampoo, and conditioner, shaving cream, a razor, and clothes into the bag. I throw in the book my uncle gave me to read when I first arrived. I hope to share it with Brenda, as my uncle did with me.

I wish I'd thought of getting Brenda some clothes from her house last night, but I didn't.

"We'll pick up some clothes and anything else you need once we get on the road," I tell her. "Let's get some lunch before we leave."

We go into the kitchen, and I make ham sandwiches and chips.

I look in the food cabinet and take a few cans of tuna, Vienna sausages, Spam, Cheese Whiz, and crackers. I know he won't mind.

Then, I write my uncle a note:

"Thanks for taking care of me and for the duffel bag you gave me for my birthday. I'm gonna hit the road for a while and see where home is for me. I'll check on you when I come back this way. Your nephew, Chris."

I look Brenda in the eye and ask, "Are you sure you wanna do this, kid?"

She nods. "Okay, I think we might have to change our names; people will look for you once they realize you are gone. Will you think about that while we drive?"

She nods her head again.

Brenda settles in the passenger seat, and I ask her where she would like to go. She shrugs her shoulders.

I open the United States map, point, and say, "This is where we are now. Will you point on the map where you want me to drive?"

She lays her finger on California. Far, far away.

I tell her stories as we drive, hoping to make her feel comfortable and safe. First is *Robinhood*; he stole from the rich and gave to the poor. Next, *Huckleberry Finn*— a naughty boy full of adventures. Lastly, *Bonnie and Clyde* who robbed banks and fled across the country.

After a while, she opens up a little and says, "My mom tells me bedtime stories. Do you know *Goldilocks and the Three Little Pigs?*"

"Yes," I heard them from a lady who babysat me when I was little. Do you like the stories I'm telling?

"Yes, can you tell me more?"

"Did your mom ever tell you about Peter Pan?"

She shakes her head no.

"Okay, so Peter Pan is a boy who lives on the island of Neverland. Peter saves lost boys and brings them to safety."

Chapter 6: AKA (also known as)

I like Chris; he doesn't look at me the same way the bad men look at me. I can't explain how they look at me, but I know if they're not good.

I'm glad he saved me from the bad guy. I'm always afraid to be alone in my room.

"Chris, can we change our names now?" I ask.

"Yeah, we want people to think we're brother and sister. Let's say we make our last name Slater. Your name could be Ellie Slater, Bonnie Slater, or Maryann Slater. Do you like any of those?"

"I like Bonnie. Can you be Clyde? Like the story you told me."

"No, honey, that would be too flashy for us to be called Bonnie and Clyde. How about Carl Slater? Do you like that?" Chris asks.

"Okay."

"So, now we need to have a backstory."

"What's a backstory?" I ask.

"Well, we have to make up a pretend story about growing up together and why we aren't with our parents," he says. "You got any ideas?"

"Can we say we ran away?"

"No, if we say that, they will send us back," he says.

"Oh."

"Okay, how about this, we tell people our parents died in a car accident, and we're traveling to California to live with our aunt and uncle. Can you remember that story and pretend that it's true?"

"Yes. How much longer to California?"

"If we drive straight through, I guess it will take about two or three days, but I can't drive that long. Unless you wanna do some driving," Chris says.

"I can't drive!" I say. "I'm only twelve years old!"

He laughs and says, "Just kidding..." "How about we drive for a few hours every day, then park and sleep at night until we get there? Will that be okay with you?" he asks with a smile.

"Yes, but where will we sleep?" I ask.

"Well, believe it or not, this camper-van has a foldout bed in the back and a pop-up room on the roof," he says.

"One on the roof?" I say.

"Yes, on the roof. We can stay overnight at state parks, rest stops, and RV parks. They all allow van camping, and sometimes they're even free."

"Okay."

"Hey, Bonnie, I want you to hear a cool song, one of my favorites by The Mamas and the Papas, called *California Dreaming*," Chris says and pushes in the 8-track tape.

Chapter 7: Dear God

Chris Finch, April 16th, 1972

Brenda/Bonnie and I became friends. I know it sounds weird because I'm eighteen, and she is only twelve. But we relate on a level that most people will never truly understand.

I don't think of Brenda/Bonnie in a perverted way. Although I suppose some people will think so. I told her we could be family and that I would be her big brother and look after her.

We drive from Orlando to Tallahassee. I know, not far, but we got a late start, and I want to set up before dark.

"Brenda, I mean Bonnie, keep your eyes open for something good to eat, and let me know if you see something." Five minutes later, she says, "Look, Chris, ummm, Carl, I mean... there's a place called Big Boy Burger! Can we stop there?"

I see what caught her eye: a massive statue of a chubby little boy with black hair in red and white checkered overalls and blue shoes, holding a plate like a fancy server with a hamburger. Brenda was smiling, I think.

The hostess at Big Boy was an older lady with bleach-blonde hair coiled on the top of her head. Her name was Regina. She sits us at a booth, and I ask her if she knows anywhere, we could camp free or boon-dock around Tallahassee.

"I have no idea. Let me get my manager for you, sweetie."

The manager approaches and says, "Regina said you and your sister are looking for a place to go boon-docking. I go a couple of times a year to the Appalachia National Forest; there is a campground called Brown House. It's about thirty minutes from here. There isn't a charge for camping, but you'll have to purchase a parking pass." He gives me directions.

Heading to the campground, we stop at the Roses Discount store to pick up brown hair dye, scissors, towels, sheets, blankets, pillows, bathroom supplies, old maid playing cards, and some clothes for Brenda. Then, we stop at the A & P grocery store for fresh vegetables, fruit, cereal, milk, bread, and sandwich meats, to put in our little fridge.

The Brown House Campground ended up being an excellent place for an escape. Camping is allowed anywhere, so we picked a secluded spot by a quiet little stream. There is no running water, electricity, or sewage available, hence boon-docking, but we were prepared. I bought a couple of gallons of water, one to drink and one to flush out the toilet before we leave.

"I can't believe we are spending the night in the woods under all these huge trees; they're so pretty," Brenda/Bonnie says with her face to the sky.

I smile, and my heart swells.

"Hey Carl, can I sleep in the rooftop bed tonight?" Bonnie asks.

"Sure, that means I get the back of the van, and if you like it up there, it can be your permanent room," I say.

"Okay."

"Hey, I have an idea. Are you hungry for some Oreo cookies and milk before we go to bed?" I ask.

"Yes, please. Chris, sorry… Carl, I miss my mom and dad."

"I thought you might be sad. Do you want me to take you home?" I ask.

"No."

"You want to talk about it? "I ask.

"No."

"Okay," I say.

We go to sleep, listening to the outside sounds of the night. The crickets, cicadas, grasshoppers, and katydids almost sound like an elegant choir.

Breakfast consisted of Frosted Flakes and milk. Afterward, we go outside and take a walk by the stream. Walking back to the camper-van, I ask, "Brenda, both of us need to cut and dye our hair so we look more like brother and sister. Is that cool with you?"

"You can cut and dye hair?"

"I sure can. I've been cutting my own hair for a long time. However, when it comes to coloring, I do need to refer to the instructions."

So, that afternoon, we sit outside at the picnic table while I cut and dye her hair.

Afterward, I open the TV antenna on top of the camper, and we sit at the dinette table, listening to the TV and playing *Old Maid*.

Suddenly, Brenda says, "Hey, that looks like where I live!"

I look up at the TV and see live footage of a burned-down home with an enormous red maple tree and a worn-out tire swing in the front yard. The reporter comes on the screen, looking solemn.

"Reports have been confirmed that arson was the cause of a home burning down on Mercy Drive in Orlando two nights ago. There is one dead body that has not been identified. Frank and Jenny Larkin are in critical condition and have been taken to the hospital. Unfortunately, we have not located their twelve-year-old daughter, Brenda," says the reporter as they project a screen-size photo of Brenda on TV.

"Please call 880-423-TIPS if you have any information that may help find Brenda Larkin. There is a local search team preparing to search the five-mile radius. If you would like to volunteer, they will be meeting at North Point Church on the corner of Abbott's and First Ave from 9 o'clock this morning until 5 o'clock tonight," concludes the reporter.

Brenda says, "Will they find me?" I watch her face, full of confusion.

"Do you want them to find you?" I ask.

"No," she replies as she stares at the TV.

She doesn't cry, but her face is turbulent with emotions. I want to hug her, but I know she is not ready for anything like that and maybe never would be.

It seems she wants to say more, so I wait. It isn't easy.

"Carl, did you burn my house?"

"I'm so sorry, Bonnie. Sorrier than you'll ever know. I did light a fire in your room. I was trying to burn evidence of the body in the closet." She turns away from me.

"Bonnie, please look at me; I didn't mean for the whole house to catch fire. I saw three smoke detectors and thought it would wake your parents before the fire spread through the house."

Did I mean to kill them? I wondered. Maybe I did. Maybe I was so mad I didn't care if they died. Oh God, what is wrong with me?

"What about my mom? Is she okay?" Her tears begin to flow.

"Your mom is in critical condition, meaning she is hurt but still alive and in the hospital."

"Can we go see her?"

"Yes, I'll drop you off if you want me to. You can walk into the hospital and tell someone your name. Your real name, but honey, I can't go with you."

"Why?"

"Because the police will put me in jail for taking you away and burning the house."

"You helped me."

"Yes, I did help you, but I wasn't supposed to take you away from your parents."

"I wanted to go. My parents didn't care about the bad men. You saved me from him, from them."

"Are you ready for me to take you to the hospital?"

She remains still and quiet. Then, she says, "No, I don't wanna go back. I was always alone and afraid."

"Okay, we'll let's put a little distance between us and Florida. Your face is all over the TV."

She nods her head okay.

We look at the map together and plan our next stop: New Orleans, Louisiana. I've been to two places in my life: Paragould, Arkansas, and Orlando, Florida. Bonnie says she has only been to the beach. Now we are heading clear across the country to the West Coast.

Dear God, I hope I did the right thing; I can't take it back. Nor do I want to; I couldn't stand to think of her trapped in that home. I knew too well how that felt.

Chapter 8: Person of Interest

"How is the Brenda Larkin case coming, Detective Sellers?" The captain asks as soon as he enters the precinct.

"Well, the twelve-year-old girl's body still hasn't been found, alive or dead. Chris Finch is my main lead and suspect right now."

"Tell me," My captain says.

"There are four people who left the party around 11:00 pm and two that left around midnight. Their whereabouts are accounted for, and alibis have been checked and are solid. Each one put Chris still at the party when they left. Yet, Chris told me in his statement yesterday that he left the party around 9:00 pm."

"Okay then, get him in here," the captain responds.

"I will when I find him. I'm headed over to his uncle's house right now."

"Keep me updated, Detective."

When I arrive at the uncle's home, I see a Mustang Fastback in the driveway. I take this as a good sign and knock on the door. An older man answers, and I show him my badge.

"Good morning, sir. My name is Detective Sellers. Are you Donald Finch?"

"Yes, sir. How can I help ya?"

"Sir, I'm looking for your nephew Chris Finch. It's my understanding that he resides at this address."

"Yes, sir. He does, or at least he did. So is Chris in some trouble Detective Sellers?"

"Not at this time, sir. We'd just like to speak to him. He may have been one of the last people to leave a party where a house burned down two nights ago."

"Oh, well, when I got home from a meeting yesterday, there was a note on the counter saying he was going to hit the road and travel for a while."

"What time was that sir?"

"After 1:00, I had lunch before going home."

"Was this 'hitting the road' expected?" I ask. All my alarm bells are going off.

"Expected? Yes and no. He told me when he turned eighteen, he planned to travel and find his place in life. We even purchased a camper-van for him a couple of months ago. He talked like he may head back toward Arkansas because Florida never felt like home. I didn't know it would be right after he turned eighteen. I was just a little surprised about how suddenly he left."

"Could I take a look at that note, sir?" I ask, my heart pounding.

"Sure, come in and sit while I fetch it," he says.

The note is short:

Thanks for caring for me and the duffel bag you gave me for my birthday. I'm going to hit the road for a while. I'll check on you when I come back this way.

Your nephew, Chris

"Do you mind if I keep the note, sir?" I ask.

His brow furrows, and he looks me in the eyes. "Detective Sellers, are you sure he isn't in trouble? He keeps to himself, with no incidents with the law. He's lived with me since he was fifteen when his dad passed away."

"Right now, he's not in trouble. We hope he can provide information or insight about what happened the night of the party. We're just being thorough, sir. Do you mind me askin' what happened to his father?"

"He died in a house fire, smoke inhalation. The boy's whole life burnt up in a snap."

"I see," I say, my alarm bells intensifying. "What part of Arkansas is he from?"

"He and his dad lived on the outskirts of Paragould on a farm. Not sure he'd go back there, bad memories and all, but he told me he missed the mountains. You know, the foothills of the Ozarks."

"Yes sir, I know 'em; been there, beautiful country. What kind of camper-van did he get? I've had my eye on buying one of those things for years." I say.

"It's one of those German VWs." Donald replies.

"Do you know when your nephew got home the night before last?"

Mr. Finch is getting agitated at this point; I can hear it in his voice and see it in his facial expression.

"No, sir. I don't know what time. I go to bed early, and our rooms are on opposite sides of the house; he comes and goes as he pleases. Now if you don't mind, I have a busy day," he says.

"Okay, I understand; thank you for your time, Mr. Finch. Here's my card; please let me know if you hear from Chris."

He shut the door in my face.

I relay the conversation to the captain when I return to the station.

"His uncle mentioned his father died in a house fire. That's two fires around the same person in the past three years; that's suspicious. I'm calling Paragould Police Department to see what I can find out about him."

"Good job, Detective. Find that boy. This could be kidnapping, added to the arson and murder charges if he has the girl," says the captain.

I spend an hour on the phone with Sheriff Gilmore of the Paragould Police Department, who worked the Lee Finch death and fire in 1969.

"Well, Detective Sellers, I gotta agree; the similarities are there. The night Chris's father died, and his house burned down, I couldn't outright see anything that might prove my thoughts or feelings about Chris, but he seemed off. He played the part well if he was faking crying. I suspected he might be, but I couldn't be positive. I had him come to my home to stay overnight because he had no relatives in town. I contacted his uncle the following morning, so he spent the night at my home. He spoke very little. The next morning, he had breakfast and lunch before his uncle showed up. I kept the water glass he was using, put it in a baggie, and checked it into evidence. As I said, he seemed off. The glass should have his fingerprints," says Sheriff Gilmore.

"Can you get those fingerprints into the system, you know, on a hunch?" I ask.

"Yes, I'll circulate a BOLO, reporting he is a person of interest in an arson, murder, and kidnapping case out of Orlando. With him growing up here in Paragould, the guys will be on a heightened alert. I'll call if anything comes up." says Sheriff Gilmore.

"Thanks," I say and hang up, thinking we may be onto something.

Chapter 9: Ramble On

Carl Slater (aka Chris) 1972

Laissez Les Bon Temps Rouler

After driving for two hours, we stop for a snack and gas.

"How far is New Orleans?" Bonnie asks.

"Not sure. I've never been, but according to the map, the drive looks pretty far." I say.

The filling station attendant says, "I've been to New Orleans. It's about a six-hour drive from here."

"You know where we might find camping or boondocking?"

"Yes, sir. Rest Dem' Bones Campground is pretty close to New Orleans, maybe about 15 minutes 'fore you get there. My da's took me there a couple of times. Damn good crawfishin' on the property if you wanna try it."

We make it to the campground late that afternoon and drive into New Orleans the next day. We find parking under a bridge a few blocks from the French Quarter.

We walk down Canal Street and find Bourbon Street in the French Quarters. Bourbon Street is a fully functioning street, open to car traffic during the daytime, with bars, stores, and restaurants.

However, the road is blocked at night and becomes one large walkway for pedestrians and party-goers.

The street smells like spilled beer and piss, which is gross, and there were tons of tourists.

Bonnie looks up and takes my hand.

I've heard on TV and the radio news that the crime rate in New Orleans is horrific at night, including murder, rape, aggravated assault, human trafficking, prostitution, and even sexual abuse of children is off the charts. Bonnie and I will not be in the French Quarter at night. Instead, we will stay safely tucked away in our camper-van at Rest Dem' Bones Campground.

We turn off the main strip and wander down the side streets. I start thinking about how we can earn money to keep going. We have to get to California. We need money to eat and gas to get there. We aren't completely broke, but it won't be long before we are.

I see a sign on the front of the Central Grocery and Deli that reads, 'Home of the Original Muffuletta Sandwich.'

"Do you want to try a Muffuletta Bonnie?"

"What is it?" she asks.

"I have no idea," I reply, smile, and open the door for her.

We approach the counter, and I ask," Sir, what is the muffuletta?"

"Ahh, my father and I are from Italy, and the muffuletta is an Italian sandwich my father invented. It's a variety of Italian meats, with a special olive salad topping on freshly baked Italian bread," he beams.

"We'll take one."

We sit at a small table in the back of the store, and I cut a piece for Bonnie. It is beyond yummy, and she agrees. We finish the entire sandwich.

"Bonnie, I was thinking, I want to make a little money while we're here. We can sit on a curb and put a little sign beside us asking for money. Would that be okay with you?"

She nods yes, but I don't know if she understood what I was asking or why.

I get a small poster board and box from the Central Grocery and make a sign. It reads, '*California Bound. Can you help? Willing to work for cash.*'

Leaving the small box open for change and dollar bills, we place it next to us on the curb and sit in St. Ann's Square.

Watching people is fascinating.

Every day near PJ's Coffee sits an older man on the sidewalk, holding a cup to collect money from a passerby. He has lots of wrinkles on his face and has a tired, worn appearance, like he's lived a hard life.

An even older plump woman walks around St. Ann's Square throughout the day, singing *Amazing Grace*, and people walk up to her and hand her money.

Bonnie asks, "Why doesn't she sing on the radio? She sings so pretty."

"Looks like she's had a tough life, Bonnie. I'm not sure how some people make it on the radio, and others don't. She may not have had opportunities to share her gift until later in life."

We pass a young girl, maybe eighteen, sitting on the sidewalk with a sign that reads, "I'm not a bad person; I just need help."

She looks miserable, I think.

Bonnie says, "I want to help her."

"We'll bring her lunch later, but no money; I saw tracks on her arm."

"What's tracks?" she asks.

"It means she does drugs. One day the drugs will probably kill her. I don't want to help her kill herself."

"You mean drugs like my mom and dad's medicine? They always told me it helped them."

"Well, I don't know about that, honey," I answer.

One woman sets up a speaker on the sidewalk and sings *Dream a Little Dream of Me*. She sounds like Ella Fitzgerald and has a fancy magician's hat laid upside down a couple of feet in front of her, and it is already full of tips. She takes pride in her singing and makes an effort to look presentable, wearing clean, well-worn clothes and a hat for people to place their donations. We speak to the shopkeeper behind her setup, and he says she's a familiar sight in the area and that people often come from far and wide to hear her sing.

One of the street acts attracts twenty or thirty people at a time. It's incredible; they do magic, music, and stunts that keep the crowd involved through the entire skit.

In front of Cafe' Du Monde is a three-person jazz group playing *When the Saints Go Marching In*.

Sitting with the sign feels weird. Some people walk by and look at us like they feel sorry for us; they would look away. Some look disgusted and stare us down as they pass by. Some look kindly; the kind people always drop money in the box next to us.

No one offered us a job, and after about eight hours, we return to our campsite for the evening. We count our money;

— $38 in one-dollar bills. Then, someone dropped a ten-dollar bill, and we had almost $12 in change.

The next day, I take my mom's guitar with us. We sit in a corner, and I play. I perform my favorite acoustic songs, beginning with *Summertime*, *Fly Me to The Moon*, *Sunny*, and last but not least, my favorite, *All of Me*.

As the day goes on, Bonnie begins singing along with me; that's when we start making our best tips and even draw a small crowd!

The payoff is incredible. We make $173.44 for six hours of performing the first day and even make more each day for the rest of the week.

Someone called us street performers today! Say what? Not only that, everyone who passes by us smiles or nods as we sing and play the guitar. It was so much fun, and I was working, not asking for handouts. Playing my guitar and singing makes a vast difference in the way people view and treat us.

We see the same street people each day and eat muffulettas and beignets.

Sunday afternoon, we decide to be just regular tourists. We plan to move on tomorrow and try to make it to Houston, Texas.

We walk along the New Orleans Riverwalk. It runs along the Mississippi River and offers incredible views. The wide, paved walkway has benches, fountains, and lush greenery. We sit on one of the benches and watch the turbulent waters pass us by.

The sky is blue and sunny, with a few clouds and a cool gentle breeze coming off the river. It is so very peaceful.

Cafe Du Monde is a couple of blocks away, so we stop for coffee and chicory and the best beignets in New Orleans topped with half an inch of powdered sugar — unbelievably yummy.

"Can we go for a ride on one of the red and yellow trolleys? They look fun!" Bonnie asks.

"Heck yeah!" I say.

We hop on the Canal Streetcar, that takes you down Riverfront and St. Charles. Sitting in the back of the streetcar, we stretch out and enjoy views from all sides.

At one point, a filthy, hobo-looking guy gets on the streetcar. The guy rambles down the aisle, and as he passes each seat, he asks for a cigarette.

Finally, he makes it to the back and approaches us. "Hey, you gotta a cig, man?" he asks, shaking his head yes.

"No sir, I don't smoke," I say.

"You a tourist?" he asks.

"My sister and I are passing through," I say.

"Tourist," he reiterates and laughs. It is a full, joyous laugh that makes you want to smile.

"Do you live here in New Orleans?" I ask.

"Native-born, through and through," he says. "I was born over dere in da Lower 9th Ward, Desire, Holy Cross neighborhood, ya know dat place? I been dere ma whole life. I'm get'n outta here one day, yas siree I am."

He sits in the seat in front of us, turns around to look at us, and keeps talking. Boy, does he smell bad!

"Well den, can ya buy me sumpin' to eat?" he asks.

"I'm sorry, but we barely have enough money for us to get sandwiches at Central City Grocery before we hit the road. I wish I had enough to help you." I say sincerely.

He looks at me, breaks out into a massive smile, showing missing teeth, and says, "What's yo name?"

"My name's Carl."

"Well, den Carl, it's okey dokey, son," he says and takes a large wad of bills from his pocket. "I told ya, I'm savin' to get outta here."

I can't believe the amount of money he flash's and wonder why he asked for help he didn't need. Then it dawns on me; he's made this his job.

"Where are you going when you get out of here?" I ask him.

"I'm going somewhere with sand, sunny beaches, and low crime. Thinkin' I gonna getta a condo right dere on dat ocean, son."

"Well, that sounds like a mighty fine plan, sir," I reply.

"Where you an ya sister goin?" he asks.

"San Diego, California, to stay with our aunt and uncle."

"SanDiegoCaliforni!" he says but makes it sound like one word. "Woo wee, my kina place, mayhap I see ya dere one day," he says. Then, he looks at Bonnie. "Wha cha name, little sister?"

"I'm Bonnie," she says as the streetcar approaches our stop. We stand up.

"Well, dere, Miss Bonnie, take care of dat big brother!"

"Thank you, and good luck, sir," I say as we walk down the aisle of the streetcar.

"We make our own luck, Carl," he calls after me. Only now, he has a deep, strong voice, suddenly sounding thoroughly educated when he spoke those words.

Then he smiles and winks our way.

Houston, we have a problem.

Houston is our next stop. We pull into a Stuckey's right off the interstate around Beaumont, Texas, to gas up and eat lunch. A pretty, curly red-headed girl with a sweet southern drawl waits on our table. Her name is Camryn, and she looks about sixteen years old.

She brings Bonnie a coloring book and says, "Darlin', you remind me of my sweet little sister." Boonies beams. "Where are ya'll headed?" She asks.

"My sister and I are headed to California to visit family."

"No joking?" she asks.

"No joking," I reply.

"I sure would love to go with ya'll." She smiles. "I'll be right back with your water, sugar."

Two booths from us sit's an older man, maybe 60 years old, with a beer gut, a balding head, and a massive disrespect for females.

Every time our waitress passes his table, he makes inappropriate comments toward her.

His last comment to the waitress is so abrasive and idiotic it makes me wanna spaz.

He says, "Girl, you look like a nice snack. Can I take you home for dessert?"

Did he think she would like a come-on line like that? I can tell she is trying to avoid his table as much as possible, which she should not have to do!

"Camryn," I call her over. "Would you mind bringing me a steak knife to cut my hamburger in half?"

"Oh, I can get the cook to cut it for you," she says as her hand reaches for my plate.

"No, no, that's okay. I'd rather do it myself," I say, closely guarding my plate and smiling.

Fortunately for me, after Mr. Annoying finishes eating, he gets up to go to the bathroom. I follow him. I walk into the bathroom and lock the door behind me.

Unfortunately for Mr. Annoying, he is facing the wall, using the urinal. This puts him in a very awkward and vulnerable position.

I walk up behind him and quote word for word what he said to our waitress. "Girl, you look like a nice snack. Can I take you home for dessert?"

He turns to look at me, his face flushed.

Upon hearing his own words said back to him, he asks, "Who the hell do you think you are?" He turns to face me fully as he zips up, only to find a steak knife in my hand, aimed about a half inch from his throat.

"I thought the same about you, Mr. Low-Class Redneck. That is your name, isn't it?" I say as I touch his throat with the blade.

I push him back against the urinal and wall and, with my other hand, I press the knife to his skin.

His mouth opens to answer, but I push the knife a little deeper. He looks scared shitless; good thing he had already peed, or his pants would be soaking wet.

He hasn't said a word yet. His mouth just hangs open, he seems stunned and dumb.

"Now, you're gonna go back to your table and apologize to that young lady. She's a waitress, not a prostitute looking for a sleazy guy with a stupid one-liner so she can make a few bucks. And then, Mr. Low-Class Redneck, in that sorry excuse of a brain of yours, you will remember never to speak to any young lady that way again. Do you understand, Mr. Low-Class Redneck?"

He nods his head yes, quickly.

"Know this, I have a gun, and I will find you and shoot your dick off, then your balls for good measure. Do you understand?"

He nods again, but his eyelids have begun to squint, and his lips are pressed hard together.

"Tell me, say it out loud. Say this word for word; say: Pardon me, Miss, I shouldn't have talked to you like that, and I'm very sorry."

He says it through gritted teeth as I press the knife against his neck, leaving a pink line, "Pardon me, Miss, I shouldn't have talked to you like that, and I'm very sorry."

"Good job. After you apologize, I want you to tip her real good and walk away. I'll be leaving right behind you. And Mr. Low-Class Redneck, do not come back here."

I leave him in the bathroom and walk to our table, my heart pounding. A couple of minutes later, he comes out with an ashen face.

When he sees the waitress, he asks her for his check and then repeats my words to her, word for word.

She looks surprised and brings him the check. He lays a ten and a five on the table and walks toward the door. We walked out behind him.

"See you later!" I yell to him across the parking as he gets inside his old beat-up Ford truck with a Confederate flag in his rear window. He blares his radio and flips me the bird as he spins out of the parking lot.

"Who was that?" Bonnie asks.

"Just a guy I met in the bathroom," I say.

"How far are we from Houston?" Bonnie asks.

"We're getting close."

"Okay, I found a campground," she says.

I've made Bonnie my co-pilot. While on the road, she watches for signs as the world passes. I want her to know that I depend on her to find places for us to eat and spend the night. That's her job.

"Hugo Point Campground," Bonnie says as we pull into our new campsite. The trees are beautifully aligned and hang over the road like an arch to pass under.

It's peaceful, with a small bridge over a cove, and the water is breathtakingly clear. We stay at a waterside campsite that evening, walk to the bridge, then hike up to the watchtower to see the sunset over the bay.

As we watch the sun fall slowly from the sky and the day turning into the night, I ask, "How are you, Bonnie? I mean, we've been gone from Orlando for over a week. Are you homesick?"

She says nothing for a little bit, then, "I miss my mom and dad, but I'm not homesick."

"What do you mean?" I ask.

"I played in my room most of the time by myself. I'd ask mom and dad to play with me, but they were always too tired or too busy. I wonder if my Mom misses me."

"I know she does. I can call the hospital and ask about her and your dad. Of course, I have to be careful, but I think I can pull it off."

The following day I make the call to the hospital in Orlando and am told that Mrs. Larkin has been released and is doing well. Mr. Larkin is still in intensive care and will be in the hospital for an undetermined time. He will be going through multiple skin graft surgeries and occupational therapy as well.

We go for a walk in Market Square Park. There is an outdoor venue with local crafts, music, and a farmer's market. We buy fresh lettuce, tomatoes, strawberries, and cucumber.

"Can I fix dinner tonight? Bonnie asks.

"Sure. What are we going to have, Bonnie?"

"Fried bologna, mashed potatoes, and a salad?" she asks.

"Bonnie, that sounds like the yummiest meal in the world!"

She smiles, then starts singing, and I join in.

"My bologna has a first name; it's O-S-C-A-R.

My bologna has a second name; it's M-A-Y-E-R.

Oh, I love to eat it every day, and if you ask me why I'll say.

Cause Oscar Meyer has a way with B-O-L-G-N-A!"

We head to the campground.

Devil's River

The following morning as we drive to Del Rio, Texas, I admire the vast open space in front of us, with no trees to block the view. I take in the Texas open skies' depth, width, and beauty. Incredible. I'm in awe of the enormity.

My new favorite song is playing in the background, *Take It Easy.* Bonnie and I are singing along.

Bonnie says, "I found a campsite. It's San Pedro Campground."

We arrive in Del Rio before dark, get gas and groceries, and wash our clothes at a laundry mat. One of the locals introduces herself as Pam.

Pam says, "I haven't seen y'all around here before." She has a funny look on her face.

"Yes, ma'am. My sister and I are headed to the San Pedro campground tonight. After that, we're driving to California." I say.

"Sure enough?" she says and looks at Bonnie. "Are you alright, my darlin'?"

Bonnie smiles a winning smile and says, "I'm doing good. I can't wait to see the campground; it looks like it's next to the Devil'sRiver!"

"Why are y'all camping your way to California?" she asks, still looking at Bonnie.

"We're goin' to live with our aunt and uncle. They live in San Diego. Our parents died a few months ago." Bonnie says. "Mom and Dad left us this camper, and Carl says it seems the best way to get there."

"Well then, sounds like a mighty fine plan. It's a nice campground. The main camping area is inland, but it also has walk-in sites located on Devil's River."

"We want to stay next to Devil's River!" Bonnie says.

Pam smiles and says, "San Pedro Point is about a four-mile walk from the parking area, but you can put up a tent. It's one of the few areas on Devil's River that's public land. Most of the land by the river is privately owned and extremely protected, with shotguns, by the way."

"Good to know! Thank you, ma'am." I say.

"Just don't expect too much. It's primitive camping, mostly used by paddlers on the river. My husband and I canoe down the river sometimes and stop there for a break, it's not fancy." Pam says and waves goodbye.

We park at the main campground and sleep in the camper overnight.

The next day after breakfast, we load our backpacks with water, food, towels, pillows, and blankets. We decide we will sleep under the stars tonight. We hike to the point and edge of Devils River.

"Tonight, we will sleep under the stars," I say.

The trail is worn and rocky, and winds along the peaceful river. We find a shallow area with slate rock for entry into the

115

river and go in to cool off. It was so cold! After the swim, we lay on the rocks and dry off with the sun's warmth.

Arriving at the paddlers' campground, Bonnie and I find a nice camping spot under a Cyprus tree near the river bend. We hang our backpacks high on the tree limbs, so animals don't get into them.

This place is a hidden beauty that runs through a rustic landscape. The river is so clear you can see through to the bottom. I watch fish swim past us, wishing for a fishing pole.

Later in the day, we meet a group of twenty-year-olds setting up camp for the night. They have a cute Collie dog named Freckles, who plays frisbee with them most of the afternoon. We are invited to join the frisbee throwing and Bonnie is having a blast with Freckles, she can catch the frisbee in her mouth, fetch, sit and a bunch of other tricks.

"How can she catch the frisbee so good?" Bonnie asks one of the girls.

"Well, I spend a lot of time with her. I've been teaching her tricks since she was a puppy. I have an obstacle course for her in my backyard," Jennifer says.

"Cool!"

"Yeah, Freckles is cool!" Jennifer said.

Later a young man named James says, "Would you guys like to have lunch with us? We're grilling hotdogs and hamburgers! Please come and join us."

"Sure!" Bonnie replies excited.

At dinner James says, "We are going to canoe the complete length of the river over the next few days."

"Wow, how long is the river?" I ask.

"Roughly 92 miles," he replied.

"Whoa!" I say.

After dinner Bonnie pulls out her Nerf football for us to play toss. A little while later, one of the young girls, Mary, asks Bonnie if she could join. Bonnie looks at me nervously, and I nod for her to go ahead.

After a bit, Bonnie seems to loosen up, so I leave them to play on their own.

Later, Bonnie says, "I told Mary about our mom and dad today. She asked why they weren't with us, so I told her."

"Did it feel weird to tell her?"

"No, it felt real. It's almost like I believe it's real now," she says.

"Did she ask any more questions?" I enquire.

"No, after I told her they died in a car accident, she seemed sad."

"It's good that she didn't get too curious, but we'll need to figure out a couple more details, just in case someone does. The lady at the laundry last night seemed a little suspicious too," I say.

That evening at dinner, we learn that Mary and her brother, James, are on this trip to honor and spread the ashes of their dead parents. No wonder she understood Bonnie's explanation so quickly

Mary introduces everyone. "These are our friends: Gina, Jennifer, Camille, Celeste, Will, and Ken. They wanted to be a part of spreading our parents' ashes, so we have all been training for this trip."

James says, "Our parents were on a week-long trip, their 25th anniversary, and the first time we weren't on a trip with them."

Mary says, "We'd both left for college. They had been planning this trip for a couple of years."

"What happened to them?" I ask.

"Dolan Falls is where they were found. The police told us later that people would be paddling along, and the river's horizon is flat, the water smooth, so many people are unaware that a fifteen-foot drop is coming right past the horizon. Then, it's too late," James says.

"The officials said it most likely wasn't the drop that killed them, but the water at the bottom of the falls that pulls you back into the current. The water pulls you under and pins you against the rocks at the bottom. There's no way to get loose," Mary says bravely but lets out a small whimper.

I thought, *how brave — or maybe stupid of them — to come on this trek*, although I understand why.

The teens leave the following morning at sunrise. They get into their boats and wave goodbye. Bonnie and I eat doughnuts, sit by the river, and watch them go.

Bonnie asks, "Carl, what happened to you when you were younger?"

I don't want this conversation, but I know it's long overdue.

"I will tell you, but it's horrible, and I don't know if it's too much for you to hear. You're only twelve years old. You may be too young to understand some things."

"If I don't understand, can I tell you?

"That's fair," I say. "Bonnie, do you know what 'rape' means?"

"I'm not sure," she says.

"So, my dad, well, he raised me alone cause my mom died when I was born. He must have really hated me. He neglected me as a baby and left me alone without human touch or interaction. As a young boy, when I was about five years, he began beating me with his belt. I wasn't doing anything wrong as far as I knew. This continued until the age of thirteen, then the abuse changed. The first time it happened, I thought he was fixing to belt me as usual." I stop talking for a moment to gather my thoughts.

"Bonnie, he did to me what that bad man was planning for you that night. That was the first time my dad raped me, and then, he began doing it all the time, and I didn't know what to do or how to stop him."

"How did you get away from him? Did someone save you like you saved me?" she asks

"No, Bonnie, when I was 15 years old, I killed him. By then, he was no longer my father. I only saw him as a perverted rapist."

She was very quiet, her brows furrowed, and she looked deep in thought. "Was I raped, Carl? Is that what the bad men did to me?"

I shake my head yes.

We sit in silence for a long time.

"Do you still think about him? Are you sad that you killed him now that you're older?"

"No, Bonnie."

There is silence again as minutes roll by.

"Carl, why did you set my house on fire?"

"Honey, this is hard to say, but your mom and dad neglected you in a major way. What happened to you should never happen to any kid. But, sometimes, knowing what is happening and not doing anything about it is as bad as the person doing it."

I look at her, and she remains silent. I don't think she really understood me.

Nevertheless, I continue, "When I pushed the bad man, all I could see in my head was my dad. I felt anger and rage fill my head. I probably would have killed him, even if he hadn't fallen backward. Instead, I lit your house on fire to hide the bad man's murder."

She's still sitting there, looking at me in silence.

"Bonnie. I don't know if I'm a good or bad person. I've ended the lives of people who do evil things. You'd think that would make me good, but it could send me to jail for the rest of my life."

"You saved me. That was good."

"Yeah, Bonnie, but even doing that would put me in jail for a long time."

"Why? You've said that before," she asks.

"Because I took you, a twelve-year-old girl, from your home. They would consider that kidnapping."

"Carl! You didn't kidnap me, I wanted to go, and I would tell them that!"

"Bonnie, I took you away from your family. It wouldn't matter what you told them because you are only twelve years old and not considered old enough to make those decisions."

"Oh" is all she says.

We stand by the river that morning, throwing rocks across the surface of the water, seeing who could make the most skips across before sinking. Again, I hope I made the right decision.

We lay on our blankets that evening, staring at the millions of stars above.

Bonnie says, "I'm sorry your dad was bad and hurt you."

"Me too, honey."

"Hey Carl, can we get a Collie puppy that I can train to do tricks? I love Freckles!" She looks very hopeful.

"I think so, Bonnie, one day. We will need to settle down and have a real home with a big backyard and a fence. Then we could have a puppy. Would you like that?"

"Yes!" she says, "And when we do, I'll name him Del Rio!"

Sun City

El Paso, Texas, was next. It's a small, cute city with lots of unique shops. They say the sun shines here 300 days a year, so the nickname 'Sun City' has stuck.

We are camping at Tom Mays State Park, the foothills of Franklin Mountain. It's a gorgeous day as we head to the downtown square of El Paso.

"Look, Carl, an ice cream store called Wonder Scoops! Can we try it?"

121

"Let's check it out!" I say.

We walk into the ice cream shop, and a tall, kind of dorky kid with glasses and blonde hair greets us. "Howdy, ya'll, welcome to Wonder Scoops!"

"Hi there, I would like a chocolate ice cream in a sugar cone," I say.

He smiles, "Indeed, sir, it comes with whipped cream and sliced almonds on top. Is that okay?"

"Perfect, and whatever she wants," I say, gesturing to Bonnie.

"Do you have butter pecan?" Bonnie asks.

"Yes, that's my favorite ice cream, too! It comes with whipped cream and cherries on top. Is that okay?"

"Yes, and sugar cone, please," Bonnie says.

"I haven't seen you all around these parts. Are you visiting El Paso?" the young ice cream scooper asks as he prepares our cones.

"Yes, for a couple of days," Bonnie says.

"Have you ever been to the El Paso Zoo?" he asks.

"No," Bonnie says. "I've never been to any zoo."

"What? Well, you're in luck; we have the best zoo in the United States. Are you guys here long enough to go?"

"Can we go, Carl?" Bonnie asks.

"I don't see why not. We aren't in a hurry."

"My dad is a vendor there and always gets free tickets. Please take these." He hands me two free zoo tickets.

"Really?" I ask.

"Yea, if you can't use them, give them to someone else before you leave town."

We take the tickets and ice cream cones and thank him. Then, we continue window shopping until we find a cute shop called "Yours to Own." Out of curiosity, we go inside.

The store is bright with colorful neon signs with catchy slogans, postcards, local artwork, T-shirts, keychains, and other trinkets. It's an exciting place, a lively and upbeat atmosphere filled with unique and memorable items. The shelves and display cases are neatly arranged, and in the back corner of the store, a jukebox is playing.

Bonnie picks up a beaded necklace with a round silver pendant and a miniature wooden horse in the center. The shopkeeper notes this and says, "That pendant and necklace were handmade by a local Indian artist named Jacy. His name is etched on the back."

"That's a funny name," Bonnie says.

"His name means the moon. Jacy puts all his artwork on round pendants like the moon. It's part of his signature."

"Do you like the necklace, Bonnie?" I ask.

"I love it, Carl!" she answers.

I smile and pay the cashier, and Bonnie hugs me.

It is my first real hug, and I am surprised by her demonstration of appreciation and trust.

We visit the El Paso Zoo the next day. Neither of us have ever been to a zoo. An attendant hands us a booklet as we pass through the gates and says, "This is a guidebook about each exhibit. Take it with you and read as you go."

I had no idea how much we would learn about animal families and how similar their behaviors are to humans.

The first exhibit is birds. The Bald Eagles were the main attraction, but there were also Sparrows, Pigeons, and Parrots.

"I'll read the first set of facts," I say, flipping through the guidebook. "Most birds are social and live in groups called flocks. Most species are monogamous and spend their lives with only one mate, and the mates work together to raise their young."

"What is 'magamous?'" Bonnie asks awkwardly.

"Monogamous? It means they choose one bird to be with always and have babies together.

"Like, the Waltons?"

I felt a chuckle in my body. "Well, yes. The Waltons are an example of that kind of relationship. I know we didn't come from families like that, but just because our families weren't capable of giving that kind of love doesn't mean we can't. Bonnie, we get to choose who we are."

"Okay, Tigers next," I say. "They do not form families consisting of a father, mother, and offspring; neither do they form packs of family members.

"Rather, the tiger is a solitary creature. Usually, the male will only be present during mating and, occasionally, the birth of the cubs. The mating process usually takes several days, during which they copulate frequently to ensure fertilization. Then, the male will move on to another territory to mate elsewhere."

"They don't have a wife but make babies, right?" Bonnie asks.

"You got it, Bonnie. People call these kinds of men 'bachelors.' That means not being married."

Then came the elephants.

"Aww," Bonnie says. "Look at that elephant in the water bathing the baby elephant with her trunk! That's so cute!"

"Okay, your turn to read, Bonnie."

She reads, "Elephant families have a matriarchal head, meaning an older, experienced lady elephant leads the herd. A family usually consists of a mother, her sisters, daughters, and their babies (calves).

Female family units range from three to twenty-five elephants. While elephants do not mate for life, a female may repeatedly choose to mate with the same bull, and bulls are sometimes seen as protective of females. However, most bulls are solitary."

"That means the females are the head of the family and care for the children," I say.

The next enclosure had big trees, many monkeys, and a few baboons.

"My turn. Fun facts," Bonnie says, "A group of monkeys may be commonly referred to as a 'tribe' or a 'troop.' Once born, baby monkeys are primarily cared for by their mother. Often, a young monkey will ride on its mother's back or hang from her neck. The baby is considered an adult between four and five years old. Although the baby monkey can sometimes be cared for by both parents, only if the male monkey wants to."

"That means most dads don't care for the baby monkeys?" Bonnie asks.

"Yes, and I think we found your dad," I reply. "Do you wanna eat? I'd love a hot dog and french fries."

That evening, we watch the sunset from high ground. The sky is magnificent, with multiple shades of oranges and pinks all melded together. The colors are deep and mixed with light, making it look like a raging orange ocean in the sky — unbelievably beautiful.

As the sun dips below the horizon, I say "Bonnie, I've been thinking about today. We are more like animals than we realize."

She says, "I want to be a bird, like an Eagle."

"I want to be an Eagle, too."

Before leaving town the following afternoon, we go by Wonder Scoops to get another ice cream and thank the young fella who gave us the tickets again.

However, we find the store closed, with crime scene tape across the door and a policewoman guarding the entrance.

I ask the police lady, "What happened?"

"We had a robbery and murder here last night," she says.

"We were just here the day before yesterday. Who was murdered? Did you catch the guy?" I ask.

"We have video and a BOLO out on the suspect, he's a local, and we all know him from multiple infractions; he won't get far. The video shows him waving his gun around, demanding money. The employee immediately handed him the cash and backed away, but the guy shot him anyway and ran. Here is a photograph of the suspect, have either of you seen him?"

126

The man looked to be in his mid-thirties, with choppy black hair, pale white skin, and squinty eyes. His nose was too big for his face, and a porn mustache rested below it.

Bonnie and I both shake our heads no.

"The boy that was hurt, did he have blond hair and glasses?" Bonnie asks.

"Yes, he did. Do you know him? Is he a friend of yours?" the policewoman asks.

"No, we just got ice cream the day before yesterday, and he gave us tickets to the zoo," I say.

"Well, I'm sorry, but he died on the scene. That boy didn't have a chance. The suspect shot him right through the heart," she says. "We have three search parties leaving in a half hour if ya'll want to join in the search."

We were shocked; we had just talked to him and now he's gone, like forever. It seems surreal.

"Carl, why would something like that happen to someone as nice as he was?"

"Bonnie, honey, I don't know. The world isn't fair. I will never be able to explain why bad things happen to good people, but it does."

The policewoman says, "We'll catch him; drug addicts usually end up dead or in jail."

"Bonnie, we can stay and help?"

"Yeah, I wanna help," she replies.

The policewoman gives us the meeting address of one of the search groups. We spend half the day searching the Rio Grande River trails. Finally, Bonnie and I find him around five o'clock.

The border ledge that runs along the river is sometimes rugged ridges, canyons, and even grassy banks. In one area, where the ledges and high above the water, you can lean over and see both small and wide crevices in the rocks.

We find him in a perfect hiding place. The crevice he chose to hide in is about five feet high and four feet wide. It wasn't easy to see him; you had to be specifically looking down the side of the ledges.

I climb down the side. He is comfortably passed out and stoned out of his mind. A needle, drugs, and arm paraphernalia was lying beside him.

"Bonnie, I'll be right up. I'm going to make sure this guy doesn't go anywhere."

"What are you going to do, Carl?" Bonnie calls out.

"I just told you, I'm going to make sure he doesn't go anywhere. He is totally wasted on some heavy stuff. I'll be up in a minute."

I slide my upper body under the shelf so that I can cover his mouth and nose with both hands. His body reacts to the lack of oxygen, but without his brain helping him, the fight to live lasts under two minutes.

When I climb up, Bonnie asks, "Did he get what he deserved?"

"Yea, he did, Bonnie."

We continued along the path heading back towards town.

Later, we hear whistles and a horn from far off.

"I think one of the search teams found the guy," I say.

After that, we go to have dinner at Cafe Central in town. The rumors were already circulating amongst the locals.

"Yeah, my team found the guy; he was hiding in a hole along the river shelf. He had overdosed. The damn junkie had a pocket full of heroin," says the man at the coffee counter; "Jerry" was stenciled on the front of this work shirt.

"At least the taxpayers didn't have to feed this dipshit on death row," remarks the cafe cook.

The Old Pueblo

We stay the night and then drive for six hours to Tucson. We find a primitive camping area, mostly dirt, rocks, brush, and cacti scattered everywhere. The campground has no designated camping spots, so I pick an area with a beautiful view of the mountains. That evening, we watch the orange and pink skies as the sun set.

After dinner, I say, "Bonnie, looking at the map, I think if we leave around 10:00 am tomorrow, we could make it to San Diego before dark. Do you want to leave for California in the morning or stay in Tucson for a day or two?"

"We could be there tomorrow?" she asks.

"Yeah," I say.

Then, Bonnie begins to bellow out a song to one of her favorite shows, *The Beverly Hillbillies*. With her right arm bent and swinging like a sailor, she sings:

"Well, first thing you know, Old Jed's, a millionnaire,

The kin folks said, 'Jed move away from there.'

Said, 'California is the place you oughta be,'

So they loaded up the truck and they moved to Beverly,

Hills that is. Swimming pools, movie stars."

"California, here we come," I say.

Part Five: Patrick & Chester 1972-1975

"The battle between good and evil is endlessly fascinating because we are participants every day,"

Mark Twain.

Chapter 1: America's Finest

Carl and Bonnie, San Diego, California

"I love this place," I told Bonnie this morning.

"Me too, Carl," she said.

We're in San Diego, California. I've been working temp jobs through a hiring service. I do whatever they can find for me—walking dogs, mowing lawns, working as a mechanic, laying house foundations, and whatever else I can find.

The homes in San Diego are nestled in canyons and perched atop them, as they snake down toward the sea. The city itself is full of college students, beach bums, surfers, military, and people like us, wanderers who have fallen in love with the city.

When we first arrived, it was late spring. I bought a ten-year-old 1960 Rambler, and we found a place to settle with the camper-van. Now we leave the camper parked in one place. Our beach campsite is quiet, clean, and close to the beachfront.

I told Bonnie, "We have to figure a way to get you into school for the fall. In the meantime, I have a couple of books we can read together. I'm thinking of one chapter for each book every day. It's what my uncle did with me when I first moved in with him. Did I tell you that he's a family psychiatrist?"

"No, what does that mean?" she asked.

"It means his job is helping children and adults that have suffered abuse at the hands of a loved one or someone they trust.

"My uncle Don was abused as a child by his father, my grandfather, who I never met. Instead of becoming angry and an abuser later in life, like his brother, my dad, he chose to leave his father's home to seek help. He was hungry to find a better way of life. Eventually, he was able to work his way through college. He majored in psychology, and it taught him how to heal, which also taught him how to help others. Maybe I can help you because of what he taught me," I said.

A few weeks later, I was repairing a driveway at a bungalow near our campground.

I started working on it that morning when the owner left for work. When she came home at lunchtime, she said, "I'm impressed with what you've completed, young man. Most people would drag this job out for a full day. It looks like you're almost finished."

She held out her hand and said, "My name is Aparna Elias."

"My name is Carl Slater, ma'am."

"What are you doing working temporary jobs, Carl? It seems to me that you have a good work ethic."

"My sister and I just moved to California, and I'm looking for a full-time mechanic's job," I said and smiled. "I'm doing temp work until I find one."

"How old is your sister?" she asked.

"She's twelve. We lost our parents in a car accident and moved here to be close to our remaining relatives: an aunt and uncle. I'm her guardian."

"I'm sorry to hear about your parents," she said. "Where will you guys be going to school in the fall?"

I said, "Oh, I graduated from high school in the spring of this year. Bonnie is supposed to be going into eighth grade, but when our parents were alive, they were like 'hippy' parents." I acted slightly embarrassed, then said, "They raised us in a commune, where we lived with other families. When we were old enough for high school, they allowed us to choose, and I chose public school. I have my diploma. I'm worried about enrolling my little sister because she has no education records. Do you have any advice or direction to point me?"

"Where do you and your sister live?" Mrs. Elias asked.

"We have lot rental at the Tiki Beach RV Resort," I said.

"Why aren't you staying with your aunt and uncle?" she asked.

"They have a tiny apartment, and we didn't want to impose. Besides, the VW camper-van our parents left us is in great condition, and we have plenty of room. Bonnie has her room on the rooftop, and she loves it. I sleep in the back of the van, and it works for now."

Mrs. Elias said, "I have to say, I think you are one of the luckiest guys I've ever met. I'm the president of a private middle school. Also, we are in your school district, near your home. So, Carl, I may be able to help you. Schools can place your sister based on her date of birth since you don't have school transcripts. Although, she will be required to take placement testing, which is in her best interest."

"We can't afford a private school Ms. Elias."

"Carl let's get your sister in for testing. Bring her by; I'm there every day. If she tests well, she may be eligible for a scholarship. If not, I'll be happy to advise you on the next steps you should take going forward."

"Yes, ma'am! Thank you, Mrs. Elias, I don't know what to say."

"You don't have to say anything. Help someone you don't know when you can, and I'll be paid in full," she said.

We've been here two years now, and the norm is sunny, not too hot or cold. Why would anyone ever leave? I can't believe we drove across America. It feels like so long ago.

Bonnie is now fourteen years old and in ninth grade, getting As and Bs, and as long as she maintains her grades, she keeps her scholarship.

"Do you want to go for a walk on the beach?" I ask her after school.

We go for walks on the beach almost every day. She tells me about the school, and I tell her about my work. Then, some days, we find a bench along the beach walk, and I play my guitar, and we sing and earn tips. It's a feeling of freedom and happiness to me.

I say to her, "You're growing up way too fast; I can't believe you're already fourteen."

"It's weird to me, too," she says.

"Bonnie, my job at A-1 Auto is ending. My boss's son is graduating high school this year and will work with his dad full-time."

"So, are you going back to temp jobs?" Bonnie asks.

"Yeah, but don't you worry. We'll be okay, just like before," I reply. "I saw a guy I used to work with laying foundation a few days ago. His name is Doug; he gave me his phone number and told me to call him if I needed work. I'll give him a call this afternoon."

That evening, I walk to the pay phone to call Doug. After several rings, Doug picks up the phone and says, "Roadkill Cafe. You kill it; we grill it!"

"Hi, Doug. It's Carl, I'm officially looking for a job."

"Hey, dude. Yeah, alright. Can you meet me at Charburgers in an hour? We can eat, and I'll tell ya about the job."

"I'll see you there," I say.

Chapter 2: I'm a Criminal

Carl Slater

Doug waves me over to the booth, I sit down, and he pushes a burger and fries in front of me. Then, Doug blurts out, "Dude, I stake out homes and then rob them; I wondered if you wanted to get in on it."

I say, "Wow, I wasn't expecting that. I don't know, Doug; I've never robbed anyone before. Well, other than my dad when I was a kid, and I don't figure that counts."

Doug says, "Maybe not, but it's about the same. Just pretend it's your dad's house. I've thought about telling you this for a while because I know you need the money. Look, I only take what I can fit in a backpack, never more. I look for jewelry, cash, and small electronics. Whatever can be pawned easily."

I just look at him, so Doug continues his spill; he says, "My dad owns a security business. I've worked for him forever, and he's taught me everything he knows. Picking locks, disconnecting alarm systems, and even cracking safes. I could teach you."

"I don't know, man. Taking other people's stuff seems just wrong. No offense," I said.

He says, "None taken, but we won't take from anyone who can't afford to replace what we take. I only choose homes that are in excellent neighborhoods. Carl, if they can afford huge homes and expensive cars, they won't miss a little jewelry or cash. Go with me; one job, dude."

Curiosity is a bitch. I meet him the following day, and we drive to a park in a classier section of town.

Doug says, "This is the neighborhood next to the one we'll rob. We leave our ride here. If anything happens, like someone walks in and catches us, we run in separate directions and meet back at the car tonight, 7 pm. Otherwise, we fill our backpacks and walk back."

We're both dressed in jean shorts and bright-colored shirts for the beach. Doug's is yellow with a tweety bird on the front, and mine is a Pink Floyd band shirt, sunglasses, baseball caps and backpacks.

As we walk, Doug talks. "I've been watching this home for a few days; the mail and newspapers have been piling up. I haven't seen any activity in or outside the home, including lights. I've also watched the neighbors leave for work around 8 am each morning. We should be good unless the owners come home from vacation at the same time we're inside. Now that would suck. That's when we would run. We are looking for things of value that we can pack in our backpacks, jewelry, watches, purses, wallets, cash, electronics, cameras, guns, knives; you get the picture?" he asks.

"Yeah, man'" I reply.

We approach the two-story home and follow the path leading up some stairs to a screened front porch. My heart is pounding both in fear of being caught and excitement about what I might find.

Doug says, "I think the best way to go in is always through the front door if possible." He goes right up the door, plays with the doorknob, and opens it. We hear no alarm.

"Let's split the house down the middle for our search, I'll take a right, and you take a left," he says and walks away.

We had been standing in a foyer, with the stairs to the second floor in front of us. I turn left into the dining room, go through the kitchen and laundry room, up the back stairs to an office, then to the main bedroom and bath.

My first robbery brings me a diamond and opal ring, two gold necklaces, one gold bracelet, a Sea-Dweller dive watch, and $50 in cash from a sock drawer. Doug had asked me to look for a safe, but I don't see one.

We meet back in front of the home. Doug has a backpack full of stuff, but mine is half-empty. Everything I have taken is small.

Doug asks, "Did you find anything? Your sack looks light."

"Yeah, I did, but it's small stuff," I reply.

He says, "Look, I don't know what you need, dude, but always fill your pack!"

I walk through the house again and find some 8-track tapes, one of them by Elton John with his new hit, *Benny, and the Jets*. Going into the kitchen, I have a brilliant idea; I can take food like I did when I left my uncles! That will help us so much; that's what we need. We slip out the back door facing the beach. It is a breathtaking view.

We walk along the beach, back to the beach access path that leads to the street.

"Brilliant, Dougie," I say.

He nods and smiles, "Yes, yes, I am, don't you forget it!"

This is how I started my life of crime—unless you count burning down two houses, killing my dad, and killing Brenda's dad's sicko friend from the party. But I don't count those. They deserved what they got; they were evil people.

We work together for seven or eight months, and he teaches me how to do surveillance on homes, pick locks, disconnect alarms, and, the most challenging part, crack safes.

In early December, Doug says, "Hey, bro, my dad needs me to watch his shop for a while. Unfortunately, he had a heart attack, and is in the hospital. He's going to have heart surgery; I'm not sure when I'll be able to go on rob jobs again."

"Dude, no worries; just let me know if I can do anything for you or your dad," I say.

That's when I begin doing rob jobs on my own.

It's almost Christmas now, and if I pick the right home, Brenda and I could be set for the rest of this year and into 1975.

We have a tabletop Christmas tree that we've decorated with long strings of popcorn that we threaded with a needle to wrap around the tree. On Christmas Eve, we'll have freshly baked cookies from the bakery and milk for Santa. Brenda always makes homemade presents from her craft books and wraps them in newspaper comics for me.

Last year, it was an old bottle that she covered with strips of masking tape and then painted with shoe polish. I use it for a vase and pick wildflowers for her when they bloom. The year before, she decorated an oven mitt with a hand-drawn Christmas tree, and she used sequins for the Christmas balls.

This year, I bought her number one on her Christmas wish list: a Cadillac skateboard with a new style of urethane wheels. They came on the market last year, and the kids in our part of California are going nuts over them. Skateboarding has become super popular, and her best friend, Alicia, got one last year. She'll be psyched.

Chapter 3: The Basement

Carl Slater, Christmas Eve

This house on the beach is much like the first one Dougie took me to, but a little fancier. There are about 17 miles of beach and plenty of homes.

Yesterday, I walked the beach and observed a man walking out to his car with a suitcase in his hand, and I haven't seen him today. I will see what I can find if his car has not returned tomorrow morning.

I disconnect the alarm and walk into the home. All I can think is this house is humongous and gorgeous, and the man or woman has excellent taste. Everywhere I look, I see someone who buys quality in every item they own—nothing but the best.

I find a safe in the main bedroom downstairs that is relatively easy to break. I see several men's fine watches, gold chains, and $8,000 cash. I couldn't believe my luck; my heart was racing with excitement. Finally, I hit the mother load and was only in the first room.

I pass through the living room. I pick up one of those new battery-powered cassette players with some cassette tapes, mostly classic.

The kitchen pantry is full, and I finish stuffing the backpack with boxed and canned foods, then top it off with meats from the refrigerator.

I could have left then—I should have left then—but I was curious to see the rest of the home. There are four bedrooms and three baths on the second floor; two look like boys' rooms, and one for a girl; the fourth is an office.

In the office, there is an enormous mahogany desk. It is neat as it can be, everything in its place. I search the office drawers, find a gun in a locked bottom drawer, and take it. Why do people think locking a drawer even matters?

A Doctorate Diploma is hanging on the wall behind his desk:

"The Regents of the University of California, Berkley have conferred upon the nomination of the council of the graduation JASON ALEXANDER HILL having demonstrated ability through original research the degree of doctor of philosophy with a Ph.D. in Developmental Psychology."

No wonder he has such a nice place. I look around his office; the photos are minimal, primarily exotic places he's visited. None with people. The furniture, wood/industrial, very simple. The walls are antique white.

There's an abstract painting on the wall across from his desk. It's central to where he sits. It's beautiful but in the wrong way; chilling. The painting fills you with stillness, dark grays, black depth, white shadows, and deep reds. Combined, the colors give me a feeling of coldness and deep sadness. I sit and look at the painting for longer than I'd like to admit.

I go down the back staircase in his office that leads back to the main level. Once there, I see a door I hadn't noticed before. I wonder if this is a basement; those aren't common here in California, like in the South. However, I find it locked when I try to open the door.

Usually, if you find a California basement, it's small rooms tucked below grade to the house, with the boiler, water

143

heater, ductwork, and electrical panel. A basement that is a living area is virtually unknown. So, why is it locked?

"Screw it," I say out loud. I pick the lock and head down to look. I can't find a light switch to turn on until I reach the stairs' bottom. I flick it on and look around. What I see is horrifying and appalling.

To the left of me is a cage or cell built from the floor to the ceiling. It's made of iron and welded together very well. It was like the ones you see on tv. It reminds me of the *Andy Griffith Show* jail cell, except it was dark and filthy, and the floor was hard-packed dirt and stone. It smells awful, like rotten garbage with raw onions and fish as its main filler.

Beside the cage are torture tools hanging on a wall rack, I see a hangman's noose, handcuffs, chains, a split whip, knives and a demon's head mask.

Moving beyond my initial shock, I begin to look deeper into the cage in the back corner; I see a dirty, skinny, scared little boy shrunken into a ball in the corner of the cell. I hope what I am seeing is an illusion. But it is not.

I approach the cell, and the smell gets more potent. Finally, I realize the smell is him. I know he has to be scared to death, so I approach him slowly and carefully. When I speak to him, I hope and pray I sound non-threatening.

"Hey there, kid, my name is Carl. I'm going to get you out of there." He seems to retreat deeper into the corner if that's possible. He pulls a dirty blanket up and over his body. He is small, and his face is gaunt. I pull out my tool for breaking locks and free it in about 60 seconds. Now for the tricky part: coaxing him out of the cage.

"I'm not here to hurt you, kid; I'm here to help you. I promise. Please let me take you out of here," I say. "I have a camper, and I can take you far away from here if you want to go with me."

He doesn't move.

"Would you like to go with me?" I ask.

No response.

"I have a friend named Bonnie, and she's fourteen years old. She lives with me. She's so nice and will help take care of you."

Silence.

"Where is your mom?" I ask. No answer.

"Is the man who lives here your dad?" He shakes his head no.

"Do you want to leave this house?" He slowly nods his head yes.

"Then come to me, please. I won't hurt you; I promise."

He slowly gets up from the corner. Then, with his blanket balled up and hugged in front of his chest, he walks toward me. His tiny, fragile body has lacerations; some were deep and smooth, others jagged. His hands have dirt packed under the long, broken nails, and he is wearing dirty white underwear. I can see where he had been trying to dig a hole, but the earth was too hard to get very far without a shovel. He has blonde hair, blue eyes, and a deep dimple on his right cheek. His body odor is horrific.

"Can I pick you up and carry you out of here?"

"Yes," he says in a very scratchy voice.

I pick him up into my arms, carry him upstairs, and ask him which room is his. He points, and I have him put on some clothing. Then I grab more clothes, shoes, and a photograph of whom I assume are his mom and dad.

He is scary light to carry; I bet he weighs eighty pounds, max. We get into the Rambler and head towards the camper.

All I keep thinking is, *I'm going to kill that motherfucker, that sick, psycho bastard.*

While driving, I say, "I told you my name's Carl. What's your name, kid?"

"Patrick," he replies very quietly.

"Patrick, do you have a last name?"

"Deshaun. Patrick Deshaun," he says.

"Patrick, were you kidnapped or something?"

"No, I live with my foster dad. My real mom and dad died in a car accident two years ago."

Foster dad? The person you are supposed to trust. Why does this not surprise me? Why?

"Does he keep you down in the basement like that all the time?"

"He didn't at first. I had a foster brother, Michael, and a sister, Veronica. I think he might have taken them down to the basement, too."

"Why do you say so?" I ask.

He sits in silence for a minute or so, then says, "One day, he asked if I wanted to see them, and I was excited, but we didn't leave. Instead, he took me to the basement. I've been there ever since. I think they died there because he says, 'They are here with us; don't you feel their presence?'" Chills go down my spine.

"When did you last eat, kid?"

"I'm not sure."

I pull into the McDonald's and order four double cheeseburgers, fries, and apple pies.

He gobbles down two of the double cheeseburgers as we drive to the camper-van, and I tell him about Bonnie.

When we enter the camper, Bonnie trips out.

"What ... who ...?!"

As she takes in his appearance, she immediately goes to Patrick, kneels, and hugs him. "Are you okay?" she asks.

"Are you Bonnie?" he asks.

"Yes," she says, "and what's your name?"

"I'm Patrick," he says.

"Well, Patrick, I bet you want to shower and wear clean clothes. Let me show you where. Then, I'll grab you something to change into."

I toss Bonnie the backpack and say, "Some of his clothes are in there."

Bonnie takes Patrick to the Campground showers so he can have more room to move around. We only use our small shower in the camper if we have no other choice.

After his shower, he puts on speed buggy sweatpants, a matching shirt, and a pair of slides for his feet.

Patrick seems wary but content when Bonnie brings him back to the camper-van.

"Thank you," he says and starts crying softly.

"You're welcome," I say. Bonnie hugs him, and he lets her.

I speak to Bonnie later that night while Patrick slept with a light snore. "Look, I'm not sure what 'foster dad' will do when he gets home and sees Patrick is gone. Maybe he'll report a kidnapping; perhaps he will run, but he must know trouble is coming. He may even try to turn the situation around and blame me. Who knows? He is obviously smart," I say. "So, we're gonna have to leave San Diego. Are you okay with that, Bonnie? I know you are happy with the school here, and I don't want to mess that up, but we can find another happy place."

"I know we can, too," she says.

The following day, I hear Bonnie talking to Patrick. She says, "Patrick when I was twelve, Carl helped me, too. We went on the road and traveled to so many places and gave ourselves a fresh start. Would you like to do that? Go with us on the road? Or do you want us to take you to a police department or something?" Bonnie asks.

"I want to go with you, not the police," he says.

"Just think about a new name you like, okay? You can't keep the same one because everyone will be looking for you," Bonnie says.

"I know a name I like. Can you call me Saul? That was my dad's name." Patrick asks.

We agree that Saul is a perfect name, and now his name is Saul Slater.

I leave to get pizza for dinner and buy a Christmas present for Saul before all the stores closed for the night. I get him the same gift I bought Bonnie, but a different design.

They eat pizza while watching *Rudolph the Red-Nosed Reindeer*. Then, they have cookies and milk during *Santa Clause Is Comin' to Town* and fall asleep during *Frosty the Snowman*.

I start formulating my plan. I want "foster dad" to die. Well, not only to die but to suffer and be found out for what he is. It seems he is a man of means that could continue his charade for many years and never be under suspicion.

Chapter 4: Retribution

Carl Slater, Christmas Day

The following day, the kids start riding the skateboards around the campground right after eating bowls of Captain Crunch. I let them play until lunchtime.

When I call them inside for lunch, I say, "Bonnie, if you guys want to keep riding after you eat, you can. But stay inside the RV park. I have some loose ends I need to tie up before we leave, and I'm not sure when I'll be back. Will you and Saul be okay?" I ask as I give them leftover pizza.

"Yeah, Carl, don't worry about us."

"There are peanut butter and jelly or ham and cheese sandwiches for dinner if I'm not back yet. Are you okay, Saul?" I ask.

He nods his head yes and looks at Bonnie.

I leave and go to the payphone to call Doug.

"Hey, Doug, how's your dad doing?" I ask.

"The surgery went well; he's home and healing. The doc said he's not ready to return to work, but soon. The good thing is he closes the shop for the week of Christmas every year, so I'm scot-free until after the first. After that, we can make some moves!"

"Good! I'm glad he is getting better," I say. "Look, I wanted to call and let you know that I'm going to be leaving town soon, for good."

"What the hell, man!"

"Yeah, I know, dude, but some things have come up, and I wanted to ask if you want to buy my Rambler."

Doug says, "I'd love to own that ride! But what is the price?"

"Can you meet me at Char-burger? We can discuss face to face."

Around an hour later, we meet, and I catch him up.

Doug says, "So you're saying all I have to do is hide in the corner of a dark, dingy, smelly cell in a dark basement, under a dirty blanket until someone comes, but you're not sure when he'll come. Then you will sneak up behind him when he does show up, and what? What are you going to do? And, If I do all that, I get the title clean and free?"

"Yep," I say.

"Well, I got to say that sounds creepy, but I'm in! I want that ride, so when do we go?"

"We have to go now."

"What? Now? It's Christmas Day, bro!"

"Yes, remember the part where I said I don't know when he will come home?"

"You coulda given me some warning, man; what if he doesn't come home for days?"

"Then I guess you'll pay for the car in days instead of hours."

"What about my dad?"

"You said he was recovering well."

"Yeah, I guess I did. So, what do you have against this guy?"

151

"He hurt a kid, so I'm going to hurt him."

Doug hops in the car with me, I plug in *Bad Company*, and we drive to Jason Alexander Hill's home.

I take Doug to the basement, revealing to him what I saw the first time there. I tell him about the boy and his story.

"Holy shit, man!" Doug says.

I pull two 45 semiautomatics from my backpack and hand one to Doug. I had packed one for each of us in case we needed them. I acquired these from past rob jobs. I also brought some snacks and water in case we're here for a long time.

The plan is simple: an eye for an eye, as they say. I had prepared a homecoming like no other, and we waited.

I hear him opening the basement door about seven hours later. As he walks down the stairs, I crouch under them. Doug is hidden in the corner of the cell under the dirty blanket.

When the fuckhead deviant gets to the bottom of the stairs, he stops and stands there for several minutes without saying a word. Then he flips on the light.

"Hello, Patrick. I'm back," he says.

Silence. Seconds go by without any movement.

"Awww? I haven't been gone that long; don't be mad. I brought you a special Christmas Day dinner," he says, wagging the bag towards the cell.

Silence.

He steps deeper into the room and walks toward the torture wall. He sets the bag on the corner table and turns toward the cage.

"I told you I brought something for you. Aren't you going to say thank you?"

Silence.

"Okay, play hard to get." He puts on the demon mask and walks to the cell to unlock it; as he passes the torture wall, he grabs a whip.

His back is to me when he opens the cell door. I step up behind him and press a gun to the back of his head.

"Hello, Mr. Jason Alexander Hill." I cock the gun, and he freezes.

That was Doug's cue. As he stands up, the blanket slides off his shoulders to the ground, and he advances and holds the Ruger 45 pointed at the child molester's chest.

"Drop the whip to the ground before I shoot a hole through your head," I say.

He does.

I handcuff his hands behind his back. I turn him around and pull the mask off his face so that I can look him in the eye.

He looks ordinary, like your quiet next-door neighbor. I say, "You have no idea how much I will enjoy this."

"How you like that, you fuckin' sadist!" Doug yells.

"Doug, go see what Christmas surprise he brought for us," I say, pointing to the bag, "and then help me set the stage for his last Christmas dinner."

Doug says, "Oh, man! It looks like he brought pigs' feet. Real nice of you, Jason! I bet a twelve-year-old boy would love this!"

"Bring those pigs' feet and pull that table over," I tell Doug.

"Where would you like the table?" Doug asks.

"Put it in the center of the cell. We will set a stage where detectives and police will talk and marvel about for years to come. Please, my friend, also bring me the knife, wire pliers, and cassette player from my backpack. I want some wicked music with my torture; let's see, put on *Deep Purple, Burn*, and let's jam."

I put the demon mask on and go to work.

He begged, pleaded, and tried to get loose. When he felt the pain, he screamed, begged, and cried; until he didn't.

Chapter 5: Breaking News

Carl Slater

I needed to clean myself up before going back to the camper-van. We leave the crime scene out the back door and go swimming in the ocean to wash away evidence on our bodies.

Next, we drive to a nearby boat dock and sink the torture tools, including the demon mask.

We sit on the beach for a long time; we have little to say.

Finally, Doug says, "Dude, I think you got your revenge."

"Yep," I say.

"If anything, ever catches up with you, I never knew you, dude."

"Yep," I say.

"Alright then, you ready to go? It's almost morning," he asks.

"Yep," I say

Doug drops me off at the RV, and I say goodbye to my friend and Rambler.

We leave San Diego later that afternoon. However, cooler weather is coming, so we've decided to stick to the southern states.

"I'd like to go back to Del Rio and camp by Devil's River again if that's okay, Carl," Bonnie says.

"Yeah, that was a nice place. Great idea! We'll head that way.

The first thing on my agenda is to cut and dye Saul's hair brown like ours and give him a John Lennon haircut; it's a good look for him.

We stayed a week at Tom Mays State Park Campground. I explain to Saul that he would be introduced as our younger brother. The parents' part was easy for him to remember because his parents had died in a car accident.

While there, we stop at the ice cream shop we visited last time we were here. We ask for the cemetery address of the young ice cream scooper who had tragically been murdered.

At the gravesite, Bonnie says, "I wish I'd known you better. I'm here because I remember your kindness, and I will try to be as kind to others as you were to me."

We go out early on New Year's Eve for a special dinner at Cushing Street Diner. Unfortunately, the Cushing Street diner has several TVs around the dining area, and the breaking news spoils our evening.

That was the day the police found Jason Alexander Hill. News stories spread over every network.

"This is CBS News reporting a breaking story," says the animated reporter. "A man has just been found dead at his residence in La Jolla today. Mr. Hill was reported missing by a colleague who assumed he had been traveling. When Hill never returned to work, the colleague notified the police. I have spoken with two of his colleagues, and they both said he was a professional and expert in his field of study, but neither had social interactions with him. I have also spoken with Mr. Hill's neighbors, who relayed that he has been an excellent neighbor."

NBC reports, "It appears Jason Alexander Hill was found dead in a homemade iron cell in his basement. Foul play is suspected. Then, three images were on the screen. He is said to have three foster children under his care. Their whereabouts are unknown. The children have been identified as Mike Stone, age eight, Veronica Roberts age ten, and Stephen Deshaun, age twelve. Please call the crime line at 1-800-423-TIPS if you have any information on this case."

Saul jerks his head upon hearing his foster dad's name and asks, "Is that...?"

"... It sure looks like it," I say.

His eyes begin filling with tears, and he stares at me.

"Are you alright, Saul?" I ask; I can see fear in his eyes.

"Yes, it's just ... I wished he would die, and I hoped he would die ... did I cause him to die? Did God answer my prayers? Is it my fault he died?" Saul asks as the tears roll down his face.

Bonnie says, "No, you didn't cause it, Saul. And God may or may not have answered your prayers. But know this: you are not to blame, not ever. He is better off dead. Kids are safer without him in the world."

As days pass, more information becomes available, and reports continue over the next few weeks.

ABC reports, "This is breaking news from our onsite reporter Julie. Can you hear us, Julie?"

"Yes, Cindy, I can hear you. Detective Hammond is said to be updating us at any moment. We have been receiving reports for days that the police have discovered several bodies buried in this La Jolla basement." The camera crew pans to the outside view of the home.

Detective Hammond approaches the reporters. "Ladies and gentlemen of the media. A letter was left on a table in the basement, and it has been verified that it is the homeowner's writing. He claims responsibility for the bodies we have found buried."

CNN reports," We have been given an exclusive by a source that will remain anonymous. All reports have said that Jason Alexander Hill was found dead in a homemade iron cell in his basement. What has not been provided is his condition. We now know his arms were handcuffed and pulled toward the ceiling by chains. He was lifted off the floor. Our source now says he had over 100 deep cuts, punctures, and whip marks all over his body. He had no fingernails and had been hanging for days, with his tippy toes barely touching a 2x2 inch box." There is some hesitation from the reporter. "Should I say this?" she asks someone off-camera, then hesitates and says, "His mouth was full of...pigs' feet? When they took the pigs' feet out of his mouth, all his teeth and fingernails fell to the floor." The reporter looks sick; she stands up and walks off-camera.

Fox News spokeswoman reports, "Detective Hammond has requested we report the following vital information. We have unearthed six bodies in the La Jolla Beach home. The victims are currently being identified, and we do not have the authority to reveal their names. Jason Alexander Hill is the original homeowner and is said to have been a foster care dad for the past several years. I can only say that the police are still looking for Stephen Patrick Deshaun, who is missing from home and has not been found."

A 5x7 photo of Stephen Patrick appears on the screen. "Deshaun is twelve years old and was one of the current foster children. It has been verified that he is not one of the

158

bodies we have uncovered. However, he is missing; please call the crime line at 800-423-TIPS if you have any information on this case."

Chapter 6: Finding Home Again

Carl Slater

Del Rio

We leave on New Year's Day and head to Del Rio. We set up in the RV area and add a tent close to the sliding door on the passenger side of the van. Del Rio is quiet—off the grid.

After a couple of days, I go to the high school and enroll Bonnie in tenth grade. Then, I go to the middle school to enroll Saul in seventh grade with the same story I used for Bonnie.

It's been a few months now, and Saul is having a hard time in school. He's struggling to concentrate in classes, has difficulty retaining information, and is also having trouble sleeping because of nightmares.

Some nights we find him curled up into a ball. He whimpers, moans, or sobs uncontrollably, and when he wakes, he's often yelling, "No, no, no!"

Bonnie is able to soothe Saul back to sleep by reading or singing soft songs to him—like a mom would do, I guess.

He's beginning to understand what's happened to him and learning that it's not his fault. He understands he's safe with us.

He struggles anyway—we all do, to one extent or the other. We are heading to Sedona when schools are out for summer. It's only a couple of weeks away.

"The views are stunning," I say. There are red sandstone cliffs like cathedrals that surround us as we set up our campsite.

Bonnie says, "Carl, do you know they have something called vortexes in Sedona?"

"Yea, I remember you and Saul talking about it. What is a vortex?" I ask.

"It's like places where the earth seems to be alive with energy. Like an energy center radiating from the earth. It's supposed to help with physical healing and mental inspiration," Saul says.

Bonnie said, "Vortexes are found at sacred sites throughout the world—the Great Pyramid in Egypt, Machu Picchu in Peru, Bali, Stonehenge, and Sedona."

We drive into Sedona and wander around the touristy area. On our way back to camp, I notice a store called Copper Gun & Rifles, so we go in. I speak to the owners, Ronnie, and his wife, Shay.

"I'm Carl, and this here is my sister Bonnie and brother Saul. I'm looking for an outdoor shooting range for some target practice. Do you know of any places close by?"

"My wife and I go to a sandpit off Beaver-Head Flat Rd. It's kinda popular to us locals; not a lot of tourists know about it." Ronnie says.

Shay looks at Bonnie and asks, "Where are your folks?"

"They passed in a car accident a couple of years ago," Bonnie says.

"I'm sorry to hear that, Bonnie," she says and looks over to me.

"Are you doing okay taking care of these two?" she asks

"Yes, ma'am; they're good kids."

Then she looks at Bonnie again and smiles. "Keep an eye on your little brother while your big brother practices today."

"I will!" she replies.

"We'll be safe, thank you," I say.

We pick up lunch at Indian Springs Sandwich Shop and head to the outdoor shooting range.

It is an incredible day, with temperatures in the low seventies. We have music playing on the radio as we drive to the shooting range. *Led Zeppelin, Kashmir.*

Sweet jams.

I want to teach Bonnie how to shoot a gun. She turned fifteen almost two months ago and should know how to defend herself.

But I come to find out that Bonnie is a natural badass. I have to say I'm not surprised. I give her a Remington 20-gauge shotgun first. Then we move on to a 44 Remington Magnum. She is hitting the bullseye target 90% of the time.

That evening, Bonnie says, "Oh my gosh, I loved shooting guns today. It was so much fun! Do you think I was pretty good?"

"Oh, hell yeah!! You are a natural sharpshooter, Bonnie," I say.

Back at the campsite, I teach both Saul and Bonnie how to clean the guns.

"When can I learn to shoot?" Saul asks.

"When you turn fifteen, Saul, but I'm teaching you to clean guns now, so you have a head start," I reply.

He rolls his eyes.

Kids, I think and smile.

That night, Saul had a slight fever and sore throat. I give him aspirin and make him some salt water to gargle with—he hates it. He is a little better by the next morning, but I worry about his immune system.

We all go to get checkups. The doctor tells Saul to take vitamin C and iron tablets daily, at least until his next checkup. Overall, we're in good shape.

We stay in Sedona for three weeks. During that time, Saul and Bonnie become experts at starting fires, throwing knives, and climbing rocks. Saul learns to dry shoot. "No bullets for you," I tell him.

One night, after reading our third chapter of *Torch in the Dark*, Bonnie starts to cry—she is angry. She misses her parents, not as they were, wild and partying, but as she wished them to be. She feels they didn't care enough about her to stay sober, to watch over and protect her.

"They were so self-centered," she says. "If I ever have kids, I'll treat them with so much love. I'll take them everywhere with me, and nobody will lay a hand on them."

"Bonnie, you will be the best mom," Saul said. "You act like my mom already. My parents were good; although I'd get mad at them, I always loved them. Then they died, and that freak became my foster dad. You guys know I have flashbacks when I'm awake and nightmares when I sleep?" Saul says. "Will they ever go away?" he asks.

163

"I didn't realize you were having flashbacks, but we know about the nightmares. I'm not sure if they will go away, Saul. But I hope, in time, they will. Let's make a pact. We will talk to each other when we have flashbacks or nightmares. Maybe the more we share, the better things will get." We all agree.

"Carl, what's the plan? Are we staying here or going? What are we doing?" Bonnie asks.

"I'd like to go live in Arkansas and settle like we did in California," I say.

"Anywhere is good for me," Saul says.

"Will we get a puppy?" Bonnie asks.

"When we have a house and fenced-in yard. Don't worry; I haven't forgotten. We just need to find the right place."

"Carl, can we go to the Grand Canyon before we leave Arizona?" Saul asks.

"Do you wanna go too, Bonnie?" I ask.

"Uhhhh, of course I want to go. Who do you think put him up to asking you?" Bonnie says.

"Okay then, let's go before it gets too hot. How about we get everything together tonight and head that way tomorrow? I'll find out where to boon-dock around the canyon on our way out of Sedona in the morning," Carl says.

"Shazam!" Saul exclaims. "My family was supposed to go on a trip to the Grand Canyon before the accident happened. When I was locked in that cage, I would daydream about us going there together. It helped me through many of the days and nights in the darkness."

The next morning, we get up and watch the sunrise; the sky turns a bright orange as the sun rises, reflecting off the red rocks. Truly outstanding—one of the most mesmerizing visuals I think we will ever see.

Bonnie takes me to the side, "Carl, I'm feeling weird this morning; my stomach is hurting and cramping." She looks scared and embarrassed. I know she doesn't want to tell me these things, but who else was there? Not Saul.

Bonnie says, "When I went to the doctor, she asked me if I had gotten my cycle. We learned a little bit about it in health class this year, but I didn't know for sure what it would feel like. The doctor explained, and I think this is what she meant."

"I'm not sure, Bonnie, but when we go to say goodbye to Mr. Ronnie and Ms. Shay this morning, you can ask Ms. Shay. She will know about all the girl stuff. Would that be okay while I talk to Mr. Ronnie about our trip to the Grand Canyon?" I ask.

We had become regulars at their gun shop over the past three weeks and even had lunch with them a couple of times.

"Yes, that will be good," she says, relieved.

Thank goodness both Ronnie and Shay were at work this morning.

"We wanted to stop and say goodbye. We are heading to the Grand Canyon for the rest of our summer vacation," I say.

Shay says, "Fun! Ronnie and I have gone several times, but our best experience was going to the bottom of the canyon, a place called Phantom Ranch."

Bonnie quickly interrupts, "Miss Shay, can I talk to you for a few minutes about something private?"

Shay and Bonnie walk over to the waiting area and sit down to talk about girl stuff. I start thinking maybe Bonnie needs a mother figure in her life. Why have I not thought of that before?

"Now," Ronnie says, "you can park the camper-van at the Bright Angel Lodge. You'll need to check in with the rangers inside the lobby and let them know the three of you are hiking down and spending the night; it's a safety precaution. You'll all need a backpack with a change of clothes, three bottles of water, some lunch, snacks, and a blanket each. Do you have pup tents?" Ronnie asks.

"No, just one big tent," I reply

"I have some pup tents on the survival aisle. Let me give you three as a going-away gift. It has been so great to know y'all. They are small enough for each of you to have one hooked to your backpacks. You can sleep under the stars," Ronnie says.

Shay and Bonnie disappeared into the backroom for a little while. When they back out, Bonnie seems a little flushed, but happy.

As we are leaving, Bonnie hugs Shay and thanks her. I'm glad Bonnie had someone to talk to when she needed.

Rim to River

We stand on the rim of the Grand Canyon. Looking over the railing makes my stomach drop. The view is extraordinary; it literally makes you feel humble and in awe. It's a place that, once you see it, you can never accurately describe it. You have to go there—actually stand there on that ground—to feel the expansiveness of the land below and all that is around you.

It's genuinely unimaginable; no photograph can ever precisely show what you see and feel.

As we trek down the Bright Angel path the next morning, we are mindful of three things: drink a lot of water, don't fall off the edge of switchbacks, and don't step in mule poop.

"Holy smokes, are you watching the faces of the mule riders? Watch—they look so excited and yet frightened every time a switchback comes up," Saul says. "Watch, watch ... the mule walks out to the very edge of the trail, overlooking the canyon, and the rider's eyes squeeze shut. They are terrified, and then the donkey stops and makes the switchback turn and goes the direction of the path instead of walking off the edge." Saul's expression was of total amazement.

"It probably feels to the rider that he's going off the edge each time; I'd rather hike than trust a mule," I say.

We stop at Indian Gardens about 5 miles down the canyon, refill our water bottles, eat our packed lunches then continue on our way.

It takes over five hours total to get to the bottom of the canyon—a total of 9.3 miles—but it is worth the descent.

Once at the bottom, we leave the path and take a bridge crossing over a stream. Since we arrive early in the day, we set up camp and change to swim clothes. A few swimmers are in the cold stream that ran off the Colorado River. It feels amazing.

The Phantom Ranch Canteen is a two-minute walk from our campsite, and the dinner is wonderful. Afterward, we wander around the floor of the canyon, surrounded by the towering canyon walls, until sunset.

I wake up at about 3 am and crawl out of my pup tent. The stars fill the night sky with zero city lights to interfere. It looks like billions of stars.

I wake the kids. "You guys have to get up and see this."

"Whoa! I've never seen so many stars—not even in Sedona," Bonnie says, wonderstruck.

We sit alone under the stars in silence as we absorb the strength and energy of that place.

Bonnie says, "There has to be a God."

Saul replies, "Agreed!"

The following morning after breakfast, we begin our hike back up the canyon. Seven hours later, wiped out, we come to the top. We are utterly exhausted and completely satisfied with our achievement.

As we head back to the camper-van, I say, "One day soon, we'll find a safe, stable home. You guys can finish school and maybe go to college?"

"All I want is a house with a fence and dog," Bonnie says.

"I just want to be with you guys; I don't care where we go," says Saul.

Once back in our safe place, Bonnie falls asleep on the long bench and Saul in the back of the van, so I crash up top.

I wake around 9 am from the best sleep ever! I close the camper top and hit the road, letting both kids sleep in.

The Duke City

We find free overnight camping spots at the Silver Skipper Resort & Casino in Albuquerque.

168

There are two other RV campers, a semi-tractor trailer, two tents, and a Station Wagon settled in sites for the night.

I find temp work the next morning and am sent to a construction site to do foundation work for a week, then an auto repair shop for a couple of weeks while a worker was healing from an emergency appendectomy surgery.

"What is an appendectomy?" Saul asks.

"Good question. Let's go to the library and find out," I say.

"Cool!"

We spend the afternoon finding books. The librarian, Martha, was in her twenties, wore cat-eye-shaped glasses, and was super smart.

"Why did you become a librarian?" I ask.

Martha replies, "My grandmother read me books every night at bedtime since before I can remember. She told me books are life. You can become anything you want to be when you read. The hero, the villain, an innocent bystander, the observer, or even the storyteller. I can read for hours. I couldn't think of a better job," she says.

"I didn't get to know my grandmother; yours sounds really great," I say.

"What happened to her?" she asks.

"I don't know," I say, uncomfortable with personal talk. "Hey, I heard a hot air balloon festival is happening tomorrow morning. Do you know anything about that?"

"Yes!" she says. "The balloons lift off at sunrise. It'll be so fun to watch! I'll get you a flyer."

I find Bonnie and Saul at a table in the corner, absorbed in books.

"I want us all to get up to watch balloons lift off in the morning." I show them the flyer. "I'm thinking we can wrap up in blankets and sit on the roof of the van to watch."

"That sounds fun! Can we make a picnic breakfast?" Bonnie asks.

"Of course, we can! We'll stop at the grocery on the way back home."

We eat frosted flakes and strawberries as we sit on top of the camper-van, waiting on the balloons to rise.

The first hot air balloon slowly lifts from the ground and rises into the sky, gently climbing into a smooth glide across the sky. As bright-colored hot air balloons ascend, I see the excitement and wonder on the kids' faces. This fills me with hope that everything will be okay.

"Woohoo!" Saul says. "How cool is this?"

"I counted thirteen balloons," Bonnie says. "They are so beautiful."

Before we knew it, they had all lifted one by one until the sky was filled with elegant balloons.

We watch them float away, and I wonder what it would be like to drift above the world, look down and see us, all like tiny ants.

After that morning, we begin to hang out on the top of the camper in the evenings for sunset.

It's interesting that no one seems to look up when they're walking. They don't seem to notice you.

There is a woman living in the parked station wagon and her son. They walk by every evening on their way to the truck stop down the road for dinner. She has a mean spirit and seems to be drunk most of the time and is always yelling at the boy about something. The boy is maybe twelve years old.

Tonight, as they were walking past our camper, I hear her say, "If it weren't for you, I'd be married by now." The boy just dropped his head down and kept following her as they passed by. He never talks back to her and never looks up.

This morning, when I saw her walking towards the casino down the road, I decided to walk over to the station wagon and talk to the boy.

I knock on the door lightly. "Hello in there, I'm in the camper-van." No answer. "I was wondering if you had some band-aids? My sister scrapped her knee, and all we have is toilet paper for the bleeding."

"I'm not supposed to open the door to strangers or get out of the wagon," he finally replies.

I say, "Okay, well, if you have some band aids, I'll walk away, and you can set them outside on the ground, and I can come back and get them."

"Okay."

After a few minutes, I retrieve the band aids and go back to our camper-van. I watch the station wagon the rest of the day, but the little boy never comes outside, and his mom doesn't come back until dusk.

I wonder how this boy goes to pee when she's gone? At least when Bonnie was younger, and I had to work, she stayed in the camper and had food, a television, books, and a bathroom.

When his mom finally returns, she opens the back door to the station wagon, and the boy comes out. They begin walking towards the truck stop, I'm assuming for dinner.

The mom stops walking just past our camper and yells at him, "I'm tired of you complaining that I'm gone all day; you are never happy with anything! You're a sorry excuse for a son." Then she pushes him to the ground.

He gets up, dusts his pants off, and proceeds to follow her. I can see he is embarrassed and trying not to cry—trying to be a tough guy. I want to kick this woman's ass right there, but I keep my cool.

I send Saul to talk to the boy the next day, but it is more of the same. "I'm not allowed to talk to strangers or open the door for anyone," he says and stays inside the wagon all day long, coming out only when she comes back in her drunken swagger.

The boy looks our way when he passes us today. I notice he has on the same clothes as the past two days, along with a black eye.

The following day is the same. I'm not sure what the woman is doing all day long at the casino; she doesn't seem to have money to blow. The station wagon was in okay shape, but it was old.

I decide to go to the casino and spy on her. She heads to the penny slots right away. As the building begins to fill with people, she starts flirting with any and all available men. She has drinks with them and plays slots with them and ends up in the man's car for at least 30 minutes. Then, she comes back inside and starts over.

I believe she's a prostitute; I counted six men today.

I wonder if the boy would want to leave her and travel with us. I decide to try and talk to him one more time, but of course, he doesn't answer me at all at this point.

Later, I send Bonnie back to offer him some lunch. He doesn't answer.

Today, as the boy and his mom walk through the campground to the truck stop, she keeps yanking his arm and telling him that he's no good. She is low-class, loud, and obnoxious.

"Okay, I've had enough," I say to Bonnie and Saul. "Let's take him and leave."

Saul asks, "What if he doesn't want to come with us? He won't even answer the door for us. How will we get him to go?"

"You remember telling me about the science teacher you had that did the spy experiment in your class last year, Bonnie?" I ask.

Bonnie gives me a disappointed look. "Do you mean the chloroform experiment that got him fired? That's not a good idea."

"Bonnie, he's being abused!" I say, frustrated.

"I know he would be better off with us, but if we just take him, we'll scare him. He may run away from us, and then he'd be worse off. He doesn't know us."

Saul says, "Bonnie, you didn't know Carl, and I didn't know either of you, but I was glad you guys took me away. He must be awfully scared of his mom. He can't be happy living like he is."

"How about we drive into town, go to the library, and see if there's a book that tells us how to make the chloroform? If

173

we find one, we pick up supplies and make it. If not, we don't. Then, we find another way," I say.

"Well, how do we get him to open the door?" Bonnie asks.

"I got an idea about that," I say.

"I don't know, Carl. Is this any of our business?" Bonnie asks.

"Would you rather I minded my own business when I saw what was happening to you or to Saul?"

"No, Carl, but it isn't the same."

"Bonnie, we've seen the emotional and physical abuse he is going through. She hits him, pushes him, curses him, no telling what she may do to him in private. He stays in the car all day, at least eight hours, with no bathroom and lying down. It's not good. It will only get worse; you know it never stops and never gets better. Do you think it's okay?"

"No, it's not okay," she concurs.

"Let's take him," Saul says. "Moms are supposed to protect and love—not hurt!"

After the boy's mom leaves the following day, Bonnie walks to his station wagon.

She knocks frantically on the van door. "Is anyone there? Please help me, my boyfriend is hurt bad, and I can't leave him to get help. So please, please, please help me!!"

Knock, knock. "My name is Bonnie; if you could just go to the truck stop or casino and call an ambulance for me while I stay with him, please! I think he may be dying."

He opens the door, and Bonnie leans into him and slides the washcloth with chloroform across his nose and mouth.

He is out like a light. I pull up beside the station wagon, and we slide him inside and drive away.

I wonder what his mom would think—what she would do. Will she think he ran away? Will she even tell the police that she's lost her son? Will she look for him? These are all questions we will probably never have answers to.

I drive straight for twelve hours. When we get to Shreveport, we park at the Horseshoe Bossier City Hotel & Casino. "This looks like a good spot to hang for a day or two," I say.

The boy is lying on the rear bench seat, covered with a blanket and a pillow under his head. He hadn't moved for the whole trip.

"Do you think we might have used too much chloroform on him?" Saul asks.

"No way, we were super careful with the measurements," I say.

"Let's go get some food," Saul says. We go through the drive-thru at McDonald's.

Bonnie gently shakes the boy's leg and says, "Hey, kid. I have a hamburger and french fries for you. Are you hungry?"

He begins to move his body slowly, trying to get some circulation through his limbs. He sits up and looks at us but doesn't say a word. He eats the food and then goes back to sleep.

The next morning, I make cereal and milk for everyone. The boy sits up. He still has not spoken; he looks dazed and confused.

"Good morning, kid. You want to talk about why you are here?" I ask

The boy nods his head yes.

"My name is Carl; what is your name?"

"Chester," he says in a hoarse voice.

"Okay, this is Bonnie and Saul. We're family. So far, so good?"

He shook his head yes.

"How old are you?"

"Twelve."

"Do you go to school? "

"Not since 4th grade."

"So, since you were nine years old?"

"I guess," he shrugged.

"How long have you lived in that station wagon?"

"I don't know, since 4th grade, I guess. Mom said we lost our home because I was bad, and my daddy left."

"Where else have you lived other than your station wagon?

"I don't remember where; we've been in the wagon for a long time, and we drive to different places."

"Is the woman your mother?"

"Ya."

"Where is your dad?"

"I don't know."

"How often does your mom hit you?"

"When I'm bad."

"When are you bad?"

"If I leave the van or open the door of the wagon. If I talk back to her or do anything without asking her first."

"How often are you bad?"

"Mom says I'm bad every day."

"Do you have any other family?"

"I don't know, I've never met any other family, and my sister died."

"How old was your sister?"

"I think she was two years older than me, but she took care of me every day, and then she was gone. Mom said she thinks she went to heaven."

"How long has she been gone?"

"Maybe a year," he says.

"Chester," Bonnie says, "would you like to stay with us and become a part of our family?"

He looks at us and starts crying. "Why did my mom have me?" he asks.

"I don't know how to answer that," I say.

Bonnie scoots next to him and just sits with him for a while.

My third victim, they will say. After our heart-to-heart, he chooses to stay with us. We all breathe a sigh of relief.

We talk to him about changing his name. "What name would you like us to call you, Chester? Pick any name you want," Saul says.

177

"I like the name 'Matthew.' My sister used to read to me from a tiny Bible that a church lady gave her, and her favorite part was about a guy named Matthew. I never want to forget my sister."

"I really like that name," Bonnie says.

"So, what happened to your sister?" Saul asks.

"I don't want to talk about it," he says.

"Okay, but if you ever do want to talk about her, you can talk to us," Bonnie says.

Rachet City

The next day, we drive deep into Shreveport, looking for a shady-type pawn shop where I can sell jewelry without a ton of questions.

I find one, go in, and scope the place out. I feel good about it, so I pull out a small bag of jewelry from my pocket that I have been saving since San Diego. I ask the owner to give me an estimate of its worth and what he would pay for the items. "I don't want to pawn them; I want to sell them," I say.

The owner's eyes light up when he sees the quality of the rings, necklaces, and bracelets. I give him two of each. I am hoping to learn how this guy deals with people.

"Well, sir, what will you take for them?" the pawnshop owner asks.

"I want to know what you think you could give me first," I reply steadfastly.

"With this being a pawn shop, I won't be able to give you its full worth, son. But give me a second to look at them." He pulls out a loupe and turns on the light.

After a few minutes, he says, "I can offer you

$1500.00"

I already knew what they were worth, and I knew I'd never get their full value. I say, "I was thinking more around $2500."

"I can go $2000," he says and puts his hand out. We shake. "Do I need to worry about these diamonds being on a list of stolen goods in Louisiana?"

"No sir; not a chance." I never sell stolen jewelry from the same state or city that I steal from.

The owner smiles and says, "Partner, come back anytime. My name is Nathan, I'm the only one who works here besides my son, and he is only here for protection. He's in the back with a gun, watching us; you'll never see him."

I nod and say, "I'm Carl." I take the money and say goodbye.

We go back to the Horseshoe Bossier City Hotel & Casino for overnight parking.

Getting fake IDs was a little tricky, so I do what any good criminal would do: I go back to the pawnshop and talk to Nathan. I sell him another $1000 in jewelry and ask him if he knows anyone with the specific skill of creating a fake driver's license.

"Yeah, I know a guy. He's very professional, the ID will pass, but if you ever get caught for anything that would put you in jail, they'd figure it out. He also sells birth certificates

179

that can be used to get legit licenses, but you wouldn't be able to pick your own names, and they cost more."

"What are the odds he could get certificates with our first names?"

"Give me a list of names and approximate ages, and I'll see what he can do. Those will cost you $500 each; it takes a lot of work."

I give him our list of first names with the relevant ages, hoping he could pull it off or at least come close. Then, two days later, Nathan gives us an address, and we go to meet the man. His name is Freddie.

Freddie says, "Lucky you, I was able to find Carl Parker Jr., Bonnie Smith, Saul Gilmore, and Matthew Harris's birth certificates. Will those work for you?"

"Yeah, we'll make it work," I say.

"Okay then, we have a deal. The birth certificates are authentic, and you can get a state driver's license or identification cards with them. You just have to have an address."

I hand him $1,500 cash.

"Thanks, man. Are there any good lunch places around here?" I ask.

"Yeah, the Shrimp Buster; it's a hole in the wall, but I betcha you'll go back every time you're in town. It's like a Shrimp Po' Boy, but better," he says and smiles.

Freddie was right; it was the best I've ever eaten.

That afternoon, we drive about three hours to the Ouachita National Forest. We park our camper at the Golden Buck Campground, which is very close to Wandajo,

Arkansas. We set up our big tent and the three pup tents. Bonnie makes a fire ring, and we cook Oscar Mayer Weiner's over the flames and eat Wise potato chips with sour cream and onion dip.

Bonnie begins to sing:

> *Oh, I'd love to be an Oscar Mayer Wiener*
> *That is what I'd truly like to be.*
> *'Cause if I were an Oscar Mayer Weiner,*
> *Everyone would be in love with me.*

I begin to laugh. *What's up with her and Oscar Meyer commercials*, I wonder.

Chapter 7: Ouachita National Forest

Carl Slater

I bought a Pontiac GTO at a reasonable price; it's seven years old and in good shape and makes life more manageable when we need to go to town for school, supplies, and work.

I got a full-time job as a mechanic the second week we arrived in Ouachita Forest. I enrolled Bonnie in eleventh grade and Saul in eighth for the fall, which starts in two weeks. I can't believe how fast everything is changing.

Bonnie says, "Matthew, they'll put you in seventh grade, same as Saul. The first year will be tricky, trying to get you caught up, but we'll help."

I wait until the first day of school to register Matthew, hoping the school office would be overwhelmed and Matthew might slip in without much questioning—and it worked! Principal Stackhouse put him in a class immediately.

My work hours are Monday through Friday at Mountainside Auto Repair. They allow me to arrive at 8 am and leave to pick the kids up from school at 3 pm. So, for now, we have a relatively normal everyday life.

I take Bonnie, Matthew, and Saul to the dentist, and he says, "Bonnie needs braces. She doesn't have to have them, but her teeth may look like shark teeth if she doesn't get them. Saul needs two fillings, and Matthew needs wisdom teeth extracted."

Bonnie gets her braces and, one year later, gets them off—a few days before her senior year begins. Her teeth are perfect, and I'm glad we made the sacrifice.

Matthew has a rough start the first year he attends junior high school. There is a bully named Derek and his little gang of friends. They constantly call Matthew "slow poke" or "dumb duck," making him feel bad about himself. Finally, one day in spring, they corner him in the locker room after gym class. He comes home with a black eye and bruised chin, but not only that, he comes in with heart and determination not to be a victim.

"I want to stand up to Derek. I want to know that I can kick his ass."

"How about taking weight training classes over the summer?"

That's where Matthew meets Luke Reed, the junior high school football team captain. They worked out together and became fast friends.

Luke tells Matthew, "I take grappling classes a couple of times a week in the evenings. Do you want to come with me as a guest?"

By the time Eighth grade starts, Matthew has put on twenty pounds, grown two inches taller, and now has a muscular build. He looks like a different kid and exudes confidence. Derek and his little gang decide not to mess with Matthew anymore, when they realize he's buddies with Luke and the rest of the football team.

"Bonnie, has Saul talked to you about his drama classes?" I ask.

"Yeah, he said he tried out for a part in the school's Christmas play."

At the same time, Saul comes tromping through the woods. "Hey, guys! I have good news. I'll be the Grinch this year!"

"You're that every year!" Matthew says.

"Yuk, yuk, yuk," retorts Saul.

I say, "Congrats Saul! I have good news, too, you guys! I found a cave this morning while I was hunting. It's a short hike into the forest, but the cool thing is a waterfall hides it. The woods surround the small clearing, so it's like a hidden treasure. We can make a base camp there for a while. I explored the inside, and it was huge and had many chambers. We would have much more room to sleep and could make it more like home. Although it's been cool using the pup tents and connecting the big tent to the rear of the camper-van to make a bigger space, I think this place will be much better."

"Yeah, and besides that, Saul snores!" Matthew replies.

"I do not snore!" Saul says sheepishly.

"Okay, whatever," I roll my eyes. "I want you guys to come with me to see it. What do you think?" I ask.

Bonnie says, "Well, I would love more privacy from all you boys!"

"Oh yeah? We'll be glad we don't have to leave the camper whenever you need to change clothes!" Matthew says, sticking out his tongue. Even though he is fifteen, he sometimes still acts like he's ten.

We hike to the cavern the following day. When we come upon the small waterfall and pool of water that lays below, the kids go crazy. The boys run and jump into the water, while Bonnie walks to the edge and slides in.

"The water feels so good!" cries Saul.

Matthew and Saul fist-bump and start splashing water at each other.

After about 15 minutes, I gather everyone to the edge of the pool of water.

"So let me tell you about this place. The mountain stream exits there." I point to the top of the waterfall. "There is an abundance of vegetation, mostly ferns and fungi, up there. The waterfall covers the face of the cave. I wouldn't have noticed the cavern if I hadn't decided to swim by the rocks over there." I point to the other side, about 50 feet away. "That's where we will climb into the cave, behind the waterfall."

"Adventure!" says Saul.

I can't help but smile, "Well, yes! I went into the cavern to explore, and there was lots of natural light in the entranceway, but the cavern is enormous and has several chambers, small and large. There's also a little stream and a couple of pools. The pathway throughout the cavern system is wide but winding and becomes smaller and dimly lit the further you get from the entrance, so once we go in, please be careful."

"Can we go in now?" asks Matthew.

"Why not? Let's go for it!" I reply.

"Yay!" say Saul and Matthew in unison.

We climb up a few rocks behind the waterfall and into the mouth of the cave. The opening is about six feet tall and six feet wide, so we go in one at a time.

"Oh my goodness, this is perfect, Carl!" Bonnie says.

"So cool!" says Matthew.

Saul yells 'hello' for the echo, and we join in.

"Do you think we can move our stuff today?" Bonnie asks excitedly.

"If everyone votes yes," I say.

The vote is unanimous, and we move our sleeping bags, pillows, and personal stuff to the cavern.

The walk back and forth to the RV takes about 10 minutes. The forest beyond the camping area is super thick with no trail, so Carl makes trail signs for us to follow to the cavern:

- Two stacked rocks mean this is the trail.

- Two stacked rocks and one rock to the right side of the means turn right.

- Two stacked rocks and one to the left mean turning left.

"The very first thing we do is build something to cover the mouth of the cave. Anybody got ideas on what we can do?" I ask.

Matthew has a brilliant idea. He says, "We can build a flat wall like we do for stage props to block the mouth of the cave. We will need some materials from the hardware store, some wood, wooden planks, hinges, and French braces. Last year I helped build a lot of stage props, so I can show y'all how!" He is so excited.

We did it! It's not perfect and took some work, but it encloses the cave, and we have a door in the center of the wall to come in and out. This will keep the outdoor elements outdoors.

We use battery-powered lights and have scrounged and salvaged building supplies, boards, and beams from disposal areas in and around town. Of course, people discard what they consider useless, but we find uses for many things.

Then, we find a wood stove for cooking, and it's also a reliable heat source. Finally, we funnel the pipes outside to ventilate smoke, which keeps the cave nice and toasty over the wintertime.

We hunt for food on weekends, mostly squirrels and rabbits, with traps or our bows and arrows. We catch fish and sometimes turtles from the Ouachita River and look for mussels and crawfish under rocks and logs.

We have tons more food sources where we live: hickory nuts, walnuts, pecans, wild mushrooms, and berries.

We always have SPAM, Vienna sausage, and potted meats on hand because it doesn't spoil and is good emergency food.

Turning our cave into a home has been a slow process. We now have a thin mattress on a wood slab in each bedroom.

We have picked up bookshelves, chairs, and even desks from the thrift store and added battery-powered lanterns throughout the cave.

Outside, about 500 yards deeper into the woods, we set up a crude, camouflaged but comfy outhouse inside our old tent. We cut out the bottom of the tent after digging a hole in the ground three feet wide and five feet deep. We cover the hole with a makeshift wood box that has a cut-out in the middle with an actual toilet seat over the hole—not bad if you ask me. We pour the ash from our wood-burning stove into the hole for decomposition, but it's not so effective on the odors, for that, we use lime.

I've been making good money at work, but the kids have a lot of needs. I've done three rob jobs over the past two years, but only when we needed help. I drive two hours away from home base, just enough to get new clothes, shoes, and school supplies for the kids. Since the braces, I've run out of backup money, but at least we don't owe anyone.

Saul and Matthew both started ninth grade this year. Matthew is lucky; he has had both Bonnie and Saul to get him up to speed in school, and he is now thriving, even though last year was rough.

After getting settled one evening, Bonnie asks, "Would you let me come on a rob job with you, maybe on Thanksgiving or Christmas break, when we are out of school?"

"Are you sure you want to do that, Bonnie? I've never wanted that for you," I say. "We're doing fine."

"Please, Carl, I want to help out. I can't get a job because of school and chorus practice, but I've always wanted to go on a rob job with you. I think I'm old enough, don't you?" she pleads. "Please, I'm in 12th grade!?"

"Let me think about it, Bonnie."

Part Six: Michelle, 1977-1979

"Family isn't always blood, it's the people in your life who want you in theirs: the ones who accept you for who you are, the ones who would do anything to see you smile and who love you no matter what,"

Maya Angelou.

Chapter 1: Whisky and a Carton of Cigarettes

Carl Slater

"Good morning, guys. How does it feel to be on Thanksgiving break?" I ask.

"It's GRRRREEEAAAT!!" Matthew says, even using *Tony the Tigers'* folded arms with a thumbs up. *What a goofball,* I think and smile to myself.

"Serious talk. I want you guys to know where things stand. There are things we've been able to do over the past two years that make me proud. Everyone is healthy. We've all been to the dentist, and our teeth are good! The only negative is that we've depleted our savings. We've been stable, and school is good.

"Only thing is, at this point, we are living paycheck to paycheck. So, Bonnie and I are going to drive a few hours away for a rob job," I say.

"Why so far?" asks Matthew.

"Because being far from home is a good rule of thumb. We'll pick a higher-end neighborhood in a faraway city, play private eye, and stake out the home to be sure no one is around. We should be able to get in and out in 15 minutes. We'll head right back home after," I say. "I'll need you guys to hold down the fort."

"Cool!" says Matthew.

Bonnie says, "Saul, while we're gone, will you teach Matthew to hunt with the bow and arrows and set traps for food? Then, after you catch something, teach him how to skin and prepare the animals?"

"Yeah, I got it. You can count on us," Saul says.

Carl says, "We will only be gone for 48 hours or less. Remember, if anyone comes around here, keep low-key. If they find the cave and try to approach by climbing up the rocks, one of you will need to yell down at them. Just say, 'Please, respect our privacy.' Be prepared to act if needed. You guys have a rifle, just in case," I say. "I don't think it will come to that. It's winter, and most people will not climb behind waterfalls anyway.

Bonnie says, "ONLY use the rifle if you feel you're in danger." She hugs them, and we leave.

Bonnie and I drive to McAlester, Oklahoma, roughly 200 miles from our base camp.

We drive around until we find a home with several newspapers in the driveway. The house we choose is a brick two-story with a fancy circular driveway in an upscale neighborhood.

We watch the residence overnight, and there is no movement the next day. We are both ready to go home, so we go into the brick house that evening after sunset.

I pick the lock, and we go inside. I'd prepped Bonnie to know what to look for.

"Here we go. Start your search upstairs, and I'll start downstairs. We will meet back here in 15 minutes. If you see any headlights pull up, come straight down, and leave out the back door, and head back the way we came and wait for me."

"What if you get caught?" she asks.

"I won't get caught, but if I'm not there five minutes after you arrive, leave!" I say.

"Okay."

I find a gun cabinet that has two rifles and a handgun with ammunition and in a hidden compartment that I find by accident, $2,700 in cash. There were also three small jewelry boxes, with an 18c gold Diamond Solitaire engagement ring, a Designer Bracelet, and a Cartier watch.

"WOW!" I say out loud.

I look quickly at clothing sizes; the men's clothes are too big for the boys or me, but a few women's sweaters could work for Bonnie, so I grab a couple of options. Next, I check the dresser drawers but find nothing. So I go into the bathroom, grab a couple of towels, a whole bottle of shampoo, conditioner, shaving cream, and a man's razor. I also loot the medicine cabinet.

The living room is very classy, but it has items I am not prepared to take with us.

I see a cassette player on the kitchen island and grab it and the tapes next to it. Then, I look in the pantry and pick up cereal, chips, cookies, and several boxed and canned foods. In the refrigerator, I see batteries and throw them in my backpack.

I fix Bonnie and myself a turkey sandwich with potato chips and put them on paper plates to-go.

In the meanwhile, Bonnie picks out some clothing and shoes for the boys and packs them in two school bags from the kids' rooms. Next, she packs a Smokee CB talking radio in her backpack and the brand-new Kenner Star Wars figure collection for the kids. The box includes Luke Skywalker, Princess Leia, Chewbacca, and R2-D2. To top it off, she adds a blanket and pillow.

"You good?" I ask.

She said, "Yes, the boys will hit the roof when they see what I found! I crammed as much as possible in this bag; no more room."

"Okay, I made dinner. We should hit the road; I want to go home!"

Bonnie smiles as I hand her the sandwich. "Looks yummy, thanks!"

As we are leaving, the phone rings, and it scares the shit out of us! The answering machine picks up, and the person on the other end of the line begins leaving a message: "Hello, Lori, I'm checking to see if you and Phil want to have dinner with us when you get home from Chicago. Let me know, my sweet friend!"

"Shit, let's get outta here!" I say.

We go back home and share the spoils. We had a great Thanksgiving.

On Christmas break, Bonnie and I go to New Boston, Texas.

We find another gorgeous home—it is more like an estate. It has high ceilings, massive columns, and floor-to-ceiling windows. We find $1800 hidden in a hat box in the women's closet, nothing else. Most things they own are beautiful but not a need for us.

The hard winter is upon us, and it will be our first real winter in the cave; we aren't sure how it's going to feel inside, so we decide to grab blankets, warm coats, gloves, hats, and long johns, and we clean out the food cabinets. On the way out the door, Bonnie sees a cassette tape case and takes that too.

Driving home, we pass a young blond girl hitchhiking, so we pull over to give her a ride.

"Hey there, where ya headed?" Bonnie asks.

"Well, I don't care where I go; I just want outta Texas," she says in a deep Texas drawl.

"What's your name?" I ask.

"Michelle," she replies.

"How old are you?" asks Bonnie.

"Sixteen," she lies.

"I figure you for about fourteen, honey," I say.

"Are you a runaway?" Bonnie asks.

Her face turns red. "I reckon you could say so. Are you going to turn me in?" she asks.

Bonnie laughs and says, "No, girl! Get in the car, and let's go. Is anyone looking for you that we need to know about?"

"Heck no! He probably isn't awake yet; he usually sleeps until noon and then gets drunk again. It may even be a couple of days before he notices."

"Why are you running?" I ask.

"My grandpa traded me for a bottle of whiskey and a carton of cigarettes," she says.

She is fourteen and has reddish-blonde hair and blue eyes. She is about 5'3 and petite, maybe 110 pounds, and seems too mature for her age.

"The man that he traded me to is old as dirt. He's a gambler and loans me out to other men for money. I have to get as far away from him as I can," she says with her head down.

"Okay, honey, enough said. We're going to Arkansas; if you want, you can come to stay with us for a bit. We have room, and it's safe."

She asks Bonnie, "Are you boyfriend and girlfriend?"

Bonnie laughs. "Heck no—he's, my brother."

"Oh, that makes sense because you look similar."

"I'm glad we look similar. But no, sweetheart, he is my brother and friend," Bonnie answers. "We have two other siblings at home; surprise, none are blood-related. But we have chosen each other as a family. My name is Bonnie, and he's Carl. It's nice to meet you."

She becomes one of us on our drive back to base camp over the next few hours. Finally, we pull up to our campsite and get out. I say, "We park our car here, and that is our camper-van and pup tent village."

"Y'all live in a camper-van?" she asks.

"We have in the past but decided we needed more space. So, we recently acquired new accommodations in the forest. We have to walk there from here, you'll see. It's not far," Bonnie replies.

She gives a hesitant look and says, "Y'all aren't taking me in there and killing me, are you?"

"Yes and chew the meat off your bones. No, silly; we found the perfect hideout—a cavern—and we all have our own space," Bonnie says.

As we approach the cavern, Michelle is in awe. "It's beautiful, the stuff of dreams!" she exclaims.

After introducing Saul and Matthew, we give her a cavern tour. Michelle picks a spot to crash, and we give her a pillow and a few of our blankets to settle in for the night.

"Since you're staying with us for a while, you need to know somethings, we rob houses, Michelle. We only take what we need, and sometimes a little more, but we always share everything among ourselves, and we only take from people who can afford to lose a little," Bonnie says.

"Yeah, but I also work to make money. Sometimes, we just have to do what we must to make ends meet," I say.

"The boys have been hunting while we've been gone, and until they are older and able to work, that's how they contribute," Bonnie says.

"Settle in and take a few minutes to yourself, then come to the front of the cave. There is a room to the right that we call the family room. It has lots of cool flat rocks to sit on and a small fire pit to warm the area. That's also where we usually eat. Are you hungry?"

"Famished," she says in her Texas accent.

That night, we grill a rabbit that the boys caught on the wood stove. We have it with fresh grilled squash and canned green beans from our spoils at the fancy house in McAlester, Oklahoma.

Michelle fit right in with our family. She is a tremendous cook and likes things in order. We asked her to pick a new name when she decided to stay.

We now call her 'Sherry.' Her Texas drawl is sweet as sugar, and she is smart as a whip.

Chapter 2: Then There Were Five

Carl Slater

The first weekend after the thaw came, we all go on a road trip to Shreveport, Louisiana.

It's crazy how quickly time goes by; Bonnie will turn sixteen in two days. I've decided to give her the GTO for her birthday.

My main reason for coming to Shreveport is to get Sherry a birth certificate.

"Hey Bon, can you and Sherry follow in the GTO?" I ask.

"What? I can drive by myself?" Bonnie asks, and her eyes light up.

I smile and say, "Yes! Just be careful, and happy birthday, Bonnie; you can keep the keys to the GTO — it's yours!"

"No way!" she exclaims. Sherry and Bonnie give each other a high five, hip-bump, and smash their hands together like patty cake.

When we first get to Shreveport, we park the camper-van at Horseshoe Bossier City Hotel & Casino and join Bonnie and Sherry in the GTO.

We find a payphone and I call my contact. "Hey Freddie, it's Carl. Are you still able to acquire birth certificates for me?" I ask.

"Yea, man, it's been a while. It's good to hear from you," Freddy replies.

"We just arrived in town and will be here two days. When can we hook up?" I ask.

"I can meet you at Shrimp Busters tomorrow for lunch, say 1:00 pm? What name and age?"

"Tomorrow at 1:00 pm works, and her name is Sherry. She is fifteen but will turn sixteen later this year.

"Okay! I'll see what I can do."

"Oh, Freddie, I want us to go to an outdoor shooting range this afternoon. Do you know one?" I ask.

Freddie laughs. "You're joking, right?"

"Why do we need to learn how to shoot?" Sherry asks. "Not meaning I don't want to; I do want to. But why?"

"Because you should be able to defend yourself, Sherry, and if you ever want to do a rob job with us, you will need protection," Bonnie says.

"Have any of you ever gotten caught?" Sherry asks.

"No, not so far, but Carl plans well, and we always have an escape route. Sherry, this is not a family requirement," Bonnie says.

The next day, around eleven, we return to Shreveport and drive to my favorite pawn shop. The owner, Nathan, smiles when I walk in. "It's great to see you, Carl!" he says.

We conduct our business. Nathan buys all the jewelry I have to sell. Then we head to the Shrimp Basket.

"Sherry is now Sherry Huey. Welcome to the land of the living, Sherry," Freddie says and smiles.

For the next two days, Bonnie and I take the GTO and stake out an estate on the outskirts of town. We learn that no one was home.

We go in on Sunday morning — Bonnie's sixteenth birthday. It takes us 22 minutes to get in and out, with our backpacks full. We find over $13,000 in cash and some exquisite jewelry under a fake floor plank.

We come out with our regular bounty of money, jewelry, cassette tapes, books, blankets, medicine, and food. It is time to go home. About two blocks from the mansion, a police car speeds past us. I quickly turn off the main road. Bonnie pulls out a map and starts giving me directions back to the casino, keeping us on backroads.

"Oh, my goodness," Bonnie says. "Do you think that police car was going to the mansion?"

"Maybe," I say. "But how would they know?"

"I'm not sure; I cut the phone lines and electricity right before we went in. It should have been clear," replies Bonnie.

"The police may not be looking for us. They could be headed anywhere. Let's chill and get back to the casino," I say.

"Right on, Bonnie. Listen, when we get back, I want you to gather everyone in the camper-van and start rolling out of town, head up Hwy. 29. I'll give you guys five minutes. Then, I'll hit the road and drive the GTO on the same route. If someone saw us robbing, casing, or leaving the house, and police are on the lookout for our GTO, it will be only me who gets caught."

After dropping her at the camper-van, I give them a few minutes head-start. As I turn onto Hwy. 29, I see several police cars far away in my rearview mirror, pulling up to the intersection I'd just gone through less than 30 seconds ago. My heart is pounding; I am unsure what they are looking for. It probably isn't our GTO, or they'd be chasing me. I keep my speed steady and head toward the cavern— home sweet home. We have to be more careful.

Chapter 3: Birthplace of Elvis

Carl Slater

I come home from work today excited to share some news with the family.

"Guys, I'm taking the week off work. I want us to go to Tupelo, Mississippi. There's a huge Music Festival this weekend. It goes on for three days, the fundraiser for the Elvis Presley Memorial Foundation. Next Friday, it will be a year since he died," I say.

"I loved him. I'm going with you!" Bonnie says.

"I think he's still alive, but I'll go for the music," Saul says.

Sherry says, "Ha-ha. I'm in too."

"Well, I don't want to be here alone, so let's road trip!" says Matthew.

"Alright,' I say. "There will be so many good bands playing at the festival for the foundation to honor him. It'll be held at the Tupelo Fairgrounds, where Elvis first performed after releasing his first top selling song, *Heartbreak Hotel.*

"When are we leaving?" Bonnie asks.

"Tomorrow; we'll drive to Tupelo and get a ten-day campsite. Then, we can drive back on Sunday. The festival begins this Friday, so we'll get tickets for all three days. Then Monday, I'll see about getting a temp job for the week while you explore the area. Know what I mean?" I ask.

"Let's take the camper-van, pup tents, and the GTO," Bonnie says.

Once we arrive in Tupelo, we settle at Presley Lake Campground. The camp owners had recently changed the name of their campground in his honor.

The music festival weekend turns out to be fantastic. We take blankets and a picnic lunch and stay for hours listening to all the different bands. We sing along to many of the popular songs, but Free Bird is the hit of all hits, and we sing our hearts out along with thousands of others. Not one of us had ever been to a concert before, and I believe we spoiled ourselves with this one.

I go to a staffing service for a temp job. I want Bonnie to be in charge of the family for a while.

The temp agency sends me to B&B Concrete, and I am hired for five days. While I work at the concrete company, Bonnie finds a couple of small, secluded homes, one on the east side of town and one on the west side. Bonnie takes Saul, Matthew, and Sherry on their first rob jobs. They find a few things, but the take is minimal — perfect for their first.

It's been eight days since we left Arkansas, and tomorrow is my last day at work.

Bonnie says, "Carl, I found the perfect home for us to rob. Their routine is extremely consistent, if it's okay with you, I think we should enjoy the weekend together. We can make our move on Monday, then hightail it back home. Tomorrow's your last day at work, right?"

"Yeah," I say. "Mr. Jenkins asked if I would come back and work another week. I told him no, that I had to move on. Then he asked me to meet him for drinks after work tomorrow night."

If I had not gone out with my boss the next day, the family would have enjoyed the weekend in Tupelo before the rob job on Monday. But then, we would never have met Leslie Jenkins.

Part Seven: Samantha & Leslie, 1980-1981

"I've discovered an unyielding strength within me, empowering me to confront this darkness head-on. No longer burdened by shame or haunted by sleepless nights, I am resilient. I refuse to deny the reality I've faced or indulge in mind games. The person I once was, naive and oblivious, has transformed into someone brave and unapologetic. I've come to understand that I possess the audacity to defy this horror and emerge unscathed, for I am without fault,"

ADC

Chapter 1: New Year's Eve

Samantha Archer (Sam), 1980 - 1981

The trip to my grandparents' house was long, but it was worth the drive to spend all this time with my cousins. It's been great, but I've had the missing girl, Leslie, on the back of my mind. I worry about what happened to her and decide to say a prayer for her.

It's great being with all my cousins again.

Everyone is inside the church singing in the New Year together. It's fun, but it's getting late, and I'm sleepy. I walk across the lawn to my granny and pawpaw's house.

One of the parishioners is sitting in his truck, and he calls me over. His name is Mick, and he has always been pleasant to us kids, but he's a little weird.

Mick adopted a boy named Ty, who I became friends with last year while visiting for the holidays. But I haven't seen Ty this year.

"Happy New Year! How has your family been doing this year, Miss Samatha?" he asks as he pats the passenger seat. "Hop up!"

I climb into the passenger seat of his truck. "We have been doing good, Mr. Mick."

"Awww, you don't have to call me Mr. Mick. It's just Mick to you. Where are you headed?" Mr. Mick asks.

"To the parsonage," I reply. "Why aren't you inside singing?" I ask.

"Oh, I have this new radio I got for Christmas, I just put it in my truck this morning, and I thought I'd come outside for a little bit to see if it's working well. The church is packed tonight, huh?" he asks.

"Yes, sir."

"Remember, you can call me Mick! Do you realize I've known you since you were six? I believe that permits you to call me by my first name," he says as he reaches over, pats my leg, and leaves his hand there. I am wearing a dress, and his hand feels weird sitting on my leg.

I am uncomfortable, so I say, "Okay," and turn toward the door to leave.

"Hold on, Samantha, where ya' going so fast? Let me show you my new radio first, then you can go," he says. His hand is still on my leg — not tight, but he is not letting go.

I don't know what to do. I am afraid and say, "I need to hurry, Mr. Mick; David's meeting me at the parsonage."

"Oh yeah, isn't David your cousin? "

"Yea."

"Well, we can see him when he leaves the church. Why are you in such a hurry? Is he your kissing cousin?"

"What?" I ask, thinking, *what is he saying?*

"You know what I'm talking about, Samantha," he says, and I feel his hand sliding up my leg. I am paralyzed at first, but I push away from him, turn, and jump out of the truck. I run to my grandparents' house. I'm not sure what just happened, but I am scared and feel sick.

Why do I feel like I did something wrong? I feel bad, dirty, and ashamed. Why do I feel this way?

I'm afraid to tell anybody about what happened. What if Mick says I'm lying? I know he will because adults aren't supposed to touch kids like that.

If he says he didn't do it, what will happen then? Will everyone believe him? I'm just a kid. He'll probably say I made it up. I don't want people to think I'm a liar.

I make up my mind to pretend it never happened. I'll never go near him again; if I see him, I'll walk the other way.

I couldn't wait to get home the next morning, New Year's Day of 1981.

As time passes, I chalk the incident up to a bad dream. The bad dream is now in a shabby, taped-up box and pushed to the back of my mind in self-storage.

Unfortunately, I now have a more challenging time trusting men. The encounter taught me something about dark ideas and evil thoughts. Some people pretend to be good, then hurt others to satisfy themselves. I'd not experienced that before, but I have now. I will no longer be easily fooled. I will watch people, I will pay attention, and I will learn.

Two years later, on our Christmas vacation, I went with my pawpaw on visitation rounds. He goes to see sick church members' homes and prays with them.

We went to Mick's house, of all places. But, of course, I didn't know he was one of the sick people we would visit, or I would not have gone.

When I came face to face with him, I felt God had exacted vengeance for me — if he did that. I think he just might. The left side of Mick's face was covered with Shingles. I wonder if I smiled.

Chapter 2: I Will Miss the Cave

Leslie Jenkins (Lea), 1980 - 1981

A lot has happened since I decided to stay with Carl and the others. It's been almost three years since they took me, and I came to live in the cavern. Now, it looks like we are moving.

The music is blaring. Carl is angry, but when is he not lately? He is usually the coolest cat and laid-back, but something is going on with him. Maybe Bonnie will know what it is.

I ask Carl, "Where are we going?"

He answers, "Not far."

Really? I think to myself.

Bonnie rolls her eyes and says, "Lea, we're going to a place called Mount Yonah just northeast of here and a few miles from where Carl grew up in Paragould. He knows the area well and some places we can boon-dock."

"Will we be going to another cavern?" I ask.

"No. We'll have to squeeze into the camper-van and GTO for a day or two. Carl said he plans on trading in the camper-van for a bigger RV."

"Why are we leaving?" I ask

"There was an arson in town yesterday; a house burned down with the owner inside. Carl is distraught. I think he went too far."

"What do you mean?"

"Carl said the owner, an older man around sixty, walked in on him while he was in the living room. The guy threatened Carl, turned to pick up his phone, and said he was calling the police. Carl moved quickly and pushed the man forward, trying to get him off the phone and get away. The man fell forward, face-first, into a glass table; a piece of it cut his throat and face, and the man died. Carl did what he's done in the past. He lit the place on fire to cover up evidence. The whole place went up in smoke."

"Oh no," I say, frightened.

"No, kidding. Do you have your backpack ready?" Bonnie asks.

"Yes."

"Will you check on Sherry for me? We're leaving in five minutes."

"Yeah, sure," I say.

The cavern in the Ouachita National Forest covers about 1.8 million acres in central Arkansas and southeastern Oklahoma. The rugged mountain ranges are primarily forested and have almost everything we need.

Carl shouts over the music, "Hey Matthew, shut off the music and pack the player in your backpack."

Matthew gets ticked off at Carl for bossing us around and making all our decisions, even though Carl is the oldest. Then again, Matthew is in a rebellious teenage stage right now, and Carl is like his dad, so it seems normal.

Carl's new favorite song is playing: At the Devil's Ball by Berlin Irving. I think I like it.

Shortly after my introduction to the family, I began working on skills to help the family survive and learning what is valuable and essential for survival.

I'm unsure why, but I want to make Bonnie and Carl proud. I ask Bonnie if I can go with her and Saul for my first robbery.

As we sit in the woods surrounding the home, Bonnie says, "I've been coming here every morning for a week watching this house. Everyone leaves before 8 am. I don't know when they will return, but they won't be back before 10 am, because that is how long I've stayed each time I come. We are good."

We wait for them to leave. Sure enough, at 7:55 am, they drive away. We give it about 10 more minutes to be sure no one forgot anything and came back home.

"Let's go, Lea. You get to pop that cherry," Saul says, laughing. He is seventeen too. He doesn't have the rebellious thing going on, but he is also Carl's right-hand guy, so maybe he doesn't have a reason to.

Saul became a part of the "family" two years after Bonnie. Saul was the second person Carl took in, and I think he is as special to Carl as Bonnie is — not that we aren't all special.

I feel privileged to be with Bonnie and Saul today. We didn't have to break glass or kick in the door; the owners must have felt safe out in the country because they left the backdoor unlocked.

Bonnie confirms instructions as we walk into the kitchen area. She says, "We're looking for specific things. Jewelry, cash, medications, first aid supplies, batteries, and music if you can find any."

I say, "Gotcha." I hope I sounded confident. I'm thirteen years old, and I am scared to death that the people will come back; my heart is racing.

"Lea, you get the bathroom beside the kitchen and the living room. Saul, you get the kitchen. You know what we need. I'll get the other bedrooms," says Bonnie.

I go to the bathroom first, grab all the medicine and vitamins, and scoop everything into my backpack — aspirin, random prescriptions, ointments, and band-aids. Then, I grab unopened toiletries from the bathroom closet, shampoo — shaving cream, soap, and toothpaste.

There are cassettes by the couch in the living room, with a portable cassette player next to it on a side table. It is full of tapes, and my heart skips a beat. *Carl will be so happy*, I think, scooping them into my backpack. Unfortunately, I don't see anything else we need or that looks of value that I can carry back to the hideout.

Bonnie returns from the bedrooms with jewelry, blankets, and men's and women's clothing.

"Nice wardrobes today," she says as she puts on one of the coats and walks around like a movie star. It looks super warm, with some fluffy white fur on the inside and leather outside.

"My pack is full. How did you do, Lea? Do you have any room left in your pack?"

"I think I did good, but I have little room left."

"Then go into the first bedroom to the left; see if there are any shirts, jeans, or shoes that might fit you or Sherry, to try and finish filling your bag."

We all meet back in the kitchen with our stash. Saul has his backpack filled with can goods, jars of jams, peppers, pickles that the wife or husband enjoyed jarring, and a few fresh vegetables. He also found some batteries, which is vital to us because we have no electricity at the hideout; everything is battery-powered.

"Guess what," he asks, acting like a giddy girl that hit the jackpot. "I found cash hidden in a pancake box! The wife must be saving for a rainy day. I think there is at least $400!"

"Not bad; Carl will be happy," says Bonnie. "Okay, guys, let's get out of here."

We leave for our long hike back to the cave. Along the way, we talk about robbing people. It had been my first time, but Bonnie had been at it for many years. Saul had, too. They shared stories about almost getting caught in the past — my worst nightmare.

Even though I knew what we were doing was wrong, and those people would come home and be very upset and sad; I felt like I had contributed and was a part of something bigger. I had helped the family.

Later, at dinner, Carl congratulates me. "Lea, good job today. You are a natural!" Then he hugs me; it is a side hug, and I feel safe.

Today, we are moving. Sherry is packed, and we are heading out. I will miss this cave; we all will. I hope we can come back one day.

Chapter 3: Yonah's Ridge

Samantha Archer (Sam)

I'm watching reruns of The Hardy Boys & Nancy Drew Mysteries. I have a girl crush on Nancy Drew and a boy crush on Joe Hardy from the Hardy Boys series.

I have a centerfold poster of them both on my wall from Tiger Beat magazine.

I hear the front door open. "Sam? I'm home!"

"Hey, mom, how was work today?"

My mom is a Professor at U of A specializing in Horticulture and Botany.

Her ultimate research goal is to find the least expensive, long-term way to alleviate world hunger. Lofty goals, but as she always tells me, if you are going to do something, go big.

"Work is good, honey. My research is going well; I'm onto something that looks very promising. Keep your fingers crossed for me."

"Is it something you can tell me about?" I ask. My mom is super secretive about her private research. Our basement is her laboratory; she had it renovated a few years ago and has a 'do not disturb' sign on the door when she is working.

"Not yet, Sam. One day soon, I hope," she says and smiles.

Mom begins making dinner, and I go to my room and put on my new *Pat Benatar* cassette. My favorite song is '*Hit Me with Your Best Shot.'* I sing my heart out when it plays on the radio, so my dad bought it for me.

The music is fantastic, and I think I look like her. We have the same shape eyes and face, and I recently got my hair cut short like hers.

This one song on the cassette worries me; it's called *'Hell is for Children.'* I think it's talking about child abuse. I can't imagine going through something like that.

I still have the photograph of the missing person's poster I saw when I was ten at a roadside park. It's in a special binder I made as a school project on Crime in America last year. The photograph is in a plastic sleeve, so it won't get damaged.

On the opposite page is the photo I took of two girls about my age on Mount Yonah, while hiking with my dad.

My dad is a park ranger for Craig-Head Forest Park on Mount Yonah. The Park has a 60-acre fishing lake, camping facilities, hiking, and biking trails, nature areas, picnic sites, and recreational areas. It is beautiful and also where my mom and dad met.

They were both in college; he majored in land management and forestry. Mom was photographing plants and taking samples for a project in her botany class.

He asked her, "What is your major? It looks like you're working on a project."

She looked up, smiled, and said, "Botany."

My dad told me, "I knew I wanted to marry her the minute I laid eyes on her. She is the most beautiful woman; her smile captured my heart, and her light blue eyes locked it away forever.

216

I love to hike and enjoy nature with my family; we are all outdoorsy people, and on that specific day in 1983, my dad and I were walking trails and photographing wildlife.

We were taking a quick break for lunch, and I was sitting on a large boulder rock on the side of the trail; my dad was resting beside me.

I had just finished gobbling down a ham sandwich; I had been hungry. After I was done, I picked up my camera and looked through the lens, waiting for the perfect shot. I did not know what that shot would be, but the backdrop was exceptional. So, I was waiting as my dad finished eating his lunch.

Soon, I see a beautiful girl around my age walking on the trail. She stops and bends down to look at and smell some flowers; she is leaning over some aster and yellow jasmine. She has long brown hair and very delicate features. It's a fantastic shot and the lighting was perfect, so I took the photo.

Then another girl, maybe nineteen or twenty, walks up behind her and prods her to move along. I look up.

I snap a few candid shots when they started coming up the trail toward me. I should have asked if it was okay, but they didn't make eye contact as they passed, so I decided not to bother them.

I drop the film at the pharmacy and pick the photos up a few days later. I was excited and filled with anticipation, wondering what kind of photos I'd gotten.

Of course, the best shot I got from the entire roll of film was the profile photo of the girl smelling the aster and yellow jasmine. The candid shots are pretty good but without any real substance.

As I look closer at the candid pictures of the girls walking toward the lens, the long brown-haired girl's face looks oddly familiar. For a minute, I assume it is because I love the profile photo, but then my heart speeds up. "Oh crap." My heart is hammering now as the realization sets in. "It can't be," I say to myself.

I run home as fast as I can. When I reach my bedroom, I pull out the first photo I'd ever taken on my camera in 1978 at that rest stop in Mississippi. I hold the photos side by side.

There she was, walking on a path at Mount Yonah. She was older, taller, and weighed more, but her face was the same. The hair was long and brown instead of blonde. She was wearing a tank top, and I saw what I believed to be a strawberry-shaped birthmark. If it's not her, I swear, it's her twin. I have to show my mom and dad.

They agree the similarities were exceptional. That evening we call the sheriff's department and make an appointment to see Sheriff Gilmore the next day about a possible lead in a cold case from 1978.

When we arrive at the police department, Sheriff Gilmore meets us in the lobby and takes us to his office.

"What's this about?" he says as he glances at his notes. "A 1978 missing girl from Tupelo, and you have pictures?"

Dad says, "Yes, sir, we were traveling in December of 1978 and stopped at a rest area where there was a Missing Person's flyer poster of a girl my daughter's age. That caught my daughter's attention." He nods toward me, "She had just gotten a new camera for Christmas, so she took a photo of the flyer in case we saw her."

"Is that right, miss?" he asks.

"Yes, sir," I reply.

"Can I see the photo of the flyer, young lady?"

I hand the photo to the detective, who studies it for a long time.

When he finally looks up, he stares directly into my eyes and asks, "You believe you saw this girl last weekend at Craighead Forest Park?"

"Yes, I do, sir."

"And you have a photograph of that girl?"

"Yes, sir." I hand him the three photos I took on the ridge. He takes them and again looks at them for a very long time. Then he holds the old and the new side by side.

"Well, I'll be damned. It sure looks like it could be the girl. Of course, not a hundred percent sure, but it's enough to warrant a call to Mississippi. Give me a few minutes to make a call, folks."

Sheriff Gilmore placed a call, and within a few minutes, he was connected to Detective Pace, the original Detective on the Leslie Jenkins case. Within minutes, Sheriff Gilmore had permission to run the girl's photos on the newspaper's front page and send Person of Interest bulletins to the local newspaper and tv stations.

"They say this is the best lead they have had in years. What is your name again, young lady?" Sheriff Gilmore asks.

"Samantha Archer, but you can call me Sam."

"Well, Miss Samantha Archer, have you ever considered going into police work? You have an eye for detail that we could use."

"Yes, as a matter of fact, I want to study to become a Private Detective when I go to college."

"Samantha Archer, you can use me as a reference; just tell them that Sheriff Gilmore in Paragould, Arkansas endorses you."

Chapter 4: Person of Interest

Lea (Leslie Jenkins)

We moved to Mount Yonah area. Carl and Bonnie went to Hot Springs in the GTO a week after we arrived at Mount Yonah and bought a used 1977 GMC '26 RV. It's much bigger than our camper-van and will be the main sleeper for Bonnie, Sherry, and myself.

The floor plan has one bedroom with a full bed and one with bunks. Both rooms have storage. The kitchen has a stove and sink, a small living room and dining area, and last but not least, a small bathroom equipped with a shower.

We kept the camper-van and tents for Carl, Matthew, and Saul to sleep in.

Carl works at Christian Brothers Automotive as a mechanic, and Bonnie is a clerk at A & B Pawnshop.

In the spring of 1982, Sherry, Matthew, and Saul all graduated from high school, and I completed ninth grade.

But, with all the good luck we've had, we had trouble again in the summer of 1983. Not by one of us making a robbery mistake; we had not robbed any homes in a long time. Instead, we were caught on a camera by an amateur photographer that believed she recognized me.

What are the odds of that?

Carl was in Paragould with Saul on the afternoon the news broke. They had stopped at a pub called 'Never Too Late' and were picking up fish and chips for dinner.

Carl says, "I looked up from the bar while we were waiting for our order and saw on TV that there was a search for a girl, and a person of interest, in the case of a missing girl from Tupelo, Mississippi, from 1978. I saw Lea's face across the television. It scared the shit out of me."

Saul says, "Yeah, when Carl told me to look at the tv, all I could say was, 'It looks like we need to gas up the RV.'"

"We saw a newspaper box as we left the pub, and Saul purchased a newspaper," Carl says as he lays the paper on the table.

My face is on the front page, next to a photo of my younger self. There is also a smaller photo of Bonnie and me walking on a trail.

The caption reads:

"Is this Leslie Elsa Jenkins?

Looking for this person of interest, have you seen her?"

I am mortified. "I can't believe my face is on the newspaper's front page. "Holy shit!" I say. "I remember that location and smelling those flowers. How the hell did someone get my photo?

"Lea, do you remember that damn teenager sitting on a rock, shooting nature pictures? I never saw her aim the camera at us, but she must have," Bonnie says.

"I remember her, but barely. I can't believe it's all over the tv and in the newspapers." My heart is pounding. "How could anyone even notice or think it was me? It's been five years," I say out loud.

"I don't know, Lea, but you must be more careful. It's time for us to bug out," Carl says.

"Yeah, we've worn out our welcome in Arkansas; it's time to go," Bonnie says.

"Carl, can we go to a beach, lake, or maybe even a river? I want to be near water," Saul asks.

"Me too," says Sherry.

"Sure, but we all need to brainstorm together and agree. I think we all should have something to say about where we go," says Carl.

"Lea, with your photo all over the papers and TV, we'll need to cut and color your hair. So, do you want blonde, black, or red?" Bonnie asks.

"Ugh, I don't want to change my color. Bonnie, will you pick the color for me?"

"Of course, red it is then," she says.

Carl says, "I think we should go with a red hair mohawk and black highlights, then we can pierce your eyebrow and add a tattoo to your neck. What do you think?"

"I think you're crazy!" I say.

Bonnie smiles and winks. "I got you, kid. I'll be back in a flash. And don't worry; this will all die down. But, first, we have to get away from this area without anyone else noticing you."

I give her a thumbs up.

Carl does all the haircuts in our family; he always has since I've known him. First, he smiles really big at me and raises his eyebrows up and down in a funny but menacing way. Then, he brings out the scissors and cuts my hair while I stay utterly still, hoping I won't end up with a mohawk.

Chapter 5: Don't Freak

Carl

We get pulled over, leaving Paragould. The last thing I remember Bonnie saying to Lea before we left was, "Don't worry, this will all die down."

Lea and I left in the RV. We followed the camper-van and the GTO.

I say, "Hey, Lea, don't freak, but an officer got behind us at the last light and is following us." I glance at the rearview mirror. "Listen, if we get pulled over, you must be someone else. Remember, you are not Leslie. You are Lea. Put on those reading glasses," I point to the console. "Also, put a piece of gum in your mouth, and, if you have to speak to him, chew your gum obnoxiously, be confident, and show no fear. You look very different with your hair colored and those glasses," I reassure her as the cop flashes his lights. "Damn. Okay, the cop just turned on his blue lights; we're pulling over," I say.

The police officer walks toward the RV on my side, and I roll down the window. The officer approaches, "Where are you headed, buddy?"

"Florida sir, we're headed home. My sister and I have been visiting relatives in Tennessee," I respond.

"Alright, sir, I pulled you over because we're searching for a missing person."

The policeman hands me a photocopy of a beautiful, young, brown-headed girl admiring some flowers against a gorgeous background of mountains and the two candid shots.

"Do you recognize or know this girl?"

"No sir can't say I do," I say, passing the photos to Lea, who was in the passenger seat.

"Nah," she smacks away at her gum. "I'd remember her; she's beautiful," she says, then blows a bubble, smiles, and returns the photo to me. As I return the picture to the officer, he says, "Sir, I need to ask you and your passenger to step out of the vehicle."

"Okay," I say.

"It's just you and your sister?" The policeman asks.

"Yes, sir," I reply.

"Do you mind if I look around in your RV?"

We comply. The policeman looks around in every room, including the bathroom.

When he comes out, he says, "Thank you for being so helpful, sir."

Lea continues chewing on her gum and popping bubbles obnoxiously.

"If you do come across this young lady on your trip home, please contact our police department," he says and hands me his card.

"We believe she was kidnapped in 1978 when she was ten; she would be around 15 or 16 now."

"Okay, will do, sir," I say.

"Have a safe trip," he says, returning to his patrol car.

We don't wait for him to leave; we pull out and head northwest.

Over the next few years, we traveled in the summers and settled down so Lea could go to school during the school year. She will graduate this year!

We added on a Fifth-wheel travel trailer so we could unhook and have another ride, which means that we will also have to buy a truck to pull the travel trailer. Damn the sacrifice.

We chose an Airstream Sovereign Travel Trailer and a Ford F-150 truck to pull it. Matthew decided to call the Airstream "The Bullet."

When we went to pick up The Bullet, we took the camper-van for her last trip to trade her in. Not gonna lie; Bonnie and I were both a little sad.

We loaded our stuff into The Bullet. Then, Bonnie, Lea, and Sherry drove to the Ford Dealership to pick up our truck.

Part Eight: 1985-1988

"For I know the plans I have for you," declares the Lord, "plans to prosper you and not to harm you, plans to give you hope and a future,"

Jeremiah Twenty-Nine: Eleven.

Chapter 1: Promotions

Samantha (Sam)

"I can't believe I'm attending Florida State University!" I say to my mom.

"I know, honey. We need to go shopping! Have you made a list for your dorm room?" She asks.

"Yes, it looks like the only things I need to buy are a mini fridge, coffee maker, bed sheets, a blanket, and a Futon," I reply.

I'll be on my own for the first time, and it's somewhat terrifying but exciting too.

"Okay, we can go shopping whenever you're ready — let me know." She adds, "Hey Sam, I also have some great news to tell you."

"What is it, Mom?"

"I've been offered the lead pathologist position with PureAgra, in Atlanta, Georgia. The job is based on my private research, crop improvement through microbiome manipulation.

"Is that the research you've been doing in the basement since I was, like, a kid?" I ask.

"Yes! Isn't it exciting?" Mom says. "I'll be in charge of and given free rein to continue my research with all the financial backing I need."

"What? That's cool, Mom! Are you going to take the job?"

"Well, your dad and I have talked about what we would do if I did get the offer."

Dad chimes in, "Yes, sweetheart, we think you should take it!"

"That's amazing, Mom. I'm so proud of you!"

"Thank you, honey. We'll be developing new types of plants that are resistant to diseases in hopes of contributing to our society, particularly in food and nutritional production. This position with PureAgra will also mean I'll be closer to you at college! How could I not take it?"

"Have you talked to Kat and Mark yet?" I ask.

"No, we know it will be tough for Kat. She has friends from kindergarten that are still her best friends. I think she'll be upset initially, but she adapts well," Mom says.

Dad says, "I think Mark will be fine. He's only in 6th grade and doesn't have the same deep bonds as your sister does with her friends. Except for his buddy Marcus."

"Well, I love that you finally get to do what you want, Mom, and get paid too!" I say.

We had a family meeting when Kat and Mark got home from school.

"What the heck, you can't just move us! Our friends are here! I'm not going! I'll stay with Marcus and his parents. They love me!" Mark protests.

"Mark, we'll be okay," Kat says. "We can visit our friends in the summer and maybe even on holidays if it's okay with Mom and Dad."

Mark angrily stares at Kat. "I can't believe you're on their side!" he says and storms off to his bedroom.

I say, "Well, Mom, it looks like he doesn't take change very well, after all."

I leave and go to Mark's room and knock. "Hey, Mark, it's me, Samantha." He opens the door for me, and I sit on the side of his bed.

"So, it looks like we're all moving soon." I gently nudge him.

"I don't want to go!" he half-ass yelled.

"Look, Mark, the family is heading to Atlanta, but you still have some summer left here. Enjoy it with Marcus. In the fall, you'll be starting a new school. It will be the same thing happening to me since I'm going to college. We won't be together, but you will be closer to me in Atlanta than in Paragould. It will be a good thing, Mark," I reassure him and give him a huge hug.

After a couple of seconds, he hugs me back. I love that little boy.

Chapter 2: Dark Reflections

The Family

The years are flying by. We are now in Oregon. Saul, Matthew, and Sherry have turned 21, and Lea just finished her senior year. It's summertime again!

Today, we're all getting ready to hit the road. Sherry's cooking breakfast and Bonnie asks me, "Carl, will we ever get a real home with that dog you promised me when I was twelve?"

"Promised, did I?" I smile. "Yes, Bonnie, I promise we will settle down and stay somewhere for good one day. But, of course, that is if you still want me around."

"I'll always want you around, Carl," she says, then hugs me and kisses my cheek. I am surprised and touched by her show of trust and vulnerability.

She has gradually learned to trust the rest of the family and me through the years.

Matthew asks, "Do you think we will all stay together? Most families find mates, move on, and have their own families."

"Well, we aren't your typical family. If one or all of us want to find another life, then all of us should agree to support that," I reply.

"I agree," says Lea, and so does everyone else.

Saul says, "Carl, since we are close to California, can we go and visit my parents' graves in San Diego? They're buried in the Greenwood Cemetery, but I've never been to their grave. The douchebag pervert Jason Alexander Hill never took me. He said it was stupid and my parents wouldn't even know I was there. So, I've been afraid to ask you guys, worried you might think the same. Is it a dumb idea?" He pauses. "Maybe he was right, but I want to go for me, take flowers, maybe say a prayer?"

"I think that's a great idea, Saul." Sherry says and hugs him. Everyone agrees.

We go to the gravesite with flowers first, then drive to La Jolla, where Saul had been locked in a cell. The home is now abandoned and creepy.

The exterior is tagged with graffiti, the windows are broken, and the yard is overgrown with weeds. It was a bad place then, even though beautiful on the inside at the time. Now, years later, its exterior reflects the true horrors that went on behind the walls.

"It seems like a bad dream," Saul says." Starting with my parent's accident and ending with my torture in the cell in that basement. Then you came into the basement, Carl. You were my hero. I prayed to God every day to send someone to help me. Do you know that? Have I ever told you that?" Saul asks.

"Uh, well, I don't think you officially told me all that, but yeah, you have thanked me. "Thing is, I've often wondered if it was God; I mean, I was doing a rob job — would God send a thief?" I ask.

We walk around the property for a bit, then go down to the beach for a walk. Saul tells Lea, Matthew, and Sherry what happened to him in captivity. Saul has never discussed it in detail, and I never felt it was my place to drill him or get more information than I already knew.

232

As he speaks, chills go down my spine. He had been tortured, sodomized, and starved. We find a spot on the beach to sit as he pours his memories out like crappy wine.

He recounts, "I would curl myself in a ball, in the back of my cell, and sob and sometimes scream to God to please save me. I was so frightened every time I would hear the door upstairs open, and I knew he was coming downstairs. I never knew what he would do to me next. He played games, dressed in weird black leather, sometimes in girls' clothes, and even wore a villain costume."

"He would tie my hands and feet to some stakes he had hammered into the dirt floor. My mind would scream no. The worst was when he'd put on that demon mask. As soon as he would put it on, I knew what was coming. He always had a knife in his hand and would make tiny cuts on my arms to show me how sharp the blade was. Then he would hold the knife to the back of my neck and do horrible things — things too embarrassing to talk about."

I say, "I want to kill him again!" I was so angry.

"So, you did kill him?" Saul asks. "I thought so, but you never told me it was you. Thank you."

I say, "Saul, I saw your prison, please remember, it's not your fault. A grown man took away a twelve-year-old kid's innocence, his freedom, and his childhood. You trusted him. He failed you horrifically, Saul. You are free now and can be and do whatever you want. We will support you."

Bonnie says, "Saul, you're strong, smart, honest, and kind. You are not like Jason Alexander Hill, and don't ever let what he did to you taint who you are. He wanted you to break you. He wanted you to be weak, damaged, and feel dirty. At leaset, those were the things I struggled with the most. We survived Saul."

"Amen," says Sherry. You get to choose who you are, Saul! Don't let him ruin that for you"

"Truth," says Lea.

"Dude!" Matthew says and hugs him.

We sit for a while longer, then I say, "Hey, let's go grab some lunch! I want to go to Char-burgers for old times' sake."

While eating at Char-burgers, I think of Doug and call his old phone number. I couldn't believe it, but he was still around.

"Roadkill Cafe. You kill it; we grill it!" Doug says.

"Doug, it's me, Carl! I can't believe you're still using that same ol' phone line!"

"Carl? Wow, how have you been, man? It's been twelve or thirteen years since I last saw you, right?"

"Yeah, Doug. I'm in town with my family and wanted to say hello if I could find you. Are you doing good? Your dad?" I ask.

"I'm doing great, but my dad passed a while back. Hey, why don't you come over this afternoon? We can hang out and cook dinner on the grill. You have a family now?" he asks.

"Yes, Bonnie and I have added to our family; we are six now," I say. "We would love to come by, but I don't want to intrude, dude'."

"Whoa, you're taking care of five kids?"

"Well, they aren't kids anymore, Doug. Hell, Bonnie is in her twenties!"

"What? Man, I knew her when she was eleven or twelve!"

"I know, we've been gone a long time," I say. "Well, my dad left me the family cottage on beach access road no.19 in San Luis. Come on over, bro. Bring your crew. I want to catch up and meet the family," Doug says.

We left for Doug's house.

When he answers the door, I say, "Dude, I wouldn't have recognized you if I saw you on the streets." I hug him and say, "You cut your hair, you're clean-shaven, and it looks like you have got your shit together!"

Doug chuckles and says, "Yeah, I got a good job years ago; the owner liked me. This man taught me everything he knows about running a successful business — his business. I'm now his partner and the General Manager of a restaurant called Merseas at the Port of San Luis. It has a super cool location. You drive onto a pier to get to the restaurant. I love it."

"Dude, I'm so proud of you!" I say.

"After you left that Christmas Day, I felt sick about what we did for months. Especially with all the coverage for the first several weeks." Doug looks nervously toward Saul, who is not paying attention to our conversation.

They are all looking at the unbelievable view of the dunes and ocean from Doug's back patio.

"Carl, I still haven't come to grips with what we did that night. Not completely. You know, I never did another rob job after that night. I mean, I know you believe what we did to that man was right, and I'm not condemning you for how you felt. I felt the same way at the time. He was an evil man and deserved death, and I know that. Later though, it was hard to live with myself. I cleaned up my act and decided to go on the narrow path. I go to church and have accepted Jesus as my Lord and Savior, and I feel I've been forgiven."

"Wow, okay, that's cool, man. I'm just glad you're happy and living your best life," I say.

"Yes, I am, it's a simple life, and I feel free. I even have a sweet girl I met at my church that I hope to settle down with one day," Doug says.

I say, "Well, so you know, he's my higher also. Uncle Don taught me about Him. I don't go to church, but different strokes for different folks."

We stayed with Doug for two weeks and went to the beach. It was like a vacation from our wandering, and we just relaxed. I even read the latest Stephen King book and vowed to read more frequently to become a constant reader.

On our last morning, we had breakfast, walked on the beach, and then left town in our small convoy before noon. I hope it will not be our last visit, but deep down, I feel I would never see the West Coast or Doug again.

"Hey Carl, can we go to the campground where you guys found me and took me in all those years ago?" Matthew asks. "And is it weird I wanna go? I'm not trying to copy Saul; it just got me thinking. I'd like to see where you found me, my memories very blurry."

"No, dude, it's not weird. I tell you what, it's about a 12-hour drive, let's stop halfway and eat and sleep tonight. We'll get there sometime tomorrow."

"I'm not sure what I will get from going, but I think I should go," Matthew says.

We pull into the Isleta Resort & Casino, a camping area, around dinner the next day, and park lakeside.

Matthew says, "When Mom and I were here, I remember walking to the truck stop for dinner every day, but I don't remember much else."

"That's probably because your mom left you in your station wagon all day, and you weren't allowed outside. The only time we ever saw you was when you both walked to the truck stop in the evenings," Saul says.

"Matthew, would you like to go there for dinner tonight, or would you rather we go somewhere else?" Bonnie asks.

"Yea, let's go there," Matthew says.

When we walk into the truck stop, Matthew asks the waitress, "Do you have a girl named Hailee that works here?"

The woman looks surprised. "You know Hailee?"

"Yes, ma'am," Matthew says.

"Well, Hailee is my daughter, and my sweet girl went to college and became a pediatric doctor up in Westville. She even has her own practice. We are so proud of her. She has made herself a good life, married another doctor, and they have two pretty girls named Camryn and Cindy."

Matthew says, "I'm glad to hear that. I knew her when I was about eleven or twelve years old."

"What's your name, son?" she asks.

"Ma'am, I'm sure she won't remember me, but my name is Matthew."

"We talk every day. I'll let her know you came by."

She sits us at a table. Matthew says, "I remember me and my mom would always eat in that corner booth over there," he says and points. "I'd always get the blue plate special, Salisbury Steak, and French fries. The same waitress, Hailee, always waited on us; she was very kind to me. I remember her sometimes giving me a soda or dessert for free because my mom wouldn't buy those things."

"It's easy to remember people who are kind to us," Bonnie says.

Matthew says, "When my sister Dana was still with us, my mom always left her in the station wagon while we went to the truck stop for dinner. Dana always cried when we left, but Mom was hard. I would beg her to take Dana with us, but she would always say Dana has to earn her keep. We'll bring dinner back for her. I would think, what does 'earn her keep mean,' but was afraid to ask."

"Can you tell us what happened to her? Do you know what happened to her?" Lea asks.

"I think I do. One night, we came back from dinner, and the side door of the station wagon had been left open. There were drops of blood on the ground that led away from the station wagon, then suddenly stopped. I started crying and calling Dana's name until my mom slapped me and told me to stop being a baby.

"As I sat on the ground, I remember saying to Mom, 'But there's blood, Mom!' My mom looked at me so hateful and said, 'You don't know anything, Chester, but one day you will, this life ain't easy, and your sister is gone. Maybe she'll be back. Maybe, she just ran away, or maybe, she's just off whoring around. Either way, you hush now and keep that trap shut!'

"I didn't know what whoring meant, I was too young at the time, but I think I kind of knew, deep down." Matthew's face is contorting, and he looks as if he is about to cry.

We remain completely quiet and let him regain his composure.

"Anyway, my sister never came back. A few days later, Mom told me the police found a young girl's body in a ditch on the other side of town. Mom said, 'It's probably your sister.'"

"Was she upset?" asks Bonnie

"No, not at all, and I felt a knife of lonely pain deep inside me. I knew then that mom doesn't care about us at all."

Sherry asks, "How are you sure it was your sister? I mean, what if she's still alive somewhere? Or has been taken, like you? I told her I know, because the next day I snuck out of the Station Wagon and walked to the truck stop to see what I could find out while my mom was at the casino. I was so scared she would catch me, but I needed to know if what she said was true."

"You snuck out? We could never even get you to open the door for us!" says Bonnie.

"I know. I'm sorry," Matthew says.

"Don't apologize!" Bonnie says.

"Anyways, Miss Hailee sat me at a booth and asked what I was doing at the truck stop without my mom, and why wasn't I in school. I told her my mom homeschools me until we get settled down somewhere. Which, of course, was bullshit, but that's what she told us to say if anyone asked.

239

Hailee took my order, and when she came back to check on me, I asked her if she had heard about the teenager getting killed nearby. She said she had heard about a young girl and wanted to know why I asked. I explained that I heard people in the campground talking about it and wanted to know what happened. She looked at me kinda funny, but came back with a newspaper, my apple pie, and ice cream. She cleared her throat and began to read the story. I don't remember word for word, but the headline was 'Teen Found Dead.' The article said a female teen was found in a drainage ditch and that she was wearing a brown and white beaded necklace with a peace sign pendant. That was my sister's necklace. We made it together one day when it was raining, and we had nothing else to do."

"Oh no!" Sherry says, "I'm so sorry!"

"It's okay. When Hailee looked up from the paper, she asked the same thing. I told her, yes, I'm ok, and I quickly wiped away a tear. It's just sad, I said. I was so thankful a real adult could see me. You know, Hailee was the only adult I ever trusted until I was taken away by you guys." Matthew says.

"Dude, are you okay?" I ask.

"Yes." Matthew smiles. "Thank you. I've held all that in for a very long time."

Sherry says, "I'll tell you what I think. But, first, we should have apple pie and ice cream in honor of Miss Hailee." Everyone agrees.

As we return to the campground, Saul says, "I feel like I understand you better, Matthew; you know we can't pick our blood relatives. It's not your fault that your sister died. You were too young to understand all that was happening. I love you bro."

I ask, "Does anyone want to go hang out on the rooftop of The Bullet tonight?"

They did.

The following morning at breakfast, I ask, "You guys up for a trip to Houston? I chatted with Sherry last night, and she has some unresolved issues she would like to flesh out as well."

"Good God! It looks like we are on a therapy trip." Bonnie says, laughing. "But I'm all in!"

Saul says, "We don't have a specific destination at the moment, so I vote yes, of course."

"Me too, yes," reply both Matthew and Lea.

"When we picked up Sherry, she was hitchhiking, close to Boston, Texas, but she was running from Houston. So, our destination is her grandfather's house. The man who sold her for alcohol and cigarettes."

We arrive in Tomball, Texas, and park the RV and the Bullet at the Spring Creek Park Campground.

We all pile into the GTO and head to Houston and Sherry's grandfather's house, about a 45-minute drive.

Sherry says, "I'm afraid my grandfather will be there. I'm not sure how I'll feel when or if I see him. He was pretty old already, an alcoholic and heavy smoker; maybe he's already dead. But if he's not, what will I say to him? So why am I even going back? I feel the need to put that part of my life to rest, but maybe we shouldn't go."

Saul held her hand tight, saying, "It's going to be ok; we are here with you. Don't be afraid."

After that, I notice Sherry settle down as Saul continues to hold her hand.

We drive through the streets of Houston, quite an amazing city, but the area became very seedy when we got close to Sherry's grandfather's home. I felt a sense of heightened awareness in the car, and anticipation.

Her grandfather's home was a piece of shit; it was an old shotgun house that looked broken down, worn, and needed paint and repairs. We drive past his home and find an abandoned lot with three houses/shacks. Bonnie backed the GTO into the dirt driveway leading to the property.

"You guys have 10 minutes. You better do whatever needs to be done, quick and efficient," I say.

Lea nods as Sherry, Saul, and Matthew join her outside the car. "We'll be back," Lea says.

Bonnie and I wait patiently over the next nine minutes, then she says, "Sixty seconds left."

"Thirty seconds, why is my heart pounding?" Bonnie asks.

"It'll be ok, Bon," I say as I slowly ease out of the abandoned lot and inch towards the house.

Twenty seconds left, and Sherry comes out of the trashy house. It looks like she's been crying as she slides into the back seat. Bonnie crawls into the back with her.

Fifteen seconds left; Matthew comes out. He vomits in the shrubs, heads to the GTO, and slides into the back seat without a word.

Ten seconds left, I hear a gunshot, no, two gunshots — holy shit. After that, I think we have to go!

In five seconds, Lea and Saul walk out calmly and get in the front seat.

Lea says, "Let's go, take backroads, and get outta town." We head back to Spring Creek Park Campground.

After a few minutes of driving in silence, I ask, "Can anyone tell me what happened in there?"

"Alright then," Lea says. "Sherry's pervert grandfather opened the door with a cigarette hanging out his mouth. He said, 'whadda ya want?' Sherry asked him if he remembered the granddaughter that he traded for whisky and cigarettes."

Saul interjects and says, "He looked her up and down in a super creepy way. I wanted to punch him. I swear, the man just stood there staring for 30 seconds before he said, 'I should have gotten more from the trade, you turned out to be a nice piece of ass.'"

"What a piece of shit," Carl says.

Sherry says, "After he said that Saul pulled his gun and held it to the pervert's chest. Saul backed him up until he tripped and landed in a dirty recliner. Then Saul called Lea over and told her to wrap his mouth and body with duct tape.

Matthew says, "After Lea bound him, Saul aimed his gun at the man's crotch. He looked at me and said to pull the old geezer's jeans off. The old man was shaking his head at me in terror. I looked at Saul for a long second, deciding, then I did as Saul requested."

Sherry says, "I walked over to my grandfather. I said to him, you raped me and traded me to a psychopath, for cigarettes and a bottle of whisky. You took away my childhood, my innocence, and my trust, and for that, I will never forgive you."

Saul says, "I asked Sherry if she'd said her peace, and she told me she had. I looked at the perv and said, 'Tell me, old man, how does it feel knowing you only have three and a half minutes left to live?' He just started shaking his head no like crazy. I told him too bad, that he was about to experience how it feels to be raped."

"Bonnie, you look shocked," Lea says, "and yes, Saul did that. The perv was raging, screaming, and crying, but it was muffled underneath the tape I'd wrapped around his mouth. He struggled, boy did he struggle, but the pistol stayed."

Sherry looks at Bonnie and then says, "I looked at my grandad and knew he now understood what he did to me. Then I walked out of there."

Matthew says, "I was next to go. I was getting sick to my stomach and thought I was gonna throw up."

Saul says, "Then, it was just me and Lea left. I told Lea, 'I got this, go.'"

"And I told him no; I wanted to stay," Lea says. "Saul nodded at me, then he says, and I quote, 'Ok, old man, ask forgiveness from God; it's now or forever hold your peace. Three, ... Two, ... One.' He pulled the trigger twice, and we walked out."

We got back to the campground and headed southeast the next day.

Chapter 3: The Sunshine State

Carl

Bonnie asks, "Carl, it's been seventeen years since we left Florida. Do you think it's safe to go back?"

"I don't know, maybe we'll stop by my uncle's house, and I'll ask if anyone is still looking for us."

We stop at Rest Dem' Bones Campground and spend a week in New Orleans, going into the city daily. Bonnie and I street-perform for extra cash on Friday, Saturday, and Sunday.

After a lengthy discussion, everyone agrees that Florida should be our next state to explore and search for a home. So, Bonnie and I go to Orlando, and the rest of the family head to West Palm Beach. We will meet them there.

Bonnie and I roll up to my uncle's house in our GTO. My uncle's old Mustang is in the driveway, but there is also a 1988 Porsche 911 Carrera.

"I'll be right back," I say.

My uncle answers the door. "Hi Chris, it's been a long time," he says and smiles.

"Is that your Porsche?" I ask.

"I know it seems excessive, but I only have a few more years to blow my money."

"You deserve to have some fun, Uncle Don, excessive or not," I reply. "I have a friend in the car, so I can't stay long. But we were passing through, and I wanted to say thanks,

Uncle Don; thank you for taking care of me as a kid. You were kind to me. Is there anything I can do for you — anything you need?"

"No but listen; I got something I need to tell you about," he says. "The day after you left here, Detective Sellers came to ask some questions about you. He said you were a person of interest in a murder, arson, and possible kidnapping case. They were very curious why you had all of a sudden left town. I told them that you had just turned eighteen and wanted to travel a couple of years, that you had been planning to do so for the past six months."

"That's right. Is that all?" I ask.

"Well, he started asking about your friend Frank and when you last saw him. He said your boss at the shop said you were with Frank the night his house burned. They never found the little girl, Brenda, and he found it odd that you left work the next day without notice and never returned."

I nod my head.

"When they discovered that you had purchased a camper-van, he seemed very suspicious of you. Finally, he gave me his card and asked me to give it to you when you returned."

"Do you think they're still looking for me?" I ask.

"Yeah, I do, at least Detective Sellers. The last time he came by was about six months ago. It seems he comes around just about every year," he says.

"Can I have that card if you still have it?" I ask.

"Sure, Chris. I'm happy you stopped by. I don't know if you had anything to do with what happened back then, but I'd rather not have to lie about you. If the detective ever does drop back by, I'll tell him you stopped by, and I gave you his card. But Chris, if you do happen to know anything about this business, you should get in touch with him or leave town," he says and hands me the detective's business card.

"Thank you, Uncle Don. I'll take your advice." I give him a quick hug and leave.

I tell Bonnie about our conversation.

"Can we drive by my old house before we leave town? I've wondered what was left of it and if my mom and dad are still alive and live there. They probably aren't, but I'd like to know."

"Yeah, of course, Bonnie. It makes me super nervous because of the detective, but I know this is important for you."

The neighborhood is trashed, seedy, and unredeemable. Bonnie's home is still in shambles from the fire and years of neglect and has a 'no-trespassing' sign posted. The yard is completely overgrown and empty.

"Are you okay?" I ask as we sit in front of her old house.

"Lots of mixed emotions. I can't believe the old tire swing is still hanging. I remember sitting in that old tire for hours, avoiding going inside my house. I realize now that I was a terrified little girl. All the memories have faded, but the feeling remains."

"Do you want to talk about it?"

"No, we should probably go. Thank you for bringing me," she says.

"Tomorrow, I'll call the detective to find out what happened to your mom and dad."

"Okay," she says.

"Let's go then," I say.

We drive to the Lion Safari Campground in West Palm Beach. It's right next to a drive-through animal park.

When we get to the campground, Saul and Sherry are playing horseshoes. Matthew and Lea grill sausage, onions, and peppers on the campground grill for dinner; it is a cute little common area with hammocks, fire pit grills, and picnic tables. The boom box is playing *Living on a Prayer by Bon Jovi*. Cool song; I gotta learn that one.

"Dinner's ready. Come eat!" Lea calls.

While we are eating, Matthew asks, "Can we drive through the animal safari tomorrow?"

"Vote time; all in favor, raise your hands," I say. All hands go up. "Yay! Animal safari!" Sherry exclaims.

There are seven sections to the animal preserve, and we make it through all of them — the lions, giraffes, monkeys, and zebras. Then, we eat hotdogs, corndogs, french fries, and ice cream for dessert.

"Let's stay for a couple of weeks and do some surveillance of beach homes. Then, maybe, we'll make some cash and mosey down the Florida coastline," I say.

That afternoon, we go for groceries and pick up a local map. At night, we start planning our "rob jobs."

We split into two teams and watch our chosen homes for their routines over the next few days.

Team one is Bonnie, Saul, and Lea. They watch a two-story Mediterranean-style home as they sunbathe on the beach.

248

Two older adults occupy the house. Like clockwork, they leave together each morning and go for a long walk on the beach. Every day is the same; they are gone for 45 minutes.

Team one sneaks in and out of the home in record time. The theft goes seamlessly; they walk away with expensive jewelry and $1750 cash from a floor safe. Each also tops off their backpacks with groceries and new CDs.

One day later, team two, Matthew, Sherry, and I, go into the home we had been watching on the opposite side of town. It is an Intracoastal neighborhood; the home style is Spanish with lush landscaping. We go in through the side entrance and split up. Matthew and Sherry take the upstairs, and I begin in the downstairs main bedroom and then make my way to the kitchen.

They must have had a silent alarm because, after a few minutes, I hear a car pull up in the front. My heart begins pounding; I look out the window and see a police car.

I call out to Sherry and Matt, "Cops!"

My heart is pounding as I exit the kitchen back door, and run to our designated rendezvous point, which is where we left our car parked at the Cash and Carry. I wait. Our rule is five minutes, then whoever is in the car has to leave.

I'm panicking in a way I've never experienced before. I'm worries, scared, nervous, and afraid for Sherry and Matthew. That's when I hear a gunshot. My heart sinks.

What if they don't make it out? I think. *What if one or both of them are dead?*

Not even twenty seconds later, Sherry runs to the car and jumps in; she looks so freaked out.

"Matthew was still in there when I ran out the back door. I heard him coming down the stairs, and several seconds later, I heard a cop yelling and a gunshot. I didn't turn around," she cries. "I was so scared; I was afraid someone was shooting at me! Then I realized maybe Matthew — maybe he got shot!" Her eyes widen, bulging and troubled.

At about that exact moment, Matthew comes running toward us. He is holding his shoulder, and there is blood. He dives into the car's back seat, and I slam my foot on the gas, screeching out of the neighborhood.

"He shot me!" Matthew says in miserable pain.

"Is the bullet inside of you?" I ask,

"I don't know; it hurts so bad!"

"Let me look," Sherry says and twists around in her seat to look. "It looks like there's a hole in the back of your shoulder and the front. I'm pretty sure it went through and through."

We make it back to the campground without getting caught. Bonnie, Saul, and Lea go into action the moment we walk in. They had been waiting for us but not expecting what they would see.

Lea takes charge. "Bonnie, get the first aid kit. Saul, wash your hands and help me."

Bonnie gets some painkillers and antibiotics from the first aid kit and gives them to Matthew.

Saul and Lea begin cleaning the wound and patching it up the best they can as Saul moans in pain.

We get the full story from Saul after he is bandaged and has a little pain reliever in his system. He says, "The cop entered the kitchen and saw me heading out the back door.

He told me to stop, and I turned towards him. I was planning to back my way through the open door and make a run for it. The problem was, I had taken out my gun, and he saw it; I saw his eyes widen. The gun was in my hand by my side. I wasn't going to use it, but when I turned to run, he shot me — the damn cop shot me!"

We leave town quickly and in the dead of night on the backroads. Bonnie drives the GTO between our campers in case someone has noticed her car leaving the robbery scene. I am worried that the car could be identified. Shit! We always plan escape routes, and it has worked, but I forgot to cover up the license plate. In hindsight, that was stupid.

After we make it to Miami Beach, Florida, and find the Francis S. Taylor Wildlife Area, we set up camp. It is close to Miami, but not too close.

"I think we should stay put for a while, and this looks like a good place. I'll go out in the morning to a temp service and get a job. The same goes for each of you; find what you like to do," I say.

"My heart's desire is flipping burgers," Matthew says, smiling. Bonnie punches him, and he laughs.

Saul heals from his gunshot wound. Lea did the best she could, but the scar is pretty nasty.

I find a mechanic job at the Four Brothers Auto Repair — super clean with modern technology. Lea is in night school for business and works at Elite Security Resources. Sherry got a job in home security sales, selling home camera systems, and learning to be an on-site technician. And Bonnie starts today at Winston Gun Shop as a firearms instructor. She says, "They want me to try and start a women's shooting league, said I'm the best woman sharpshooter they've ever seen. It felt good for a stranger to see my skills and want to hire me on the spot. I can't wait to start."

Part Nine: Changes 1988-2001

"The universe doesn't give you what you ask for with your thoughts - it gives you what you demand with your actions,"

Steve Maraboli.

Chapter 1: Alibi Investigations

Sam

I've been attending Florida State University in Tallahassee for two years. My goal of becoming a private investigator is within reach. I will have a BA in criminal justice by 1990.

Gilchrist Hall is a women's residence hall built in the 1920s. I share my dorm room with two girls. One has a boyfriend and goes to his dorm most nights; the other seems to always be in our room studying. The library is my best place to learn; we can access computers there!

I work at Alibi Investigations as an intern. My boss is Allie Caine.

I work on my missing person case on my own time. There is new testing called DNA that a lot of agencies have been using, and it sounds good for my case. I'll have to see what my boss thinks. I'd like to try it for Leslie Jenkins.

My mom has been on my case about going to Pawpaw and Granny's for our family New Year's Sing.

"Sam, you are working too hard. It will be weird if you aren't with us for Christmas; we always go together."

"I know, Mom. I'm sorry; school and work are so overwhelming right now. Before I can graduate, I'll need 4,000 hours of paid investigative work. That is why I'm working so hard. Plus, I'll have to pass a two-hour multiple-choice test on laws, regulations, terminology, evidence handling, and undercover investigations. Mom, I really need to stay on top of things here," I say.

"Sweetie, I hear you, but everybody needs a break. So please try to come, even for a day or two."

"Okay, Mom."

Mom sighs.

"I love you, Mom. Give Dad, Kat, and Mark hugs and kisses for me."

Getting off the phone with Mom fast was pure luck; she is quite the talker. I listen, and she talks.

Saturday morning, I head to work. We open at 8 am, and I'm early, as usual. So, I stop by The Black Dog Cafe to pick up coffee.

I see my boss, Allie Caine, answering the phone. "Alibi Investigations," she says.

I slip a coffee across her desk; she likes it black and bitter.

"Oh," she says to the caller, "you will want to speak with Samantha about that. One moment, please." She hands me the phone, smiles, and off to work I go.

Later in the day, Allie says, "Thanks for the coffee this morning. You have no idea how much I needed that today!"

My boss is a great PI but has a little alcohol problem, so she always needs coffee!

"Allie, you know how whenever I have a few minutes to spare, I continue to work on leads to find Leslie Jenkins, right?"

"Of course, I do. That is one of the reasons I chose you as a co-worker. I love your drive and persistence," Allie replies.

"Have you heard about the new type of testing called DNA?"

"Yes, I have."

"I'd like to go to Tupelo and talk with Leslie's mother. It would be helpful to get her DNA into the national database."

"I back you 100%, Samantha. I hope, one day, you will find out what happened to her. Plan that trip out; when that time comes, we can adjust your work accordingly," Allie replies.

Chapter 2: Graduation

Sam

I've earned my BA in criminal justice. It's the spring of 1990, and I'm graduating top of my class.

My whole family came to Tallahassee last night to celebrate my accomplishment. They stayed at my apartment, and though crowded, I wouldn't want it any other way. It was wonderful having my own place where they could come — it felt like home.

Katrin is now twenty and in college herself. She is going to design school. She has quite an eye for fashion and is currently at the top of her class. Mark is 16 and a Junior in High School.

I ask the morning after the graduation ceremony, "Did you guys remember to bring bathing suits to swim in the pool?"

"I did," says Mark.

"Me too!" says Katrin.

"Sweet, we can go swimming after lunch. Our apartment complex has a diving board and a slide; we'll have fun! Then tonight, we'll see *Alabama* and jam on *The Charlie Daniels, Devil Went Down to Georgia* at The Civic Center!"

"Seriously? That's lit, Sam! Are all of us going?" Mark asks.

"Mom and Dad have seats, but we will stand in the pit, which is right in front of the stage!" I say.

"Gucci!" exclaims Katrin.

Everyone changes to go swimming. We have pizza delivered for lunch and go for ice cream after. What a great day!

The concert that evening *was* 'Gucci' — a memory that'll last a lifetime.

On Monday morning, I go to work at Alibi Investigations, eager to talk to Allie about my hopes for a future partnership.

A young lady I had not met answers the phone when I walk in. I say hello, then knock on Allie's office door.

"Come in!" she calls.

I notice she already has coffee, so I sit the cup I had brought her on the desk.

"Awww, thank you, Sam. But you know that is not your job anymore, right?" Allie asks.

"Well, we didn't speak about what I would do after graduation, but I hoped to continue working for you," I say.

"Yea, Sam, I don't think that will work for me. I'm so sorry, dear; I thought you would want to move on to bigger and better things when you received your BA."

"Okay..." I say.

"Sam, I have loved having you as my assistant. You have been the best, and I hope the new assistant will be half as good as you," she says.

"Oh, my goodness, I'm so sorry, Allie." I am apologetic and stumbling with my words. "I just assumed I would still be working here; I never even thought of leaving. You've been my mentor and friend. I'm going to miss you," I say.

"Let me walk with you to gather your belongings," she says.

"Oh my gosh, I feel so awkward, Allie. I assumed too much; I'm sorry." I am hurt deeply, confused, and embarrassed. Although the new assistant isn't at her desk when we walk by, and I am glad, I feel like I am on a walk of shame.

"It's okay, Samantha. I put all your things in the research room. I wanted the new assistant to feel like this is her own space, right?" she asks.

"Right." I shake my head and numbly follow her through the research room door. I walk in and am perplexed; four people are standing right inside the door. Pam, our research lawyer; Stephen, an older PI who had retired from the police force; Ben, our financial investigator; and the new administrative assistant, whose name, I learned, is Michelle.

I am thinking, *where did all the research cabinets go? Why is everyone standing here?* I'm trying to take all this in, and then I realize they are all congratulating me.

They part down the middle and reveal a desk. There's a nameplate with my name on it! It reads, 'Samantha Archer, Private Investigator.'

After being Allie's intern/assistant for the past three years, she has made me her partner. That's what I had hoped to talk to her about when I came into work today, but it seems she had already thought about it and made it happen.

Everyone is saying, "Congratulations, Sam!"

There is a hummingbird cake waiting for me, and on this cake, it reads, 'Samantha, will you be my Biz. Partner?' I am relieved, happy, and crying all at one time.

"Allie, Thank you so much! Yes, I would love to be your business partner."

Everyone claps, and we have cake!

Chapter 3: Terror

Carl

Time passed, and before we knew it, we had been in Miami for ten years. I'm not sure why we are all still here or why we are still together.

We are adults; each of us has had people we've met at work, school, or even church that we've hung with and dated, but nothing seems to stick. Yet, we always come back around to each other.

We are still living on the outskirts of Miami, in the middle of nowhere. Our RVs are parked in a field surrounded by trees. I watch the sky slowly evolve from dawn into the day when I wake up this morning. The sky is clear, deep blue with no clouds, and I think it will be a good day. Thing is, we never really know.

When I go inside, Sherry and Saul are up and making breakfast. I turn on the Satellite TV for background noise and help myself to Captain Crunch and milk.

Then suddenly, something happens across the screen that will change our lives forever.

The day is September 11th, the day when nineteen Islamic extremists associated with a terrorist group called *Al Qaeda* hijacked our airplanes and carried out suicide attacks in the U.S.

Two planes flew into the twin towers of the World Trade Center, a third plane hit the Pentagon, and a fourth plane crashed into a field in Pennsylvania. We later learn that almost 3,000 people died during the attacks.

261

We are watching everything unfold live on tv and sit in disbelief.

Sherry says, "What's happening?"

Bonnie says, "Oh my God!"

I say, "Shhhhh, just watch."

Saul asks, "Is it a freak accident or what?"

Matthew says, "Holy shit!"

Lea says, "What the hell!"

It's like a movie; it doesn't seem real. People are running in terror, crying profusely, dazed, and confused. We watch people die on live tv. This is real, and we are dumbfounded.

Sherry says, "How could this happen? Has something gone wrong with the control towers?"

Matthew replies, "Could this be on purpose?"

After the second airplane hits, I say, "I think it is intentional, Matthew."

The news anchors begin speculating that it was an attack of some sort. Then, as we and the world watch the events unfold in New York, a third plane — American Airlines 757 — circles over downtown Washington, D.C., and crashes into the west side of the Pentagon Headquarters at 9:45 a.m. Jet fuel from the airplane causes a devastating fire, which leads to a structural collapse in part of the U.S. Department of Defense headquarters.

About 15 minutes later, the south tower of the World Trade Center gives way and crumbles in an unimaginable cloud of dust and smoke.

Again, people are running, screaming, and crying; all of this is caught on tv. You can barely see through the cloud of dust; it is almost black. We watch as people are struggling to breathe. We continue seeing people die, some even jumping from windows. Finally, the tower collapses, and our hearts break.

It is 10:30 a.m. when the north building collapses, and only six people end up surviving, although the news reports there were about 10,000 people who made it out before the collapse.

As we sit glued to the tv, we find out about the fourth plane. It was Flight 93 that was hijacked about forty minutes after leaving Newark Liberty International Airport in New Jersey.

The plane had a delay taking off, so passengers began learning of the events in New York and Washington on their cell phones.

After realizing their plane had been hijacked too and what their likely fate would be a brave group of passengers and flight attendants planned an overthrow of power. If they were going to die anyway, they would not let the terrorists fly them into another building.

Later, the reports told us that one of the passengers called his wife and said, "I know we're all going to die, but three of us are going to do something about it. I love you, honey." Then, another passenger said, "Are you guys ready? Let's roll" over an open line.

One flight attended called her husband to hear his voice and to explain their plan. She was in the galley filling pitchers with boiling water. Her last words were, "Everyone's running to first class. I've got to go. Bye."

The passengers fought the four hijackers, and it's believed they attacked the cockpit with a fire extinguisher. The plane flipped over and dropped at around 500 miles per hour toward the ground. It crashed in a field near Shanksville, Pennsylvania, at 10:10 a.m.

All forty-four passengers died.

No one knows what the specific target was for flight93. Some think the White House, the U.S. Capitol, some Camp David, or maybe one of several nuclear power plants on the eastern seaboard.

Months later, we discovered that 2,996 people died in the 9/11 attacks, including nineteen terrorists on four airplanes. That figure includes 343 firefighters and paramedics, 23 New York City police officers, and 37 Port Authority police officers evacuating the buildings and saving people trapped on higher floors. At the Pentagon, 189 people were killed, including the 64 passengers on American Airlines Flight 77.

The world stopped for weeks. Afterward, we lived through months of recovery, heartache, and anger in America. The skies above us were eerily quiet. No planes or helicopters to make a sound. We didn't realize the amount of noise coming from the skies until it was silenced.

Chapter 4: I Have a Lead

Sam

I can't believe it's been ten years since I became a partner.

We have grown our business, and my personal investigative work has been on the back burner. I don't think about Leslie as much anymore, which makes me sad.

On a break between cases, I finally make time to go through old Tupelo newspapers, now on microfilm, looking for anything unusual happening in 1978 around Leslie's abduction. I keep hoping to find something — anything — that may have been overlooked. *Nada* — until now. I hit the intercom button for Allie's office.

"Bet you never thought you'd hear this, but I've got a lead on Leslie," I say.

"Seriously? I'll come to your office so you can tell me about it," Allie says.

When she arrives, I say, "Okay, Allie, I noticed two robberies in August, the week before Leslie's abduction. The robberies were unique and stopped after Leslie's home was robbed, and she went missing. I think it was the same person or persons who robbed her house. My theory is he, she, or they, took her because she could identify them."

"So far, so good. What did you find that made the connection of the robberies unique or peculiar?" asks Allie.

"In each robbery, the items stolen were obviously jewelry, which isn't uncommon, but get this — all the other stolen items were so random. They took medicine, clothes, bedding, food, toiletries, and music tapes. So, I'd say, not so typical."

"I agree; that's different."

"Yeah right! So, I started calling robbery divisions throughout the state of Mississippi, asking them if they have any robberies with a similar pattern of operation.

"Nice!" she acknowledges. "Do you have a pattern of locations and dates?" Allie asks.

"Yes!" I say.

"I had no doubt you would find a new lead one day; you are a smart girl! Would you like me to help you organize these leads? I'd be happy to give you a set of fresh eyes."

"Would you, please?! I would love your help."

The next day, Allie posts a massive map of the United States on the wall facing my desk and outlines the state of Mississippi in marker. Then, I begin putting stick pins in each city with similar robberies. Again, I see a pattern as I push each pin into the map.

This week, I'll begin making more calls. Arkansas, Alabama, Georgia, and Florida.

Chapter 5: Animal Trials

Dr. Stephanie Archer

"Good morning, Sam! Are you sitting down?"

"Sure, Mom."

"Good, I have big news! My research team is announcing that we've been approved to begin animal studies on my project!"

"Congratulations, Mom! I'm so proud of you."

"Thank you, sweetheart. I'm on my way to PureAgra now," I say.

"Okay, call me later and let me know how it goes. I love you, Mom."

"Okay, Sam. I love you, too."

My stomach is in knots as I begin my speech. We are in the conference room of PureAgra. Its capacity is 300, and the room is full.

My team stands with me on stage as we share the good news for our company and its future.

"My fellow colleagues, on behalf of PureAgra, I'd like to thank you all for coming today. We have been working on what we are now calling 'The World Project.' This project is the result of almost thirty years of research and patents. The US government has green-lighted our research and has also awarded project funding," I say.

Everyone applauds loudly.

"I'd like to introduce The World Project team to all of you: Dr. Raj Campbell, Dr. Steve Mayo, Dr. Natalie Bailey, Dr. Joshua Grimes, Dr. Natalie Bailey, and myself."

Roaring applause.

"Our society is evolving, and our food system has grown into a global system of immense complexity. The world has progressed from hunter-gatherer, agricultural, and then to the industrial stages for providing food and medications. Yet, we still have hunger. We still have people right here in the US that can't afford groceries to feed their children."

Silence

"Our commitment to The World Project is the advancement of food through plant life, in hopes of ensuring a safe and abundant food supply for the world, not just the United States."

Everyone applauds.

"We are looking ahead; it might take five to ten years, but we will be the leaders of the future. This project is highly classified, and everyone here today has been granted top-secret classified status. This means as part of this project, each individual who accepts his or her job responsibility will sign the industrial security policies and directive contracts. Please read the fine print before you sign. It is imperative that you know the consequences if your contract is broken."

Chapter 6: Intentions

Sam

We have been clearing cases left and right. The work we do at Alibi Investigations has been intense and extremely fast-paced. Allie hired another investigator; his name is Blaise. He used to be a police detective, now retired, but he wants to stay in the game.

The map on my office wall is still there. That constant reminder that Leslie is still somewhere, dead or alive. Each week I take one day to research any recent robberies matching the M.O. and put more pins on the map.

"Good news, I got a message from Detective Lambright in West Palm Beach this morning. They had a robbery with the same M.O. as our robberies, but this time, the owners had a silent alarm, and an officer arrived in time to catch a boy leaving through the back door. The policeman left his name and number for you to reach out to him," says Blaise as he hands me the number.

I intended to call that morning until an extremist group called *Al Qaeda* hijacked four airplanes and carried out suicide attacks against the United States. After that, all flights shut down, and the world stopped.

There was so much devastation. Our police and firemen were inside the buildings, alongside the people they were trying to rescue when the towers collapsed.

Every city in the U.S. was on high alert and shocked by the attacks. We needed to fight back and save the people buried under the building. We all felt helpless. All I could concentrate on was helping those around me who were falling apart.

It shook America and searching for Leslie was pushed to the background of my mind again while our country figured out what response we would take against the terrorists.

Part Ten: Leslie & Mom,

2001-2015

"Go on, take the money and run,"

Steve Miller Band.

Chapter 1: The Wrong House

Carl

We stayed a while longer in Miami and lay low while the United States began to heal and pull itself back together. We watched the news, played cards, went to the beach, and discussed how America would respond.

Life in the U.S. slowly started to become somewhat routine again, and when spring arrived, we took out a Florida map and began to discuss our next destination.

"What about the Keys," Saul asks.

"Too small," I say. "How about Naples?

We head to the Belle Meade Campground near Naples, Florida.

The campground is in a remote area. There is a gas station and store nearby, but not many campers, except on weekends.

Saul, Matthew, and I got jobs with Naples Staffing. We begin building homes with Kurtz Homes the very same day. It is solid and consistent money, and the contract lasts three years. We stay.

Matthew met a girl; her name is Dana, and she is sweet, but she isn't one of us. She comes to the campground several times a week for dinner and to hang out, but it won't last long. I can tell she isn't the right one.

Lea met a girl, too; her name is Maggie and she's cool but a little clingy, and she likes Lea a lot more than Lea likes her.

Lea needs to have her space and some 'me' time, and Maggie wants to consume every minute.

Time flies by. We work, eat, and play, but we do not steal. Then, when our contract is up, we are offered another but decline.

After three years, we all agreed; this would not be our home.

Next, we drive to Dee River Campground in Inverness, Fl. I love the old oak canopies. We park beyond the grassy areas where campsites are well-marked and choose a more primitive place. We like our privacy, if possible.

Lea, Bonnie, and Matthew get temporary jobs grading oranges at the farmers' market.

Sherry, Saul, and I stake out a private estate with electronic iron gates. The property has a main house and a guest house.

Fortunately, the land is out in the middle of nowhere, with no homes nearby. We watch the road for incoming and outgoing cars from the woods. There is no traffic whatsoever.

Three days go by with the same results.

"Maybe they are on vacation," I say.

"Maybe so; let's go in tomorrow. Sherry, you up for some security action?" Saul asks.

"Of course." She smiles.

"I think we should just hit the main house," I say. "Keep it simple. Sherry can get us through the gate. Then, if anyone drives onto the property while we are there, we can go out the back door, walk around to the front and say the roofing company sent us to do an estimate."

Sherry disconnects the alarm, electricity, and phone lines.

We go in through the front. Sherry and I go toward the bedrooms, and Saul goes toward the kitchen.

Suddenly, we hear, "Holy Shit!" It was Saul. My heart drops, and I think, *is someone here? Are we caught?*

"Hey, you guys, get in here!" Saul says.

Walking into the kitchen, I see at least fifty mason jars filled with pot. "Oh my god!" I say.

"What the hell, look at this shit! I'm talking tight red buds!" Sherry says.

"We're in a drug dealer's home," says Saul. "Holy shit!"

Besides the table are sixty-gallon-size bags of marijuana stacked alongside several smaller baggies full of what looks like acid. I'm not sure if it was acid, but they were little squares of paper with cartoons on them. There are also pills, maybe speed and valium.

The windows in the kitchen are all covered in black-out curtains.

"What do we do, Carl?" Saul asks.

"Well, we find some money and run like hell. We do not want to be here if someone comes home."

Then in the background, we all hear a shotgun chambering a round. I hope it was one of us. Then a deep rough voice speaks, "Everybody, stay right where you are. I've already alerted the owner of this house, and he'll be here right shortly."

I look toward the voice and see a very tall, heavy man with many tattoos aiming a shotgun at Saul, who is closest to him.

"Look here, sir, I think we made a big mistake," Saul says. "We didn't know this was a drug dealer's home, and we wouldn't want to piss someone like that off."

"We were looking for a little cash, some food, and maybe some clothing. We don't even do drugs," I say.

"Please, let us walk out of here. We haven't taken anything. You'll never see us again. I promise," Sherry pleads.

And as he looks her way, Saul barrels into him in two seconds flat. He is knocked off balance, and I pull my gun, aiming at the guy's chest. "Drop your rifle," I say, "NOW!"

The giant man does so, and then he smiles. That is not a good sign — not at all. I keep my aim on the center of the man's chest.

We have to decide what to do, and quickly.

"Okay, so now what are we gonna do?" Saul asks.

"Well, the way I see it, we are screwed either way. If we run, he has seen us, and he'll look for us, then kill us. If we stay, we're dead," I say.

"I think we tie this guy up, find the money quick and get the hell out of here. We'll take our chances and get lost. We're pretty good at that," Saul says.

Sherry and Saul use duct tape to tie the man to the chair, and Sherry tapes his mouth. They do this quickly while I begin the search for cash.

"Wait, wait, wait, Carl," Saul says, "Check all the kitchen cabinets, refrigerator, and freezer first. This whole operation is in the kitchen. It would make sense the money would be as well."

We do as Saul says and realize that he is brilliant. All the cash is shrink-wrapped and stacked in the freezer. "Cold cash — you get it?" Sherry says, joking.

I roll my eyes and say, "You guys grab as much cash as possible and put it in our backpacks and a garbage bag." I point to the box of bags on the countertop. "Then you two head out; I'll be right behind you."

"You sure, man?" Saul asks.

"Yep, I'll be there in a minute," I say.

Grabbing the cash is fast and easy. Sherry leaves with a garbage bag of money and her backpack, but Saul hangs back. "I'm not leaving you alone on this," he says adamantly.

I look at the guy we had wrapped up with tape. "I wish you hadn't come in on us," I say. "I hate that you can identify us. We have managed to remain unseen for many years. Do you know why? Because we watch our homes for days to be sure no one is coming or going. We only take what we can carry in a backpack and never return. Where the hell did you come from?"

The guy's eyes just smile.

I think for a second, deciding. "I guess it doesn't really matter," I say, and I shoot the man point-blank in the forehead. I turn away and light a match to the curtains. "Let it burn down to the ground," I say.

As I am walking out, there is a sound in the next room, and I see Saul crouched down behind a chassis lounge, waiting.

After about 30 seconds, I see another tattooed dude with a gun. He is coming around the corner. When he sees the curtains flaming up, he lets his guard down and runs towards them.

I take my second shot; he goes down and does not get back up.

Saul looks over at me but doesn't say a word. I check both men before leaving, and there are no pulses.

"Saul, I was afraid if I didn't kill him, we'd be hunted forever," I say.

"We still might be. Let's hope that was the only two around and that there are no hidden cameras," Saul says.

When we arrive back at the campground, Lea, Bonnie, and Matthew listen silently to our story.

Lea says, "The police will be looking for suspects because of the fire and dead bodies. And the drug dealers associated with those guys will want their money back."

"Shit, that sucks," Matthew says.

"Looks like we took over 300,000 dollars," Bonnie says. "That's more money than we've ever come across."

"We need to sell the GTO at a used car lot," I say. "I don't know if we were caught on camera at any point, anywhere, on or around the drug dealer's home, but we should cover our asses."

We leave town immediately and drive to Lake City, Florida. Lea, Bonnie, and I go to buy a new ride and sell the GTO. Everyone else waits for us in the parking lot of Wal-Mart.

First, we drive to a new car dealer and buy a 2005 White Jeep Grand Cherokee with tinted windows. Bonnie picks it to replace her GTO.

We pay cash, and I use my uncle's address to send the title, so he'll know to hang on to it. Then, we drive across town and sell the GTO at a small used car lot.

"I think I might cry," says Bonnie. "We've had this car forever, I love it, and it's been everywhere with us."

"I know what you mean, Bonnie. I truly do. But we have to suck it up!" I say.

As we leave the car lot, Lea asks a question that was a long time coming. "Carl, do you remember when you first took me?" she asks.

"Yes."

"Do you remember telling me that one day I could go back and see my mother?"

"Yes, are you ready?" I ask.

"Really?"

I'm excited as our convoy drives to Tallahassee and stops at Big Boys for dinner that night.

Bonnie says, "You guys, this is where the adventure of our lives started. Carl and I came here a long time ago. Afterward, we went to the Brown House Campground."

"Good memories," I say. "I can't believe you were only twelve years old."

"I felt so much older at the time," Bonnie recalls.

We spend the evening hashing over our lives together.

Carl asks, "Does anyone want their share of the money, or are we still doing the family thing?"

No one says anything.

"Does anyone want to strike out on their own? If so, don't be afraid to say so. I want to make sure we are all on the same page."

Bonnie says, "Raise your hand if you want to stick around for now."

Everyone raises their hands.

"Okay then," I say. "We need to keep moving, and Lea wants to go and see her mother. I promised her when she was twelve years old that when she was older if she wanted to go home, we would take her. So, let's take a trip to Tupelo, MS."

"I can't believe I'm going to see my mom!" Lea says.

We leave our RV set up at Brown House Campground the following day and hop into the Jeep Cherokee.

We find Lea's mom quickly. She still lives at the same address.

Chapter 2: Tupelo

Sam

I finally call Leslie's mom, Vanessa Jenkins. She agrees to meet with me, so I pack for a trip to Tupelo.

"Allie, I'm taking a few days off next week. I've got to try and get something of Leslie's to do DNA testing."

"Smart girl! I wish we had this technology years ago!"

"Me too, girl!"

I arrive the following week. Ms. Jenkins invites me into her home. She tells me about the day Leslie went missing, the day and night before Leslie went missing, and how she grew up. I tell her I saw the missing poster at the rest stop when I was twelve. She hugs me and cries.

I look at her and say, "I intend to find your daughter for you, Ms. Jenkins."

Vanessa says, "Samantha, I'm no longer waiting for my daughter."

"Why?" I ask.

"Well, dear, Leslie's kidnapper sent me her PJs with a note. Leslie wrote that she would see me again. That was twenty-six years ago. If my daughter were still alive, she would have come to see me by now. Leslie would be 38 years old. No one could stop her. I don't believe she will return and may not even be alive."

"When did you receive the note and PJs? There is no mention of it in any of the research I've had access to." My heart is hammering.

"The note came three months after her abduction. The police believed it was a ruse."

"But you didn't think so?"

"No, it was my daughters' handwriting, and the kidnapper also sent her pajamas with the note. So, yes, dear, I believed I'd see her again at that time."

"Ms. Jenkins, I'd like you to take a look at a photo; I believe I saw her at Yonah's Ridge one day when I was hiking and photographing nature with my dad. I was only fifteen and didn't realize it might be her at the time, but when the photo came back, her face looked incredibly familiar to me," I say and show her the photograph.

She says, "Yes, I was aware of this photo and the news coverage afterward. Detective Pace called me the day it was released and asked me to come to the station to look at the photo. I said to him, 'that is my daughter; I'd know her anywhere.' But again, Detective Archer, that was twenty-one years ago. I do believe that was her, but something must have happened."

I ask to see Leslie's room, and Ms. Jenkins escorts me; it is dusted and clean but is otherwise the same as the day Leslie left. Ms. Jenkins retrieves a plastic bag for me when I request to take her hairbrush.

She says, "Take whatever you would like, Samantha. But so that you know, I bought a memorial at Lakeside Cemetery for her. I go every year now; on the day she went missing and on the holidays. I feel sure she is gone. I would know if she wasn't," she says.

It feels surreal sitting there in her bedroom. I close my eyes and think about when I was twelve. She was twelve also, and I think about how scared she probably had been. I get teary-eyed and almost lose my composure.

I get up and look around the room. I find Leslie's hairbrush, put it in the baggie, and return downstairs.

"Thank you, Ms. Jenkins," I say.

I drive to the police department to speak to Detective Pace, who worked on her case many years ago. He was waiting for me in the lobby.

"Ms. Archer, it is my pleasure to meet you. Are you the same Samantha who photographed what we believed to be Leslie Jenkins up in Yonah's Ridge, Arkansas?"

"Yes, sir," I say.

"I thought so," he says, "you called our missing persons and our robbery division not too long ago also."

"Yes sir, I did," I confirm. "I just visited Ms. Jenkins, and now I'm hoping I might gain some insight from you and your cold files on Leslie."

"Ms. Jenkins is such a dear woman," he says. "I'll pull the cold case files."

We go over everything as if I was entirely new to the case. He is extremely thorough and patient with all of my questions.

"Any chance I can see the pajamas and the note from Leslie?" I ask.

"Yes, of course," he says, pulling the large envelope from the evidence box. "I pull this evidence box at least once a year and scour it, hoping to see a lead, something I've missed."

"I understand; I can't seem to let Leslie go either," I say. "Detective Pace, Ms. Jenkins gave me Leslie's hairbrush from her bathroom. Is there any chance that you could do a DNA test and put her results into the police database?"

"Yes, but you know Ms. Jenkins and I both believe Leslie is most likely dead?" he says.

"I do," I say as I hand the detective the baggy.

"Okay, I'll submit the sample for testing," he says.

Two weeks later, Detective Pace calls. "The DNA results came in, and we got a hit on Leslie Jenkins's DNA right away; it's linked to a murder from a crime scene in Houston, Texas, from 1987," he says. "The DNA was found on duct tape that had bound the victim."

"That doesn't necessarily mean she killed him, though. Does it?" I ask.

"Well, let's just say the odds are not in her favor," he replies.

I've always thought of Leslie as an innocent victim. I had hoped to find her — to save her. What happened to her?

Chapter 3: I'd Know Her Anywhere

Lea

I ask the family to drop me off two blocks from my mom's house and wait for me.

I say, "I need to see how Mom will react to me, and I don't want you all to end up in jail before the day is done."

"Agreed!" Bonnie says.

"Give me one hour. If I don't return by then, you'll know Mom let me in the house. Then you guys come back and get me in a week. Okay?" I ask.

"We'll come back for you, don't ever doubt it, Lea!" Carl says, and I leave them.

I am extremely nervous as I walk up to my mom's door. I feel like I could puke. I can't believe she is in the same house.

As I knock on the door, I feel utter terror — unrealistic, but I feel it all the same. My head is saying, *what if she doesn't want me anymore? What will she say when she finds out I'm a robber? Will she still want to hug me? Does she still love me?*

My mom finally opens the door. She looks shocked as she stares into my eyes. Then, she reaches out to me, pulls me into her embrace, and begins to cry as she hugs me tight.

As we enter the living room, she says, "I knew you were my Leslie the moment our eyes met."

We hug and cry and hug some more. Finally, she says, "I never gave up on you, kiddo."

There are a million questions to be answered.

I tell her about the day I was taken and why. I tell her about the hole in the cave and how I wouldn't listen to them and kept telling them how I wanted to go home. Then, I tell her the basics of our screwed-up family over the past 26 years.

"I didn't think it would be good to bring them here. I was afraid you might kill them," I say.

"Yes, that was a good idea." Mom smiles.

"Mom, I've been to every state in the US except for Hawaii and Alaska. We travel everywhere."

"Did they hurt you, Leslie?"

"No, Mom, they have never touched me in the wrong way or mistreated me. They want to be good guys but sometimes do bad things."

"Like what, honey?"

"Like taking me away from you. They thought they were saving me from Dad. They thought they were saving you from Dad."

"What?"

I explain to her that Dad was planning to 'get rid' of her so he could move back home and have me to himself. "Carl said Dad was a sick man."

She sits, stunned. "You believe this… Carl? That he was telling you the truth?"

"Yes, Mom. It's the only logical reason for them to take me. They didn't ask you for money. They didn't rape me or kill me. They thought they were rescuing me. They put me in school, fed me, and made me feel like family."

"Leslie, I don't think your father had it in him to get rid of me," she says. "He was sick mentally, and alcohol ruined his life, but murder? I'm not convinced he would do that."

"Well, Mom, Carl was convinced," I say.

"Honey, I do have to let you know your father died of liver failure a few years ago. The doctors said it was alcohol poisoning. He lost his job and ended up drinking himself to death. The bastard."

"Mom!"

"Well!" she says. "He did, and he was. But would he have tried to kill me? I don't know, Leslie, that's reaching."

"Carl was a temp worker here in Tupelo when he met Dad at B & B. Dad was his boss for ten days, and Carl went out with Dad drinking on his last night, the night before he took me. We planned to rob a home in Double Gate the following Monday for food and money, then leave. But when Dad told him his secret, they changed their plans and snuck me out of town. They don't call it kidnapping."

"Leslie, come to me, my child." She hugged me like crazy, so tight. "I'm not sure how I feel right now; quite honestly, it is many different feelings. Above all, I'm happy you're here, but I think you have Stockholm syndrome. Part of me wants to believe all of this, and part of me wants to turn them in," she says as she laughs and cries.

"I thought as much. That's why they aren't with me," I say and smile. "I told them to give me some time alone with

286

you if I made it inside the house. They will come back in a week to pick me up."

"You mean they were waiting for you when I opened the door?"

"Yes, they dropped me and parked down the street to be sure I got in. Is it okay for me to stay?' I ask.

"Are you kidding? Of course, you can stay; you're my child always and forever. Besides, I owe you Taco Bell and Fenton's Ice Cream."

"You remember that?" I ask.

She smiles. "Always."

That evening I say, "Mom, I need you to know what has happened in my life. Some things have been beautiful and amazing, we've traveled extensively, and I've lived in such unique places. I want you to know about all of it. But we've also had some hard times and made some tough decisions. These won't be fun to hear, but I want you to know what I've been through."

"I want it all, honey — the good, the bad, the ugly, and the pretty. I've waited for this day for a very long time," she says.

I start at the beginning and tell my mom everything I can remember, including the murder of Sherry's grandfather, for which Saul and I were personally responsible.

There is a long, uncomfortable silence from my mom. Then she pulls me to her and says, 'I love you, my child." And she holds me tight.

After that story, everything else I had to say was like girl scout stories.

I stay the week with my mom, and she seems to be trying to forgive Carl and Bonnie, but I doubt she ever will.

My mom is a hell of a woman — so brave. I tell her many stories about our lives, how we live, everything.

We laugh and cry. She promises not to reveal her knowledge to Detective Pace, or anyone else for that matter, for fear that I will go to jail.

Then, on the seventh day, I was getting ready to go. Carl is on his way to pick me up when we hear a knock at the door. My mom goes to answer and comes back a few seconds later and says, "Honey, go to my room and close the door and be really quiet. I'll come to get you as soon as I can."

I did so, and when Mom's company left, she tells me, "That was a private investigator at the door. I invited her in because she contacted me last week about coming to talk about you. Her name is Samantha Archer. Honey, she shared with me quite the story. She's been looking for you since age twelve because of a missing child poster. Leslie, she has never forgotten you and told me you are the reason she became a PI. She told me she was the girl who took your photo at Yonah's Ridge when she was fifteen. She said she will never give up looking for you. I tried to throw her off the hunt by saying I gave up on you and believe you are not alive. But, honey, she asked me if she could look in your room. She's hoping that she can get something of yours that may be able to provide a DNA sample. It's some kind of genetic testing."

"Did you give her something?"

"Yes, she took your old brush; I thought if I denied her, she would become suspicious," Mom says.

"It's okay, Mom," I say.

Later in the evening, the family comes for me. However, they don't come to the door. Mom says she's not ready for that. I hug and kiss mom goodbye and promise to come to see her soon.

As I slide into the car, Carl says, "Sorry we're a little late; I saw someone at the front door of your mom's house earlier this afternoon. The lady was flashing an ID badge; I thought it was maybe the police. I freaked out a little. I didn't know if your mom had called them or if it was a coincidence. I decided to leave to keep the rest of the family safe. I hope I was right. "

"Carl, of course, you were right to leave. I would never want the rest of the family caught because of me," I say. "But, about the woman… have I got a story to tell you!"

Chapter 4: Tallahassee, Home for Now

Lea

After leaving Tupelo, we drive back to Tallahassee.

I say, "We have enough money for several years as long as we're conservative. I say we stash it and go to work until we develop a master plan so we can all retire."

"Can we stay in Tallahassee while we figure out our end game?" Sherry asks.

"That'd be great, but can we live in a house like regular people? I'd love to see what living in a home is like," Matthew says.

"What if one of us decides to go off alone or get married?" Saul asks.

"Well, can we all agree that if anyone just wants to take their cut and move on, they have our blessing?" Carl asks.

"I like it," Bonnie says.

"Me too," everyone agrees.

"How about a vote for living in a house?" Bonnie asks, and everyone agrees.

We stay at the Brown House Campground while Carl and Bonnie begin to look for a rental property big enough for us all. They find a place in the country, on the outskirts of Tallahassee. It is the perfect place to rent — an old country farmhouse. The yard is fenced and even has a huge barn where we can park the RVs inside.

Five years have passed since then and Carl is now working for a Domestic Violence Shelter. He's been there for over five years now and does whatever needs to be done. He is head of security and operations.

Carl says, "I'm so proud of these moms who've had the guts to walk away from abusive husbands and take their children with them."

Carl doesn't get paid much at the shelter, but we are all working — no robbing. The drug money has been put away for the future, and we haven't spent a dime.

Bonnie works at a gun range and is the Lead Instructor teaching beginners' lessons. Sherry is working at Secure Home, which is an alarm company, she is an on-call technician.

Matthew works at a liquor store, and since he doesn't drink, he is the best employee Pop's Liquor has ever had.

Saul is working with a construction company, building homes.

Me — well, I work for Loomis Armored US, LLC. I'm in the security and safety division, so I get sent to many different locations, and I'm learning about possible vulnerabilities in the system.

We're all hoping retirement is around the corner, but none of us want to rob houses anymore. The drug lord's home was the last straw, for all of us.

I've noticed that Bonnie and Carl have become noticeably closer since we have been living in a house. They are like two old friends that sit sweetly together and watch movies or listen to music. When there are issues in the house they are always discussing and finding the solutions together. I think we all saw them as our dad and mom figures as we grew up. I wish they could see how great they would be together.

Bonnie finally got her Collie puppy, and she named him Del Rio. She has taught him tricks like Freckles, and he follows her everywhere.

Sherry and Saul have also become very close; they haven't told us they like each other as a couple yet, but we have all noticed how they are looking at each other.

Me? I'm still looking for the perfect girl; I know she is out there somewhere.

Chapter 5: Human Trials

Dr. Stephanie Archer

It's been six years since we began the animal studies for my project. I was excited to share the news with my family, and I'm now ready to share even better news with everyone!

"Good morning, ladies and gentlemen," I say and step closer to the microphone. "Our mission began with the pursuit of crop improvement through microbiome manipulation, working to find a food source that will grow easily in all climates, be cost-effective, and ultimately taste good," I say. "Dr. Bailey?"

"Thank you, Dr. Archer. We have several patents on our designer plants that are rich in nutrients and earth elements and have healing compositions to combat diseases. We hope to contribute meaningfully to our society, particularly in food production. In our first phase, we posed some questions to be answered. Does it taste good? Is it viable in all weather conditions? Can we prove that our food source has dietary and health benefits? Is it possible to start a grain-free food for our dairy industry and raise healthy animals free from outside protein inputs? Lastly, is it disease resistant? We say YES to all the above."

Everyone applauds.

Dr. Bailey smiles. "Our next testing phase has been green-lighted by PureAgra. We'll begin human studies within the next month. We want to thank you all for the hard work you have put in to get us to this point. Thank you for coming today and enjoy your lunch!"

Next is lengthy applause and lots of talking as everyone is served lunch.

The World Project Team sits at a round table in the front of the room. Dr. Stephanie Archer, Dr. Raj Campbell, Dr. Steve Mayo, Dr. Natalie Bailey, and Dr. Joshua Grimes all feel exhilarated.

"Stephanie and Natalie, I believe you guys have stolen the show," says Dr. Grimes.

"A toast," says Dr. Campbell, "to hard work and dedication!"

"Cheers," replies the rest of the table.

"And the fun begins," says Dr. Mayo with an excited look and a huge smile on his face. "We are looking to start with thirty-two participants from each state; we had better get busy!"

"Amen, brother," replies Dr. Campbell. "I'll contact the newspapers to begin the search for participants in each state and give them the criteria and guidelines they will need to follow."

"I think we can begin phase one of our trials within three to four weeks," says Dr. Bailey. "I will set up days and times for us to meet with the monitors and teach them the protocols."

The next day, we begin preparation for phase one — the first application on humans.

Chapter 6: Sabbatical

Sam

Spying on cheaters is not exciting work. You sit for hours, waiting to take photos of two people entering a hotel room, to do the wham-bam; thank you, ma'am.

The work I dreamed of is sometimes exciting, occasionally awful, but mostly ordinary. It's not all the action I had hoped it would be.

Alibi Investigations is booming with business; we handle small-time and high-end clients and have a 98% closing rate on our cases. In the past two years, we've added two junior private investigators, Ryan and Ava; two administrative assistants, Julia and Nicky; a top-notch research lawyer, Jake; and a second financial investigator, Aiden.

"Hey, Allie, can I take some time off without worrying about leaving you guys in a bind?" I ask.

"Of course, go, Sam," Allie replies. "You don't need my permission; we're partners, for God's sake. Take a sabbatical, chase down threads."

"I'm not sure how long it will take, Allie."

"That's fine, and I'll get all the cases you're working on transferred to Ryan and Ava. Go, girl!"

"Thank you, Allie!" We hug, and I head to my office to begin preparations.

The following week was packed as I headed to my last lead on the pin map, West Palm Beach, FL. It was about a seven or eight-hour drive after stopping for lunch and gas.

I arrive around 3:30 pm and check into the Marriott Suites at Rosemary Square.

I call the Police Department and make an appointment to talk to Detective Bennett. He contacted me about a robbery ten years ago, and I had planned to drive to West Palm then, but 9/11 happened. Everyone's lives and priorities changed after that, and time passed.

"Detective Bennett, please tell me what happened when you arrived at the robbery," I ask.

He says, "I went in through the front door and worked my way through the home. I heard a noise from the kitchen; I saw a young man heading towards the back door as I approached. I shouted, 'STOP. Police, stop where you are!' The boy hesitated, stopped, and turned to look toward me. He had a gun in his hand, and I said, 'Put down your gun.' I thought he was bringing his arm up. It turned out that he was turning to reach for the door to flee. Unfortunately, I had taken a shot that hit him in the shoulder, but he kept moving. I called dispatch and went after him. He left a small blood trail, but I lost him. The dispatch call only delayed me by ten to fifteen seconds," recounts Officer Bennett. "The only things taken were jewelry, music CDs, men's clothing, and half the pantry, mostly canned goods. So weird, but that's what made me reach out to you. I remembered your phone call and the unusual M.O.; it was the same weirdness."

"I think this is how these guys live or survive," I say. "I don't think they have jobs. They seem to move around and steal other people's stuff. I've never gotten very close to them, but sooner or later, I always find the next step. Can you tell me about your follow-up investigation?"

"We canvassed the neighborhood and found that the local JAX liquor store had surveillance video," Officer

Bennett says. "The video footage was not great quality, but three individuals were walking past the Ajax liquor store, about two blocks from the residence and five minutes before the silent alarm went off. We were able to extract still shots of the suspects, but no one in the area knew them nor recognized them."

"Do you still have the video footage and still shots?"

"Of course, it's in evidence; walk with me. I'll get the photos and the video set up to show you."

"Thank you," I say and follow him.

As we watch the footage, I see two males and one female walking past the liquor store. One of the males looks older than the other two suspects.

Detective Bennett points to the younger male, "This is the guy I shot in the shoulder; here is the description and sketch of him." He handed me the BOLO.

The female in the video does not look like the girl from my photos at Yonah's Ridge.

I was bummed.

"Do you have anything else?" I ask.

"We have an eyewitness statement from Timothy Waldner; he is a homeowner in a close-by neighborhood. He said a suspicious vehicle was in the neighborhood park about an hour before the robbery. He stated the vehicle was a white Jeep Grand Cherokee. Three people got out of it: two males and one female. They sat at a picnic table for about 20 minutes, then walked away from the park and left the car."

"Did anything come from that lead? Did the witness confirm it was the same group that walked by the liquor store?" I ask.

"Yes, he did. We put a BOLO out on the vehicle and got a few tips about the car, but they were just dead ends, nothing to follow. The sketch of the male suspect was good, and we got calls, but nothing came of them either," he says.

"Do you mind if I follow up with your old leads?" I ask.

"I'd love your help, Ms. Archer. Here's the case file. Please make photocopies of anything you deem relevant and return the case file to me before you leave the building," he says and points me to the copy machine.

After making copies, I return to my hotel and lay the information on the bed. I spent most of the day at the police station and I'm hungry and tired.

The next morning, I go visit Mr. Waldner, the eyewitness. The neighborhood is upscale and very well-maintained. I knock on the resident's door, and an older man in the 60-70 range answers. I tell him why I'm there, and he invites me in for coffee. We sit in the sunroom, and he tells me what he knows. It isn't much.

Afterward, I walk across the street to the neighborhood park. It has lovely landscaping, picnic tables, and a children's playground.

The parking lot is a perfect location for someone to leave a getaway car. I can see why they picked it.

I go to the home where the shooting occurred to speak with the owner, Mr. Labrasciano. He invites me in and expresses his distaste for how the robbery was handled.

"I think that officer was overzealous, and I told him so," says Mr. Labrasciano. "There was no need to shoot someone in my home. In fact, after that break-in, I decided to use my alarm only at night while I sleep. If someone needs clothing, food, and money, let them have it."

"What exactly did they take, sir?" I ask.

"Well, on my dresser, in my trinket dish, I had a watch of nominal value and a pair of gold cuff links. My wedding band was there also, but they left it in the dish. They took about $50 that I had in cash on my nightstand. From my closet, they took several pairs of jeans and button-up shirts. I wouldn't have noticed this, except I always shut my closet door, and it was wide open when I came home. From the living room, all that was missing was my CD case. Besides that, they took all my canned and boxed foods from the pantry. Like I said, not worth getting shot or dying for."

"Yes, sir, I agree."

We talk about the package store a few blocks away.

He says, "I know the owner, Chris. I'll give him a call and let him know you're coming by."

I thank him for his time. From there, I decide to walk to the package store. The owner, Chris Delahanty, welcomes me. I ask him about the day of the robbery and what he remembers.

"The police came in and asked about my video cameras outside and inside my store. They asked to see the videos of that day, so we pulled the footage and watched," Chris says. "I know almost everyone that comes into this store. We're a close-knit community, and we don't have a ton of tourists in this part of town. People who aren't from around here stand out, so it was easy for me to pick out the three people that walked by my store.

I'd never seen them before. The police took the tape with them and said it was evidence. I wish I could show it to you."

"That's okay. The detective showed me the footage yesterday. Was anyone else on the video you didn't know?" I ask.

"No, not on foot. Just those three."

"You said not on foot, did you notice any unusual vehicles in the area?

"Yes, that week a white Jeep Cherokee drove by my store in the mornings when I was opening up. I'd never seen it before and didn't know anyone in the area that owned one. Later, I'd see them pass by again around three in the afternoon."

"How many days do you think that happened?"

"It was at least three or four days in a row.

"Can you describe any of them?"

"I wish I could, but no, I didn't see any of them close up," Chris says.

"Then, you don't know that was the same people in the video?"

"No, not sure. Just a feeling, I guess."

"Okay, thank you, Mr. Delahanty."

I leave slightly discouraged.

That evening I go to dinner at Bradley's Saloon and listen to a phenomenal band called A1A that sounds like Jimmy Buffett.

The next day, I follow up on a phone tip from the owner of Lion Country Safari campground in West Palm Beach. Ms.

Kaufman reported that the Jeep Cherokee from the robbery had been staying at her RV park for a week before the theft. Ms. Kaufman meets with me the following day.

Ms. Kaufman confirmed the phone tip. "I believe they could be your suspects. They were here for one week. During that time, there were two home robberies in the more expensive and exclusive parts of West Palm, one of which you are following up on."

"What do you mean two robberies? I only know of the one."

"Well, another was the cross-town the day before your robbery. No shooting, but from reports in the news, both reported having stolen food, and the news anchors said they almost certainly were connected. One reporter, in particular, came out and asked me a bunch of questions. I'm sure she followed up on all the other leads as well. She was smart, that's for damn sure," Ms. Kaufman says.

"What is this reporter's name?" I ask.

"Her name is Jodie Mouton, and she is a reporter for The Palm Beach Post."

"Ms. Kaufman, do you remember faces or anything else that may have stood out?"

"I remember the driver of one of the RVs because he came in and paid for the camping sites, then later came back and got Safari discount tickets for the next day for six people. He talked to me for a while about the zoo. He was nice, and I had no problems with him or his people. I remember so well because the reporter arrived two days after they left. She asked me to dig up the registration for the spot they were staying in, which was two spots."

"What did he look like?"

"He was maybe in his 40s — white, dark brown hair, shoulder-length, smooth face, no facial hair. He was wearing a trucker hat with a Saints logo, and he was maybe 5'10"."

"Can you remember the campers or other vehicles they were using?" I ask.

"No, I remember the Jeep Cherokee, and one of the RVs was drivable, and the other was a fifth wheel connected to a truck, but I didn't pay attention to the brands," she says.

"Okay, thank you, Ms. Kaufman, you've been a huge help. If you think of anything else, please give me a call." I hand her my card.

I reach out to the Palm Beach Post, Jodie is not at her desk, but they take a message and say she will get back to me within twenty-four hours.

I call Detective Bennett and inquire about the first robbery, and he says it was in a different district and they don't have access, but he gives me the precinct's phone number.

I decide to drive and meet the Officer who handled the other robbery. He says there were no witnesses. He reaffirms the MO was similar, if not dead-on, with the other robbery. He says they canvassed the area but couldn't find anyone who saw anything unusual. Therefore, he had nothing to add to her investigation.

The following day, Jodie calls me and invites me to the Post. She sets a meeting for lunchtime, and we sit in a conference room. She clears half the table and lays out all her data. We collaborate for two hours, each exchanging information and leads. I believe it's time to head back to Tallahassee.

Part Eleven: 2016-2021

"What separates us from the other killers is that we only kill bad people,"

Vigilante.

"Some people just need killing,"

Barry Eisle.

Chapter 1: West Virginia

Carl

A couple of weeks ago, we all had time off and could hang out together. As we played cards, listening to *Heathens by Twenty-One Pilots*. I bring up a subject that changes the course of all our lives. Not that we knew that then.

Lea came across an article in the paper that says the company PureAgra is looking for participants for a study a of a new food product that may help with health issues and satisfy appetites. The trials are beginning phase one in a couple of weeks. They're opening spots for healthy adults ages thirty to fifty. The trials are being held in one city in every state. In Florida, it's Tallahassee. How lucky were we?

Saul, Sherry, and Matthew decided to submit applications, and all three were accepted for phase one. It could be up to a four-year paid study if all goes well.

Three weeks later, all three moved to the PureAgra campus for onsite studies. The participants stay on campus during the weekdays and come home on weekends.

They signed all necessary documents that said they couldn't share information when they were on leave from PureAgra. Ha, good luck with that.

Over the next four years, Saul, Sherry, and Matthew continued to be involved in each phase of human studies.

Matthew met and fell in love with a woman named Andrea from his study group. She has light brown skin, dark brown eyes, and a petite body. Her smile lights up the room when she walks in. He has been bringing her home when they have time off.

As crazy as it may sound, Sherry and Saul officially became a thing. Well, more than a thing, they plan to get hitched when the PureAgra trials are completed, which should be in just a few weeks.

I say, "As you all know, while you guys have been busy with food trials, Lea, Bonnie, and I have been working on our exit plan from Tallahassee."

Bonnie says, "Carl's been researching land and homes while Lea and I have been working on detailed plans for the Loomis robbery. We need everyone to be ready because as soon as your trials end we'll only have two weeks to hit Loomis and head out of town."

"What about Andrea? Can she come with us?" Matthew asked.

"That's up to you Matthew. She can go with us, or you can make up a story for why we must leave in a few weeks. Or you can stay with her. You have our blessing, no matter what you decide," I say.

"I want to take her with us," Matthew replies.

"Then it shall be done!"

"Are we all in agreement on the robbery?" Bonnie asks.

Everyone agrees.

We all look at the final five choices of homes to buy, and agree on a large cabin near Joan Gap in West Virginia.

I say, "It's a basic build, a large cabin with a basement, six bedrooms with five full baths. It has a deck and fire pit area, but that's as fancy as it gets. Clean and simple. It can sleep up to eleven people if needed. Fortunately, the seller said the mountain cabin is 20 miles from civilization or other residents, and that we would need a four-wheel-drive vehicle to reach the location. The good news is, the closest city is Petersburg, West Virginia, and it was voted one of the coolest little mountain towns in the country."

"How far away are we from a beach?" Saul asks.

"We have access to Lanier Lake, it's just minutes away. It has beaches, kayaking, fishing, hiking, and boating. It's not the ocean but will that work for you guys?" I ask Saul and Sherry.

"That's cool," Saul and Sherry agree.

"If we're successful with Loomis, I'd like to build a campground at the beginning of our property for travelers like us. As well as creating a haven for battered women and children. It would be a way of laundering our cash and keeping townsfolk from asking questions about our cash flow. What do you guys think?"

"That's awesome! Can we go ahead with the sale, sight unseen? Pay for the place in cash?" Lea asks.

"Yes, I can call the realtor and let her know we want to proceed with the sale. Agreed?"

All agreed.

Chapter 2: Last Job

Carl

Saul, Sherry, and Matthew finish their contract and commitment to PureAgra successfully. Countdown, two weeks, and we head to West Virginia.

We all sit down together to discuss our exit.

I say, "Lea has examined and photographed the Tallahassee Loomis Depot. As a supervisor, she's obtained detailed floor plans and camera locations. She has our entry and exit plans laid out."

Lea says, "We'll leave town the night of the robbery, so I need to establish an alibi ahead of time. Otherwise, I'll be their prime suspect. So, I'm giving my two weeks' notice tomorrow. I'll invite my co-workers to a farewell party the evening of the robbery and leave in a cab "quite drunk," *wink, wink,* around 11:30 pm. The cab driver should be able to drop me off at home no later than 12:00pm. I'll be ready to hop in a van with Carl and Saul."

"What van?" Matthew asks.

I say, "We're going to sell our RV's and truck over the next couple of weeks. They are still in good shape, but we need an inconspicuous vehicle that can blend in with traffic. We're thinking a work van would blend. We also need to sell our furniture on Craig's List."

"We are looking at a buying a used 2011 Ford E350 Van. This will be one of our getaway vehicles, the other will be our Jeep Cherokee," Bonnie says.

"What will we do?" Sherry asks.

"You, Matthew, and Bonnie will follow us to the facility in the Cherokee," Lea says. "Let's not forget to duct tape over the license plates of our vehicles. We will park the Cherokee a few miles from the facility, and you guys will join us in a van."

"We've copied Lea's keys; they will gain us access to the facility," I say. "She has already timed the security cameras and determined how long they can be avoided.

"On Friday nights, the vault is left open due to the large quantities of money being moved. I know the bags will contain the highest denominations. I also know where the recording devices and security cameras are located. We'll turn them all off and have 30 minutes to load, hopefully millions, of dollars into our van and get out of town." Lea says.

"Guys, our cash is dwindling. Buying the cabin and our getaway vehicle will empty our savings. We'll have around $55,000 left. But, if this robbery works, we will be set for life," Bonnie says.

I say, "Heads up. You all know that I've met some amazing ladies at the battered women's shelter. A few have let their guard down enough to tell me their stories. Before I leave this city, I will go see these husbands who beat and raped their wives and children. There are five, whose names and addresses I know. I also know exactly what they did to their women and children. I plan to see these husbands face to face, the night before our robbery."

Chapter 3: Vigilante

Carl

We plan to settle in WV, where we've acquired a home, and become law-abiding citizens-ish.

So many years have passed since I began work at the Tallahassee Women's Shelter. It's a tough job, heart-wrenching. Through time, I've built great friendships working here, one being with Elizabeth Jackson, a domestic violence attorney. She once lived in this shelter as a child.

"Tonight, I am going to wreak havoc on some abusive men. Saul? Matthew? Are either of you coming with me tonight?" I ask when the day gets here.

"What are you gonna do to these guys, Carl?" Matthew asks.

"You're going to kill them, aren't you." Saul says without it being a question.

"Look, you guys, the things I'm going to do to them are an eye for an eye. These men have never paid the price for their actions. The law has worked to their advantage; they've never spent a day jailed. Always out on technicalities."

"I don't want you to kill anyone, Carl," Mathew says.

"I know, Matthew. You don't have to do anything, but you could drive me. Would you be okay with that?" I ask.

Matthew nods. We have kept him out of robberies ever since he was shot and almost got arrested many years ago.

"Saul, you good?" I ask.

"I got your back, boss," he says and smiles.

We arrive at the first home around midnight, Matthew stays with the van on the side street.

Saul and I break in through the back door. The man has a woman with him in bed, they are asleep. I quietly chloroform the woman. Saul gently removes the woman from the bed. He takes her outside and puts her in the backseat of the car in the driveway.

Standing over the man, I shake him rudely awake and say, "So, you want to beat someone with a bat, huh?" The man wakes and backs up in bed, trying to get away from me.

He doesn't make it far. He smashed his son's arm so badly he will never be able to shoot another basketball or anything else for that matter. The wife will see her scared face every time she looks in the mirror. I beat him with the baseball bat and while thinking about the broken body parts his son and wife live with each day. Then, I set his home on fire. Starting in the bedroom.

At the second home, the man is alone. I shake him awake and say, "I heard you like to sneak into children's bedrooms."

His eyes bulge, and his mouth is wide open, scared. I hit his head with the bat, but not hard enough to kill him, just to knock him out. When I shake him back to consciousness, he is handcuffed to the bedposts, no clothes on and I have tied his legs apart with ropes and taped his mouth shut.

"It took me a while to figure out an eye for an eye on this one," I say as I pour pure honey on his private parts. "Then it hit me," I say as I remove the lid on another jar. "The Maricopa Harvester Ant. Do you know this ant species? These ants are unique and cost me a pretty penny, but they are worth my trouble. They will kill you by poison, it only takes a few hundred stings for this ant to kill a human, and once one stings you, the others will follow. They smell the alarm pheromones in the sting so death will be fast, but not too fast."

I show him a syringe. "This will immobilize you, but you will feel them," I say as I put the needle into his arm and press the plunger. "The ants will take you like you have taken others — *unwilling.*" His eyes are pleading, and he is screaming underneath the tape that binds his mouth shut.

I open the jar and pour the ants all over his privates. I set a timer to burn down his home, I don't want the firefighters to save him in time. I want him to suffer for a while as the ant's burrow away. Then he can burn.

The third man is alone and bare-butt naked. When we wake him, he jumps out of bed and reaches for a gun on his nightstand. We have already checked, and I raise his weapon in my hand and point it at his head.

"Now, sir, be still and tell me, how did you scare and hurt your wife and children?"

I let him realize his situation for a few seconds, then hand Saul the gun as he passes me the hot frying pan. I beat him with that frying pan as he tries to get away. Ultimately, he is burned and has blackened eyes, a broken jaw, teeth, arms, hands, legs and toes. His house burns down while he lays broken on the floor. Unable to move.

The fourth man has a woman and two kids living with him out in the country. We chloroform the man, the woman and children. We remove him from the home and put him in the bed of his covered truck, that's sitting in his driveway. I hold the gun pointed in front of his eyes, put one of my hands over his mouth, and wake him. He jerks awake quickly frantically, then goes very still as I tape his mouth shut.

I straddle him, my knees holding down each arm while sitting on him. "Your ex-wife told me you would force her to have sex and strangle or suffocate her with a plastic bag over her head while you were getting your rocks off. She said she would pass out, and you would revive her, then do it again. She said sometimes you would rape her three or four times in one night."

I smother him with a plastic bag over his head and as his body fights, I say, "I brought a friend for you."

I bring him to death's doorstep, then I revive him each time and do it again. Until I don't. Then, I say "Oh, your friend is here!"

Saul hands me a cage for this specific moment. I crawl out of the back of the truck. The man is still alive, but without any fight left. Once out of the back, I open the cage and shut the back of the truck. Time for them to be alone. It cost a ton to get the reticulated python, but my friend Freddie, always come through. I pull the cover over the bed of the truck and leave.

The fifth house is hard to get to because all the houses are close together. I ask Matthew to drop us off and park on the street behind the house.

"Should I come and help?" Matthew ask.

"How about we all go over together and once we get inside you head back to the car?" I asked.

"Okay" he replied.

I sent Saul to the back door while I went to the front. After a few minutes, I motion for Matthew to come to me, and he does.

"Saul went to the back door and hasn't come back yet. I want to check on him and make sure he's okay. Do you mind standing here for a minute? If anyone comes to the door besides me or Matthew, just pretend you are looking for a guy named Joe."

"Okay, okay, sure, Carl," he says.

I walk away from Matthew and head into the back yard

By the time I get there, Saul has made it inside and opened the front door to find Matthew waiting, instead of me.

I hear a gunshot, and rush through the back door headed towards the sound of the gunshot. I see Matthew slumped on the living room floor and Saul kneeling beside him. There is also and a man in the hallway who hasn't seen me come in, he is holding a gun pointed at Saul.

"You m'fucker!" I say and shoot the man's gun shoulder, then both legs. Saul jumps up, rushes the man violently, takes his gun away, and holds it to his head.

"You will die tonight; you will die!" Saul rages, his face filled with the desire to kill.

I rush over to Matthew, trying to get him to respond. "Come on, Matt ... please don't go, man." But when I feel for his pulse, I know he's already gone.

I work on him for a few minutes anyway, doing CPR, hoping. I'm trying to get him back, but it is useless. The shot was perfect — too perfect.

I rise and walk over to where Saul has the man pinned down. I can see hate in the man's eyes. I smile at him, then search the house to be sure no one else is there. We tie his wrists and ankles and tape his mouth shut.

Then, we move him to the bathtub in his room. He is struggling with all his might to get away. Now, his eyes are pleading, *please, let me go.*

"Saul, you may not want to be here for this. I'm going old school, as in Scarface," I say.

Saul remains as I take out my hunting knife and go to work.

We start to leave. I have Matthew in my arms, and Saul has just lit the bedroom curtains on fire. We are walking towards the back door, and I notice headlights pulling up in the front driveway.

It is a police car. There were no sirens; someone called 911. The neighbors probably heard the gunshots.

"Saul, go out the back door, NOW!" I demand. "I'll lock the front door deadbolts and delay them."

"Okay, I'll meet you at the car," Saul says.

Saul runs, and as he leaves out the back door, I sit Matthew down and bolt the front door, hoping to buy some time.

Yeah, I was not so lucky; I never made it out. The police busted down the door just as I had gotten Matthew back in my arms.

"Police, stop right where you are!" the first policeman says as he rushes into the room.

I stand with Matthew's body, turn around to face them, and say, "Can you call an ambulance for my friend?"

The second policeman radios for an ambulance and fire department, and then he begins searching the rest of the home.

The first police officer says, "Lay the body down onto the floor, sir, then slowly place your hands behind your head."

I do, and he cuffs me.

Barney Fife comes back from the bedroom and says, "Shit, Franklin, there's a guy in the master bathroom cut up really bad. I'm pretty sure he's dead."

Officer Franklin says, "Sir, you have the right to remain silent. Anything you say can and will be used against you in court. You have the right to an attorney. If you cannot afford an attorney, one will be appointed for you. Do you understand your rights, sir?"

"Yes, sir; I do," I reply and think, I hope Saul follows our protocol and leaves in five minutes. I don't want them to catch him too.

The firefighters arrive and rush inside and put out the bedroom fire.

Barney Fife shoves me into the back of the police car. I sit while the crime scene people, and the coroner come and go.

I thank God that Saul made it out, but my heart is broken for Matthew. He wasn't supposed to go in the house. Why did he go in the house? It makes me sick to my stomach, Matthew's death was on me, and I deserved life in prison or death for that.

Chapter 4: Revise the Plan

Lea

Saul came home. He was a wreck, and he was alone.

His voice was high-pitched and hysterical. We couldn't understand anything he said at first. Sherry hugged and held him close. He was shivering all over, and she didn't let him go until he stopped crying.

I took charge. Something went very wrong tonight.

"Bonnie, can you get Saul a glass of water and a shot of whiskey?" I ask.

"Sherry, please make your fiancé a hot bath and get him some clean clothes. There's blood all over him."

I cup Saul's face in one hand and tap him lightly on his cheek with the other hand, hoping to bring him around. "Saul, Saul, look at me, Saul. It's Lea, where is Matthew, and where is Carl?" I ask.

He looks at me, his eyes full of tears, ready to overflow again. He is overwrought with emotion, and his voice comes out in gulps of air between hurtful words.

"I ... don't... I don't know what ... what happened to Carl," he says. "But Matthew ... he's... he's... he's dead!" He begins to cry again.

"Are you sure Matthew's dead?" Bonnie asks as she sits the whiskey down in front of him. Saul nods his head.

"Take the shot of whiskey, Saul," I say.

"I don't drink," he says.

"You do tonight," Bonnie says. "We need you to calm down; take it." She shoves it in front of his face.

He takes it, and it does calm him down a little.

Sherry returns to the room and says, "Saul's bath is ready."

You could see how shaken Sherry was, seeing her boyfriend like this. Saul was usually her rock, and now Sherry would have to step up and be his.

"Sherry, take him to the bathroom, but don't ask questions; help him wash and soak for about 10 minutes. Then help him into some clean clothes. When you're finished, we'll have another shot ready for him."

In about 15 minutes, Saul was seated at the little card table we had kept for our last few days in Tallahassee. He is calmer now. Sherry had given him three Tylenol for his monster headache.

He takes the other shot, clears his throat, "I was surprised when I opened the front door and saw Matthew standing there. He stepped inside the entrance to whisper to me that Carl had gone to the back door to check on me. I was turning away from Matthew because I saw sudden fright on his face. A man came around the corner of the hall into the living room; we must have woken him. He was carrying a gun, and because I had turned to the side, instead of shooting me in the back, the man shot Matthew dead in the chest." He began hyperventilating and we waited for him to calm.

"After that we killed the guy in the master bath. Carl called it Scarface style, remember that movie we watched? We did that. When we were leaving, we saw police pulling up in the driveway. Carl told me to go out the back door, he said he would delay them. He didn't make it to the car in five

319

minutes, then I waited five more. He never came." Saul said and began to cry.

After a bit, he asks, "Could I please go lay down now?"

"Yes," I say. "Sherry, take him and come back when he falls asleep. We'll wait until you get back to discuss things," I say.

When they leave the room, Bonnie says, "You want a shot, Lea?" None of us drink regularly, but I was thankful we had the whiskey available that night.

"Absolutely," I say.

We sit and wait for Sherry about ten minutes. While waiting I ask, "Bonnie are you okay? I know how you feel about Carl, you love him more than anything."

"I'm so scared," she says. "Just so damn scared."

Sherry comes back about that time and says, "He's out like a light."

We are all scared. Sherry pours another shot and turns it up.

Bonnie asks, "Lea, should we still go forward with the plan? Matthew is dead, and Carl, well he must be in jail, or he would have met up with Saul; right? What do we do?"

I say, "If Carl were here, you both know what he would say. Get the job done and go."

We begin revising our plan for the heist, which is now more critical than ever..

Chapter 5: Serial Killer

Lea

The next morning, Carl is all over the news. He is considered a suspect in the other fires and murders that happened last night. The police are saying they think he is a serial killer.

Sona Sara, our local CBS news anchor, reports, "Last night, in a normally quiet neighborhood, two men were murdered. One was the homeowner, and the other was a suspect. There is another suspect presently being held behind bars. His name is Carl Parker Jr., we believe that Carl Parker Jr. and his partner, Matthew Harris, entered the home late last night. The homeowner woke up and shot Harris after he entered the home illegally. Parker responded to the death of his partner by killing the homeowner.

Please get in touch with us at the number scrolling across the screen if you have any information regarding this case."

We were all watching the television and drinking coffee. Then, finally, Sherry says, "Lea, did you reach out to Matthew's girlfriend yet?"

"Yes, I called Andrea; she is broken-hearted. I called the morgue, too, and they confirmed that a person carrying the ID of a Matthew Harris is dead. They are waiting for someone to identify his body, and I asked Andrea to do it, and she said she would."

"Well, what did Andrea say?" asks Bonnie.

"Andrea asked if we knew what happened last night. I told her I had no clue. I said 'that was a boys' night on the town. Saul stayed home with Sherry because she wasn't feeling good.' I lied to her. Then I asked if Matthew had called her, to tell her what he was doing.

Andrea said, "No, I was working last night, he doesn't call me when I'm at work." She replied, "Is Carl guilty of murder; of what they are saying on the news about him?" Andrea asked.

"No, I don't believe he is guilty, but if he did do it, he must have had a good reason. The police are missing something. Carl nor Matthew would ever do something like that. We have all shared a home for years, and none of us have ever been in trouble!" I tell her.

"Then Andrea began rambling questions, …. "Are you guys still leaving? Will Matthew have a funeral? Who will bury him? What about Carl?" Etc.

"Yes, we are still leaving. We have to. We all committed and signed employment contracts with Lost Creek Oil Field, which established rights and responsibilities, as well as the start date, which begins this Monday morning."

"What about Carl sitting in jail and Matthew? He'll need to be buried. Aren't they important to you guys? I thought you were family." She said, very upset.

"We ARE family Andrea, and they would want us to go and do what we must. I will send you money through Venmo for Matthew's clothing, shoes, and flowers. He did not want a viewing, just a small graveside prayer service. I'll set up the service for next weekend. We'll drive back and help you bury Matthew. We'll also try to see Carl, if they'll let us."

"What if you can't come back?" She asked.

"I don't think that will happen, Andrea. I'll prepay the funeral home for all their services, the gravesite, flowers at his grave, and his casket. We'll take care of everything except his clothes. You'll take care of that."

"Then, she started asking about Carl. Do you think they will let him out on bond? Can he get bail money?" She asked.

"My goodness, that girl can ask some questions," Bonnie said, interrupting me.

"Ya, think?!" I replied.

I told her, "I contacted Carl's friend Elizabeth this morning, she's a Domestic Abuse Lawyer. She told me that she knows the best Criminal Lawyer around. Her name is Jillian Coker. She's going to see Carl today." I said, "Don't worry about Carl; we will handle things. You take care of Matthew for us."

Andrea said, "Ok," sniffed, and blew her nose loudly.

I asked, "Have the police questioned you yet, Andrea?"

"No, not yet."

"Just be honest with the police, honey. You come over on weekends and hang with Matthew in his man cave. They may think we are somehow involved with what happened and try to dig out things that aren't there. Just keep it simple. I'm only saying this because it will most likely look suspicious to a detective that we leave town right after Carl gets jailed and Matthew gets shot. Even though it was already planned."

Then I asked, "Do you think I'm being paranoid?"

She said, "Well, I think you're right. In all those detective shows on tv, they always suspect family and friends are involved first. Yes, Lea, I will stick to the basics."

323

Saul was still a wreck but better than last night. We clued him in on what we discussed the night before, and he agreed, but with hesitation. "We can't leave Carl," he said.

"I know how you feel," Sherry said. "None of us want that, but we have to follow through with our plans for now. We execute the Loomis robbery, then go to West Virginia and get settled. Carl would want us to continue without him; you know that."

"I agree. If the robbery is successful, we will have plenty of money and can be sure to help him." Bonnie said.

He looked at each of us solemnly. "Ok," he said, "for Matthew and Carl."

We had a lot to do this morning, so we began.

"The plan will stay the same, but we now have two less people. Going into Loomis will be Saul, Bonnie, and myself. Sherry, you will remain at the loading dock, be our lookout and take out the runner when the time comes. We will all be on handheld radios, but remember you guys; if you must speak, do not use names, and please disguise your voice."

We cleared our house, taking the table, chairs, and excess clothing to the Goodwill. We kept three mattresses and loaded them into the back of the van, taking half the insides out of each bed.

We hoped to fill the three mattresses with cash tonight. We kept some stuffing in garbage bags and would add it back into the mattresses after we hid the money. Then we scrubbed the house down, removing as much evidence of our lives as possible.

We packed one suitcase of clothes and one bathroom bag for each of us. We put them in the Jeep Cherokee, along with some snacks and a cooler of drinks. Bonnie and I will be driving the Cherokee.

Saul and Sherry, the van.

We will be starting over. Completely.

Part Twelve: 2021-2023

"In real life, the hardest aspect of the battle between good and evil is determining which is which."

George R.R. Martin.

Chapter 1: Collaboration

Sam

"CBS reporting, this is Sona Sara with your morning news. The police have just released an update on last night's killing spree. The suspect being held, Carl Parker, Jr., has been identified as Chris Finch." His photo becomes the background on the screen.

My phone begins ringing; I mute the television. "Hi, Samantha. It's Detective Kantor."

"Hi, Detective. What can I do for you?" I ask.

Detective Kantor is my liaison at the Tallahassee Police Department.

"Samantha, it's been a hectic morning here at the station. We've had several law enforcement agencies reaching out to me wanting to share intel on this Chris Finch, aka Carl Parker. I'd like to invite you to a 9:00 am meeting at our headquarters tomorrow morning. Can you come?"

"I would love to, Detective Kantor." My heart is beating like crazy. I can't believe this—finally, some serious collaboration.

"Good. I've received calls from two Detectives, Seller and Pace, also a Retired Sheriff Gilmore. Each of them brought your name into our conversations. You have made yourself well known while looking for this Leslie Jenkins, Samantha." She said.

"Somehow, all this connects with Chris Finch, and we need to figure it out. Bring your files and research on the Leslie Jenkins case and be prepared for a long day."

"Thank you, Detective Kantor; I'll be there."

The following day, I arrive early with a carton of coffee from "The Black Dog Cafe".

The conference room table has tent name cards for seating and a pad of paper and pen in front of each seat. After everyone arrives, Detective Kantor brings the meeting to order.

"Thank you all for coming. I'm sure you all are happy to see I invited Private Investigator Samantha Archer. I know that all of you have met with her at some point during investigations. I am her liaison at the police department here in Tallahassee. She has been invested in a hunt for Leslie Jenkins, who she has suspected was kidnapped by the man we know as Chris Finch for a very long time. She will know how to add to this investigation. Each of you reached out to me very quickly after finding out the real name of our suspect, Chris Finch. I want to do this as efficiently as possible, so let's start with the year each of you interacted with Chris Finch, aka Carl Parker, Jr. As you see from the information you provided me over the phone, I have you sitting chronologically. Sheriff Gilmore, can you please begin?"

Sheriff Gilmore, Paragould, AR

"Good morning," Sherriff Gilmore begins. "I'm Retired Sheriff Gilmore of Paragould, Arkansas. Chris's father, Lee Finch, was burned to death in his home when Chris was fifteen years old. Chris's story was that he woke up and smelled smoke, his father's room was on fire. He couldn't wake him up, so he dragged his father out of the house but couldn't revive him. The official records read that a cigarette caught the curtains on fire, and because the house was made of old wood, the bedroom went up quickly, and his father died of smoke inhalation. That's what the coroner's report reads."

"Why the doubt?" Detective Kantor asked.

"I didn't find anything out of the ordinary about the fire itself. The house is built of sticks; I've seen those go up quickly around here. I didn't rule out foul play, though. The boy was convincing enough with his story — it was believable, he even cried a bit. But I think that's when I felt something in my gut saying it smells fishy. The tears seemed... a bit inauthentic. I took him home that night to stay with my family while we located his next of kin. The following day, his uncle drove up from Orlando and took him home. As I said, I'm not naïve, so I put a glass he drank out of while he stayed at my home into evidence later that afternoon. It gave us his fingerprints to put on file, but I never found any evidence that tied him to starting the fire or killing his father."

"Do you now suspect he killed his father and burned his home down?" I ask.

"Yes, I've got an idea he might've. The second time I ran into Chris Finch's name was three years later.

"Detective Sellers reached out to me about Chris Finch. He was a person of interest in arson, murder, and possible kidnapping case in Orlando, Fl. There have been two fires and several deaths in three years, with the same person present in both places. Pretty suspicious. I put a BOLO on him and a missing ten-year-old girl, Brenda Larkin. Again, two fires and several deaths in three years, with the same person present at both, is suspicious. I believe this is where you come in, Detective Sellers," he concludes.

Detective Sellers, Orlando, FL

Detective Sellers says, "My cold case file is about fire, death, and kidnapping. This family was throwing their daughter a birthday party. Chris Finch was there. His boss told me he had attended the birthday party. Late that night, around 2-2:30 am, the place burned with one adult dead, two in critical condition, and the daughter missing. I went to the deceased male's workplace the morning after the fire to talk with his boss and coworkers about the night before.

"When I spoke to Chris, I asked him what the exact time was when he left the party; and who was at the party. I needed names. Chris said he left around 9 pm and didn't know anyone except Frank, his coworker. Chris said there were about ten adults, including him. Chris had nothing to offer, so I moved on to other coworkers. I made my inquiries throughout the day and eventually located all the party guests — except one. Four guests I interviewed left around 11 pm, and two left around 12:30 pm. All their alibis checked out. Get this, all six people said that Chris was still at the party when they left."

"Did you go back and talk to Chris?" I ask.

"I tried, but he wasn't at work the following morning, so I drove to where he lived with his Uncle Don," Detective Sellers recalled. "His uncle said Chris was gone; he left a note saying, 'I'm going on the road. Next time I'm in town, I'll stop by.' I don't remember word for word, but that sums it up. His uncle Don told me that Chris had been planning on leaving after his eighteenth birthday, but his uncle wasn't expecting him to leave on the day after. His boss didn't either. Chris never gave him any notice. The uncle rambled on and told me about the fire Chris's dad had died in three years before in Paragould.

"From there, I called Sheriff Gilmore in Paragould and asked him to put out a BOLO on Chris and the missing girl, Brenda Larkin, but nothing ever came of it. He became the highest on my list of persons of interest, and I've been searching for him ever since. I even go to his uncle's house every year to see if Chris has returned at any point."

"What about Brenda Larkin? Any leads there?"

"No," Detective Sellers replies.

Detective Pace, Tupelo, MS

"What do you have, Detective Pace?" asked Detective Kantor.

"I have a 1978 cold case for robbery and the kidnapping of Leslie Jenkins. Samantha knows this one better than anybody, but I'll share what I've got in case something gets missed. No murder or arson is surrounding this one, as far as we know. Leslie just disappeared during what looked like a robbery. We ran out of leads, and it became a cold case. In 1983, I got a call from Sheriff Gilmore about a possible Leslie sighting in Paragould. At the time, a fifteen-year-old girl, whom we all know as Samantha Archer, had caught Leslie on film with her camera while hiking Yonah's Ridge. Sheriff Gilmore sent her photo to me. The mother, Ms. Vanessa Jenkins, confirmed it was her daughter. Sheriff Gilmore put a BOLO out for her in Paragould and surrounding areas. It was in the newspaper and on tv. We received many possible leads but found dead ends."

"What makes you think she is tied to Chris Finch?" Detective Kantor asks.

"Samantha's the best one to work through that one," Detective Sellers replies.

I take my cue. "When I was in 11th and 12th grade, Sheriff Gilmore hired me and allowed me to investigate closed cases to see what I could learn from them. A closed case happened in 1969, where a house burned down, and a boy's dad died of smoke inhalation. There was a slight possibility that the boy killed his father, but there was no evidence to support it, so the case was closed. I asked Sheriff Gilmore about the case, and he told me what had happened. Then, Sheriff Gilmore said, 'This case sounds familiar and like another case few years later. What was it?' he said and pulled out some notes. He found that Detective Sellers from Orlando had called him about kidnapping, murder, and arson. The main suspect was an eighteen-year-old boy from

Paragould, Arkansas. His name is Chris Finch. It was thought at the time that he might head towards Paragould because he grew up there."

"This Chris Finch was suspect in a fire and kidnapping in Orlando, and you feel they were tied together somehow to Leslie?" Kantor asks.

"Yes, stay with me here; he had been involved in two house fires within three years, and both fires had dead people. The first was his home, and his dad died. The second was his coworker, where one person died, and their twelve-year-old daughter went missing, believed to be kidnapped."

"So, another twelve-year-old was kidnapped. Is that the connection you are making with Leslie?" Kantor asks.

"I know it sounds a little crazy, but what are the odds Leslie would end up in Paragould, Arkansas? Where Chris grew up. Could it be this Chris Finch is the kidnapper of both girls? I know it's a far reach, and I have very little to tie the cases together, but in my gut, I feel it."

"What else do we have?" Kantor asks.

"I needed a photo of Brenda. There were two girls in that photo on Yonah's Ridge. I figured if Chris Finch is involved, Brenda might be the other girl, and that should make my fragile theory a little stronger. So, I contacted Sheriff Gilmore first and asked him to reach out to Detective Sellers about getting me a photograph of Brenda."

"Yes," replies Sheriff Gilmore. "I called and spoke to Detective Sellers right away."

Detective Sellers says, "I told him I would check, and within 24 hours, I confirmed that someone had taken a photo of Brenda in front of her birthday cake on the night of her birthday party. The camera had been on the kitchen counter when the back of the house burned down. The fire department arrived at the home before the kitchen and dining room went. The camera was confiscated, and the film was developed and added back into evidence."

"So," Sheriff Gilmore says, "I asked Detective Sellers to send the photo of Brenda our way. I told him it may help verify one of my colleagues' theories. When the photo arrived, I reached out to our forensic artist. He said he could provide the same updated images as are featured on America's Most Wanted.

"The process is called age progression. They added a few years, then a decade, to Brenda's photo to give us a general idea of how Brenda's appearance could progress through time," Sheriff Gilmore says.

Detective Gilmore says, "I called Samantha right away. We have a winner, Samantha; this photo progression is a dead ringer for the Orlando girl in the photos with Leslie at Yonah's Ridge!"

"I got to tell you; I was ecstatic! My heart was jumping with joy. I was right! I felt like I'd been chasing ghosts for many years and thought they might be my ghosts." I say, smiling. "The robberies that I found in Tupelo around the same time as Leslie's disappearance started me on this adventure of mapping robberies all over the country. I thought for some time that Leslie was in the wrong place at the wrong time and was taken by the robbery or robbers. They became relatively easy to track once I noticed the unusual, unmistakably unique M.O. for the robberies, but it was hard to know where they would go next."

"Well," Kantor says, "reporters have been splashing news of Chris Finch, aka Carl Parker, Jr., across the front pages of every paper in the United States. Two strong tips have been called in from the Tallahassee Domestic Violence Shelter; one said that Chris has been working for them for years, although they knew him as Carl, and that he was never a problem and never got in any trouble with the police.

But to be clear, the second tip was, each man that died that night was the husband of one of the women who had stayed in the women's battered shelter," Kantor shares. "Sounds like a huge connection to Chris right there. We still need concrete, physical evidence that he did the deeds."

"Yes, and the Tallahassee Democrat newspaper is having a field day. This morning the headlines read Vigilante in Tallahassee! They're making him a damn hero." I say.

Kantor says "There's the gun that Chester, aka Matthew, had on him, but it hadn't been fired and had been reported stolen from a Land Lakes, Florida, robbery. We have the gun that killed Chester, the homeowner's gun. We didn't find the weapon that killed the homeowner. Chris did not have a gun on him, and we didn't find any other gun at or around the crime scene."

"Do we think there may have been another person?" I ask.

Everyone nods. It is a definite possibility.

"Detective Kantor, may I meet with Chris and interview him?" I ask.

"That's a great idea, Samantha, although he has to agree to the interview. I'll put in a request for you. You may get more out of him than anyone."

The meeting lasted five hours, and the circumstantial evidence against Chris Finch grew. Detective Kantor had discovered that Matthew Harris's real name was Chester Willis. His prints were on file, and although he was assumed to be a runaway, there had been someone who had to report him missing in 1975 through snail mail, which included his favorite book. The note said, "The boy were taken or mayhap ran away.

The police expected to find more on Chris as they searched the database with his fingerprints. Instead, there was no evidence that he killed anyone, before tonight. His fingerprints were found at two robberies but as they searched all the way back into the 1960s, they found nothing.

Chapter 2: The Heist

Lea

The night after Carl was arrested, I go out with my coworkers for the farewell party to establish my alibi. I pretend to drink like a fish and act like I am wasted. One of my coworkers calls a cab to take me home around 11:30 pm.

The cab driver drops me off at home, and as soon as he is gone, I hop into our Jeep with Bonnie. Saul and Sheryl follow in the van.

The planning stages were critical, and we went over them together that morning. I told them, "I copied my Loomis keys the day before I gave my two weeks' notice because I knew the Loomis protocol would be to take away my access during the last two weeks of my employment. The keys will be like magic and gain us admittance into the facility. We will dress in ski masks, common mechanic jumpsuits, and gloves. We'll need to use walkie-talkies. This is how it needs to go down; Saul will go in first. You're tasked with making it to the security room undetected."

Saul said, "Yes, and then, I'll rush the security guard and chloroform him. Then, use his handcuffs to secure him in the room, disconnect the landline, and grab his cell phone and gun. Then wipe the drives, break the computers." he said.

"Yes, the room is sound proofed," I said.

"Once the cameras are taken down, the computer wiped and destroyed, you will use the walkie and let us know you made it and meet us at the loading docks."

"Got it," Saul said.

I said, "The guard inside the vault is the filler, and each truck receives a specific amount of money for delivery tomorrow. The filler stacks the money on a flat hand-truck for each armored truck. He's the beginning of the assembly process. The second guard is the checker. He receives the money from the filler and verifies it's correct. He then pushes the money to the third guard, the money mover. The third guard picks up the order number, verifies the money then takes it to the correct holding cell for loading in the morning. We have to take out the money mover."

"Like kill him?" Saul asked.

"Let's try to avoid that," I say. "Bonnie and Sherry, wait for the money mover at the holding cells. As he comes through the door, Bonnie, you will hold a gun to the side of his head. Sherry will chloroform him. I know which orders will contain the highest denominations and non-sequential bills. We'll have 10 minutes to load the van with hopefully millions of dollars and get out of town. We're done if we don't make it out in that time. The other guards will begin to question where the Money Mover is."

Everything goes accordingly. We find one of the three hand trucks I wanted. Sherry backs up the van to an empty dock, and Saul and Bonnie fill the van. The second hand-truck is four docks down to the left, and the third is right next to it. We fill the van with an estimated fourteen million dollars and lay the mattresses on top.

We make it out with the cash, but I am freaking out, it took eleven minutes. We hear chatter from the other guards on the walkie-talkie as we leave, police are being called this very moment. Good news, no one died, and no one's caught us, yet. There will be two guards who will have awful headaches in a couple of hours, it could have been much worse. Saul and Sherry drive the van, Bonnie and I follow in the Jeep Cherokee. We go straight through to WV on backroads, stopping only for gas. News of the robbery is all over the radio.

Chapter 3: Never Black and White

Sam

I was granted access able to meet with Chris Finch on Saturday afternoon. That was fast.

As we sit across from each other, I have an unexpected feeling of comfort. He is handsome in a way, and he looks me straight in the eyes; they are a piercing light blue, direct and seemingly with intent.

"Hello, Mr. Finch. My name is Samantha," I begin. "I'm not the police. I'm an independent private eye and want to ask you some questions. Off the record, of course."

"Shoot, and call me Chris… or Carl," he says and smiles. It is an easy smile and kind. Knowing what he has been accused of, I had a preconceived notion of who he was, and it genuinely surprises me that he is so likable.

We are sitting in a private visitation room, and guards keep a watchful eye, but I am told that no recording devices would be in operation.

"I have a very personal case that goes as far back as 1978. There was a girl that went missing in Tupelo, Mississippi," I say. "Have you been to Tupelo, Carl, or is it, Chris? What do you prefer?"

"Either is fine, but since my cover has been blown, let's return to the original."

"Chris, it is then," I say.

"Samantha, I have been all over the U.S. I'm sure I've driven through Tupelo, Mississippi, at some point, but I don't remember the year," he says.

"There is a girl that went missing, Leslie Jenkins. I think you will remember. I need to know if you know her and if she is dead or alive."

"Why would you be interested in a 40-year-old case? Why would you think that I may know her? That seems weird," he questions.

"I saw her photo on a missing poster in 1978. It shocked and scared me because I was the same age as her. My heart was sad for her, and I wanted to find her. So, I took a photo of the missing poster with my camera. When I developed the film from the trip, I put the photos in my first photo album. The missing poster is on the first page. Five years later, I saw her in Paragould, Arkansas. That's where you're from, right?" I ask.

"Yes, I am."

"Well, I was hiking with my dad and taking random photos, and I took some of her smelling flowers and then with her friend. I didn't realize it was Leslie until I had the film developed. Then I knew it was her.

"Recently, I discovered that the friend she was walking with was a girl who had also been kidnapped. She was from Orlando, Florida, and her name was Brenda Larkin. That's where you lived after your dad died, right? Orlando, Florida?"

"Yes, I did." He does not look nervous, worried, or guilty.

"When I started actively searching for Leslie Jenkins," I continue, "I found something I believe is a key to her mystery. I found some very unusual robberies in Tupelo the week before her abduction, and her house was one of the robberies. These robberies, well, they have drawn my attention for years. They have a certain M.O."

"What do you mean?" he asks.

"In every robbery that I have noted throughout the United States, these specific robbers, always without fail, take food, music, clothing, and everyday household items from the bathrooms. The only thing these robbers have in common with your typical robber is that they also take jewelry, guns, and money, if available. I have been tracking these robberies for many years but have always been one step behind."

He sits for a long while, not saying a word.

"You think these robbers took your Leslie, and I am the robber? You also think I kidnapped a girl named Brenda. You think these things because I'm connected by the cities I lived in and circumstances," he says.

"I do."

"Samantha, I can tell that you truly care about what happened to your Leslie Jenkins. I'm intrigued to know more about that. It's amazing to me that you never gave up on her. I wish I could tell you I know Leslie, but I cannot," he says.

I look at him long and hard. *Could not or will not,* I think, then move on.

"Can you tell me why you're accused and charged with five murders?" I ask. "The police have verified that all five men killed were husbands of wives from the women's battered shelter you've worked at for the past four years."

"I can tell you that my friend Matthew was shot and killed. I can also tell you I was trying to take him out of the home so that they wouldn't blame him for the murder of the homeowner. I almost made it out," he says and smiles.

"Chris, I'll be more direct. Did you kill those men and burn their homes down?"

"Why would I do that?" he asks.

I am beginning to get flustered. Everything answer he gives is vague and mysterious.

"Listen, Samantha; I will be going on trial within the next two weeks or so. I understand you want something that can help you with your case. I can't give you anything. I do want to thank you for sharing your suspicions. All I can say is that I see why you would think that I could have been involved. Other than that, I love your passion," he says.

"Wow, okay then. One more thing, please?"

"Sure," he says.

"In 1983, on Mount Yonah, I saw Leslie alive. I took the photo of her and the other girl Brenda. I went to the police, and they blasted it all over the news and papers. Were you back in Paragould, Arkansas, in 1983?"

"You are tenacious, Samantha. I can't say if I was there or not. I've never kept a travel diary."

"Really?"

"I'm sorry, Samantha. I wish I had answers for you." He smiles gently and says, "Guard, please take me back to my cell."

As I'm walking out of jail, my mind is confused. My brain is trying to understand. I like him, not in a romantic or even a crush kind of way. I play for the other team, as some say.

I can't even understand why I like him. Is he the guy? There is no actual evidence. I know I'm reaching, but the coincidence is enormous, and some believe there are no coincidences. Do I believe that? Do I really think this guy I just met kidnapped two twelve-year-olds? I have no feeling whatsoever that he is a pervert. I would recognize that certain creepy look from a man. I can always sense when a man is not right, almost like I can smell his intentions.

With Chris, I felt nothing of the sort — quite the opposite. Although he told me literally nothing, I think I can trust him. What is wrong with me?

I requested to see him throughout the pre-trial, trying to get to know and understand him. Unfortunately, he always seemed to get more information from me than I did from him.

Chris is facing life in prison or death if convicted of first-degree homicide on five charges.

Three days before the trial begins, he says, "Sam, I want to share something with you. I don't want you to be shocked at trial."

"What is it, Chris?" I ask.

"My defense lawyer, Jill Coker, and I have decided I will testify in court. Sam, when I do, I will be straightforward about what happened that night and why. The jury will have to decide what to do with my testimony. I wanted to inform you beforehand, so you won't be shocked or caught off guard. No one expects me to testify, especially the prosecution, so please keep it to yourself."

"Are you guilty of all they are accusing you of?" I want to know.

"Samantha, it's never black and white. Did I kill them? This is not the only question. When and where they were killed have been answered. Keep asking questions, why were they killed? Who were they? What did they do? All of this will come out. My testimony will be clear, and the jury will have much to consider."

"You won't tell me now, though, will you?"

"No, Samantha, you will learn when everyone else does. I care about you, Sam, and I love your passion for truth, and I wonder, will we still be friends after all this? I hope we will. You have been a breath of fresh air at a horrible time in my life. I hope that I can do the same for you one day."

Chris's court trial was huge, televised, and the courtroom was packed. In addition, the streets before the courthouse held hundreds of people holding signs with their opinions.

Some believed he was guilty as hell and wanted the death penalty.

Others believed, although probably guilty, he had killed for a good reason. Vigilantes are sometimes considered heroes. It was about a 50/50 turnout.

In the courtroom, you could feel the emotion and electricity in the air. The gallery sat in anticipation when the defense called Chris to the stand.

When he testified, his lawyer stood up, walked before him, then faced the jury; she asked, "Chris, did you kill these men?"

Chris responded, looking at the jury, then at the court, head held high with truth exuding from him, "Yes, ma'am."

Then he continued, "These men were child abusers, women abusers, rapists, and perverts. I was given first-hand accounts from the victims in the safe haven where I worked. They were not innocent, yet there were no consequences for their unspeakable actions to their women and children.

"The women's lives will never be the same. They will never truly trust or feel safe anymore. These women and children will always be afraid that their abuser will find them one day. They hide in fear while these men live in freedom. I believe this is an injustice within our system. Some people say I'm a vigilante. That is true. I have taken matters into my own hands and acted as judge. I wouldn't go back and change things, even if I could, except for the death of my friend, Matthew. He was only my driver that night. He had no clue what I was doing inside the homes."

His lawyer asked, "So, you admit that you killed these men intentionally, is that correct?"

"Yes, ma'am."

"When asked if you were guilty or not guilty, you pled not guilty. Are you now admitting your guilt? Why did you plead not guilty?"

"If I had pled guilty, I would not have had the chance to share the evil these men did to their women and children with the world. It would have been swept under the rug. The truth about them would not have come to light. I believe it was right to eliminate such scum, such evil in the world."

"To be clear, Chris Finch, you are pleading guilty to the murder of five men," Jill replied.

The courtroom was buzzing. Chris was right; no one expected him to testify or admit his guilt. "Yes, I am guilty of killing monsters."

345

When the trial ended, the jury stayed sequestered in an unknown location. The people were passionate about this case. Finally, after two weeks of deliberation, the jury returned with a verdict. The courtroom was silent as the foreman stood to read the verdict.

It was plastered across the papers and the news within minutes of the jury's verdict.

VIGILANTE Chris Finch FOUND GUILTY

FIVE Counts of Second-Degree Murder!

I'm relieved, and I'm not sure why I feel the way I do. In the end, Chris Finch seems to have had a sympathetic jury. Instead of first-degree murder, he was charged with second-degree murder on all five counts.

They gave him fifty years, ten years for each count of second-degree murder, but with eligibility for parole in ten years. When the jurors were asked later, they agreed on leniency. Many people are outraged by the decision and the sentence, but what can you do as a regular citizen? Become a vigilante too? Isn't it ironic? Don't 'cha think?

I still don't know if Chris is my guy for the robberies. There is no objective evidence for a connection, only supposition.

I will continue to look for Leslie, but I admit, I may have been on a wild goose chase.

Part Thirteen: 2021-2023

"Wherever there is abuse there is also corruption. Politics, philosophy, theology, science, industry, any field with the potential to affect the well-being of others can be destroyed by abuse or saved by good will,"

Criss Jami.

Chapter 1: PZK and Halle

Dr. Stephanie Archer

The World Project was finally brought to the public in February 2021 as a food source for the world. The plant was genetically engineered through microbiome manipulation and named Pazak or PZK.

It was a humanitarian project that I developed and patented while working with PureAgra. As a result, the new plant is resistant to all environmental diseases.

PZK is the manipulation of potato, zigzag vine, and kudzu fruit. It is super easy to grow in abundance and is tasty.

This successful food source and has been given to the poorest families across the United States, as well as countries around the world. Because of the enormous success, Dr. Grimes, one of my fellow research scientists, had an idea to develop a PZK supplement.

I disagreed with the idea, "Dr. Grimes, I know you believe this will be a great use of what we have created, but supplements don't have to pass any tests to get on the market. I don't want PZK to become tainted. If you consider doing trials and testing on the supplements, I'll agree and back you completely."

Dr. Grimes said, "Dr. Archer, I understand your concern. However, we must act quickly, or someone else will find a way to use what we've created."

With Dr. Grime's deep connections at the White House, the US government authorized the seizure of my patent. It was easy to do because PureAgra sustained itself with government funding.

I was given the Humanitarian Award; we had saved the world from starvation, but the formula was now in the government's hands to do with as they pleased.

PureAgra put Dr. Grimes in charge of developing the new supplements to go on the market. I elected to stay as a part of the team so that I would know what was going on.

The PKZ was ground like coffee and combined with small amounts of chili pepper, nutmeg, seabream, phytoplankton, and psilocybin mushrooms, this became the Halle supplement.

The promotion of the new supplement was fantastic; before long, it was in every household in America and worldwide.

The feel-good nutritional products spread far and wide. Halle was all-natural and had become the most sought-after nutritional product, with the benefits of staving off diseases and illnesses and even reducing weight gain.

Until it didn't, and Halle became a huge problem.

The side effects began appearing in 2022, and more than 25% of our population became sick.

In late December 2022, a woman in Chicago complained of an earache. Her doctor found a seedling plant growing inside her inner ear. He was mystified. Within two weeks, the woman went utterly insane.

The Chicago Morning Post reported the story, "What had happened to this poor woman? It is a mystery."

Newspapers, tv stations, and the internet sensationalized the story, and by doing so, rumors began to spread.

In February, a Washington woman was rushed to the hospital. She had a collapsed lung. Her name is Pryia Michaels and she had been battling emphysema for months, and when her condition deteriorated, she was preparing herself for the possibility of a cancer diagnosis, but the X-rays revealed she had a plant growing in her lung.

We were notified right away, of course, but not wanting the publicity, those who made the decisions chose to make a non-disclosure agreement, a confidentiality clause, that prohibits both parties from discussing the details of the claim, and we offered a settlement. As a result, Ms. Michael's became quite a wealthy woman.

In March, a 75-year-old man was also treated for a growth in his lung.

In April, a woman from Nevada began having unexplained headaches and later learned that she had a plant form deep inside her ear canal. It had partly flowered and had grown to nearly 2 cm long before being surgically removed. The warm and humid conditions in the ear canal are likely to have encouraged the growth. Although the plant was removed, she was later sent to an insane asylum. She lost her mind. Again, not wanting the publicity, they chose to make non-disclosure agreements with confidentiality clauses prohibiting all parties from discussing the details of the claim and settlement.

The news began to spread fear. Those who thought there was nothing to the rumors started to change their minds.

We know as scientists that most plants will not grow into your flesh. Our bodies are not exactly hospitable to chlorophyll-manufacturing green plants. But these plants do, specifically inside the lungs, as the warm moist environment is suitable for sprouting seeds that need warmth, moisture, and oxygen to germinate. You'll find the same conditions in the stomach, but it also has hydrochloric acid, and hydrochloric acid has no trouble dissolving seeds.

We were called to an emergency meeting with the management and owners of PureAgra.

"You all know why we are here today. Dr. Campbell, will you please begin?" asks our CEO, Jim Morgan.

Dr. Campbell says, "The strange plants found growing in the lungs and around the heart as well as the growths found in the ears and brain, could possibly be coming from the Halle nutritional supplements. Although there has not been enough testing to be positive."

I say, "I can't believe the FDA hasn't pulled Halle yet; we need to be proactive. We should go on TV and warn people about the possible side effects. It has only affected approximately 30 people, but if Halle incubates in our bodies, we could have a massive problem."

"No way," says Dr. Grimes. "We would be ruined. It has only been a few deaths and terrible side effects. We don't know why yet, but we can do more testing to find out. We can't do what you suggest, Stephanie. We would be ruined."

"Look, Stephanie," says Dr. Mayo, "while I understand your worries, we must pinpoint the problem. We have helped so many people, and it would be frightening for them to hear about this, maybe even chaotic. I have to agree with Dr. Grimes on this one. More testing is what we need to do for our next step."

"Well, I agree with Stephanie's proposal," replies Dr. Bailey

"I believe you both have solid points. I'm not siding either way at the moment," says Dr. Campbell

Jim Morgan says, "This is extremely important, but we have so little data. Therefore, we must involve the FDA, CDC, and possibly the Chief Medical Advisor. Everyone continues with studies on the infected, and you'll be notified as soon as we get a meeting."

Chapter 2: Weird Science

Dr. Stephanie Archer

Within two days, we were invited to come to the White House. After much discussion, things did not go the way I hoped. Our directive is to return with real-time data in six months. My opinion, they are risking people's lives.

As we leave the meeting, I say, "I stand firm in believing the public deserves to know the truth. I'll be to blame if I remain impassive and let this continue." I say.

"I agree, Stephanie, but he's right we can't go against directives from the White House," Natalie says.

"I agree too. The cases are growing more and more each day. We have to say or do something," says Dr. Campbell.

"You two will be getting yourselves into serious trouble if you disregard the directive from DC," says Dr. Grimes

"Dr. Grimes is right unfortunately, the administration will strip us of our positions. We need to keep a lid on this," says Dr. Mayo.

"I suggest we leave it as is for now," Dr. Grimes says. "Stephanie, I know you want to get ahead of this with the public, and that's honorable, but we have to create a narrative that would suggest that it isn't the Halle but maybe some sort of common denominator that mixes with the product that causes it," he suggests.

"Dr. Grimes are you suggesting we fake reports?" asks Dr. Mayo. "I may agree we should wait, but I don't agree to create a narrative, as you say."

Four months later, Natalie, Raj, and I meet for lunch.

"We need another meeting with the White House." I say, frustrated.

"What can we tell them that would change their minds?" Raj asks.

"We have more data, and I'd rather people be able to decide for themselves if they want to continue taking the supplements and risk their lives and their minds," I say.

Unfortunately, over the next six months, what had been a 'few people who had been affected' has become thousands, and it's happening worldwide. The hospitals and psychiatric wards are filling up with people, psychotic breakdowns, and unusual health issues.

Chapter 3: Warning

Sam

My mom calls. "Hi honey," she says. "What I'm going to say is going to sound very strange coming from me, but I need to talk to you about something vital. Have you got a minute?"

"Sure, Mom, go ahead," I say.

"Samantha, please don't take any of the Halle supplements."

"Why? What? Is it dangerous?" I ask.

"The jury is still out, but I'm very uncomfortable with some things that have been added to make the new supplement. I'm thinking about long-term effects. The PKZ itself is good and healthy. It's only the supplement that's been created that I'm concerned about. Many of the other scientists involved in the supplement project believe my theory is silly, but I'm fighting for studies to be done," Mom says.

"Have people gotten sick from the supplements?" I ask.

"Yes, both physical and mental," Mom says.

"What are the symptoms?" I ask.

"There are two strains. The first starts with severe flu-like symptoms; as they recover, most develop a light gold ring around their pupils. They seem healthy except for the gold ring. Within 48 hours of the gold ring, they begin seeing all kinds of crazy stuff, becoming paranoid, aggressive, and dangerous to others and themselves.

"The second strain is growths. They are weird leaf-like warts on their hands, faces, and torsos. A few cases have involved plants growing out of a person's ear, inside their lungs, or nose. They too get the gold ring around their pupils and end up going crazy. We still do not know what is causing this. Every person affected has been taking the Halle supplements. No one has been able to prove or disprove it comes from Halle, but it looks that way to me..

"Would you promise me, Sam, don't eat or take the Halle supplements?" Mom pleads.

"Yes, Mom, I promise," I say. "So why hasn't the public been made aware?" I ask.

"We met with the highest authorities, and they want more testing. They're afraid we may create a bigger problem with panic."

"What higher authorities?" I ask.

"Sweetie, I didn't know where my funding came from, but I know now, it's a government-funded program. The higher authorities, babe, the White House," she says.

"Oh, my gosh, Mom! Are we talking about a conspiracy?"

"I don't know, honey," she says. "I don't think so. It seems more like a need not to fail in front of the world. If it is the supplement, we must find out why some people are infected, and others are not. I'll keep in touch. I miss you and love you."

"I miss you too, Mom!!"

Chapter 4: Spreading Madness

Sam

You will know them by their eyes. There's a shiny gold ring around their pupils, and they become super aggressive.

I didn't know he was infected the first time I saw one. He looked like a regular person until I got close to him. Then I saw the madness.

These people are filled with chaos and rage inside their heads.

When asked by a psychologist what they are seeing, one woman said, "I see two worlds overlapping. First, I see my husband clipping hedges in the yard. Then I see my husband coming in the door with the clippers to cut me. I run and get the gun out of the safe," she says, pauses and continues.

"Then, he isn't there, I look back out the window, and he's clipping hedges. I close my eyes and shake my head, thinking what is wrong with me. Then I open my eyes, and he is standing in front of me with the clippers, so I shoot him. I look back out the window, and he's clipping hedges. I look at my husband crumpled on the ground before me, and he has no hedge clippers. He is dead. I close my eyes and shake my head again. My husband is now in the bedroom saying, 'Honey, what's wrong?' I point the gun at him, and the gun goes off. I don't know what is true. Is my husband dead?"

A young father was taken to the mental ward. He said, "I was hitting the baseball with my son. He was practicing his catches. After a great catch, he stumbled towards me, but it wasn't my son, it was a kid who had been in an accident, and his eye was crushed, and his forehead was cracked open. I looked at him again, and it didn't change. It was my son, and he was saying, 'Daddy, why did you hit the ball at my face?' I picked up my son and got in the car to drive to the hospital, and my son said, 'Where are we going, Dad?' He was fine; I hadn't hit him with the ball. I can't define the real world and what is true."

I call my sister and asked her, "Hey Kat, have you had any friends or work acquaintances come down with the weird things growing on or in them? Any colleagues going crazy all of a sudden?"

"Well, my friend Ty is going insane. We had an intervention, but he acted like we were the crazy ones and began threatening us with a knife. We had to leave, and he sliced Sarah's finger off as she tried to close the door to escape his apartment," Kat said.

"Are your grocery stores posting doormen, to let people in and out?" I asked.

"No. Why?" Kat asked.

"Because my Publix was ransacked by a small party of Crazies or Experimental's'— that's what people are calling them. They think it's the world's end and are filling shopping carts and fleeing without paying. When the manager tried to stop them, he got run over in the parking lot, and some continued stomping him to the ground. I don't know if he'll live," I said.

"Omg," Kat said in disbelief.

"I know right? Our local news is running phone videos that citizens have been sending in. One is of a psycho girl and her crazy friends kicking her parents out of their home. She shot her dad in the leg and killed her mom. The dad called

358

the police, and they surrounded the home, but the crazies set the house on fire and went out the back door with knives. The police shot the psycho girl dead. The crazies turned and enveloped the cops with knives. The pack — they are now calling them — have not been caught," I said.

"Holy shit! We haven't seen it that bad here. Why don't you come stay with me for a little while until these calms down?" Kat said, "We should be together if the world is falling apart!"

"I wish I could come to you or you to me. Just be careful, and if it gets worse, call me," I said. "I'll come to Atlanta and get you!"

Chapter 5: Where's My Mom

Sam

My mom called. When I answered, I didn't recognize the phone number, and her voice was weird. My mom was terrified; I could hear it in her voice.

She spoke quickly and clearly. "Honey, it's Mom. Please listen. I'm on a burner phone, and you won't be able to call me back. I want you to know I love you, first and foremost."

"Mom, a burner phone?" My heart was beating fast; *how does she even know about burner phones*, I thought.

"Please just listen, Sam. The second thing is I want you to know I'm going public with information about Halle; it's not good. I have an appointment with Donna Love at Fox News. I was warned that I would lose my job if I spoke out or divulged any confidential information about Halle, but my colleague Dr. Campbell and I are headed to the news station right now. Honey, this goes all the way up to the White House."

"Oh my gosh. What will you say, Mom?"

"Don't eat or take Halle. It could kill you or make you crazy. Halle is the only common denominator, Sam. We don't know why some people get symptoms and some don't. But if I don't warn people, I'll never forgive myself," she said.

"Yes, I know you, Mom. I love you so much. Please be careful. You could get more than fired if they try to suppress the truth. Is that why you have a burner phone?"

No answer...

"Mom?"

"Yes, I will call you after the interview." She hung up.

That was the last time I spoke to my mom. *It has been three days now.*

No one can reach her, and she hasn't gone home.

I call Donna Love and tell her what my mom told me. She tells me to come to the station ASAP.

"We are here with Samantha Archer. She is a private investigator at Alias Investigations in Tallahassee, Florida.

"Good morning, Samantha. I've been told you have a message for the public." Says Donna Love.

"Good morning, Donna. Yes, my mom is one of the research scientists from PureAgra, that created PKZ. She and another one of the researchers, Dr. Raj Campbell, have been missing for three days now," I say.

A photo of both doctors is on the tv screen as I continue my story.

"When I last spoke to her, she was on her way to this studio to speak with you, Donna, and to make an important announcement. She told me PureAgra found a connection between Halle supplements and strange illnesses. My mom said she wants the public to be aware. Do not take the Halle supplements! She said the government is trying to bury responsibility, which goes all the way up to the White House. My mom was scared and said she would call me after meeting you, Donna. Unfortunately, I've been told that she never showed up. Please, if anyone has any information, contact Alias Investigations or the police. Our phone number is 850-518-8713."

"Thank you, Ms. Archer," says Donna. "We have called PureAgra and the White House for a comment on this interview. Both have declined to speak with us. What do you think? Let us know by logging on to our website and clicking on the link: Is there a conspiracy?" says reporter Donna.

I walk outside and realize I have started a media flurry. My cell phone begins blowing up with fourteen voicemails. It's so crazy. I had multiple threats from strangers demanding that I prove my allegations. Others who called were thanking me. I sit in my car and listen. The last message I have is from Chris Finch.

Chapter 6: Are You Afraid

Sam

"Hi Samantha, I saw you on tv. Please come and see me right away, now if possible. Don't go home," Chris's message says. "Please. It's very important." He has never called me, and his voice has such a sense of urgency.

I feel compelled, so I drive to the prison first instead of going home. I'd been given permission as a Private Detective to see him for help on his case during the pre-trial, the trial, and appeals. I am hoping I am still on the list of professionals and find that I am, thank goodness.

After we're given a bit of privacy, Chris asks, "Are you afraid?"

"Afraid of what," I ask, but I know what he will say. My brain didn't want to believe it, but I had just put myself in a risky position.

"You are in jeopardy, Sam. You shouldn't go home. There are dangerous people that have a lot invested in Halle. If it's as bad as your mom said, and you leaked the information, you're in trouble," he warns.

"Mom hasn't been located yet Chris, I had to speak out. These people can't be allowed to get away with this!" I feel like crying and am angry.

"I know; I understand your dilemma. But, Sam, I've been thinking," he says as he looks at me intently.

"Go on, Chris, tell me. What do you think I should do? Stay, Run, Hide?"

It seems Chris is wrestling with something. Then, finally, he speaks.

"Samantha. I would greatly appreciate it if you would do me a huge favor."

"What's that?"

"Everything I do is calculated, Samantha. I would never do this for anyone else, but I trust you. Please get out of town, go to my family. I want you to be safe, and I obviously can't protect you from here." He shrugs and looks around the visitor's area. "I believe you going on the national news put you in extreme danger, especially since your mom and her colleague are still missing. I don't want that to happen to you," he says. "If you visit my family, you will know I trust you with those I love most dearly. They are a protective family and secretive, but if you are willing to go, I will let them know you are coming and that you can be trusted. If you go there, you will be protected, and no one, I mean no one, will get to you."

I sit, shocked by what he is saying. For so long, I have tried to learn more about him, personally, and he would never let me in. Now he is asking me to go to his family, who is, as far as anyone knows, probably outlaws.

"My family will help you devise a plan. Trust me; they are good at planning. I know I screwed up and got myself put in jail, and my brother Matthew killed. That wasn't a plan we devised. I was impulsive, reckless, and emotional, and it was stupid on my part, and now I'm paying for it. I may even die in here. Please go, Samantha; I fear for your life."

This is all happening too fast. Is this the right play? I think.

"Do you think I'm really in that kind of danger?" I ask. "Like someone might try to hurt me or kill me?"

"Yes, Samantha, and I think it is your only play," he says. "I would never offer my family up to anyone, but you need them."

I sit and think for a long time about how scared my mom was and how she is now missing. My mom would get in touch with us if she could. So, either she's been kidnapped or killed.

"Okay, Chris, tell me what to do," I say.

"Drive to my lawyer's office and tell her I sent you. She will say, 'Then you must know his password.' You tell her 'StarCraft,' and she will give you a burner cell phone and cash for gas, food, and clothes you will need to buy later. If there is anyone you need to call before you disappear, call them outside of the prison and then drop the phone right there, crush it, and toss it in a trash can. Samantha do not tell anyone you are leaving. Act as if you are heading home. Don't blow it," he instructs.

"Okay, I'll be cool, but I'm scared."

"Oh yes, you should be. Along with losing your real phone, you need to lose all your credit cards. Cut them up, flush them, or burn them. I don't care how you do it. Be quick, Samantha. Lawyer, money, and leave. Do not go home. It would be best if you were on the road when I call you with directions. If you get done before I call, leave, and drive toward Washington, D.C.," he says.

"Chris, thank you for your help. I guess I'll finally learn about your past," I say with a smile.

He smiles back. "Maybe you will, Samantha. Remember, Jill Coker, money and leave. Got it?"

I nod my head and wonder if I will ever see him again.

I text my sister Kat and my brother Mark I say, "Hi, there! I'm in a hurry, but I wanted to say I love you. I have some things I need to do, so if you don't hear from me for a little while, don't worry. Remember, I'm a Private Detective, and this is private. Stay safe. I'll contact you soon. Love you, Samantha."

Here I go. Lawyer, money, and leave.

Part Fourteen: 2023-2024

"True life is lived when tiny changes occur,"

Leo Tolstoy

Chapter 1: Carl's Vision

Bonnie: Notes to Chris, From Her Diary

Dear Chris,

We've been in West Virginia for a little over two years, I can't believe we own over two hundred acres of forest land and that you aren't here with us.

We started developing the land from the plans you wrote before all things went to hell in a hand basket.

We divided the land into four quadrants. The main road splits east and west, as well as north and south.

The lower west quadrant is dedicated to the RV Park and is gated. You said this would be a profitable and easy financial investment and the perfect location for camping people to stay when visiting West Virginia. It has a small beach for swimming, a lake for boating and fishing, as well as, mountains for hiking. Every site has its own sewage dump, electricity, and running water.

The lower east quadrant is a family cabin community and is gated. It's built for anyone searching for sanctuary from domestic violence and child abuse. Your friend from the Women's shelter is still in our lives and will send us the people in need of protection. This development also has a community park with a gazebo, picnic shelters, playground, dog park and a large pond for fishing.

The West and East top quadrants are our private residence and starts at mile marker twelve. We have a barn left of our cabin, an archery and shooting range in the back, and a greenhouse on the right side.

We set the place up as a survivalist cabin as soon as we arrived. I hope one day you will be able to see how your vision has come to life. All the walls in the basement have been reinforced and welded together. That was the first completed project.

Lea says, "The basement is badass."

The wall on your right is set up like an armory. Our gun safe holds automatic weapons and cash. We are filling the wall with easy-to-grab shotguns, semi-automatics, and pistols. It is built to withstand fires, storms, and animal or human attacks. Ha!

I make weekly food lists and have designated the back wall of the basement for a food pantry, I have all the staples — plus.

Sherry and Saul have set up the left side wall with two generators, two freezers, and a backup refrigerator.

Saul and Sherry have also spent many days and untold hours building a six-foot critter fence around all 206 acres.

I told them we could have hired someone to build the fence.

Saul said, "Yes, but we enjoy the work."

Sherry agreed, she said "It's a labor of love. We enjoy working together and having something to do all day."

I think I'm jealous because I miss you and wish you were here. We love you.

Chapter 2: Love and Marriage

Bonnie: Notes to Chris, From Her Diary

Good morning Chris,

Today we are sitting outside on the deck, relaxing. The view is incredible. Mountains and forests for miles, unbelievably peaceful.

Good news! Saul and Sherry are engaged, they are on the porch with me as I write. Ha, ha, Sherry is holding her hand up to towards the sky to look at her engagement ring sparkle in the sun, AGAIN. She's been doing that all morning.

Lea is telling her that we can have a small wedding on our deck at sunrise — and she will officiate the wedding. Our world has become so crazy that getting ordained is as simple as filling out an online form on the internet. It seems they ordain anyone who wants to solemnize weddings now.

Hi Chris, me again. We had the ceremony this morning. It was simple, and it was sunrise. Lea officiated, and I was a witness. The words they said to each other were beautiful.

Saul told Sherry, "Every morning I get up, I am so thankful to God, because you saved me from a life of sorrow. Sherry, you are everything my heart, mind, and soul have ever desired. I want to wake up to you every morning for the rest of my life."

Sherry said, "Saul, you are the same person to me. I feel rescued as well. I would never want a single day without you in my life."

They kissed and it is DONE!

Lea and I hired a contractor to build Saul and Sherry a cottage, so they can have a regular married life. It is so cute and has its own path to and from the main cabin. They love it.

We also drove back to Tallahassee to visit Matthew's grave site. Andrea met us at the cemetery, and afterward, we all went to lunch at the Midtown Caboose.

You have 38 years left on your sentence. I'm still hoping you'll get out sooner.

Communicating through a lawyer with you is tougher than I thought it would be. I know we agreed if any of us were ever caught, this would be the plan. But I hate it! I want to see you and talk to you. Life isn't the same without you Chris.

There is a lot happening worldwide. The most disturbing news is a mysterious illness that's spreading across the nation. People are getting sick, and they have weird symptoms, and you never recover. After that, the immune system shuts down, and then you go crazy.

The World Project's nutritional products Halle have been suspected as the possible cause, but the company denies the accusations.

There's no cure, they don't even know what it is causing some people to get sick but not others. We have been staying in our bubble.

Oh, and about Lea, we drove down to Tupelo to see her mom a for a surprise birthday visit. Just Lea and I. Lea put a down payment on a retirement home for her mom, in the 62-plus community where her mom's best friend Nancy lives. She's so happy.

Chapter 3: Cell Block C

Chris

Cell Block C is full of long-timers. The boss of our cell block is Anton. We met day one of my imprisonment.

I'm assigned to cleaning duties. After work, we go to the yard for an hour. Anton is doing a bench chest press, and it is loaded. When he sees me, he racks the weight, gets up slowly, and walks my way. I don't want a confrontation and decide to make myself look pissed off at the world. He still approached.

"I hear you killed five men for beating up their wives."

I looked him in the eye and nodded my head once.

He nods back once in acknowledgment. His buddies came up behind him.

"Did you like hurtin' em'?" he asks.

"Yep," I say.

"I'm Anton, boss of Cell Block C. If you need anything, you come to me. Got it?" he asks.

"Yep," I say.

Anton nods his head and walks off.

Most inmates avoid me the first few weeks. I'm in for the long haul, and eventually, they see I want no trouble. I work hard and don't talk a lot. I'm the quiet one.

Life in prison is about habits, so it's been an easy adjustment. Every morning, guards wake us at 6 am for a formal inmate count.

We have breakfast at 7:00 am, and by 7:45 am, we're headed to our work assignments inside the prison. I work as a cleaner. It's satisfying and an independent job. I work until noon, have thirty minutes for lunch, and then return to work until 3:00 pm.

They take us to the prison yard from 3:00 pm to 4:00 pm. We, we can check our mail or spend some time on recreation.

We're taken to our cells from 4:00 to 5:00 pm, and dinner is at 5:00 pm. In addition, we have religious, and specialized programming options include narcotics anonymous, anger management, access to the gym, auditorium, and recreation yard options from 6:00 until 8:00pm.

There's non-contact visitation with individuals on our approved visiting list Wednesdays, Fridays, Saturdays, and Sundays. The visits are usually from one to one- and one-half hours max.

We return to our cell block at 8:00 pm, another formal inmate count occurs.

Afterward, we can watch television, play cards, checkers, and chess, write letters, read books, and socialize within our cell block.

At 11:00 pm, it's lights out. The next day, repeat.

Jill, my lawyer, comes on Fridays to review what she is doing for my case through appeals and other charges brought on from 1969 when I burned down Bonnie's home with her parents inside. They only have circumstantial evidence and zero physical evidence. Jill says that she believes it will probably go nowhere.

Jill is trying to get an earlier release date for me, but it's not looking promising.

"Remember, Chris, you're lucky you didn't get first-degree murder."

Chapter 4: Sam's Coming, Protect Her

Lea

"Guys, I got a call from Chris's lawyer, Jill. She relayed a message from Chris about a Samantha Archer," I say.

"Who?" Saul asks.

"She's the private detective who drove to Tupelo to talk to my mom. Remember?" I say.

"Sure, I remember." Saul says.

"Well, I just found out that she's been visiting Chris since he was first arrested. Chris says when they first met, it was because of me. She's still hunting for me. Chris believes he's led her away from that suspicion and they've become friends. It seems Samantha is in serious trouble right now and Chris wants to send her to us, for protection."

"What?" Bonnie asks.

"Yeah. Chris said Samantha is important. He told her we would help her. Also, Bonnie? He said he loves us."

"WTF," I say, confused. "Did Jill say why Samantha is in trouble?"

"Just that her mom works for PureAgra. Her mom was scheduled to give a tv interview, exposing the connection to Halle. Now, her mother is missing. Samantha decided to do the interview with the TV station and tell them everything her mom told her. Chris believes she is in grave danger, literally. He met with her this afternoon and will call us within the hour to let us know if she'll come. He'll only have a short time to talk, so his lawyer called ahead with the background information."

Chapter 5: In Good Hands

Sam

Chris called. "Hi Samantha, I'm assuming you're driving. Can you pull over? I need you to write something down," Chris asks.

"I am I have you on the speaker. I see a roadside diner. Hold on a sec, pulling over now."

He waits.

"Go ahead," I say.

"The number is 394-982-3406. Lea will be expecting your call."

"Who is she?" I ask.

"You can trust her, Samantha. She will take care of you," he says.

"Okay. Thanks again, Chris."

"Yep, and since you've pulled over at a diner, you should go in, eat some pie, drink coffee, and use the bathroom. You have a long ride ahead," he says.

I sit at the counter on a barstool. I contemplate my options. I can go back and take my chances.

Maybe the phone threats are just that — threats — or perhaps they are real. I don't know.

I finished my pie and was on my second round of coffee when I saw a news banner scroll across the tv. Missing doctors; found dead in the Potomac.

"Sir, can you please turn up the volume on the tv?"

"Yes, ma'am, I heard about them, doctors. It's been all over the news for the past hour," he says.

CBS reports, "This morning, a car was pulled out of the Potomac River. Inside were two bodies that have now been identified as Dr. Stephanie Archer and Dr. Raj Campbell. The exact cause of death appears to be gunshot wounds to the back of the heads, execution style. More to come at 5:00 pm on your favorite news station WCTV Tallahassee."

I go to the bathroom and throw up. I flush and put the lid down. Then I sit on the toilet and start crying. I'm not sure how long I was in the bathroom, but I return to the counter when I compose myself. "Can I have a coffee to go?" I ask.

"Coming up," he says. Then, when he returned the coffee, he asks, "Miss, are you okay?"

I nod yes, then use my burner phone to call Chris's family.

"Hello," says a female voice.

"Hi there, my name is Samantha. Is this Lea?" I ask.

"Yes, Samantha, we've been expecting your call. I will give you the address to put in your navigation system."

"Okay, it will take you at least 14-plus hours to get here, so I've arranged for you to stay overnight at the Hilton Embassy Suites in Brunswick, GA. Your room has been paid for. I don't think anyone can track you since you've trashed your credit cards and old phone, but we need to dump your car. There will be a White Wrangler Jeep at the hotel when you arrive. The keys will be at the desk with your room key. Just tell them your name is Sam Tipper when you walk in. The desk person will be expecting you."

"Thank you, Lea," I say. "What about my car? Do I leave it?"

"Yes, I arranged with the Jeep dealership to pick up the car tomorrow from the hotel. He said he could pay blue book value and wire the money tomorrow afternoon."

"That's okay, but I'm scared, and things are happening very fast right now," I say.

"Umm, Samantha, have you seen the news?" she asks.

"Yes, they found my mom," I say. My voice is shaking, and my eyes are full of tears again. I just want to cry.

"Yes, they did. I'm so sorry, honey. Look, I'll call you in the morning." Lea says. "Just get something to eat at the hotel and charge it to the room, then get a good night's sleep if you can."

I make it to Brunswick, check in at the hotel, and order room service and a bottle of wine. Finally, I cry myself to sleep.

My entire life is changing. My mom is gone, and I'm not sure about my future. There are a million thoughts running through my head. I use the burner and text my sister and brother as cryptically as possible.

The next morning I have a long drive. My mind is running from here to there and everywhere. But always coming back to my family.

Lea calls me after I've been on the road for about two hours. "Good morning, Samantha, do you know when you'll arrive?"

"Hi Lea, my navigation says I'll arrive in Petersburg, WV, at 6:32 pm."

379

"Okay. I'll meet you at the Cafe' Cafe' — that's the address. I work there, and I'll have a table ready, you'll be hungry. Call if you get lost or need anything," says Lea.

"Okay," I say. "I have on jeans, a white blouse, a brown leather jacket, and boots."

As I drive I also think of Chris. I have no idea why, but for some reason, I began trusting Chris even before his trial was over. I know he's guilty as charged. Yes, I do know that. It was vigilante acts against cruel men, and I'm not sure how I feel about that yet.

He's kept his life before Tallahassee like poker cards. I have to ask myself, 'Why do I trust him?' And I think, he's genuine, easygoing, compassionate, and a murderer.

My brain tells me I am taking a scary chance going to these people he calls his family, but my heart tells me it is the right move. I'm going strictly on instinct.

I arrive in Petersburg, WV, and quickly find the Cafe' Cafe'. I'm scared and nervous.

When I go inside, I immediately see Lea, and she sees me. She looks about my age, her hair is blonde in a short sassy, cut, she's fit and beautiful. I can sense her tough, confident spirit as she approaches me.

She hugs me and says, "Hi, Sam." We sit at the table. "So, heads up, I work here part-time," Lea informs me. "I'll introduce you as my best friend from high school." She smiles, and my heart skips a beat. What the heck?

"Sounds good," I reply.

"Are you okay?" Lea asks.

"Yes, there is just so much happening. I think I'm overwhelmed."

"It's okay, Sam. You are in good hands," Lea says, reaching across the table, taking my hands into hers and gently squeezing them. "So, we live about 20-30 minutes from here. Are you hungry?" she asks. "The BLTs here are amazing.

"Yes, I'm famished. I didn't want to stop except for gas stations. I ended up eating chips and doughnuts," I say.

Our waitress comes over, "Alicia, this is Sam Tipper. She is my best friend from high school. Sam, this is Alicia, my co-worker here at Cafe' Cafe'," says Lea.

"Hi there, very nice to meet you. Are you hungry, or would you like something to drink?" she asks me.

"I think I'll try the BLT with no T, and a glass of water. I've had way too much caffeine today," I say.

"I got you, sugar. I'll be right back with your water."

"Carl told me you are a private detective; what is that like?" Lea asks.

"The work is a lot of surveillance, interviewing people, gathering information, online public and court records searches. Checking for civil judgments and criminal history, evidence for clients, uncovering clues. It's not all that glamorous, but it can be very satisfying," I say.

"Why didn't you become a police detective? Why go Private Eye?" Lea asks.

"I just want to focus on finding missing persons, specifically kids, and didn't want someone controlling my career. I'm my own boss, we have cases that are all over the place, and I help work them. But, if I have a case that interests me, I can work the case's that interest me. I have a kidnapping case I've worked on for about forty years."

"That's a long time for one case," Lea says.

Samantha replies, "Full Disclosure, I thought Chris was part of kidnapping two young girls. Since I've gotten to know him, I find it hard to believe he could or would. Unfortunately, he is also a vigilante, murderer, and arson. It's a bit confusing why."

"Understood," Lea says and smiles. "Listen, as far as Chris goes, he would never harm anyone who didn't deserve it. I trust him and his instincts wholeheartedly, and if he believes you are in grave danger and need protection. You will be safe with us."

"Thank you. Chris hasn't told me anything about you all except that he trusts you," I say.

"He doesn't tell much to anyone, so please don't feel bad. Chris likes to keep things close to his chest. He's always been very private, even with his family."

Alicia returns with the BLT (no T), and I realize it's the best sandwich I've ever eaten, or I was starving. Lea cleans her section for the evening, as I finish dinner. The jukebox is playing Alanis Morissette, *I would be good*. In time, I think I will be.

Chapter 6: She's Sick

Lea

"I know you left in a hurry, but the good news is Petersburg is one of the coolest little mountain towns in the country and has excellent shopping. So, let's leave your Wrangler here at Cafe' Cafe' tonight so you can relax; you have to be exhausted from driving all day."

"Yeah, I am. I feel tired, sad, and scared. It's a lot," Sam says.

"We'll come back tomorrow to pick it up and shop for clothes and anything else you might need."

Saul and Bonnie were waiting for us on the porch. After introductions and small talk, we give Sam a tour of our home.

"You'll have Sherry's old room. Sherry and Saul are married and now live in the little cottage we passed on our way in," I say.

Bonnie says, "Sherry isn't here right now. She started getting sick about a year ago. We weren't concerned initially, but she hasn't gotten better."

"What kind of sick?" Sam asks.

Saul says, "She began having major headaches, earaches, and low-grade fevers. The symptoms didn't disappear, so we took her to Dr. Loobie in town. She sent Sherry a prescription for antibiotics, allergy, and migraine medicine and sent her home. Three weeks later, Sherry began acting frantic, disturbed, forgetting who she was. We'd heard on TV about some strange new disease spreading that causes physical and psychological problems, even death. None of us thought it would touch us."

Bonnie says, "After a few days, we went back to Dr. Loobie." Her first question was, "When did the gold ring around her pupils appear?"

"It started about a week ago, maybe a little longer." Saul says.

"Okay, I'll make an appointment for her at Mazer Research Hospital in Washington. Will you able to take her to Washington D.C. next week?'

"I'll take her the very minute you can get her in."

"Little did we know that once we took her to Washington, she wouldn't return home with us." I say.

Saul says, "She's been poked and prodded by the top doctors, including Dr. Michelle Wong, who is said to be the best of the best. We stayed in a hotel near the hospital for the first two weeks, but her mind got worse, and her obsessive inner ear itching never seemed to stop."

I continue, "Dr. Wong reported her findings. Sherry has a mass in her brain and deep in her ear canals. They're working on treatments, but she can't guarantee anything. We have been driving to Washington once a week, hoping to get answers and checking on her progress."

"When will you guys go again?" Sam asks as we walk through the home.

"In two days, we'll make our way to Washington. Would you like to go with us?" Saul asks.

"Yes, I would. Did Chris tell you guys about me? I mean, why I'm running?" Sam asks.

Saul replies, "Chris said your mother went missing right before she was about to blow the whistle on PureAgra. You then went on television to tell what she knew, which put you in big-time danger. Chris said he trusts you and wants us to help and protect you. He feels whoever killed your mom and the other doctor will want to silence you too."

"Yeah, that's about right. The thing is, they can't silence me now. The cat is out of the bag. My mom believes — believed — that Halle is the cause of all the strange new diseases and mental illness problems that are increasing each year. With the mysterious deaths and people going insane, she decided to go public which was against the company's directive," she says.

"Saul and Sherry were a part of the trials, and Sherry started taking Halle soon after it became available on the shelves," Bonnie says. "We believe what your mom says is true. I think a lot of people do. She was one of the good guys, Sam, and I'm sorry for your loss."

"Why aren't the other scientist speaking out?" Saul asks.

"They are probably scared to death, especially now," I say as we walk into Sam's new room. "This is where you'll sleep. If you need a different pillow or extra blanket, knock on the door across from you, that's my room. I know you're exhausted. When you wake tomorrow, come downstairs for breakfast and coffee." I hug her goodnight. "Try to get a good night's rest, Sam." Samantha hugged me back.

The following morning, Sam sleeps until 10:00 am. "I normally wake at 6:30 or 7:00 am," she says. "Do you guys have a spare toothbrush?"

We shop for clothes, shoes, and other necessities, and pick up the jeep. When we get home, Saul has cooked pork chops on the grill for dinner, and we have an early night.

The next day, we drive to Washington to visit Sherry at the hospital. Trying to get into the hospital is a mess. There are hundreds of Halle demonstrators in front of the gates. The distrust of Halle in mass has begun.

Signs are everywhere, and many people are chanting, "STOP production of Halle; the next to die could be me!"

"We are here to mobilize ... Fighting back against their lies!"

"No more secrets, no more lies. No more silence that money buys."

"If Halle takes one life, it is a death to us all."

"I had no idea this was going on," Sam says.

"You did this, Sam. It started after your message went out to the public," Saul says.

"It looks like you and your mom were successful in outing Halle. Hopefully, the government will respond and shut PureAgra down!" says Bonnie.

"I'm very proud of you. What you did took a lot of guts," Saul says.

We discover they had transferred and admitted Sherry into the mental health wing. But unfortunately, her behavior has gotten worse. They usher us into a waiting room on the new wing, and about an hour later, a psychologist, Dr. Hemingway, comes in and takes us to her room. It's actually a room with an observation window.

"We can't let you go in to visit her right now. She's extremely agitated and thinks a bug is in her ear is digging deep inside. We assured her there is nothing there and bandaged her ear. We've sedated her so she can rest but I wanted you to see that she is okay and being cared for."

Saul asks, "Will my wife ever get better?"

"I can tell you this Saul, so many doctors are working on this. If anyone can get better, it will be her," Dr. Hemingway says.

"Would you promise to call me if anything changes? I want to see, talk, and touch my wife. We'll stay at the Marriott. I want to be here for her," Saul says.

"Yes, I will, Saul. Leave the room number on your sign-out sheet."

We leave.

As each day passes, the news becomes scarier. There are now more than 100,000 cases of 'The Experimental's.'

"Maybe it's an incubation time," I say.

There is panic worldwide, and fear is building, which led to rumors, rioting, robbery, and murders.

Saul is able to visit with Sherry almost every day over the next two weeks. Then, Dr. Hemingway calls and says, "Saul, it's time. If you want to come see her and say goodbye to Sherry, you need to come now. I'm sorry."

We leave the hotel immediately. We are able to say goodbye to her. She isn't talkative and is highly sedated, but we say our peace. Saul says, "I love you, Sherry. I'm thankful for you, because of you, I know what it feels like to be loved." Saul weeps.

We we're asked to leave, but Saul was able to stay with her through the night. The following day, we arrive early, and Dr. Hemingway meets us when we check-in. She says, "Sherry passed in her sleep early this morning. Saul is with her now; I'm so very sorry."

Saul is devastated. Nothing is more agonizing than when someone you love with all your heart is sick, and you can't do a damn thing about it. He is heartbroken.

Part Fifteen: 2024-2028

"You do not know what will happen tomorrow. For what is your life, really? It is a vapor that appears for a little time, and then vanishes away,"

James Four: Fourteen.

Chapter 1: Spreading Madness

Samantha

The death of life as we knew it came slowly and unexpectedly. It's December of 2028, Christmas Eve — at least, I think so.

The sky is a brilliant blaze of fiery orange and red with wisps of clouds mingled in; it is beautiful. I'm thankful that something in this world has remained the same — a constant.

There has been so much death and destruction. Madness has gone rampant. The big cities that I remember driving through as a kid are no longer here, or they are filled with chaos. I've watched the cute shops, restaurants, and small towns slowly vanish. Destroyed.

I wonder why no one saw this coming. I did; I knew something was wrong with our world for years, but it eluded me to understand how to stop it.

Maybe others did see the same, but no one was able to keep it from happening.

It's like living with someone trying to lose weight; we don't notice the subtle changes in them until it's been months, and then, suddenly, we see it.

In this case, the change wasn't in months but in just a few years. We live mostly off the grid, in the woods. The woods have changed also, and what was once my fascination as a child is now the safety in which I live each day.

What's left of the small towns and big cities are rioted streets, ransacked homes, and empty grocery stores. And the Experimental's? Well, they are everywhere.

The woods are the best place to hide from them because they are afraid of the woods; we're not sure why.

The Nobel Prize was given and received by the top scientists of the World Project. The benefits of the project were shared around the whole world. But the ugly truth of the supplement was hidden from us by the need for fame and fortune of others — such arrogance.

Many who worked on bringing the supplements to the masses knew the possible dangers, but they deceived themselves into believing it was worth the risk. Deceived themselves that the good that would come outweigh the bad.

Halle was safe for us all, they said. No side effects could be found, they said. Perfect and healthy, they said.

If we had known the dangers and the side effects, and had at least been given a choice, more of us would be alive today. We would still have our homes, jobs, and a life.

Chapter 2: One of the Crazies

Samantha

It's been nine months since I moved to WV with Chris's family.

We're watching the news when a breaking story from the front entrance of the Washington Halle Facility rocked our world. Media and the public were invited to attend.

"Thank you for coming. My name is Dr. Natalie Bailey. I'm one of the remaining doctors working on a cure for those affected by Halle," Dr. Bailey says. "My best friend and colleagues, Dr. Archer and Dr. Campbell, were murdered for trying to reveal the truth about the monstrous effects that Halle has caused on so many lives. Our world has been devastated. So many of us have lost friends and family due to the horrific side effects of Halle."

A small crowd of spectators have gathered around the podium.

Natalie continues, "The last time I spoke to Dr. Archer, she was going to interview with Love Productions. Dr. Archer was working hard to find a cure for the adverse effects that Halle is having on more than twenty percent of our population. I recently found her journal and a letter with a formula she planned to test on the Experimental's, or Crazies, as they have been named. Not a vaccination, but a cure.

"I am announcing today that I have followed through with her testing and created a cure from her formula," Dr. Bailey says.

The news cameras begin panning the audience. Many are clapping and cheering, but some are nasty and angry. The crowd is getting loud and confusing, and we watch as people begin to push each other. The cameras zooms in on two men yelling at each other. One is uninfected, but the other, you can see it in his eyes. He's crazy.

In that very moment, the infected crazy, attacks the uninfected, falling upon him and ripping his throat out. Blood is running down the Experimental's chin. He is insane.

"People, listen, please listen!" Dr. Bailey shouts. "All we have to do is..."

Next, we are seeing through the eyes of another cameraman. An Experimental's is charging the podium where Natalie is giving her report. He has a butcher knife in his hand.

The camera person must have left the camera to help because the view went from Dr. Bailey to the ground. All we can see are stumbling feet, then a man dropping to the ground and being stabbed to death.

Within seconds, Natalie joins him on the ground and she's dead. There is a loud cheer of glee of triumph in the background. It sounds monstrous and makes chills go down my spine.

The uninflected begin tackling the infected, and it's anarchy next, throughout the US and possibly the world.

"We have to get that formula. We have to fight back," I say.

"Agreed. Maybe we can find Dr. Bailey's home since your mom was her friend," Bonnie says. "What PureAgra did your mom and Dr. Bailey work from?" Bonnie asks.

"They were was based in Atlanta, but moved between the facilities. Let's start with the Washington branch since it's close and a good starting point," I say.

"I want to destroy PureAgra," Saul says.

"Me too, but first, we must find the cure," Lea says.

"Yes, but we will destroy every PureAgra facility that makes Halle along the way," Saul replies.

We begin our search for the cure in the Washington PZK facility, but by the time we arrive, there are only dead bodies on the floor. The building that held the Experimental's patients and staff is destroyed. It looks like a breakout, with fighting, blood, and death.

We check the admin offices for personnel files and can find nothing on my mom or Dr. Bailey.

"Can we set it on fire?" Bonnie asks.

"Let's do it!' says Saul.

We do.

We go home and pack up our Jeeps with supplies. Bonnie and Saul take the Cherokee, and Lea and I take the Wrangler. We now have a mission. We will burn down all PZK facilities that produce Halle. If the government doesn't do something about the outbreak, we will.

We drive to Baltimore, Richmond, Raleigh, and Columbia, searching each facility, but finding nothing. They have been rioted and emptied, so we burn them down.

We finally find Dr. Natalie Bailey's home address in the personnel files in Atlanta. Saul and Bonnie quickly break into her condo and search the place. I am impressed at how quickly they get inside and how efficient they are through the search.

"Hey, Lea, I found a hidden wall safe," calls Saul.

"Okay, got it," Lea responds.

"You can open a safe?" I ask Lea.

"You have no idea, Sam," Lea replies. "You've only known us a short time. We all have unique skill sets. I am going to try."

Lea works on the safe for about 30 minutes and finally cracks it. Inside were a dozen test tubes labeled Halle Cure and two envelopes; one was addressed to Natalie Bailey, and the second was to me.

My note from the safe read as follows:

"Hey Sam, I hope you never have to find this note or the formula on the back. But you are my little detective, and I am so proud of you. If anything happens to me, I know you will search for answers, and by doing so, you will clear my name and save hundreds of thousands of people with the cure. So please reach out to your brother and sister. Try to talk them into coming and staying with you, wherever you are. I want you to know how proud I am and have always been. You are my special kiddo. I love you.

P.S. The formula for the cure is on the back of this letter. xoxox, Mom"

As tears slowly run down my face, I feel Lea pull me close. She hugs me and gently kisses me right on the lips. The kiss lingers for what seems like forever, but it is probably only a couple of seconds. My heart is pounding.

Lea steps back and says, "Let's do what your mom wants us to do. Let's try to cure this madness in our world."

I think, *OMG, she likes me!*

Bonnie says, "Hey, Sam, wake up…where did you go?" She smiles. "Here, take this." She hands the envelope to me.

I look at Lea. "How can we save hundreds of thousands of people? We aren't scientists; I don't understand this formula."

Lea takes my hands into hers and says, "We just need to find someone who does understand Samantha and that we can do that."

Then Lea hugs me and kisses my lips lightly and quickly. I'm not sure what is happening, but it is the best feeling I've ever had, even amidst the tragic events happening all around us.

I later tell Lea, "Since the first day I met you, I found you to be the most beautiful person I've ever known. I didn't understand my feelings for you, but I do now, especially after that kiss."

Chapter 3: Rapid Domination

Lea

The world has gone to shit, and I'm tired.

After the public murder of Dr. Bailey on television, our president finally declared martial law, but it was too late.

Experimental's' roamed the streets, hijacking homes, scaring, and killing people, and raiding stores until the shelves were bare.

At first, the uninfected took what they could from their homes and fled into rural areas, then eventually into the woods for shelter away from the Experimental's.

Everything happened so fast. Governments from at least three countries blamed America for the Halle disease and demanded a cure, pushing America into war.

The threats from each country were genuine, and unfortunately, our country's military wanted war. The U.S. did not like being blamed, so we bombed China, Russia, and Iraq.

It was called the 'War of the Countries' and we are to blame. No one else, we created this monster and unleashed it. We did it.

The Experimental's' have succeeded in taking over our major cities and many small towns.

Our president had a major heart attack and died, and now our vice president is POTUS. As a result, our barely functioning government has completely broken down.

We have a silent world; no one is working or producing anything. The stores have been ransacked. The uninfected are starving and hunting animals for food, but the animals are hunting them at night. I sometimes hear their screams.

The military has been hunting us down for the destruction and arson of Halle buildings, but we haven't stopped.

We continue to destroy and avenge, and many others have joined our cause in time.

War within the United States of America between each other became inevitable.

The uninfected are fighting back for control, but we are behind the curve.

The Experimental's' are half crazy madmen, and they eventually become crazy as well. Fighting — well, it is all they know. They are angry from the inside out. Halle has eaten them alive.

We find a Dr. Grimes at one of the last two remaining facilities, in Tallahassee of all places.

We're had been hoping to find Dr. Grimes or Dr. Mayo. We hoped they can help us decipher this formula for a cure.

Unfortunately, Dr. Grimes has gone insane and is useless to us.

Chapter 4: Tallahassee Prison

Lea

After the Tallahassee facility, we go directly to the prison to see Chris.

We haven't been able to reach him by phone because of the breakdown in our infrastructure. Landlines are not dependable. Neither are cell phones. Sometimes you get lucky, but most of the time, you don't. When we were able to get through, we got no answer.

We pull up to the prison gate, and the guard let us right in with only a glance of our identification.

The guard says, "It's at your own risk. Since the breakout of Halle, we don't have enough guards, and I honestly don't know how much it matters anymore. We had over 20,000 employees, from guards to doctors to support services to kitchen staff. Now, we are running out of food and barely have a kitchen staff. Our guards can't take people in and out for recreation for even one hour a day; we have such a small staff. The guards are rotating cell blocks, and the prisoners are restless. We have approximately twenty guards left, five custodians, and two doctors.

We've locked all the Experimental's' into what we call the dungeon, which is now like a crazy house. One or two die off each day, but none of the guards will go in and pull the bodies out. Our remaining staff met yesterday; we think it's time to get out of here."

Samantha says, "You're kidding me, right? What will happen to all the prisoners?"

"We will let the healthy ones out to fend for themselves. The Experimental's' will be left to die in the dungeon. Nothing will help them now anyway. So why feed them? Why keep them alive?" he asks.

I think we are all shocked by what the guard is telling us.

"Can you tell us if Chris Finch is still one of the healthy ones?" Saul asks.

The guard starts tapping on his computer, looks up, and says, "Well, I know that name. Chris Finch is not sick. In fact, he has been one of the best cell block leaders we have ever had. His people are patient, have very few fights, have no crazy demands, and are not threatening the guards.

"Cell Block C is where you'll find him. A guard inside the door will take you to the cell block, but as I said, it is at your own risk. I'm not worried about his cell block. It's the cell blocks you have to pass through."

With that, he buzzes us into the prison.

Another guard takes us to Cell Block C. It isn't as bad as he made it out to be. I'd say the same jeering and gestures that have always accompanied prisons.

When we reach Cell Block C, the guard calls out, "Chris Finch, you have visitors; come forward."

Chris walks out of his cell; all the cell doors except the exit doors are open in this block. He is a little thin but firm and muscular. He has not shaved or had a haircut in quite a while, but to us, he looks terrific. He is alive, not dead or changed.

We all try to talk to him at once, and he smiles and then laughs. "Oh my gosh, you guys are a sight for sore eyes. I've missed you all and wish I could hug each of you!" Chris says.

We talk with Chris for a long time and share with him what has gone on outside these walls. He isn't surprised the world was going to shit.

"I knew something had to be happening out there. We keep losing prison guards left and right. Prisoners are going crazy attacking each other, attacking guards. Slowly but surely, people started disappearing from their cells and never came back. Our cell block had a long talk after a few months of this happening. We decided that if we were on our best behavior, we would probably be treated better and survive another day. We only had two guys in this block get removed since all this began to happen."

Samantha says, "Chris, my mom developed a cure before she died and said it works, but we have no one who can recreate the formula. We hope to find a doctor or scientist to help and deliver it to those who need it."

"It will cure them?" Chris asks.

"We believe it will cure most, probably not all. Some will likely be too far gone," Sam says.

"Chris the guards and staff are trying to decide what to do with you guys. They are running out of food and are down to a skeleton crew. We may be able to spring you guys. Can you recruit some of them to help us?" Bonnie says.

"Let me talk to the block for a few minutes," he says and explains what's happening outside.

Chris says, "We've been incarcerated for years, and jail has been hell. Most of us in Cell Block C have been together long enough to know each other's worst and best sides. What I am proposing may or may not be an option, but I'll propose it anyway. Who would like to get the F out of here?" The guys are rambunctious and jeering in their responses.

"If I can get us outta here, we'll enter a world we don't know," Chris continues. "My friends say that the infected are being called the Experimental's, and they're everywhere. Most of them are crazy and violent, although some are just sick. My friends have a formula that could be a vaccination, maybe even a cure. They need help finding someone who can mix the formula and figure out how to distribute it so we can take back our cities. They need muscle; going into the cities, searching for supplies, and fighting off the Experimental's' is a task."

"What has happened to our cities?" one of the prisoners asks.

"The crazies, or 'Experimental's,' have taken over, killed and rioted, taken what is ours,' Chris explains. "These crazies have a disease that could be cured, but until it is, they are an enemy. We have a cell block of good men, some of whom have done horrible things, including myself, but we think outside the box. I am asking each of you, would you like to help find a way to end this madness? Would you fight the enemy for your freedom?"

"How we gonna do that, boss? We're stuck in here," another prisoner says.

"I might have a way. But if I could make it happen, who would be with me? Who is willing to fight to get our lives back?"

The men are loud and respond with a resounding "We are!"

As the men begin to calm down, Chris reasserts his leadership. "My family is here to recruit us. To hopefully get us out of this hellhole and help us regain our dignity,"

Chris comes back to the gate.

"The guys, want to help."

Chris nods. "Not all of them will do what they say. I imagine a few will run the first chance they get, but I think the rest will love a direction, and a cause to fight. See if you can get us out," Chris says. The guys have agreed to follow my leadership and yours as well. And so don't be surprised if they ask you what to do."

After talking with Chris and Warden Gunther, the Warden says, "I think this could work to our advantage. I can send the rumor that we are letting prisoners out for good behavior. It will help a ton if they see the boys from Cell Block C being given their freedom. Hopefully, it will get the prison into a more manageable situation. Come back in 24 hours, and I will let them leave with you. I want the rumor to begin circulation first."

We come back the following day, and Gunther's waiting for us. He says, "It's already working; the cell blocks are calming down. Not completely, of course. It's better, though."

The prisoners from Cell Block C are taken out of the block and paraded throughout the prison. At each block, the head guard briefly speaks to the prisoners.

"Cell Block C have been the best-behaved prisoners since the outbreak. We want each block to have an early release, but I can't justify letting you out until we have proper order inside this building. Enough chaos is out there already, and I won't add more to the problem."

After finishing his part of the plan, each prisoner from Cell Block C is given their personal belongings, some cash they had earned, and a change of clothes. They are transferred to the visitor room, unhand-cuffed, and left to change.

Chris is with us again! We can't believe what has just happened. Unprecedented times are mingled with new ways of doing things. This could be good or bad; only the future can tell.

Chris hugs each of us and kisses our cheeks. "I've never missed anything or anyone so much," he says, as he picks up Bonnie and spins her around.

Chris then addresses the prison crew of Block C. "Everyone's been worried about their families and friends. Go to your homes, find your friends and families, and bring them back. Let's meet at 5 pm at the E.J. Huey Botanical Gardens. You guys be safe; watch out for the crazies. We're going to create an army," Chris says.

That afternoon, all but three of the prisoners show back up. We have twenty-eight able bodies, ready, willing, to start an army. Some of them brought their wife, girlfriend, sibling, or parent. Our total number is forty-six people.

Saul hot-wires a prison bus and parks it in the parking lot of the gardens, and we load everyone.

Saul and Bonnie take the lead vehicle in the Cherokee; Chris drives the bus, and Lea and I drive the Wrangler in the rear position.

It takes two days to get to our home in West Virginia.

I can't believe how deserted life has become. It seems so void of life. As we pass through cities, I see abandoned buildings, wreckage, trash, and filth. There are random people, but I don't think they are normal. Most gas stations still have pumps working, and many convenience stores have been boarded up, but some have doors wide open. We drive up, gas up, and take whatever, we find helpful.

We stop at several RV Sales Lots, picking up RVs for people to have sleeping quarters. As a result, we have two Jeeps, a prison Bus, and twenty-one RVs when we reach home.

We arrive at our gate, and as we enter the front of the property, Chris stops at each quarter-mile marker going up the road toward our cabin and directs two RVs at each marker to back into the campsite and set up their campers.

"We'll return on the bus and pick you guys for dinner in two hours," Chris says.

Chris is impressed with what we have completed on our property with the RV sites, cabins, cottage, gazebo, barn, fencing, and vegetable garden. He especially loves the survivalist basement and, of course, the gun safe.

"It's good to be out, and it's good to be home with all of you. I missed seeing the skies above me, feeling sunshine on my face, hearing birds singing in the woods, and inhaling the sweet smells in the air," Chris says, then, "I should have asked, do we have enough food for everyone to have dinner tonight?"

"Hungry?" Bonnie says as she smiles. "Yes, we have plenty of food. Let me give you the tour." She takes Chris to the basement.

Chapter 5: Fight Back

Lea

Dinner was easy, grilled hot dogs, hamburgers, and big pots of pork 'n' beans. There were way too many people to make anything else on such short notice.

The barn was to the left of the cabin, and everyone gathered there for dinner.

Chris called the meeting to order.

"Welcome to freedom, my friends," he begins.

Everyone claps.

"We have all agreed that we must fight against the Experimental's and take our lives and our homes back. We also need to find someone to help make the cure from the formula Sam's mom left. It will be tricky. Let's meet back here in the barn in the morning to figure out a plan. Rest up tonight and enjoy being out of the clink."

After the last straggler left, Chris says "Sam, can you and Lea greet each person in morning? Get their name and site number on a sign-up sheet?" Let them know that Bonnie and I will be speaking with each person/family individually to identify their unique talents so we can maximize our effectiveness in this fight.

So throughout the morning we spoke to each person and explained the need to secure a vehicle, preferably a four wheel drive. "Winter is coming and we will be scavenging, everyone will take turns. Bonnie and I will take you guys to the nearest town where you'll secure your rides."

Samantha's brother, Mark, and her sister, Kat, join us and we welcome them into our inner circle.

I say, "Chris, we need organization and lots of space. Bonnie, Samantha, and I have talked about dividing people by duties and calling it a division. That will clearly divide what each one will do to prepare us.

"Divisions?"" Chris asks.

Bonnie says, "Yes, let me show you the chart. I think it will help you see our vision." She lays the chart on the huge kitchen table. "Chris, you will be our leader. The building drawn is the hospital in Petersburg. We want to use it and create a home base." She says. "We can build our army over the winter and be ready by the spring. We need organization and space, the hospital will be perfect."

"Okay, explain the chart to me." He says.

Division #1

Location: Left Side of Hospital, 2nd floor and up.

Leaders: Samantha and Lea

Strategy, Development, and Organization

Division #2

Location: Right Side of Hospital, 2nd floor and up.

Leaders: Bonnie and Kat

Recruitment, Transportation, and Supplies.

Division #3,

Location: Morgue, Main Level, and Roof Top.

Leader: Saul and Mark

Security, Fighters, and Weapons

Kat says, "I'd like to help inspire unity. Can I create uniforms for our people?"

"Like what kind of uniforms?" Sam asks.

Kat says, "I want to create a design for each division. Fighters will need lots of pockets for ammo, guns, and knives. Uniforms that match the job."

"That sounds like a lot of work. You sure you're up for it?" Chris says.

"Don't worry; I'll get volunteers to help me. We have all winter to get ready. It'll keep me busy," Kat says.

In January 2025, our Trojan horse appeared. He introduced himself as Dr. Mayo and asked for a face-to-face meeting with Samantha Archer.

Lea took Dr. Mayo into Cafe'Cafe' to meet Samantha.

"Hello, Dr. Mayo. I'm Samantha, and this is Lea."

"Hi, Samantha and Lea. First, please let me say I'm so sorry about your mom. I tried to warn her, everyone thought I was against her, I wasn't. I knew what would happen if she tried to fight the system," he said."

"Thank you for letting me know, Dr. Mayo," Sam says.

"Someone told me you are looking for a doctor or scientist to reproduce your mother's cure. I believe I can do that, and I may have a few ideas for dispersal options. Would you take my help?" he asks.

"Of course, are you kidding me?!?! You have the knowledge we've been searching for, Dr. Mayo," Sam says.

"We'll put you in Division #1, you'll be in charge of Cure Development and Dispersal systems," Samantha says. "Lea is your Division Leader."

"Dr. Mayo, our division has the left wing of the hospital building from the second floor up. We all work together to give our other two divisions everything they may need to win our country back," I say.

He nods in agreement.

"Divisions two and three will carry on your work from there. Do you understand your part, and do you agree?" I ask.

"Yes, I do," he responds. "And please call me Will."

"Okay, Will," I say, then place an open book before Will.

"Our United States of America has lost most of its leaders. We plan to wipe out the evil ravaging our nation. I am documenting every person involved in this revolution. I am also recording everything we do to in order to succeed in destroying this disease. If it all goes as planned, this book will be copied and sent to nations all around the globe so that they can take back their own countries from the Experimental's. Do you understand?" I ask.

"Yes, I do," he replies.

"Please sign the book under the director of cure development and dispersal. Read the agreement to allow all of your work to be given freely worldwide and to use and replicate the cure and distribution system," I say. He reads the document and signs it.

He looks up to Samantha with sadness in his eyes. "Samantha, I did care about your mom. We worked on the PZK project for 8+ years before it was introduced to the world. We thought we were giving the world a gift," he says.

Sam nods her head. "I know Will, and PZK was a gift, but Halle destroyed it all."

When springtime came, we were ready to begin. The cure has been developed and made into large quantities. The dispersal system Dr. Mayo came up with is an old trick from the 1970s. Dispersing mosquito repellant with truck sprayers.

One of our engineers fit trucks with the spray equipment and tanks of the liquid cure and uses it to spray a small, populated area with Experimental's. It works.

The second system is Sprayer Backpacks, which is a large tank of the cure spray with a long nozzle sprayer. We all carry one of these on our backs for any individual attacks on us, which happens every time we go out now.

Time passes quickly as we continue to fight the Experimental's'. Within two years uninfected people have come from all over the United States to learn and reproduce what we are doing. As a result, the word is out, and the country is changing.

We have been severely attacked and lost many lives. We spray them with the cure or shoot them with guns if we must. For some of the Experimental's , the treatment does not help. The percentages for the cure depend on many things. For example, 60% of Experimental's' die because it's too late, and Halle destroys their brains. But, on the other hand, 40% survive mentally, and if there is growth, it kills the growth as well. When it doesn't work, it puts them out of their misery.

Bonnie interrupts my thoughts and asks," Do you wanna attack again tonight or wait until tomorrow?"

"Ask Chris, he's the boss." I say and give her a little knowing wink. Bonnie's cheeks become light pink, she and Chris were made for each other. They have become inseparable.

Our last stronghold is the west coast. We have gone through all the major cities up to Arizona with our dispersal systems. As we go, we teach the uninfected how to make and disperse the cure.

Later that evening we meet the others in our group and sit around camp talking. Bonnie says, "We'll head into California in the morning."

Saul says, "I've heard rumors, that the entire state is Experimental's and that any Infected person that dares go, never comes back."

"I heard the same." Carl says.

"Me too. Even so, we have the cure." Sam says.

"Yep." I say with the images of the *Walking Dead* series in my head. *The hoards are coming.*

"But will we be able to get close enough to them? I don't know, I'm thinking the trucks are our best bet."

Bonnie asks, "Chris, can you play *Just Before the Battle Mother.*"

Chris nods and begins to play. One by one each person's voice blends into the song.

Just before the battle, Mother, I am thinking most of you. While upon the fields, we're watching, with the enemy in view. Comrades, brave, are around me lying, filled with thoughts of home. For well, they know that on the morrow. Some will sleep beneath the sod. Farewell, Mother, you may never press me to your heart again. But you'll not forget me, Mother, If I'm numbered with the slain.

Afterwards, Samantha says, "Thank you, guys; I really miss my mom."

"I understand. I miss my mom, too," I say.

411

"Where is your mom?" Samantha asks. "You've never talked to me about her, or your dad. It seems you know all about me, but I know very little about you, Lea."

"You're right; my mom is 80 years old now. I want to see and spend time with her when we finish our mission. I didn't get to spend much of my younger years with her, but we reconnected later, and it was as if we had never been apart."

"Oh, I didn't know. I'm sorry," Sam says. "When you go see your mom, can I come with you?"

I smile. "I would love for you to meet my mom," I say.

California has taken away a part of us. A battle fought, and many lost. Horrific memories are etched on my mind. Our minds. The journey back home is tough road, but we are close. We are in Mississippi and I'm going to stop at my mom's and check on her before we go back to WV.

Chapter 6: Lea and Samantha

Lea

When we arrive at my mother's home, my mom hugs me to death. I introduce her to Samantha.

"Hello, Samantha," she says and hugs me super hard.

"You seem familiar to me," Samantha says.

"Well, I should seem familiar to you. I've aged a ton since we last saw each other, but you're the private investigator that was looking for my daughter, Leslie."

"What???" Samantha looks confused.

My mom laughs and says, "Yes, dear, you didn't know? This is my daughter, the one you were looking for all those years ago. Leslie Jenkins."

Samantha is still confused. She looks at me. "Lea?"

I smile at her, and a dawning realization came across Sam's face. She says, "You knew! Oh my God, I found you."

"When you met Chris in his cell and shared your story with him, he told me all about you. Samantha, I have loved you ever since. Thank you for never giving up on me."

Epilogue

In the realm of child abuse and domestic violence, the landscape of laws and societal response has undergone a transformation since the 1970s. Back then, such issues were shrouded in silence and taboo, with limited legal and societal understanding. Child abuse was a hidden epidemic, with minimal legal protections in place. Awareness and advocacy were in their infancy, leaving many victims to suffer in silence. Today, we find where progress has been made, but challenges persist. The establishment of child protective services, mandatory reporting laws, and the development of child advocacy centers mark significant milestones in addressing child abuse. We now have a more comprehensive legal framework safeguarding the welfare of children and empowering them to break the cycle of abuse. While progress has been made, it is important to recognize that child abuse and domestic violence still persist today. Laws have evolved, awareness has grown, and support systems have expanded, but the scars of trauma endure. The journey towards eradicating these forms of abuse is ongoing, as we strive to create a society where every child and individual can live free from fear, violence, and suffering.

About the Author

For years, this story has resided within the depths of my mind, patiently waiting for the right time in my life to share. Perhaps it was fear that held me back or the belief that I didn't have enough time or talent. But eventually, I realized that the story deserved to be told. I hope to challenge readers to open their minds, think critically, and embark on a transformative journey.

In crafting the protagonist, I yearned to create a character who would walk a fine line between relatability and enigma, leading readers through a labyrinth of deception and suspense. It was essential for me to develop a character whose unwavering pursuit of personal justice and relentless quest to unravel the truth would strike a chord within readers, evoking deep emotional investment.

As I delved into the writing process, I couldn't help but feel the darkness within me awaken. It was the part of me that could never turn a blind eye to injustice, forever seeking to restore balance and deliver personal justice. I wrote this book for those who are unable to speak out for themselves, whose minds and emotions have been vandalized by trauma. Even in the present, there are those who remain imprisoned, their voices stifled. My intention was to create a book that would keep readers guessing while simultaneously shedding light on the darker aspects and shadows that dwell within our human nature. The consequences of actions, the complexity of morality, and the profound impact our choices can have on ourselves and others. I have a deep love for captivating stories that have the power to transport readers to a different world, where they eagerly turn the pages in search of truth and understanding. Ultimately, my motivation to write this book was rooted in my deep yearning to provide readers with an immersive experience that would linger in their hearts and minds long after they reached the final page.

Some Must Die is my first novel, and I'm currently working on my second. My home is in Alpharetta, Georgia. When not working, I'm likely hanging out with my partner, camping, kayaking, and finding quaint towns with unique coffee shops. We have two beautiful girls in college, the cutest Pomeranian dog, and the prettiest Himalayan cat ever. When chilling at home, I write, read, binge on Netflix, and never miss Survivor.

The Set List

Jailhouse Rock - Elvis, 1957
Too much Monkey Business - Elvis, 1956
Always - Ella Fitzgerald, 1956
Life's Been Good - 1978 Joe Walsh
Boom, boom, ain't it great to be crazy - Unknown
Hopelessly Devoted - Olivia Newton John, 1978
I'll Fly Away Oh Glory - Charley Pride, 1971
Dust In The Wind - Kansas, 1977
House of the Rising Sun - The Animals, 1964
White Rabbit - Jefferson Airplane, 1967
I Feel the Earth Move - Carole King, 1971
Go Away Little Girl - Donnie Osmond, 1971
I'll Be There - Jackson Five, 1970
Whole Lot of Love - Led Zeppelin, 1969
California Dreaming - Mammas and the Papas, 1965
Amazing Grace - John Newton, 18th century
Dream a Little Dream of Me - Ella Fitzgerald, 1950
When the Saints Go Marching - 1776
Summertime - Doc and Richard Watson, Unknown
Fly Me To The Moon - Frank Sinatra, 1964
Sunny - Bobby Hebb, 1966
All Of Me - Frank Sinatra, 1952
Oscar Mayer - Bologna Jingle, 1963
Take It Easy - Eagles, 1972
The Beverly Hillbillies Theme - 1962
Bad Company - Bad Company, 1974
Deep Purple - Burn, 1974
Bennie and the Jets - Elton John 1974
Andy Griffith Show Theme - 1960
Rudolph the Red Nose Reindeer - 1964
Santa Clause is coming to Town - 1970
Frosty the Snowman - 1969
Kashmir - Led Zeppelin - 1975
Oscar Mayer - Weiner Jingle, 1963
Heartbreak Hotel - Elvis Presley, 1956
The Devil's Ball - Joan Morris and William Bolcom (Berlin Irving), 2002
Hit Me With Your Best Shot - Pat Benatar, 1980
Hell is for Children - Pat Benatar, 1980
Living on a prayer - Bon Jovi - 1987
Devil Went Down to Georgia - Charlie Daniels Band, 1979
Take the Money and Run - Steve Miller Band, 1976
Heathens - Twenty One Pilots, 2016
That I Would Be Good - Alanis Morissette, 1998
Just Before the Battle Mother - George F. Root, 1863

Discussion Guide

Peer into the depths of the author's intentions and overarching themes woven throughout the narrative.

1. What messages and universal truths did they seek to convey through the unconventional family's story?

2. How does their exploration of these themes resonate with our own lives and experiences?

3. Assess the effectiveness with which the author explores and portrays these themes. Are they subtly woven into the fabric of the narrative, or do they burst forth with raw emotion and power?

4. Do these themes resonate with readers, leaving a lasting impact on their hearts and minds?

5. Challenge the conventional understanding of family and kinship as the novel invites you to reconsider deeply ingrained assumptions. How does it subvert traditional notions of what it means to be family?

6. What new perspectives does it offer on chosen families and the unconventional support systems that sustain us in our darkest hours?

7. Engage in a thought-provoking exploration of the family's fight for a dying world. How did their actions transcend individual desires and become a testament to their unwavering commitment to a greater cause?

8. In what ways did their unyielding support for one another pave the way for their triumphs, and how did it help them weather the storms that threatened their very existence?

Made in the USA
Columbia, SC
10 December 2024

48932317R00235